SPLASH ONE

Also by Walt Kross

Military Reform: The High Tech Debate in Tactical Air Forces (1985)

SPLASH
ONE
AIR
VICTORY
OVER
HANOI

A   N   O   V   E   L   B   Y

WALT KROSS

BRASSEY'S (US), Inc.
A Macmillan Publishing Company

Washington • New York • London • Oxford
Beijing • Frankfurt • São Paulo • Sydney • Tokyo • Toronto

Designed by Bedrock Design.
Maps by Albert D. McJoynt.

Brassey's (US), Inc.

Editorial Offices
Brassey's (US), Inc.
8000 Westpark Drive, 1st Floor
McLean, VA 22102

Order Department
Macmillan Publishing Co.
Front and Brown Streets
Riverside, NJ 08075

Brassey's (US), Inc., books are available at special discounts for bulk purchases for sales promotions, premiums, fund-raising, or educational use through the Special Sales Director, Macmillan Publishing Company, 866 Third Avenue, New York, New York 10022.

Library of Congress Cataloging-in-Publication Data

Kross, Walter.
    Splash One : air victory over Hanoi—a novel / Walt Kross.
        p.   cm.
    ISBN 0–08–040567–3
        1. Vietnamese Conflict, 1961–1975—Fiction. I. Title.
PS3561.R67S6 1991
813′.54—dc20   90–48327
                                                        CIP

British Library Cataloguing in Publication Data
Kross, Walter
    Splash one.
    I. Title
    813.54 [F]

ISBN 0-08-040567-3

10 9 8 7 6 5 4 3 2 1

Published in the United States of America

To Kay and Karin, who sacrificed so much so I could serve my country.

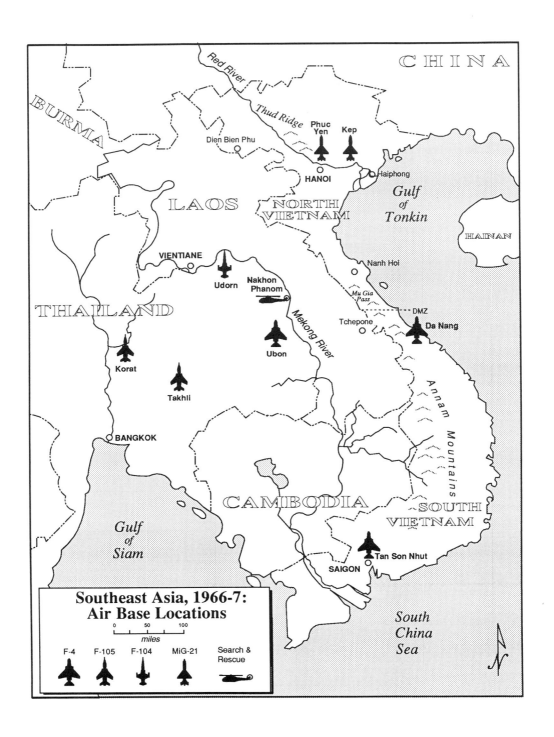

CHINA

Red River

BURMA

Thud Ridge

Dien Bien Phu

Phuc Yen

Kep

HANOI

Haiphong

LAOS

NORTH VIETNAM

Gulf of Tonkin

HAINAN

VIENTIANE

Nanh Hoi

Udorn

Nakhon Phanom

Mu Gia Pass

DMZ

THAILAND

Mekong River

Tchepone

Da Nang

Ubon

Korat

Annam Mountains

Takhli

BANGKOK

CAMBODIA

SOUTH VIETNAM

Gulf of Siam

Tan Son Nhut

SAIGON

South China Sea

Southeast Asia, 1966-7: Air Base Locations

0   50   100

miles

F-4   F-105   F-104   MiG-21   Search & Rescue

N

CONTENTS

AUTHOR'S NOTE AND ACKNOWLEDGMENTS   ix

SEPTEMBER 1941   1
LANCE FLIGHT   6
THE EAGLE ARRIVES   21
THE WING   66
THE FOUR HORSEMEN   113
THE PLAN   129
THE CONSPIRACY   172
THE EAGLE AND THE DRAGON   182
DROPPING THE GAUNTLET   205
THE TRAGEDY   229
THE TOUR EXTENSION   248
THE CONTROVERSY   254
OPERATION BOLO   271
AFTER BOLO   317
MARCH 1968   318

THE AUTHOR   322

Author's Note and Acknowledgments

"Splash One." Every fighter pilot lives for the day he can call out those words over his UHF radio. "Splash One" means that the shooter has hit his opponent's aircraft with his missile or guns and the enemy plane is breaking up or is in a final plummet to the ground.

Very few pilots experience this exhilarating moment. In Vietnam, thousands of American fighter pilots fought their way into heavily defended target areas, but only a few hundred ever saw a North Vietnamese MiG. And just a few dozen got to call out "Splash One" in the heat of air combat.

This novel is about some of those pilots and the North Vietnamese air ace who fought them tenaciously over North Vietnam in late 1966 and early 1967. It's about men who *didn't* break the rules. It's about winning by operating *inside* the artificial restrictions of limited war. It's about Operation Bolo and the events leading up to it.

The time period, places, military units, weapons, values, and operating environment described in the story are accurate and authentic. The characters and events leading up to Bolo are composite dramatizations.

Operation Bolo, the major aerial dogfight of the Vietnam War, happened on January 2, 1967. Bolo was the product of American creativity, aggressiveness, and ingenuity. It was a decisive air battle with a clearly defined outcome, fought by readily identifiable heroes. Most are still alive.

This story is inspired by the men who lived out Bolo: Brigadier General Robin Olds—one of the truly great air commanders—and three of his premier fighter pilots who have kept the legend of these times alive: J.B. Stone, Bob Pardo, and Phil Combies. All of them, MiG killers in their own right, flew the actual combat of many of the events in this story. Phil Combies, who shot down a MiG-21 during Bolo and who was later credited with a second probable kill, died during the writing of this book. He was my strongest supporter and spent many hours helping me frame the story. Throw a nickel on the grass for Colonel Phil Combies.

My special thanks to Dr. Frank Margiotta, President of Brassey's (US), a former combat pilot himself, for seeing the value in the story and publishing it. And to Don McKeon, the "hands-on" associate director of publishing. Also thanks to Air Force Colonels James ("Stu") Mosbey and Roger Gossick, who helped me research the salient details. Finally, my appreciation to the editors, Lois M. Baron, Connie Buchanan-Leyden, and Deborah Estes, whose collective mastery improved my original manuscript.

SPLASH ONE

SEPTEMBER 1941

7 September 1941 0700 hours
Nanh Hoi
Japanese-occupied French Indochina

Twelve-year-old Nguyen Tomb awoke with a knot in his stomach. He had dreaded this day for the past week, ever since he had heard his Uncle Soat, the village chief of Nanh Hoi, talking with the other elders. Nanh Hoi didn't have enough fish to meet the monthly quota demanded by the Japanese, and that meant trouble. Nguyen's uncle had recounted the horrible stories of what the Japanese had done in the villages to the south last month when they hadn't collected and dried enough fish.

It didn't matter that the Nanh Hoi families had fished the Gulf of Tonkin for fifteen centuries. And it wasn't important that the Japanese gunboats used the glass fishpots that buoyed the fishing nets for target practice. It was only important that Nanh Hoi did not have its share of fish to feed the bellies of the Japanese soldiers garrisoned at Vinh, 70 kilometers to the north. Nguyen knew this would be a very long, very worrisome day, spent repairing fish nets.

1700 hours

Young Tomb trembled uncontrollably with fear. He felt his heart pounding under his only cotton shirt. He could see the Japanese truck convoy kicking up dust along the coastal highway to the south. Three trucks this time. "Go tell Uncle Soat that they are coming," Nguyen urged his younger cousin, who loped down the dune toward the villagers who were already gathering in the main square.

Tomb too started down the dune toward the edge of the village. He loved his Uncle Soat. When Nguyen's mother had become pregnant by a Burmese fisherman who had visited Nanh Hoi, Uncle Soat had stood by her. When she had died of malaria four years ago, Uncle Soat had taken in Nguyen when the other village families had shunned the half-breed boy. Soat had taught him of the sea, fishing, and life.

Major Oishi Takeda was anxious to get to Vinh City before nightfall. The local resistance, the Viet Minh, took control of Highway One at night. Takeda jumped down from the cab of the lead truck into the choking dust of the village square. Even from 50 meters away, Tomb could see Takeda's symbols of officership: the black-holstered pistol, the knee-high, brown leather boots, and the sword.

Sergeant Nakamura, chief of the four-man local garrison, led the elders in bowing at the waist to Takeda. The officer ignored the gesture, strutting around the square like a peacock, yet carefully sizing up the villagers.

Tomb moved closer as the conversation between Takeda and Nakamura grew louder and more intense. Nguyen knew that the fat Nakamura always skimmed off the best of the daily catch for his soldiers, and he also knew that the Japanese sergeant would say nothing of it. Nguyen trembled as Nakamura pointed to Soat and the other elders, all standing behind the fat sergeant, pathetically waiting for their punishment. Why hadn't they run away last night? Nguyen asked himself. Why didn't they run away now?

Takeda's explosive outburst destroyed Nakamura's fragile composure immediately. The sergeant bowed repeatedly, fearing for his life and mumbling all the while. Soat spoke up, trying to explain quietly that the sergeant was not to blame for the scarcity of fish; it was the Japanese gunboats.

Soat's interruption seemed to enrage Takeda. Shouting profanities, he unsheathed his sword, raised it high to the right, and took one long step toward Soat. In a single motion, the Japanese swung the blade and severed Soat's head from his shoulders.

"No!" shouted Nguyen. He ran to his uncle, uncertain whether to embrace the body or the head. Takeda kicked Soat's head toward Nguyen as if discarding an unwanted soccer ball.

The almost unrecognizable skull, covered with mixed blood and dirt, rolled to a stop at Nguyen's feet. He bent and wrapped it in his shirt. As he did, Nguyen looked into the smug face of Major Takeda. He would never forget that Takeda looked pleased by his horrible act. And Nguyen Tomb would never forget the bloody sword, which Takeda cleaned by wiping it on Soat's torso. So this was what foreign oppressors did to the Vietnamese, thought Nguyen. In seconds, this occupier had snuffed out the only family Nguyen Tomb had.

At midnight, Nguyen wandered along the surf's edge in a stupor—he didn't know for how long—filled with hatred for Takeda and the other Japanese. Suddenly, two shadowy figures, dressed in black, appeared out of the darkness from his right. The larger of the two threw the small boy to the sand in one swift motion, and the second man put a knife to Nguyen's throat. Still, the young Tomb maintained his grip on the old man's head. The fluid seeping from the severed end had coagulated and dried on the boy's black shirt.

"Who are you, boy? What are you carrying?"

His voice shaking, Nguyen told of the atrocity in Nanh Hoi. His story changed the nature of this encounter. The men helped Nguyen to his feet respectfully. Together, the three walked into the scrub brush beyond the dunes. That night, Nguyen Tomb left Nanh Hoi forever. Then he became Viet Minh.

7 September 1941 1300 hours
Michie Stadium
The United States Military Academy, West Point, New York

Cadet Third Classman Clinton Radford Adams paced nervously on the sidelines with the West Point football team. He would have upchucked his lunch if he hadn't forgotten to eat. Playing for Army Head Coach Earl "Red" Blaik meant a lot to him.

"Gather around, men." Coach Blaik's steady voice drew a circle of leather helmets three deep. All eyes were on the new head coach. In just two months, the hard-nosed Blaik had integrated last season's promising plebe team with the remains of the 1940 squad—the worst in history, with a 1–7–1 record. Privately, Blaik felt good about this group, his first Army team, but still wondered how he'd let the Academy superintendent talk him out of a comfortable head coaching job at Dartmouth for this tenuous situation. Being a graduate of West Point's class of '22 probably had had something to do with it.

"There're a lot of people in the stands today, men: the Corps, your parents, your girlfriends, the alumni. They're here to watch Army win. And somebody else is here. The New York sports writers. They think Columbia's going to whip our tails. They're ready to write off Army for another year.

"You know Columbia's game strategy," Blaik continued, tapping his left temple. Then, pointing at his heart, Blaik continued, "But reach in here to win the game. You're in top physical condition, and you run the basics better than my Dartmouth teams. And remember, 1–7–1."

The players responded with two shouts of "Army Team" in unison; then they moved out onto the playing field.

Adams tripped over the heel of the man in front of him as he hurried to line up for the kickoff. The 6-foot-4, 240-pound, nineteen-year-old rolled onto the ground. The seasoned left end running past Adams didn't miss the chance. "Shit, Adams, not now. Wait 'til someone knocks you on your ass."

Embarrassed, the new starting left tackle hustled into position. One of Red Blaik's assistant coaches saw Adams straggling into line. He remarked to the neatly attired head coach, "I don't know if Adams is ready, Coach."

"He's ready," Blaik shot back quickly. He was a man of few words, but his confidence in young Adams rang true. Red Blaik liked last year's standout plebe lineman because of his cat-like quickness, blocking strength, and aggressiveness—especially his aggressiveness.

The entire Cadet Corps—all 1,920—stood up in solidarity with their new Army football team. The 7,000 friends, family members, sweethearts, and local fans soon took their cue from the Corps and stood as well. The Corps let forth its long, haunting chant, then pounded like a howitzer shell when the Army kicker's foot struck the ball.

Adams was off his mark and down the field in an instant. He was surprised at how easily he bowled over the first blocker. The second Columbia blocker, small enough to be a running back, tried a cross-body block on Adams. Clint leaped over him, took two more strides, and buried his shoulder into the lower rib cage of the Columbia kick returner. The receiver dropped hard, unprepared for Adams's ferocious tackle, and the ball popped loose, meandering toward the goal line.

Adams and the left end both pounced on the ball 1 yard deep in the end zone.

Instinctively, Adams and the senior lineman wrestled for the ball. Adams lost. The crowd roared, and the ceremonial cannon sent its percussion through Michie Stadium. Coming off the ball, the upperclassman tweaked Adams again. "Christ, Adams, nice tackle, but how about letting somebody else have a chance? Football's a goddamned team sport!"

Adams shot back, "I gave you that one. Next time you'll hafta get your own fucking ball!"

As the point after the touchdown sailed through the uprights, Red Blaik turned to his smiling assistant. "He looks ready to me."

That night, the New York sports writers had a new young tackle to spotlight. Army whipped Columbia 27-0. The Red Blaik football dynasty had begun. Clint Adams's aggressiveness catapulted him to consensus All American in his sophomore year. And it put him on a course with an opponent more formidable than the Columbia kick returner.

Lance Flight

Twenty-five years later

7 September 1966 0900 hours
Seventy miles northwest of Hanoi
North Vietnam

"Lance, let's go tactical." The gruff, raspy voice of "Big Jim" Kuszinski, the strike force leader, rang in the headsets of the American fighter pilots inbound to their target just north of Hanoi.

Sixteen F-105 fighter-bombers from the 388th Tactical Fighter Wing (TFW), Korat Air Base, Thailand, penetrated enemy airspace at 20,000 feet. The names of the four-plane flights were Lance, Cadillac, Hammer, and Buick. Most U.S. fighter-bomber flights used the names of sharp weapons or American cars.

Strike formations hitting targets in the Hanoi area often flew the same general routing the strike force was taking today, right down Thud Ridge, a 35-mile-long spine of 5,000-foot-high mountains running north-west to southeast, that thrust itself into the coastal floodplain known as the Red River Valley. The foothills of Thud Ridge, still 1,000 feet high, reached down into the flatlands a mere 15 miles due north of Hanoi itself.

Hanoi—the most heavily defended city in the world—was the north-ern crown jewel of the Red River Valley, which spread out for 100 miles to the south-southeast. The terrain around Hanoi was flat for 25 miles in three directions of the compass—east, south, and west. Air Force pilots flying into the Hanoi area from the north off Thud Ridge exposed themselves to lethal North Vietnamese defenses, and there was no piace to hide. The pilots fondly called the Hanoi area "Downtown." American aviators who flew missions Downtown were a breed apart and belonged to the newly formed and very exclusive Red River Valley Fighter Pilots' Association, better known as the River Rats.

The target this morning was the Yen Vien Railroad Yard, a small facility by American standards, across the Red River on the northeast outskirts of the Hanoi metropolitan area. Another mission, just like this morning's strike force, would hit Yen Vien in the afternoon. Because the raids were made on regular schedules, Hanoi shopkeepers knew when to close up in the morning and afternoon. The thousands of flak gunners in the valley knew when to be most vigilant—and when to break for lunch.

Kuszinski pushed a fourth stick of spearmint gum under his oxygen mask. His F-105 Thunderchief was painted with appropriate nose art just aft of its black radome—a pig trying like hell to go Mach 1, with the inscription "Polish Warrior."

Big Jim pulled double duty again today as strike force leader and flight leader—the most demanding job for any pilot in the U.S. Air Force. As the wing weapons officer, Kuszinski had the most coveted job in the 388th TFW. If it involved tactics or munitions, Kuszinski had to approve it at Korat. This was Big Jim's 76th mission over North Vietnam. The average American pilot lasted just 63 missions over the North. If his luck held for the full 100 missions North, Kuszinski would rotate home. What a deal.

More to the point, this was Kuszinski's 53rd strike mission to Route Package Six—the U.S. military planner's designation for the northernmost part of the People's Democratic Republic of Vietnam, including the heavily defended Hanoi area. The ground weenies back at Korat didn't even keep stats on how long pilots survived flying missions into Route Pack Six. It was also Kuszinski's 40th mission as strike force leader, an incredible accomplishment in itself. Everyone in North Vietnam wanted to take out the strike force leader.

Truth was, Kuszinski loved going Downtown. He was trained for it. He was good at it. And he liked being a local legend among his fellow F-105 "Thud" pilots at the Korat Officers' Club. There wasn't much back in the States for a gruff, cigar-chewing, thirty-four-year-old bachelor from Chicago's South Side. Once he got 100 missions North, Kuszinski planned to sign up for a second consecutive tour.

Big Jim adjusted his grip on the throttle and joystick. He liked the Thud for many reasons. To him, the F-105 Thunderchief was the state-of-the-art, all-weather, nuclear-capable, supersonic, low-level fighter-bomber. Most of all he knew that the Thunderchief struck fear into the heart of every Communist son of a bitch behind the Iron Curtain. Kuszinski felt good about that.

Moreover, the F-105 was single engine and single seat—his kind of airplane. When he strapped into the Thud, Kuszinski reveled in the fact that no enemy pilot flying could match his speed, payload, and low-level performance. Kuszinski was the master of his world once he pushed the throttle forward. When things got really bad in combat, Kuszinski knew what to do—hunker down, tap the afterburner for all 24,500 pounds of thrust, put the Thud on the deck, and get the hell out of trouble. What a perfect war machine for going Downtown. Kuszinski adored this beast of a plane.

Kuszinski pushed his throttle forward to increase the formation's speed to 540 knots, but he kept the strike force up at 20,000 feet. Korat Thud drivers used this tactic because fewer things could hit them up there. He flipped up three toggle switches on the weapons selection panel between his legs. Three green lights lit up, signifying that the twelve 750-pound bombs slung under the belly and wings of his Thud were armed.

He waited for a break in the radio chatter, then pressed the UHF radio button on the throttle. "Lance, green 'em up." And the other fifteen Thud pilots armed their bombs.

Kuszinski looked to his right at Lance 02, flying in loose formation 100 feet off his right wing.

"Shit, look at that son of a bitch," he grumbled into his M-1A oxygen mask. Kuszinski didn't like taking inexperienced pilots on their first mission Downtown. Yet someone had to do it. It was another chore that fell to the more seasoned strike force leaders.

The "FNG"—fucking new guy—flying Kuszinski's wing wasn't yet one of Kuszinski's breed. He hadn't yet crossed the Red River, he wasn't yet a River Rat. The Polish Warrior didn't know if the kid would choke at the moment of truth. Fifteen minutes later, all this would be much clearer. Big Jim could see that the kid's flying was getting more erratic as Hanoi got closer. "This Brannon kid is real young," Kuszinski mumbled.

First Lieutenant Chad Brannon had checked into the 469th Tactical Fighter Squadron (TFS) two weeks before with only 375 total flying hours, 123 in the F-105. Since arriving in Thailand, he had flown ten missions, all into the less stressful Route Package One over North

Vietnam's southern panhandle, just above the Demilitarized Zone (DMZ) that cut across the seventeenth parallel. The more experienced, or "old head" Thud pilots called Route Pack One "the training area." Brannon still had to pass the big test in Kuszinski's book—flying Downtown.

Big Jim again checked his young wingman's bomb-laden air machine. "Hang in there, kid," he muttered resolutely. Kuszinski couldn't help noticing that the prominent white letters on Lance 02's tail took on new meaning for this mission. Each fighter squadron had its own distinctive two-letter code. The 469th TFS Thuds had "JV" painted on their vertical stabilizers.

"Goddamned junior varsity," Jim grunted.

Kuszinski's four-ship cell led the morning's strike force. Three more four-ships followed at three-mile intervals. All these F-105s carried iron bombs to the heart of North Vietnam. Kuszinski knew he was getting lots of long-distance help from other planes: specialized F-105s called Wild Weasels that suppressed ground defenses; F-4C air superiority fighters that kept the MiGs away—called MiG Combat Air Patrol (MiG-CAP); refitted EC-121D transport planes, called College Eye, orbiting out over the Gulf filled with sophisticated electronic gear designed to alert the strike force of possible Chinese border violations; and aging B-66 light bombers converted into electronic jammers that hung back to the west and tried to blind the enemy's radar network.

Two modified C-130 airborne command-and-control aircraft (ABCCC), sporting the call signs Hillsboro and Alley Cat, also patrolled in the rear area over northern Laos. These ABCCC birds controlled all the air traffic in the Air Force route packages over North Vietnam. Several other aging medium bombers and converted cargo planes prowled about over northern Laos on classified missions. All operated with call signs familiar to Kuszinski; it was these call signs that told him the function of the support planes.

No fighter pilot knew what all of these planes were doing. That was for the bigwigs in Saigon, Hawaii, and Washington. Half a dozen mini-wars were going on in Indochina. Kuszinski was only interested in his war, the one over the North. To him, the others were merely politico-military sideshows. As he and the other Thud pilots said, "If you ain't a fighter pilot, you ain't shit."

The tactical radio net was filled with chatter. Kuszinski wondered for the umpteenth time how so many people with so little to say could be so intent on talking.

One hundred miles to the west, on the Tan refueling track, the Boeing KC-135 tanker planes that passed JP-4 jet fuel to the main force of strike bombers and escort fighters were returning to U-Tapao, their home base in Thailand about 50 miles south of Bangkok. Other tanker planes were entering their orbits to support Lance flight and the rest of the strike package when they exited North Vietnam, fuel hungry for the trip home.

"Boiler flight is feet wet to the southeast, light triple-A in the target area." Kuszinski listened as two RF-4C tactical reconnaissance planes exited the target area at supersonic speed and headed out over the Gulf of Tonkin. While passing over Yen Vien to get prestrike reconnaissance photos, they encountered light, inaccurate anti-aircraft artillery fire (AAA) north of Hanoi. The RF-4s were now starting their 500-mile journey back to Tan Son Nhut Air Base, near Saigon. The high-resolution black-and-white photos they brought back from up north would be in the hands of the intelligence specialists on the Seventh Air Force Head-quarters staff within two hours. Sixty minutes later, after the dust cleared, two more RF-4Cs would make a run over the Yen Vien railyard. Their mission: bring back the poststrike photos so the Seventh AF planners would know whether to target Yen Vien the next day. The daily ritual of death went on.

The North Vietnamese listened to the American radio chatter too. They had cataloged Kuszinski's unique voice months ago. Their intelligence operators correlated stolen flight schedules from Korat with his voice. To the North Vietnamese, Kuszinski was "The Polish Pig."

The movements of the fighter-bombers and the support aircraft were familiar to them, too. They learned the functions of each American aircraft the hard way. Now the North Vietnamese air defense controllers had Lance flight, and all the other American F-105s, on their radar screens. The American standoff jammers weren't doing much good.

Lance flight began its descent off Thud Ridge and into the Red River Valley. Kuszinski led his four-ship down to 16,000 feet, still at 540 knots. He would swing around to the northeast, then come in out of the sun. Kuszinski would start his 45-degree dive-bombing run in six minutes.

For a fighter pilot, the day's weather stunk. As Kuszinski entered the terminal caldron of defenses that surrounded Hanoi, he found it very hazy, especially in the morning sun. Murkiness resulted when the sun heated the water-laden rice paddies and mixed the rising moisture with the smoke from the Vietnamese soft-coal cooking ovens. Kuszinski had fought his war in it, but he had never gotten comfortable with it. Big Jim believed that this low visibility favored the enemy. The North Vietnamese pilots turned the haze to their advantage every time, just as the Viet Cong used the jungle against the American foot soldiers.

Kuszinski stared through the inch-thick plexiglass of his canopy, scarred by mishandling and still smudged with the greasy residue left by the plane's maintenance team. He cursed himself for not remembering to wipe it clean after his crew chief worked on a problem in the optical sight just before engine start this morning.

Inflight visibility was less than 4 miles, and the ground looked a fuzzy gray-green from 16,000 feet up. Except for the most prominent landmarks, like rivers and ridge lines, all else was virtually indistinguishable. Big Jim felt like a goldfish swimming near the surface of a bowl in which someone had dropped a half glass of milk about eight hours ago. Most of the milk had settled between him and the bottom of the bowl.

The burly Polish-American could no longer see Condor flight, his MiGCAP fighter escort. It should have been 5 miles to his left and 2,000 feet high. No flak or surface-to-air missile (SAM) activity. Kuszinski didn't take heart from that. He knew that little or no ground fire Downtown meant something else—MiG attacks. Big Jim had a bad feeling about how things were shaping up. He hoped the F-4Cs protecting his Thuds would do a better job than usual.

"This is College Eye with a yellow warning." Some American plane was getting too close to the 30-mile-wide buffer zone with China to the North. Kuszinski didn't care about that right now. He was worried about MiGs. So were his wingmen. All eyes in Lance flight were scanning the horizon.

Three tense minutes passed. Nearly 30 miles of hostile villages passed under Kuszinski's wings. Lance flight had moved well out over the Red River floodplain, 15 miles east of Hanoi. There were no hills. No ridge lines to mask an attacking plane. If you wanted to go Downtown, this was where you had to travel.

Kuszinski avoided flying over Hanoi itself. It was there that the North Vietnamese—with substantial help from the Russians, Chinese, and Cubans—continued building the most concentrated air defenses in history. By Kuszinski's measure, the caldron was far too lethal already.

Suddenly, a lone, green-camouflaged MiG-17 sliced through the Lance formation from the right, from two o'clock low, out of the sun and the haze. The tiny Russian-made fighter sprayed Lance flight with 23mm and 37mm cannon shells.

A half-dozen 23mm cannon shells slammed into Brannon's plane, and pieces flew off Lance 02's fuselage backbone. Somebody called out, "Two's hit! Two's hit!"

Instinctively, Kuszinski tracked the MiG as it blew through his strike flight. But the MiG was gone, breaking off behind and below the F-105s.

"Those little green bastards can really turn," Jim said. Just then he saw the second MiG, the always present trailer. In a split second, the second MiG pilot followed the same flight geometry as his leader. For some reason, the trailer did not fire on the Thuds. Inexperience? Jammed gun? Who knew?

"Hold fast, Lance!" Big Jim transmitted strongly. He knew his wingmen wanted to shed their bombs and pursue the MiGs. And that's exactly what the MiG leader wanted the American Thuds to do. But Kuszinski knew the MiGs were gone, at least for Lance flight.

Kuszinski's next call alerted the MiGCAP, Condor flight. "MiGs passing through Lance flight. Two to seven o'clock low. Condor, do you copy?"

Kuszinski was sure that Condor was positioned perfectly to roll off the perch from high above and in behind the MiGs. The trailer looked like especially easy prey. "Damn it, Condor, did you copy?" Why didn't Condor pick up the MiGs? What the hell were those F-4 jocks doing up there?

"Lance—"

"Got a tally on the bandits—three, five o'clock!" The radio chatter was confusing. Everyone was electronically stepping on everybody else. Condor Lead did not respond, losing precious seconds. Then, too late, Condor 01 called for confirmation. "Say again, Lance."

"MiGs, dammit! MiGs!"

But no one in Condor flight could see the tiny green MiGs, each half the size of an F-105. The haze and the MiGs' green camouflage concealed the North Vietnamese fighter planes against the lush rice paddies below. The MiGs were gone.

"Lance Lead, 02. I took some hits aft of the cockpit." The kid's plane was losing fuel rapidly. Kuszinski noted how calm Brannon's young voice seemed.

"Roger, 02. Hang tough, kid." Kuszinski knew the bombing mission was over for Lance flight. He couldn't leave Junior Varsity and continue to the target. And he couldn't send Lance 03 and 04 to the Hanoi area alone. The pilots were not lead qualified. All four Lance flight F-105s turned for home. Big Jim passed the strike lead duties to the next F-105 four-ship in line. "Cadillac Lead, Lance. You've got the strike force. Lance is out of the picture."

"Cadillac 01. Copy."

"Lance, pickle on my command." After a momentary pause. "Pickle now." Simultaneously, forty-eight 750-pound bombs dropped into the haze and obliterated some poor peasant's rice paddy.

Lance 02 called out in the same calm, but preoccupied voice, "Ah, Lead, I'm losin' gas. Won't make it to the tanker. Lance 02 has 1,000 pounds of fuel, and it's falling fast."

Kuszinski computed that the kid had only ten minutes of fuel, and the leak would shorten that time even more. Brannon's F-105 was trailing a broad white mist of precious jet fuel. The kerosene-like fluid spewed from holes in the upper fuselage. Big Jim knew that the wounded Thud must have fuel under pressure gushing all over the interior of the fuselage. If it reached the hot section of the engine, the plane could blow up in one magnificent fireball.

"Stay with it, kid. Just fly my wing." Kuszinski saw Brannon nod affirmatively. Big Jim gave Chad a silent "thumbs up"—his way of showing compassion for the young lieutenant. Brannon flipped him the finger in return. The kid has real potential, Kuszinski thought. Got to get him home.

Kuszinski hoped to nurse Lance 02 off the Red River Valley floor and far into the hills of Thud Ridge. Only then would a rescue attempt have a chance. He led the flight in a slight climb through 17,000 feet, trying to gain as much altitude as possible. Brannon would have to eject over North Vietnam on his first mission to Pack Six.

"Hillsboro, Hillsboro. Lance has a wounded 02. Get a SAR on us. Moving northwest out of the bull's-eye now." Big Jim set up the SAR (search and rescue) somewhere west of Thud Ridge. It was the best hope to recover Brannon.

"Hillsboro copy. Understand Lance 02's hit. SAR on the way." The SAR machinery ground into motion.

The enemy was still listening.

"Lance 02, flame out!" Brannon wouldn't even make it to Thud Ridge now. He would eject into the populated valley below. The kid zoomed his damaged plane upward in one last desperate effort to reach the foothills, but the attempt failed. His F-105 nosed over into a very steep glide. Like all swept-wing fighters, the F-105 flew poorly without a jet engine pushing it through the sky. Kuszinski dropped back to fly on the wing of the wounded plane.

"The damned thing glides like a fuckin' stone," Kuszinski shouted in frustration.

Kuszinski watched helplessly as Brannon ejected at 2,000 feet above the ground, still 5 miles short of the foothills, still over the Red River Valley. Kuszinski circled the area as Brannon's parachute blossomed and he drifted toward a village. Three minutes later, the kid landed in a paddy near a dike road.

"Hillsboro, Lance here. We have a good chute and a good beeper. But call off the SAR." The rescue choppers were still forty-five minutes from reaching the area. Anyway, this was too deep in North Vietnam for a successful daylight pickup.

"Lance, this is Hillsboro. Confirm you want to call off the SAR."

"Roger, Hillsboro, call off the damn SAR!"

The villagers were on young Brannon quickly, and the kid never even transmitted once on his emergency radio. Brannon and all his survival gear fell into the hands of the enemy, who would find it useful later.

Kuszinski orbited Brannon's landing area for five more minutes until his fuel ran low, and he had to start toward the KC-135 tanker. As he climbed out to the west, Kuszinski looked back at Brannon's landing area.

"See you 'round, kid." Then he turned forward and added with contempt, "Goddamn MiGCAP. What a bunch of pussies!"

0920 hours
Forty kilometers east of Brannon's capture
Kep Airfield, near Hanoi

"Red Leader, you are cleared to land."

Two MiG-17s returned to base after their attack on Lance flight. The flight leader's MiG-17 touched down on the 2,000-meter-long runway. The second MiG turned onto its final approach, 2 kilometers out.

The first MiG wheeled off the runway quickly into a revetted area, bounded on four sides by 5-meter-high, grass-covered earthen mounds. Two men waved the MiG through a small entrance only slightly wider than the jet's 10-meter wingspan. As the olive-green fighter taxied to a stop, its markings became clear. The MiG bore the insignia of the North Vietnamese Air Force (NVAF) just behind the main wing—a yellow star in a blood-red circle with a red chevron on both sides. The red numbers 3020 prominently marked the forward fuselage, just aft of the nose intake. A red band, virtually invisible in flight, covered the top third of the vertical stabilizer, signifying that this MiG belonged to the NVAF's First Air Company.

This was the Colonel's plane. Not just any colonel—*the* Colonel. The Dragon, his pilots called him. Nine red stars painted in two lines below the canopy rail singled out this MiG and its pilot from all the others in the world. Curiously, both the NVAF and the USAF painted red stars on their aircraft to signify aerial kills.

No one had ever downed more U.S. jets than NVAF Colonel Nguyen Tomb. He loved the MiG-17, and he felt comfortable in it. The plane's nimbleness and green camouflage perfectly suited the combat requirements of the NVAF.

The MiG-17F was North Vietnam's primary fighter, and it was a vastly improved design over the earliest Soviet jet fighter, the MiG-15. The MiG-17 had more sweep to its main wings for increased speed, rounded wingtips for better maneuverability, a completely redesigned tail section for better control at high Gs, and a longer rear fuselage to accommodate a more powerful engine.

A peppy aircraft even when first deployed by the Soviets in 1954, its reliable afterburning turbojet engine put out 7,500 pounds of thrust, 25 percent more than the MiG-15's temperamental VK-1 non-afterburning engine. Colonel Nguyen Tomb was not alone in his respect for the MiG-17. The Soviet Union had exported hundreds of them in the late fifties and early sixties to its Communist allies throughout the world.

With its 45-degree swept wing and modified t-tail elevator design, the MiG-17 remained inherently unstable. Mastering this plane required patience and outstanding airmanship. But once the experienced pilot learned to cope with the MiG-17's temperamental behavior in high-G maneuvers, he could use the aircraft's outstanding turning ability and superb armament—one 37mm and two 23mm aerial cannons, each with a 200-round magazine—for dogfighting at close quarters.

Tomb slid his canopy back as the engine wound down. Two maintenance men hooked a ladder over the left cockpit railing, and Tomb pulled himself up by grabbing the forward canopy frame. He paused to look over the top of the revetment at the rest of his meager assets.

Tomb commanded the NVAF's fighter forces—composed of three modestly equipped air companies flying forty-five MiGs dispersed among six bases in the Red River floodplain—Kep, Phuc Yen, Hoa Lac, and

Gia Lam near Hanoi; and Kien An and Cat Bi near Haiphong. Gia Lam served as North Vietnam's only civil airport.

He dressed like all of his MiG-17 pilots: leather flying cap; goggles; short-sleeve, open-collar, light-green uniform shirt; complemented by a darker pair of pants compressed under a lower-torso anti-G suit. This was the North Vietnamese People's Army Air Force, and Tomb was a classic patriot-warrior. He left the flashy flight suits to his counterparts in the South Vietnamese Air Force, who made an obscene practice of wearing loud flying gear.

Nguyen Tomb was all business. Ten minutes ago, he had become the only double jet ace in all of the Communist world. No fanfare, no press conferences, definitely no champagne. That would be too colonial. And Nguyen Tomb was an ardent anticolonialist above all else. He did not care that the propagandists at the Information Ministry refused to exploit his aerial successes because he was an ethnic Burmese. The red stars on his MiG were all the notoriety he needed.

He backed down the ladder and slowly removed his brown leather helmet and flight goggles. His crew chief approached him submissively and politely asked Tomb about the mechanical condition of the plane. Tomb's chief of airplane maintenance, Maj. Duc Van Do, stood nervously near the aircraft, ready if Tomb had anything for him. Tomb merely returned Duc's salute.

"The plane is still operationally ready. Paint another star on it."

"What type?" asked the young mechanic.

"With silver trim. A Thunderchief."

The crew chief set about the task of locating his paint can and adding a sixth silver-trimmed red star, signifying a U.S. Air Force kill. The four gold-trimmed stars marked Tomb's Navy kills.

This morning's slashing attack and aerial victory on Lance 02 was his easiest yet.

Nguyen Tomb was much taller, but only thirty pounds heavier than the 12-year-old boy who had fled Japanese-occupied Nanh Hoi twenty-five years ago. And he was much more familiar with war. The Viet Minh who embraced him that night on the beach had changed his life forever. As a young sapper, he had fought the Japanese for the next forty-two difficult months.

When the war ended in 1945, he had wanted to return to Nanh Hoi. But the resistance forces did not disband in those turbulent summer months in 1945, and Nguyen Tomb stayed with Ho Chi Minh as he worked to consolidate his power. Tomb remembered the joy in the streets of Haiphong the day that the resistance leaders signed the declaration of independence from the French colonialists, the same French who wanted to resume their prewar dominance of Indochina. The excitement was not just because both sides had signed the document, but of more importance, because the French had agreed to honor it.

A year of fragile independence followed for the North Vietnamese, and all the while the French were strengthening their foothold in South Vietnam. Nguyen Tomb realized that the French would attempt to control the Tonkinese again. So he stayed with the resistance for a little longer, postponing his return to Nanh Hoi again. When the French Navy shelled the Haiphong harbor in November 1946, the long anticolonial struggle began anew. For nine more long years, Nguyen and many other young Viet Minh patriots battled the foreigners.

He struggled to keep up with his studies in the makeshift jungle classrooms of the Viet Minh. He never embraced Communist ideology. In fact, he hated it. Yet he hated foreigners more. He tolerated the Communist polemics because it was inextricably embedded in his academics. It was the only way he could get the technical schooling he wanted. He knew a good education was essential to leaving the jungle resistance units someday.

In February 1953, only fifteen months before the final battle at Dien Bien Phu, Tomb got the opportunity of his life. He had impressed his superiors with his intellect and determination. In turn, they selected Nguyen and thirteen other young men for pilot training in southern China. The Viet Minh was building an air force. Heady stuff for Nguyen Tomb, who had never even driven an automobile.

Tomb's natural gift for flying showed from the start, earning him top honors among his peers—at least the eight who lived to finish the course in the poorly maintained Chinese MiG-15UTI trainers. Soon he was outflying the best instructor pilots at the Tong Me Flying School. He possessed a sixth sense that made him a master of the MiG-15UTI, the twin-seat trainer version of the Korean War–vintage MiG-15. The MiG-15 was a true combat trainer. With the 23mm cannon in the left-wing root and the crude optical gun sight in the forward cockpit, the student pilot could practice aerial and ground attack gunnery. Tomb had developed his natural talent as a marksman in his days with the Viet Minh resistance. In the air over southern China, he became the best air-to-air marksman his Chinese instructors had ever encountered.

By the spring of 1954, Nguyen had amassed 300 flying hours, a significant amount for an Asian pilot. And there was promise of action back in North Vietnam. The Viet Minh were closing the ring around Dien Bien Phu, and Nguyen yearned to join his compatriots in the final victory. He knew he and his fellow fledgling pilots could help stop the American-made C-47s from making their daily air drops to the defenders of the doomed French garrison.

But a complication kept Tomb and the other NVAF pilots out of battle with the French. Viet Minh intelligence had uncovered a secret French plan to bomb the fighter bases in southern China if MiGs appeared in the skies over Dien Bien Phu. Consequently, President Ho Chi Minh and his top field commander, thirty-nine-year-old General Vo Nguyen Giap, elected not to bring in MiG support.

Nguyen Tomb sat out the climactic battle of the French-Indochinese War on a remote Chinese airfield, 250 kilometers north of Dien Bien Phu. He was twenty-five, the physiological peak age for a fighter pilot. He would wait eleven more years for his first taste of air combat.

After the 1954 Geneva Conference gave the Viet Minh a free hand in Vietnam north of the seventeenth parallel, Tomb was assigned the task of building the fighter arm of the People's Army Air Force. He had few resources to do the job. National priorities turned to rebuilding Hanoi's industrial economy, and little came Tomb's way. Six overused MiG-15UTIs, supplied by the Soviet Union, became the nucleus in Tomb's effort for the next decade.

On 4 August 1964, the day of the Gulf of Tonkin incident, the NVAF had ten MiG-15s, fourteen MiG-17s, and thirty-five pilots of varying skill. And the entire North Vietnamese People's Army Air Force was tethered to the Tong Me Flying School in southern China. Tomb had two air companies that were not ready for combat. Gen. Vo Nguyen Giap called them into service anyway.

On 5 August, U.S. Navy fighters operating from the USS *Coral Sea* attacked the coastal defenses near the Haiphong harbor. Later that day, Tomb's superiors ordered him to deploy the first four NVAF MiGs from Tong Me to Phuc Yen Airfield 25 kilometers north of Hanoi.

For the next three months, Tomb and his pilots shuttled between North Vietnam's air bases and Tong Me, fearing U.S. attacks on the airfields. When Washington declared the North Vietnamese airfields off-limits to air attacks, Tomb moved his forces to the Hanoi area airfields permanently. How nice of Washington, Tomb thought at the time.

Well into 1965, Tomb and his pilots did little more than play long-distance cat-and-mouse games with the attacking Americans. He led his pilots on combat sorties probing for American weaknesses. Following a disciplined, conservative program, Tomb developed in his pilots the tactics and confidence they needed to engage the Americans.

Like every fighter pilot, Nguyen Tomb could not forget his first meeting with the enemy in the air, and he still patterned his tactics after that successful encounter. On 3 April 1965, four Navy F-8E Crusader fighter-bombers from the USS *Coral Sea* attacked Thanh Hoa Bridge, the key span on Route Nationale One coastal highway, 90 kilometers south of Haiphong.

That day, Nguyen Tomb led a pair of MiG-17s in a single surprise hit-and-run pass on the last F-8, just as the pilot pulled up off the target. Tomb followed the commands of the Soviet radar controller explicitly as the scope operator directed him against the target aircraft. He started firing about 5 kilometers out, too great a distance to hit anything. But Tomb had a favorable angle to overcome his slight speed disadvantage, and he kept closing on the F-8 Crusader. Tomb continued shooting until the big gray American jet filled his front windscreen. The American pilot did not expect the attack, so he did not see the attacking MiG. Most pilots shot down in air combat do not see their attackers; this one was no exception. The American did not take any evasive action. At 200 meters, Nguyen could see that he was hitting the F-8 with his 23mm cannon fire. After passing his target, Tomb and his wingman broke down and away, rapidly disengaging from the fight. His heart was pounding like a hammer in his chest. He liked the feeling.

After landing at Phuc Yen, Tomb learned that the damaged Navy plane diverted from the USS *Coral Sea* and limped into Da Nang Air Base in South Vietnam. Never mind. He didn't sleep that night. He had tasted blood in the first MiG encounter of the war. He wanted more. It seemed so easy. Tomb was pleased with his performance. He had exploited the advantage of surprise, and he had used his head. These two things made it easy. Still, he had great respect for the skills of the American pilots.

The next day was different and better. U.S. Air Force F-105s drew the duty of bringing down the center span of Thanh Hoa Bridge. Again Tomb waited for the Thunderchiefs to finish their unsuccessful bomb runs on the bridge.

He knew that the American planes would turn west coming off the target, toward Laos and home to Thailand. Based on North Vietnamese intelligence, Tomb also believed these early American strikes had no radar assistance to alert them to MiG activity. He was right on both counts.

This time he did not rely on the Soviet radar controller, except for general vectors to the target area. Instead, he trusted his instincts to see him through the attack. He rolled in below and behind the departing F-105s as they joined up while climbing to 6,000 meters. Tomb and his wingman increased their airspeed to 550 knots.

As Tomb came up under the third F-105, his wingman took the last American plane. Cannons blazing at close range did the job, and both F-105s caught fire simultaneously. Nguyen and his comrade rolled inverted and split-S'd away to safety by pulling their noses straight down, then back up toward the horizon in the opposite direction. The surprised and confused Americans did not pursue the MiGs. Instead, the American flight leader concentrated on escorting his two damaged aircraft to the Laotian border, where the pilots of the mortally wounded planes ejected safely. Tomb noted this weakness for the future.

His first kill proved easy because Tomb followed the tactics he had learned the day before. Each day he increased his knowledge, becoming a more formidable opponent. He was preparing.

THE EAGLE ARRIVES

7 September 1966 1030 hours
Operations Center, called "Blue Chip"
Seventh Air Force Headquarters (HQ)
Tan Son Nhut Air Base, near Saigon, South Vietnam

General Tom Morgan, commander of Seventh Air Force, sat in his glass-enclosed battle cab patiently listening to his weekly operations summary briefing. On the sunken floor in front of him crammed with telephone consoles, situation boards, floor-to-ceiling maps, and status lights, the Seventh Air Force operations staff went about its business in the dimly lit twilight that characterized military command centers. The unenthusiastic intelligence officer recounted the air activity over North Vietnam, code named Rolling Thunder, during the past seven days.

Morgan knew the trend all too well. The current strategy and tactics being used in Southeast Asia were not producing the results America needed, and he felt hamstrung by the rules and limits imposed by his superiors in Washington. Nonetheless, he had to do his best inside those limits.

Like many other U.S. military commanders, Tom Morgan personally disagreed with Washington's supremely rational strategy of slow and controlled escalation, designed to prod the North Vietnamese into stopping their aggression against the South. Morgan's third war in Asia reminded him that Orientals didn't give a hoot about Occidental notions of controlled escalation. They would exploit every weakness they could identify, and controlled escalation gave them time. In the Orient, time was power—power to accomplish many objectives. Few in the Western world understood the concept and the use of time as well as the Orientals. Tom Morgan understood it, and that was why he was very worried that there were too many Harvard types in the White House.

Morgan flew P-40s with Chennault's Flying Tigers, and he commanded an F-86 fighter squadron against the North Koreans. By any standard, he was an old warhorse. But this war was different. This was limited war—even more limited than the Korean War. The ambassador in Saigon had more influence over military operations than did the generals. And who had ever heard of the White House approving individual targets? And relying so heavily on American military hardware and technology? Overcontrol, micromanagement, and hardware envy in warfare took human leadership, creativity, and aggressiveness out of the equation. Morgan believed that he and his pilots should be picking the targets. His wing commanders, the Air Force's key field leaders, should have more freedom to carry out daily operations.

Tom Morgan's view of air power was simple—effective air power overwhelmed the enemy through surprise, accuracy, and sheer volume. American air power was most successful when it maximized American strengths, when it was like a raging thunderstorm. But over North Vietnam, America was applying its air forces more like a gardener watering his flowers, a few drops at a time. Morgan tried in vain to convince his superiors that applying more air power against the heart of North Vietnam was the key to ending this war. "Rolling Thunder, my butt," the general mumbled.

The briefer stopped. "Excuse me, sir. Do you have a question?"

"No. Just press ahead, son." Morgan chewed on the end of his cigar, while the slightly overweight major in the wrinkled tan uniform droned on.

Morgan's thoughts were outside the room, on the flight line. He wanted to be in the cockpit for this war too. At fifty-five, he was totally gray, and his hair was thinning. Yet he still loved to fly high-performance jet fighters. He relished the chance to show the young pilots a few of the tricks he'd learned in his 4,400 hours of military flying time, all in fighters. When he was at the controls of a plane, Tom Morgan wasn't a four-star general; he was just another old fighter jock pushing an air machine around the sky. When he landed after one of these flights, he was briefly rejuvenated. Then he was Tom Morgan again, a captain trapped in a general's uniform. To him, there was a big difference.

Morgan didn't fly the tough combat missions anymore. But at least he had the discretion to pick the men who must lead the fighting units—

and the men who must fly at the front of strike formations under these conditions. And that's exactly what he intended to do right now.

The briefing concluded. He thanked the major and dismissed the staff. As the officers filed out of the briefing room, a young captain struggled through the door against the crowd.

Morgan saw him. "What's up, Turbo?" he asked Captain Jack "Turbo" Woodside, his aide-de-camp.

"Sir, this message just came over from the Comm Center."

Morgan read the one-paragraph teletype dispatch, folded it neatly, slid it in his shirt pocket, and summed it up. "Damn."

Morgan called to his director of Thirteenth Air Force operations, Brigadier General Max Crandall. "Stay on a minute, Max." Crandall was the hard-charging, no-nonsense chief operator of American air operations conducted by Air Force units flying from bases in Thailand. Morgan trusted Crandall for a straight answer. "We're floundering, Max, just flying combat sorties, not achieving a damned thing really."

"Not like the old war, is it, Boss?"

"Not by a long shot. U.S. pilots knocked down ten North Korean MiG-15s for every American F-86 lost. Over North Vietnam, our fighter jocks achieve no better than a one-for-one exchange. We're not winning the air war; we're just sleepwalking through it."

Crandall knew that the message Morgan had put in his pocket had something to do with this discussion. "What's the latest news, General?"

"We lost another F-105 to a MiG about an hour ago."

"Damn. We're losing too many Thuds," Crandall said.

Something had to change. And fast. Morgan had a plan. Crandall knew their discussion was over. "Got to go, Boss."

Morgan and Woodside were alone in the conference room. The general picked up the red phone. A complex communication system connected him to the U.S. Air Force command post in the basement of the Pentagon. He identified himself to the duty controller who answered the phone. "This is General Morgan at Blue Chip at Tan Son Nhut. Where's the Chief, General J.P. Albright?"

"Sir, our status board shows General Albright in his quarters at Fort Myer. Would you like me to connect you?"

"What time is it there?" asked Morgan.

"It's 2230 hours."

"Yes, go ahead and put me through."

The Air Force chief of staff picked up the phone on the second ring and simply said, "Albright."

"J.P., Tom Morgan, over here in paradise."

"Tom, you old dog, how're things going?"

Morgan spoke candidly, getting right to the point. "Sir, I need your help. We've got to start knocking down some MiGs over here."

"Now wait a minute, Tom. We've been through all this before. We're not gonna break the Rules of Engagement."

"No, sir, I'm tough as nails on that with our people. I'm looking to work inside the rules on this one."

"I'm listening," the chief said doubtfully. Tom Morgan had done some creative things in the past *and* gotten away with them.

"I need someone. Someone in particular."

"All right, give it to me straight. Who do you want?"

"Clint Adams."

There was a long silence on the chief's end of the phone. Morgan knew he had to fill this void or lose the momentum. He had to make his case. "Sir, I'm not griping about the quality of commanders that Air Force personnel sends me. But I've got to be able to put the right men with the right talent where I need them. You put me here to get results."

"I'm still listening, Tom."

"They want to put Adams in as the deputy commander of operations (DCO) of the 3rd TFW at Bien Hoa, which flies F-100s against ground targets in South Vietnam. Hell, he's already commanded a fighter wing in England. I can use him best in command of a fighter wing fighting the air war over North Vietnam.

"We've got to turn things around up there. I need a combat leader in charge of the F-4 Phantoms flying missions over Route Pack Six. Someone who can make things happen, someone who can get our pilots to knock down MiGs—lots of MiGs. Adams can do the job."

"I hear you, Tom, but we've had lots of trouble with Adams. He's too much of a firebrand. He might be so much of a maverick that he might do something truly stupid and get you fired."

Then Morgan added his last shot, the guarantee he knew the chief was waiting for, "I'll ride herd on him just like I do all the others. And I'm ready to put my ass on the line."

Albright sighed. "Okay, you old fart. I'll talk to the personnel people here in the Pentagon about giving you more say in the assignment of key commanders. And, for openers, I'll have the flesh peddlers send Adams your way. You put him where you need him most." Then General Albright added, "But I'm not sure even the North Vietnamese are ready for Clint Adams."

"Thanks, Boss. I hope they're not. Owe you a beer, sir."

"Hell, Morgan, you owe me five cases already."

Putting down the red phone, Morgan reflected he would have paid much more than that to get Clint Adams into the air war.

13 September 1966 1100 hours
Fifty miles southeast of Shaw Air Force Base
South Carolina

A U.S. Air Force RF-4C, the reconnaissance (recce) version of America's hottest new fighter, the F-4C Phantom, bounced along the late morning thermals at 450 knots, 500 feet above the Carolina lowlands, nearing the end of a training mission.

"Bumpy today, isn't it, sir? Just like my ski boat hitting the wave tops out at Lake Marion," said the young first lieutenant instructor pilot (IP) from the Nineteenth Tactical Reconnaissance Squadron. He was riding in the "pit" as the GIB—guy in back. The IP had drawn a routine assignment this morning. He was the wet nurse IP for a colonel on the Ninth Air Force Headquarters staff, collocated at Shaw Air Force Base (AFB) with the tactical reconnaissance flying wing. Ninth Air Force had operational control over all U.S. Air Force tactical units east of the Mississippi.

"Turn left, heading 270, Colonel." The aircraft commander in the RF's front seat racked the Phantom into a 60-degree bank and sucked the shuddering nose around a full 120 degrees to a westerly heading. The lieutenant admitted that this particular colonel—some old guy named Adams—knew his low-level navigation.

As the RF-4C exited the low-level training corridor, the colonel pointed the plane toward home, 50 nautical miles southeast. Not much to do, so the lieutenant continued the small talk.

"You fly a pretty good air machine, Colonel Adams. Got much RF-4 experience?"

"No. It's my fourth ride. Never had a formal schoolhouse checkout," Adams answered.

The young IP was even more impressed. "What do you do at Ninth?"

"I'm the DO," meaning deputy chief of staff for operations.

"Oh, sorry, sir," the lieutenant said, as if he should have known everyone in the ops chain. "I bet it feels good to get out from behind the desk, doesn't it, sir?" A rhetorical question for any pilot not brain dead.

"Hell, yeah."

Adams sensed movement in his peripheral vision. He observed a flight of four RF-4s also returning to Shaw. The formation was cruising along at 5,000 feet, high and to his right. Almost immediately, Adams slammed both throttles into full afterburner and executed a five-G, barrel-roll maneuver—pulling up, rolling inverted, pulling through the horizon, then rolling upright and in behind his opponents—ending squarely in the six o'clock position of the unsuspecting RF-4s, one-half mile astern in perfect gun-firing position. "Bang, you're dead," breathed Adams into his mask.

The lieutenant was just catching up to his stomach, having been caught off guard by Adams's single-piece maneuver. "Ah, sir, it's just a recce bird we're flyin'."

"Yeah, too bad," Adams responded. He didn't add his basic fighter pilot philosophy—there were only two kinds of aircraft: fighters and targets. Adams peeled off and took a different route back to base.

Adams was languishing in his staff job at Shaw AFB. He'd been there for a year now; although he flew to maintain his proficiency, this was still just another staff job.

Almost any assignment would be a comedown following a two-year stint as the fighter wing commander of the 48th TFW in England at Royal Air Force (RAF) Lakenheath. Fighter wing commander—every Air Force fighter pilot worth a nickel aimed his whole career at that job. A few of the better ones became squadron commander, and a few of the best squadron commanders became wing commanders. It was the largest field command an Air Force officer could get: 3 fighter squadrons, 10 support squadrons, 75 to 100 fighter planes, and 5,000 people. Not to mention the caring and feeding of the families. All the joy and heart-ache the Air Force could pack into a twenty-hour-a-day, seven-day-a-week command slot for two years.

Now, at forty-four, Clint Adams was in the twilight of his career as a fighter pilot. It had been a remarkable but star-crossed twenty-three–year run: World War II double ace, with thirteen German aircraft de-stroyed in aerial combat; colonel when he was twenty-five years old; second place at the 1946 Thompson Trophy Air Races; right wingman on the Air Force's first all-jet aerial demonstration team; fighter squad-ron commander three times; and then fighter wing commander.

He'd developed his admirers over the years. Problem was, he'd also acquired some well-placed detractors. He knew they had kept him out of the Korean War, even though he had constantly volunteered for duty over there.

Adams was just too blunt for his own good. He was not a diplomat, and he suffered fools badly, no matter what their rank. Bad flaws for an Air Force officer in peacetime. Some people accused him of still playing tackle but without his headgear. Then there was Clint Adams, crusader of unpopular causes.

He had always been an outspoken maverick and had often found himself at odds with his superiors. Considered a visionary by many fellow fighter pilots, his ideas and warnings had gone unheeded in the Air Force of the 1950s and 1960s. The Strategic Air Command, with its long-range bomber and nuclear missiles, got top billing. The Tactical Air Forces played second fiddle, especially when it came to adequate funding.

Adams hadn't known when to stop pushing for the right kind of modern fighter forces when he had worked on the Air Staff in the Pentagon. If he had kept driving hard, eventually the high-ranking bomber-type generals would have chopped his head off. So General Tom Morgan and a few of the other senior fighter pilots had wangled a long-overdue wing commander job for Clint Adams, saving his career.

Adams proved himself again as wing commander at RAF Lakenheath. Many men considered him the Air Force's best leader of fighter pilots in the air. And he was itching for his last chance to lead air forces in combat. Privately, he feared the Vietnam War had come too late for him.

1300 hours
Ninth Air Force HQ
Shaw AFB, South Carolina

"What's up? Any calls?" Adams ambled into his office, still wearing his sweaty flight suit. He tossed his helmet bag to his executive officer.

"Something's in the wind, sir. The Old Man called for you twice while you were out." Adams hadn't had any lunch, and his exec knew it. The captain reached into the small refrigerator behind his gray metal desk for an icy Coke and put it atop the coaster on Adams's desk.

Taking the soda, Adams consumed it in two gulps, leaving only the carbonated foam to settle back to the bottom. So much for lunch. "Thanks," he said as he did a quick reversal, heading straight for the

Ninth Air Force commander's office down the hall. He tossed the almost-empty Coke can over his shoulder. His exec made a diving catch.

The suite of offices housing Lieutenant General Jack McKean and his immediate command section staff was well appointed and always busy. The general's secretary motioned Adams in to see McKean. "He's been a fussbudget ever since the Chief of Staff called about ten this morning," she whispered to Adams as he moved by her desk. Adams winked at her.

Standing on the general's upgraded blue carpet, Adams knocked on the open door and saluted as McKean looked up from a small stack of papers. McKean casually returned the salute and removed his glasses. "Where you been, Clint? Been looking for you all morning."

"Just getting in some currency flying."

"Currency, my ass. You fly as much as the line jocks. I bet you have twenty hours this month."

Adams took it as a left-handed compliment. "No, sir. Nineteen point five, but that's what it takes to stay really current. After all, I'm hoping for some authentic combat flying soon," referring to his pending assignment as the 3rd TFW DCO at Bien Hoa next month. He wasn't crazy about starting out as DCO. Former wing commanders didn't usually do that, but he was confident that he'd move up to command the F-100 wing once he got some in-country flying experience.

McKean got to the point. "Funny you mentioning that. Got a call this morning changing your assignment. Seems as if the Chief of Staff is your personnel officer."

McKean's reference to the chief made Clint Adams uneasy. He'd spent his whole career trying to make it on his own abilities, fighting envy and jealousy all the way. He'd always tried to steer clear of high-ranking influence.

"Now, sir, I didn't—"

"I know you didn't, Clint. No, it's a bigger issue. Tom Morgan versus the personnel weenies. You're the test case."

"What's up?"

"Bien Hoa's out of the picture for you now. Your orders just got fuzzier."

"Fuzzier?" Clint had been looking forward to flying combat out of Bien Hoa. He always enjoyed flying the single-seat F-100—the Air Force's first Century-series fighter and a favorite of many fighter pilots, even if it was a little old and tricky to fly. More to the point, the Bien Hoa DCO slot was finally getting him into the war.

"Now you will report directly to General Morgan at Seventh Air Force. He'll give you your orders there."

Good news and bad news. "Well, I'm still going to the war zone, but I hope it's not another staff job. No offense, General."

"That's all I'm authorized to pass on to you, Clint." Jack McKean watched Adams's expression as the younger man inventoried the possibilities.

Adams tried to find out more. "General, how'd the chief get involved?"

The general preempted him. "Put a lid on it, Clint." McKean stood, then moved around his desk to say goodbye. "Good luck, Clint. Oh, yes, General Morgan wants you over there ASAP, but you may want to arrange a rapid cram course in the F-4 Phantom before you go."

"Did you say F-4?"

"Tell anybody, and I'll shoot you."

Adams broke into a broad smile. The reference to F-4s meant that he would probably be flying over North Vietnam. "I think I can squeeze in a ten-day special at Davis-Monthan." Adams was close to the colonels who ran the F-4 initial training school at the base in Tucson, Arizona. After all, what were friends for?

The two men smiled as they shook hands. Adams took a step back, saluted McKean, and turned to leave.

McKean couldn't hold it any longer and broke into a broad smile. "Learn something about Thailand before you get in-theater. Remember, tell anybody, and I'll personally skewer you myself."

Only then did Adams know that his time had come.

1715 hours
25 Dogwood Circle
Shaw AFB, South Carolina

Laura Scott Adams stood by the window, her arms folded below her ample chest, staring out the window and not really listening to her husband.

"I know it's short notice, Laura, but it can't be helped," pleaded Adams as he stuffed the last of his flight suits into his green B-4 bag.

Laura's tall, lean figure cut an arresting silhouette. Her striking features and long dark hair belonged to a forty-two-year-old woman who had raised two children and followed her husband across the Atlantic twice and to nearly every fighter base in between. But this little surprise hurt most of all.

She had had no idea what she was getting into when she first met the handsome, famous fighter pilot that afternoon in the lobby of the Waldorf Astoria twenty-one years ago. Recently graduated from Smith College and one month into her fledgling career on Madison Avenue, she had been free to do what she wanted. And she had wanted Clint Adams, whatever the price.

It had been a good life, though it had not included the financially sweet career her Smith classmates had expected of her when they'd voted Laura most likely to succeed in the class of '45. But she'd loved Clint, helped him, and raised their children in the high desert of California and the coastal dunes of East Anglia.

It was the last assignment to England that had started to change things for her. Being a wing commander's wife was a full-time job, and having two teenagers didn't match up with the luncheons, teas, testimonials, and endless hours of volunteer work. Clint was almost never around, what with deployments to gunnery practice in North Africa, inspections, and the daily demands on his time. She finally started to resent putting their marriage and their family on hold for the U.S. Air Force. Commanding Lakenheath was sapping the life out of the Adams family. Clint had promised her it would be different *after* wing commander. She in turn agreed to be patient.

Now with Todd in his second year at the Air Force Academy and Amy settled into her senior year at Hillcrest High in Sumter, they should be enjoying themselves. She'd been trying to get Clint to plan for their retirement. They didn't have a lot saved, but her father had offered Clint an attractive executive position in his Connecticut real estate development firm. She'd always wanted to live in Greenwich and to be near her college classmates again.

But Clint wouldn't let go after they arrived at Shaw. He had long periods of bitter depression. His life was turning negative. And she and Amy were not part of it. He'd go through the motions, attending Amy's tennis matches, honor society inductions, and school plays, but his mind was always somewhere else. Laura knew he was becoming more obsessed each day with getting back into combat one last time. She figured he was working on something that would, once again, leave her out. But this time he was throwing Amy in the trash pile, too. All with one hour's notice. And that was too much.

"Do you know what this means, Clint?" she asked, finally opening up.

"Sure, honey, but there's a war on and they need me," he said lamely as he moved to take her in his arms.

Laura spun around, directly facing the window and rejecting his feeble effort to console her. "No, you *don't* know what it means! You won't be here for Amy's senior year. You won't be at the base of the stairs on prom night; you won't help her pick a college; you won't be there on awards night; and you won't be in the stands on graduation day."

"Laura, I—"

"And now you're leaving without even telling her. I'll have to do it when she gets home for dinner. You'll be on your way to F-4 training. Clint, don't we matter to you at all?"

"Of course you do, Laura. But you get to stay here at Shaw while I'm overseas, and that makes it easier for Amy." They both saw the blue staff car pull up outside.

Laura turned to him, with a hatred in her eyes that he hadn't seen before. "I *am* staying here for Amy's sake, but the moving truck will be outside the day after graduation."

"What do you mean? Dammit! What do you mean?" Clint asked, frustrated and frightened now by what he had done.

"Amy goes off to college and I go back to Greenwich. There! Is that clear enough for you, Colonel?" Laura moved past him and into the bathroom, slamming the door. This was the cruelest thing she could do to him for hurting her like this. And to her, it was the right thing.

Clint started after her, then stopped. She'd acted this way before. She'd come around. She was just hurt. He'd call her later that night from Tucson. He grabbed his B-4 bag and headed for the waiting staff car.

25 September 1966 0800 hours
Final approach, Runway 25
Tan Son Nhut Air Base, near Saigon

Two Vietnamese women, planting rice shoots in a paddy 1 mile short of the approach end of the runway, looked up to see a silver Air Force C-141 Starlifter pass overhead and glide to a graceful touchdown at Tan Son Nhut. MAC #60126 was only minutes from completing its mission, a 12,500-nautical-mile journey that began thirty-four hours ago.

Colonel Adams was riding in the jump seat between the pilot and the copilot. He'd been in the seat for the six-hour flight from Yokota Air

Base, Japan. This four-leg mission was typical of the thousands of Military Airlift Command (MAC) flights the Air Force flew daily, moving the high-priority goods from the continental United States (CONUS) to Southeast Asia.

As the Air Force's first all-jet transport plane, the C-141 was capable of carrying 30 tons of payload. Because of the long legs required to cross the Pacific, the Starlifters carried an average load of 20 tons. The rest was all JP-4 jet fuel.

The seven-man crew flew it empty to Dover AFB, Delaware, the world's largest military air cargo port. During the two-hour stopover at Dover, the three loadmasters onloaded 26 tons of ammunition—mostly 2.75-inch air-to-ground rockets and 20mm cannon shells eventually destined for one of the Air Force fighter wings in Southeast Asia. The C-141 would take the cargo load as far as the Aerial Port Squadron at Tan Son Nhut.

Following the upload at Dover, the same MAC aircrew flew the C-141 eight more hours at 0.77 Mach to Elmendorf AFB, Alaska. At Elmendorf, the C-141 took on a maximum load of fuel and a fresh aircrew while the original aircrew went into the "Elmendorf aircrew stage," resting for sixteen hours, then becoming eligible to crew the next westbound C-141. Adams had been shifting between the extra seat behind the C-141's cockpit door, where he slept restively for a few hours at a time, and the jump seat between the two pilots, where he passed the hours cruising at 37,000 feet, alternately talking to the crew and reviewing the F-4C flight manual from cover to cover.

The last twelve days had been a blur: out to Tucson for a one-week, two-flight-a-day F-4 checkout; back to Shaw for a final weekend with Laura and Amy; and then down to Charleston AFB to jump this Saigon-bound C-141.

Those two days with Laura and Amy were the toughest family time he'd ever faced, thought Clint. Laura was cold, hurt, and undeterred in her plan to move to Greenwich the next summer. She'd acted like this before, and it scared him. And Amy—she seemed so distant, so reserved. At least she had kissed him good-bye. God, he didn't need all that strife.

This C-141 flight was the fastest way for Clint Adams to get from South Carolina to Saigon, but his fighter pilot body had payed a heavy price. He was accustomed to one-hour sorties, not eight-hour marathons. And he had overdosed on fried food. After being exposed for the past thirty-four hours to the C-141's air-exchange system, which removed all the humidity, his sinuses were turning into raw leather. And he had a dry cough he couldn't shake, no matter how much water he drank. His electric razor didn't take the skin crud off his face anymore, and he needed a shower, a fact he could clearly tell by the looks he kept getting from the crusty chief master sergeant manning the flight engineer's station in the Starlifter's cockpit.

His body clock was all screwed up. He'd departed Charleston at midnight, and he hadn't seen the sun again until two hours before landing in Alaska. Then he'd stared at the setting sun for eight hours on the way to Japan. His second long night had just ended before landing in Saigon. He now appreciated why some called MAC the "Midnight Air Command." At a time like this, he was glad he was a fighter pilot.

The C-141 rolled to a stop amid the morning activity on Tan Son Nhut's substantial air cargo ramp where the long-range MAC planes unloaded their cargo. This was America's mega-base in Southeast Asia, home to the 460th Tactical Reconnaissance Wing and a long list of smaller units flying myriad support aircraft. It also housed Seventh Air Force, which ran the air war in Southeast Asia.

The Tan Son Nhut Aerial Port was the seam between strategic and tactical airlift, where cargo was transferred to smaller airlift aircraft for distribution throughout the combat theater. The ramp was crowded, busy, and looked very confusing to the C-141 pilots as they taxied behind the blue "Follow Me" pickup truck leading them to their parking spot.

The copilot with the bloodshot eyes exposed his weariness with a feeble observation, "You know, all this doesn't look like it's worth fighting for." The young captain aimed his comment at Adams, hoping that the seasoned colonel would enlighten them with some "big picture" explanation.

Adams said nothing. He was too tired to engage in a philosophical discussion. Adams thought about how bad he felt. General Morgan wouldn't be too impressed by a forty-four-year-old man with bags under his tired eyes and thinning, lifeless hair to match. The general was looking for someone with a fully charged battery.

The aircraft commander in the left seat taxied the plane to a stop in front of the control tower and shut down the four TF-33 turbofan engines. The senior loadmaster popped open the passenger door on the left forward fuselage, and several airmen scurried up the entrance ladder to complete the paperwork for signing over the cargo.

"Got any VIPs?" asked the airman from the passenger terminal.

"Yeah," said the loadmaster. "We got this colonel here."

"Okay, he's cleared off. Somebody's waiting for him."

As senior officer on board, Adams exited the plane first, looking around for a familiar face as he entered the new, confusing country. The tropical air wrapped around him like a warm, wet blanket, contrasting with the superdry, rarefied air of the plane. Almost immediately, he recognized Turbo Woodside, who had come straight to this assignment from RAF Lakenheath. The young fighter pilot aide still looked like he had eight years earlier, when he'd been an All-American lacrosse player at West Point—jet-black, crew-cut hair; thick neck with bulging veins; and a 180-pound muscled torso to match. Turbo snapped Adams a salute and greeted his old boss, "Good to see you again, sir. Welcome to Disneyland East."

"Hello, Turbo. What's a smart guy like you doing in a goat rope like this?" The two men shook hands. Adams's comment didn't warrant a serious response.

"Got any bags, Colonel?"

"Just a pregnant B-4 bag." The C-141 loadmaster took a silent cue from Woodside and carried Adams's bulging, green GI-issue bag to the open trunk of the dark blue 1965 Plymouth staff car parked on the edge of the cargo ramp.

Turbo held the door for Adams as he piled into the right front seat. Woodside drove down the flight line toward the Seventh AF Head-quarters compound. On the way there, he told Adams that things were not going well up north and that General Morgan was quite concerned about it. Clint Adams began to understand why he was there.

0830 hours
Seventh Air Force HQ
Tan Son Nhut Air Base

Turbo Woodside squinted through the bug-splattered windshield of the borrowed staff car as he turned into the heavily bunkered compound. "Sorry about the blue limo. The motor-pool people don't wash their cars much around here."

Adams shrugged.

The air policeman at the gate waved them through and saluted the staff car. Once inside the main building, Turbo led Adams past a series of checkpoints, flashing his restricted area badge to the air policemen and vouching for Adams at each stop. Eventually the two men arrived at the inner sanctum: the Seventh Air Force Command Section. General Morgan's executive officer, a paper-oriented, career-administrator colonel, waved Adams into the general's office.

Although separated in age by eleven years, Tom Morgan and Clint Adams deeply respected each other's abilities. After the customary salute and a warm handshake, General Morgan said, "Christ, you smell like hell and look like shit. How'd you get here?"

"Got on a Charleston C-141 about ten years ago. What day is it, anyway?"

"It doesn't matter in Southeast Asia. Hell, you *are* a glutton for punishment, flying nonstop MAC all the way. Have you been to Snake School yet?"—a reference to the USAF Jungle Survival School at Clark Air Base in the Philippines. All aircrew members destined for Southeast Asia went through the one-week school.

"No, sir, my orders said report to you ASAP."

"Well, compensate for it somehow. Eat a snake. Let's get down to business. How do you feel about being diverted from Bien Hoa to Ubon, Clint?"

"Did you say Ubon?" Ubon Royal Thai Air Force Base (RTAFB) was the U.S. Air Force's F-4 base in easternmost Thailand, the home of the 8th Tactical Fighter Wing. This was the first time Adams had heard exactly where he would be going. "Just happy to be in a fight again, sir."

"Good. Wish I were going up to Ubon with you. Wish I were thirty years younger, too. I want you up there because you know how to make things happen. I wouldn't say it outside this room, but I'm damned worried about the air war over the North. We can't do anything right up there."

"We seem to be operating under some severe limitations in the Hanoi area, General. Is there any hope of taking the wraps off so we can kick some ass?"

"No. We have to get things turned around using the current rules. You need to understand that from the start, Clint. Do you read me?"

"I read you, General."

"I hope so. Your job security depends on it. And I'm the policeman. Washington won't move off the dime right now. They might if we fall on our face. But the Air Force can't afford that. Hell, the country can't afford it either. It's up to pros like us. Clint, you had a hell of a reputation in the Pentagon some years back before we gave you to the 'Statue of Liberty Wing' at Lakenheath. You pissed off a lot of bomber generals with your hard-headed idea that fighters would be the decisive weapon in the next war. And they almost cut your head off when you tried to convince the civilian under secretary that we needed an internal nose cannon on the F-4."

"Yes, and now we have to fly our Phantoms without nose guns."

"You play with the cards you're dealt. But here's your chance to prove that fighters really are decisive in combat. Few men get that chance. Clint, we've got to turn things around up North. We need to get the MiGs off the F-105s so the Thuds can put their bombs on target—not into some rice paddy when the MiGs bounce them. In short, we have to protect the Thuds and knock down MiGs. Lots of them. Can you do that, Clint?"

"Yessir."

"Good, I'm counting on you. You're the combat leader that I told the Chief could do the job." The general's tone was very matter-of-fact. He reached into his desk for a cigar and offered it to Adams, who declined. Morgan struck a match, lit the cigar, and settled back in his desk chair. "Sit down, Clint." Adams moved to an empty leather chair.

"I want you to take command of the 8th Tac Fighter Wing up at Ubon." Morgan saw Adams's face take on new life, despite his bloodshot eyes. "The 8th has a multiple mission—air-to-air and air-to-mud. You still have to do both, but I'm designating the 8th *the* primary air-superiority fighter wing over North Vietnam. Get the picture?"

"Yessir; got it."

"Right now, the 8th is not clicking as a wing, just like a lot of other units in this combat theater. I just don't see that brash confidence and audacity we expect of our fighter pilots. Instead, I see caution and second-guessing. You know that's poison in the fighter business."

Adams nodded in agreement.

"I need a catalyst, Clint. You're it. If one wing gets things moving well—winning—the spirit of competition will infect the other combat wings."

"It worked that way in Europe and Korea," added Adams.

"Damned right. You catch on fast for an offensive lineman. They didn't kick you in the head as hard as the others I know. The outgoing 8th Wing Commander just completed his 100th mission over North

Vietnam, officially a full combat tour. He leaves for CONUS on Wednesday, two days from now. His vice commander, and anticipated successor, broke three vertebrae last week when he ejected from his shot-up Phantom. He won't return to combat duty. The way is clear for you to take command immediately. For now, the 8th Wing DCO is running things.

"Now, Clint, this is a limited war, not like World War II. The White House controls the strategic targets: airfields, harbors, dikes, radar sites, and more. It's all part of 'controlled escalation.' Get used to it. Hitting any of those targets would alter the nature of the war, the political balance in Asia, perhaps even the global balance of power. I'm the policeman. Anyone who violates the Rules of Engagement by hitting restricted targets has to answer to me. And I've promised the Chief to keep our people in line. And now you're the policeman at Ubon. Clear?"

"Very clear. Sir, I'd like to spend a few days here with your staff. I need to get the feel of things. I'll fly up to Ubon on Saturday—if it's okay with you, General."

"Morgan readily agreed to Adams's request, knowing each commander had to do things his own way. Morgan rose and concluded the meeting by shaking hands with Adams. "Anybody in particular that you'd like as a vice commander? The job's open."

"I'd prefer taking a look around up-country first. Will you give me a raincheck on that offer?"

Morgan nodded as he relit his well-chewed cigar. Adams saluted and turned to leave, but the general brought up one last wrinkle. "Oh yes, the current DCO, Slim Danforth, probably thinks he should be your new vice commander. Do you know him, Clint?"

"Not well. He was a doorkeeper for one of the civilian bigwigs in the Pentagon while I was down in ops in the basement."

"He's well connected in the Pentagon," Morgan warned. "A little light on flying time. Spent lots of desk time as a horse holder to old farts like me. His last job was executive officer for the under secretary of the Air Force, a fact frequently brought to my attention by visiting civilian VIPs. He was a force-feed to me, direct into Ubon. And don't ask how."

Adams smiled. "Well, he's the DCO now. I only care how he's doing that job. I'd still like to see how things look up at Ubon before recommending any personnel changes." Then Adams asked the general for one last favor. "Sir, don't tell Danforth exactly when I'm coming. I want to arrive on my own terms."

The general broke out in a wry smile. Clint Adams was commanding the 8th TFW already. "Good luck, Clint."

On the way through Morgan's outer office, Adams asked Turbo Woodside to set up transportation to Ubon for him any time on Thursday, the twenty-eighth. The young aide acknowledged and then leaned forward. "Congratulations."

"Leak this one, Turbo," Adams whispered, "and I'll personally kick your ass back to Lakenheath."

27 September 1966 1050 hours
Seventh Air Force HQ auxiliary briefing room
Tan Son Nhut Air Base

A female captain from the Seventh Air Force operations staff wrapped up her briefing to Clint Adams on the Air Force lines of organization and command in South Vietnam and Thailand.

Adams tried to ignore how attractive the captain was and questioned her. "Got any stats on the 8th Tac Fighter Wing and Ubon?"

"Yes sir. I'll give you the background papers we have. As you may know, there are three F-4 squadrons: the 433rd, 497th, and 555th. Being stationed in Thailand, you can't fly combat missions into South Vietnam, just Laos and North Vietnam."

"Just?"

"Sorry, sir, didn't mean it that way. All three squadrons are qualified for air-to-air and air-to-mud. And all three fly 'round-the-clock to North Vietnam and Laos. The 497th does specialize in night missions, flying 85 percent of their sorties in the dark. That's all I have right now, Colonel. I'll bring you the backgrounders in five minutes."

"Thanks, Captain."

A middle-aged, overweight major came forward to brief next. "Sir, I'm Major Charlie Wilson from Intell. I'm gonna brief you on the two wars you have to fight"

"Two?"

"Yep, the interdiction campaign to stop supplies moving south and the air war over the North itself," the major answered, in an unenthusiastic tone that told Adams he'd given this briefing to dozens of VIP colonels on their way to the war.

"Which one's the most important, Charlie?" probed Adams.

"The ground war, by far. The 8th TFW flies hundreds of sorties over 'The Ho Chi Minh Trail.' " The portly major pointed to the blue lines on the map of Southeast Asia. "Looks like a bad case of varicose veins about to take over all of Laos and South Vietnam, doesn't it? Your job's to choke it off. The war over the Ho Chi Minh Trail is a nonsexy, little-understood part of the air war. But it's crucial to America's success or failure in the war. This air interdiction, attacking and destroying the enemy's troops and supplies before they reach the battle, is the Air Force's most difficult mission in Southeast Asia. Stop the supply operation moving down the Ho Chi Minh Trail or risk losing the war in the South. It's that simple. But the North Vietnamese are proving very hard to interdict. They use the cover of the jungle and night ingeniously. They're winning.

"Each month we fly more sorties against the trail, and each month the tonnage moving south increases. The North Vietnamese leaders have turned their entire population and economy into one large effort to supply their troops fighting in South Vietnam. They accept tremendous loss of human life as they keep the supplies moving down the road network lacing through lower North Vietnam and Laos. Some reports estimate they dedicate more than two million people to keeping the Ho Chi Minh Trail open and the war materiel flowing.

"The political rules don't allow American ground forces in Laos, forfeiting a decisive strategic advantage to the North Vietnamese and leaving the primary interdiction campaign to Air Force and Navy air power."

Major Wilson liked briefing Adams. He felt that the colonel with his feet up on another chair was asking the right questions from the start. Wilson continued, "The Air Force and Navy fly dozens of missions during daylight hours, cutting visible sections of the trail in an effort to slow convoy movement during the following night. But the North Vietnamese labor battalions, mainly peasants, repair most road cuts in a few hours."

"Got any good news, Charlie?"

"Not on the ground war," said Wilson, "but the air war has possibilities." The major covered the NVAF air order of battle in great detail. "The NVAF has three air companies, essentially three squadrons, operating out of the airfields highlighted here." Wilson used a long pointer to touch the NVAF's six main airfields on the projection screen.

"Right now, they have about sixty-five fighters, but the number grows weekly as the Russians replace the NVAF's older MiGs with newer models. Forget the older MiG-15s; they're museum pieces. Watch out for the thirty remaining MiG-17s. They look old, but they'll eat you alive below 10,000 feet. The little bastards turn on a dime, have big guns, and respectable speed. The NVAF pilots love 'em.''

"What about the MiG-21s?" asked Adams.

"They have fourteen now. All export versions. Four 21Fs and ten 21PFs. The F model's a clear-air fighter with no radar, while the PF model has a first-generation search/track radar with a very limited 15-kilometer range. This radar, called the Spin Scan, is mounted in the MiG's distinctive red nose cone and gives the MiG-21 a rudimentary night and weather capability.

"The MiG-21PF's nearly perfect for North Vietnamese air defense because of its superior acceleration, top-end speed, high-altitude turning performance, a 600-kilometer combat radius, two 30mm cannons, and two Soviet-built K-13A Atoll heat-seeking missiles, copies of the American AIM-9B Sidewinder."

Next Wilson described a set of conditions little known beyond the combatants themselves. "With Soviet help, the North Vietnamese are developing the most proficient, best-coordinated, integrated air defense network in the world. Their equipment's not state-of-the-art, but it's extremely reliable under austere combat conditions. North Vietnamese use their weapons very well. They're fighting for national survival, and they get a continual dose of daily, hands-on proficiency. This hones effectiveness to a sharp cutting edge."

Adams already knew he'd have to fight over his opponents' territory and only when his enemy chose to engage. He was painfully aware that this was the first air war in which American pilots faced the combination of flak, surface-to-air missiles (SAMs), and fighters—all covering a very small area with just a few entry or exit corridors. Aviation history always focused on the dogfights, the sexy air-to-air war. But battle-hardened veterans knew that 90 percent of all aircraft fell to ground fire. And those statistics were compiled before SAMs and radar-controlled flak had come to the air battle.

The briefing continued. "The North Vietnamese air defense system remains off-limits to attack by U.S. aircraft. You can't bomb the valuable command-and-control nodes that make up the enemy's central nervous system. A sensible strategy would target these first, blinding the enemy and limiting his capability to defend against American attacks. Yet these installations remain on the White House restricted target list, the early warning (EW) and ground-controlled intercept (GCI) radars."

"Does that still mean the enemy airfields, too?"

"That's correct, sir."

Adams shook his head in frustration and displeasure. His experience told him that the best time to destroy hostile planes was when they were parked on the ground. The worst time to deal with enemy fighters was one at a time, when they were airborne, buttoned up, and trying to kill you. It was basic common sense. Why didn't the armchair strategists in the White House and DOD understand that controlled escalation wouldn't work against these very patient North Vietnamese? Controlled escalation: that strategic brainchild of ivory-tower intellectuals for nuclear wars was too cute for this part of the world.

Wilson pressed on with his briefing. "Washington holds back these restricted targets; they're being considered for attack later, if the North Vietnamese don't respond to our demands at this level of conflict intensity."

Adams made a few barely audible grunts. "Conflict intensity? What the hell's 'conflict intensity'?"

Adams believed, as did every first-year cadet at the Air Force Academy, that this was not the way to fight an air war. First order of business should always be to generate overwhelming offensive counterair operations: destroy the enemy's air force on the ground, close his airfields, and eliminate his ability to control his remaining air forces with radar and other means of communication.

Allowing the NVAF the sanctuary of its airfields and permitting it to operate its radar net with impunity forfeited surprise and granted the bad guys a degree of combat leverage unprecedented in modern air warfare. For some unknown reason, the political strategists in Washington had been allowed to override sound military experience and equally valuable advice. Why hadn't they listened to the Joint Chiefs of Staff?

"Sir, in Vietnam we're ignoring the major historical lesson of the Battle of Britain, where the Luftwaffe failed to destroy British radars and airfields. The Luftwaffe had the right idea. At least the Luftwaffe *tried* to knock out the airfields and the radars."

"Agree." Adams knew what this meant at the tactical level. American air power was being frittered away inefficiently. It also meant that pilots were dying while the strategists back in Washington sent "signals" to the North Vietnamese. Signals that simply were being ignored and, worse, exploited by the enemy. Maybe the geniuses in Washington really were worried about getting the Chinese or the Russians into the war.

After pondering these restrictions, and satisfying himself that they were beyond his control, Adams moved on to things he could do something about. He interrupted Charlie Wilson with a wave of his hand, "Do we know anything of the men who lead and fly the MiGs? Do we have any information on the strategy and tactics that the NVAF uses against our formations?"

As well-prepared briefers always do, Charlie Wilson patiently said, "Ah, yes, sir, I was just getting to that. We don't know much about them individually. A few names, what they wear. Some are Russian trained. But overall, you'll be dealing with a mix. A few wily survivors who learn and live to kill us. And wingmen who are easy pickin' for our fighter pilots."

"What do we know about their best leaders in the air?" Adams pressed further.

"Well, there's talk about a pilot named Tomb. In our intell shop we call him 'the Dragon.' We're not sure he actually exists, but intelligence intercepts of enemy GCI radios continually refer to him by name." Wilson talked cautiously, trying to give the objective, balanced view.

Adams didn't want that. "Look, Charlie, skip the bureaucratic bullshit. Tell me what *you* think."

"Okay, he's a shadowy figure, but I think he's for real. A few of us correlated the radio calls with shootdowns of American planes and came up with this: Tomb is probably the commander of all fighter operations. If so, he likely gained his initial flying experience in the 1950s when the North Vietnamese built what we call a fighter squadron, but he kept the squadron in China until after the French left."

Adams listened intently. He leaned forward as the intell expert talked. This was the most fascinating part of today's briefing. Adams knew that aerial combat boiled down to the skill, experience, and courage of the men at the controls of the planes.

Wilson continued. "The North Vietnamese people themselves probably know little about Tomb. He ought to be a national hero, but he remains a secretive figure. He may not be 100 percent Vietnamese. Tomb's more of a Burmese name. This may be why the North Vietnamese haven't exploited his aerial accomplishments. They don't refer to him in their propaganda campaigns.

"Our records show he's probably an air ace. Maybe their top ace with perhaps eight to ten shootdowns, both U.S. Air Force and Navy planes. He's a stealthy, fleeting figure who uses hit-and-run tactics to chip away at the American formations. Tomb can be anywhere, flying older MiG-17s one day, and newer MiG-21s the next. We believe he favors the MiG-17.

"Our aftermission debriefings with returning pilots indicate that he can outfly most Americans with his MiG-17. And he has an uncanny knack for finding the wounded straggler. He appears out of nowhere. Probably understands English and monitors our tactical frequencies. He's a consummate dogfighter who only fights on his own terms, which has undoubtedly contributed to his longevity. He can tell when you are running out of fuel. He can down an opponent with cannon fire in a close-quarters turning battle, or he can show up deep in your six o'clock position to launch a heat-seeking missile before anyone knows he's there."

Wilson went on. "Most people around this headquarters don't think he exists. But this slide's a blowup of a picture a Third World photographer took of the MiG-21 arrival ceremony held at Kep last February. We don't know for sure, but by the insignia on his uniform, this guy could be Tomb.

"We lost another F-105 yesterday. High-speed attack by a single MiG-21 from the Thud's deep six o'clock. I think it was Tomb's work. I'll wait for the electronic intell to correlate the GCI radio calls, but I'm bettin' it was him."

Wilson stopped as Adams studied the grainy black-and-white picture on the projection screen showing Tomb amid a group of NVAF pilots. As the major put his pointer on the image of Tomb's chest, Adams's thoughts were very far away. Tomb would be a worthy adversary indeed. Clint Adams understood how such a wily air commander could give the Americans fits. What a pure Asian fighting dragon, thought Adams.

"Any questions, Colonel?" asked Wilson, jarring Adams back into the briefing room.

"Yes, I have a lot of questions, Charlie, but I'll find most of the answers somewhere else. Perhaps you can answer just one more. How do you know so much about Tomb?"

The unkempt major looked around the room, even though he knew he and Adams were the only ones there. Then he remembered the young airman flipping the slides in the rear projection room. "Okay, Johnson. I'll take it from here." He waited until the back room door closed. "Colonel, I can't say much. Only that it's COMINT and HUMINT. If I tell you any more you won't be able to fly combat missions. You'll know too much to get captured."

Adams knew that COMINT meant communications intelligence, and HUMINT was the acronym for human intelligence, which could mean a number of things. Perhaps a defector. Or maybe a clandestine spy on the ground in North Vietnam. Probably something in between, like social talk gleaned and properly laundered through a friendly embassy in Hanoi. Whatever it was, Charlie Wilson was right; Adams didn't have a need to know the source. "Thanks for the info, Charlie." The career intell officer nodded and left.

Turbo Woodside caught up to Adams as he walked out of the briefing room: "I've got you a seat on a Herky Bird going up to you know where Thursday night, sir."

"Perfect. Thanks, Turbo." This news gave him almost two more duty days to study the intelligence activity throughout the theater. Adams liked low-key arrivals. A flight to Ubon on a C-130 Hercules was just the ticket.

1255 hours
Outside Blue Chip Operations Center
Seventh Air Force HQ
Tan Son Nhut Air Base

Clint Adams hated windowless buildings, so common in the Air Force operations business. Too confining. They reminded him of the Pentagon, and that made any rational fighter pilot want to puke. Outside smoke breaks helped.

It was stifling outside at nearly 100 degrees, coupled with oppressive humidity. The unnatural churning of dust, generated by the high-tempo military activity going on in all directions, only made it harder for Adams to breathe. Hell of a price to pay for a cigarette, he thought. He still felt tired. It was unnatural tiredness for him, that strange zombie-like feeling everybody got when they first arrived in Vietnam. Congenital jet lag. Only now did he remember that he'd been on the move since General McKean told him to get to Saigon. His body clock still had him back in South Carolina, where it was midnight. He ought to be in bed. Preferably with Laura.

Well, Clint Adams, this was what you worked so hard for and risked so much for, he thought—taking command of a combat wing that's fumbling through the war with little real impact. What a chance to apply some Adams-style leadership.

Leadership. Adams considered its application his profession. He'd been developing his own brand ever since he arrived as a plebe at West Point in August 1940. Clint couldn't think about leadership without remembering Coach Blaik.

Blaik was the first man Adams knew who could take a unit on its butt and turn it around in the face of adversity. The way Clint saw it, Coach Blaik did more to forge the character of his football players than did all the U.S. Army training officers assigned to the Point. Adams still considered Blaik his role-model as a leader. Imagine that—a civilian role model.

Some men avoided the hard situations that natural leaders covet. Not Red Blaik. He took over the Army football team at the lowest point in its history. The challenge of turning around his alma mater's football program was irresistible to him. A normal man might have shunned this task.

Clint Adams vividly remembered the first time he'd seen Red Blaik. Adams was still a plebe, class of '44, on that first day of spring practice in 1941. Blaik held his initial team meeting on Michie Stadium's 50-yard line.

The gaunt forty-three-year-old, 6-foot Blaik looked out of place in his impeccably tailored suit and Park Avenue fedora. All the players had dressed out in full game equipment. The fifteen plebes—Adams among them—who took their places were a promising group, and Blaik would concentrate on them. This was a lesson Adams always recalled as he moved into leadership positions in later years.

"Gentlemen, we are going to play winning football this season." Blaik paused and looked each man in the eye; then he asked, "Do you know why?"

"No, sir!" The cadets responded in unison.

"Because we will play winning football as never before in the history of West Point. We will have four priorities: hard work, top physical conditioning, basic football skills, and teamwork." Blaik paused again, looking each man in the eye a second time. This had the effect of driving his short speech into the brain of everyone present. "Now let us begin."

That first spring practice was an all-out effort. By comparison, most games were physically and mentally easier. The stoic Blaik imbued his sense of purpose into the heart and tired body of every player. This pace was repeated in the late summer of 1941.

When the Black Knights took the field for the season opener, they were ready. Army 19, Citadel 6. At midseason, a 4–0 West Point team took on Notre Dame, the nation's top-ranked team. The contest against Frank Leahy's Fighting Irish was a war in the trenches. The temperature hovered just above freezing in Michie Stadium, and a steady rain fell throughout the game. By halftime, the players were recognizable only by their position and their performance. And the best of the lot on that day was Third Classman Clint Adams, the most notable member of Army's youth corps. Army 0, Notre Dame 0.

That was the highwater mark for the year. Narrow losses to Penn and Navy followed—relative victories given drubbings at the hands of both the year before. Army posted a 5–3–1 record in 1941. Red Blaik finished third in the national coach of the year balloting.

Cadet Third Class Clint Adams was selected as an All-American left tackle—a rare honor for a sophomore. These accomplishments were forever burned into the hearts and minds of Clint Adams and the other players who took the field that last innocent fall before America entered World War II. Ten days after the traditional season finale at Soldier's Field in Philadelphia, the Japanese attacked Pearl Harbor, irrevocably altering the world and Clint Adams's future.

Adams broke his ankle before the 1942 season, which like the other "war seasons" were recorded as sports events of secondary importance. True competition, like everything else, had subordinated itself to the war.

Spending the 1942 season on the sidelines gave Clint Adams the chance to study Red Blaik, the leader. Blaik made tough, split-second decisions as a field commander under pressure, and Adams built his own set of operating rules for leading men in battle: hard work in preparation, attention to the basics, a keen sense of teamwork, and being in top physical and mental shape to do the job. He had lived by these rules for more than twenty-five years. And he always asked his men to do the same.

America's entry into the war altered Clint Adams's life as a cadet as well. The War Department needed thousands of young officers quickly. Congress approved a law reducing West Point and Annapolis from four- to three-year programs for the duration of the war. Clint Adams, newly elected co-captain of the Army football team for the upcoming fall 1943 season, volunteered with all his other classmates to graduate in June 1943. He had played only one season for Coach Blaik, but Blaik had put his mark on this young man.

Another wartime anomaly presented Clint Adams with the major opportunity of his life. The Army Air Corps needed 40,000 pilots a year to fly the airplanes being produced by the massive American war mobilization effort. West Point second classmen were given the chance to volunteer for pilot training, and Adams was first in line. The Army rapidly constructed Stewart Field 5 miles from West Point to turn cadets into pilots.

Each cadet took the same course as the U.S. Army aviation cadets marshaling by the thousands at training sites throughout the country. Flight training was normally a full-time, twenty-seven–week regimen carried out at three locations. But for the West Point cadets in Clint Adams's class, all flying training was conducted at Stewart Field and was integrated with the accelerated three-year West Point curriculum, concentrated mostly in the third year and eating up cadet weekends in the process.

It began with the primary school: ground training and sixty flying hours in the Stearman PT-17 Kaydet. The venerable biplane separated out those who did not have the stomach for flying. The cadets then moved on to the basic course, seventy flying hours in the Vultee BT-13 Valiant, a low-wing monoplane. Those who did not wash out for flying deficiency or die in training accidents moved on to the advanced course. The cadets destined to fly fighters, like Clint, flew yet another seventy hours in the North American AT-6 Texan, a high-performance, closed-cockpit monoplane with retractable landing gear.

Adams had special gifts as an aviator. He was strong enough to horse around the PTs, BTs, and ATs when they needed it. And he had the rare ability to fly them precisely when required. Above all else, in the air, he always knew exactly where he was and where everyone else was, too. He had that special gift of a fighter pilot. His instructors quickly recognized Adams's abilities. Although held back a little by the ground school academics, he finished third in his aviation class of 251 surviving cadets. Six cadets had died in training accidents.

On 7 June 1943, the Army commissioned Adams a second lieutenant on the parade field at West Point. That same day it awarded him his silver wings as a new pilot in the Army Air Corps. Coach Blaik watched from the wooden bleachers.

That afternoon, the fledgling aviator, with 200 hours in the air, left for Dover Field, Delaware, to check out in America's hottest new fighter, the Lockheed P-38 Lightning. As a Lightning pilot he began to learn the lessons of aerial combat that later served him well over Rotterdam, Frankfurt, and Berlin.

Now at Tan Son Nhut, Adams wondered as he crushed out his third straight Camel cigarette how those lessons would hold up over Hanoi against someone like Colonel Tomb.

Clint looked around his new environment before returning to another series of briefings on tactical targeting. Perhaps Ubon wouldn't be quite so steamy, so noisy, so dirty, he thought.

1455 hours
Kep Airfield
Forty kilometers northeast of Hanoi

Soviet Air Force Colonel Ivan Arkov stood in the slowly lengthening shadow of the old French control tower. Six-feet-two, slender, and muscular for a Russian, Arkov's straight brown Slavic hair and green eyes fixed his ancestral roots in the Russian steppes.

Ivan Arkov was sweating in the afternoon heat. The shade of the control tower did little to offset the oppressive humidity. He should be used to the Vietnamese heat and humidity by now, but he wasn't. Six long months in this hellhole called Vietnam and four previous years in Cuba had done little to thin his thick Russian blood.

Arkov missed the seasons of his boyhood days near Moscow. But Hanoi held compensations for a young, virile man. The benefits of overseas duty far outweighed the drawbacks of continued service away from Mother Russia: increased pay, double retirement credit, and freedom from the silly political scrutiny of the Soviet flying units back home. He enjoyed the status of being an elite and trusted officer. Few Soviet pilots served beyond the borders of the motherland. And he favored the young Oriental women who found him mysteriously attractive and generous with his extra earnings. Most of all, he liked making life difficult for the Americans who came to bomb the North Vietnamese.

He hated the American pilots. He didn't care that they were products of capitalism. He left ideology to the politicians at the Soviet Embassy in downtown Hanoi. No, his enmity was that of a proud Soviet pilot for the arrogance of all American pilots. He knew that world opinion considered American pilots to be best, while Soviet pilots were thought of as automatons, merely extensions of a rigid, inflexible air defense network.

Arkov understood that the correlation of events over North Vietnam offered a great opportunity to undermine the aura of American air power. Here he could exploit so many advantages to humiliate the Americans. The North Vietnamese fought directly above their own land, while operating modern air defense radars, a growing SAM and AAA network, and all the MiGs they were willing to put in the air.

And the foolish Americans cooperated in many ways. They came at the same time on the same routings every day. Such a chance to embarrass the Americans must be fully exploited, he thought. Yet, in Arkov's estimation, the American humiliation was not happening fast enough. More could be done to destroy the Americans' attack formations. But the North Vietnamese would not allow the Russians to operate the high-technology air defense radars, SAMs, and flak guns. This was a Vietnamese war, and they planned to win it by themselves and in their own time.

In Arkov's view, the North Vietnamese were squandering numerous opportunities every day to bring down American planes in high numbers. The North Vietnamese were not proficient in coordinating their air defenses. They were not technically skilled in operating the modern electronic radars. And they did not know how to coordinate the MiG and SAM attacks on the Yankee air strikes.

Worse, these Orientals were too timid. They were content to use sporadic hit-and-run tactics to unsettle the Americans. The NVAF judged it a successful day if the American planes dropped their bombs prematurely, away from the intended target. To the NVAF, destroying the American planes was secondary. They did not see the strategic value of bringing down many American fighter-bombers in a short time. It was Arkov's job to change that. That was why Brigadier General Alexsi Borin, the senior air attaché at the Soviet Embassy in Hanoi, asked that Arkov be assigned as the chief Soviet field training adviser to the NVAF.

He had been a professional instructor pilot and military adviser for six years. His political superiors had allowed this second consecutive overseas tour because Arkov had performed so well in Cuba. They had rewarded him with this rare advisory command opportunity to build up the NVAF.

Arkov mulled all this over for the 100th time as he watched Colonel Tomb's MiG-17 glide down the last mile of final approach and touch down on the bumpy, 2,500-meter-long runway. The MiG's landing roll was a series of jolts along the Soviet-rebuilt runway surface, made of 5-meter concrete squares squeezed together atop a poorly prepared undersurface.

The Russian didn't like Colonel Nguyen Tomb. He had said so many times in his classified reports to General Borin. Borin's reaction was always the same: "Make it work, overcome these differences, and remember it's their country and their war. And remember, Arkov: if you cannot do this, you will be replaced."

Arkov was impatient with Tomb's Maoist approach to aerial combat—guerrilla tactics in the air, hit-and-run engagements, and fleeting strikes at the Americans' most vulnerable forces. Arkov saw these attacks as mere irritants to the Americans. He believed most of the NVAF pilots were worthless cowards. Only a few had the guts for aerial combat; and those few were poorly led by the overly cautious Tomb. Tomb's approach to combat flying was alien to Arkov. The Russian was very aggressive by nature. To Arkov, Tomb was too careful, too stoic, too quiet, and much too tolerant of his pilots' failings in the air.

Arkov repeatedly pressed Tomb to incorporate his ideas for bolder, large-scale attacks. Arkov wanted Soviet pilots to lead and augment the NVAF in the air. He wanted bigger attack formations, using Soviet tactics to seriously challenge the American strike forces. Arkov himself yearned for the chance to shoot down some of the highly vaunted American pilots. He had to convince Tomb to let Russian pilots fly against the Americans. And Arkov wanted to be the first.

Arkov also found it curious that the North Vietnamese pilots preferred the venerable MiG-17 over the modern MiG-21. He saw this preference as a clear sign that NVAF pilots were basically cowards in the air. And cowardice led to timidity, which led to high losses in aerial combat. The NVAF pilots should be eager to fly the hottest new Soviet fighter. In the right hands, the supersonic MiG-21 would chew up the American formations. The delta-wing, Mach 2 plane was the finest work done by the collaborating team of Colonel-General Artem I. Mikoyan and Mikail I. Gurevich. It was the dominant fighter of the Communist world. Arkov was disgusted that these damned Orientals didn't appreciate the Soviet Union's generosity. He knew that Tomb was the key to getting the Vietnamese to fly the MiG-21 well. But Tomb favored the MiG-17. Idiot! And the others followed him like puppies.

Colonel Tomb taxied his plane into its parking place in a revetment near the control tower. He shut down the engine and slid back his canopy. He watched Arkov out of the corner of his eye as he unstrapped, climbed down, and signed a form for the ground crew chief. He moved slowly, taking twice the normal time with each task. He knew Arkov wanted to see him. Better that he should wait longer. When he could delay no longer, he began his walk toward the operations building at the foot of the control tower, 50 meters away.

Tomb was still wearing his leather helmet with the flight goggles pushed back above his forehead. He looked over at the two MiG-21PFs parked to his left. Five young pilots were sitting on a missile dolly in front of the planes. When they saw Colonel Tomb, they interrupted their training session, stood, and saluted their leader. He returned their salute and followed up with a friendly wave.

Tomb admired the clean lines and performance of the MiG-21. It was an excellent example of the Communist world's newest fighter plane. The unpainted aluminum skins of the two parked at his air base gleamed in the late morning sunlight. The large red serial numbers—#4327 and #4328—indicated that they were the next two MiG-21s assigned to the 1st Air Company after his own personal MiG-21, #4326. Tomb was disappointed in the slow progress he was making in integrating the MiG-21 into the NVAF. Still, he had some concerns about the MiG-21. He liked the plane, but he wasn't sure it was the best plane for defending his homeland.

One element of the NVAF MiG-21 program particularly annoyed him, the Russian Colonel Arkov. The arrangement was that Arkov remained to assist in the training of the first twenty-five NVAF pilots. Only five more combat-ready MiG-21 pilots, and Tomb would be rid of the egocentric Russian.

Tomb noticed Arkov getting impatient at the edge of the tarmac and expected that the Russian would press his ideas again. The Vietnamese colonel pulled a simple tan silk scarf from his trouser pocket and wrapped it around his neck as he continued toward Arkov. The maintenance people nearby watched Tomb admiringly. He was nearly a deity to them. He waved in their direction.

As Tomb approached, Arkov saluted the smaller man and asked, "How was your mission from Gia Lam, Colonel?"

Tomb casually returned the Russian's salute and continued past him toward the modest one-room, cinder-block building that served as his field office here at Kep. He removed his gloves. "The sortie was a pleasure. The sky was clear of American bombers." Then he added, "At least for now."

Tomb entered his austere office. The room contained an old wooden French desk and two spartan chairs. The mildewed walls needed paint badly. What little paint there was peeled from all four walls and the ceiling. Arkov followed him inside. "Colonel, have you given my proposal any more thought?"

Tomb knew this conversation was inevitable when he decided to fly to Kep today. "Yes, I have, Colonel."

This irritated the Soviet. He would twist off Tomb's head if he could get away with it. Arkov tried a different tactic. "I can be more valuable by flying combat sorties with your pilots. As you know, they behave differently in combat than on the training flights I fly with them."

"Yes, I know, Colonel." Tomb lit a British Dunhill cigarette. Again, he did not pursue the subject.

"You don't have any intention of letting Soviet pilots fly against the Americans, do you?" Arkov got right to the heart of the matter. "You could bring down many more bombers if Soviet pilots manned even a few of the available Mikoyans."

Tomb stood and moved to the shadeless window. Absentmindedly watching the aircraft maintenance activity on the tarmac, Tomb meted out a few more words, "Conditions are not favorable for such action, Colonel. How will my pilots ever develop the confidence to fight the Americans if they fly into battle on the wing of a Russian?"

Tomb extinguished his Dunhill, donned his cap, and walked out onto the tarmac to visit his pilots. Arkov hoped some lucky American would kill Tomb very soon.

28 September 1966 1930 hours
Tan Son Nhut Air Base flight line

Clint Adams boarded the four-engine Lockheed C-130 by walking up the extended ramp of the rear cargo door. He carried his own B-4 bag and traveled with a group of Air Force enlisted men and Army soldiers bound for one of the six stops this plane would make that night. Ubon was stop number four, seven hours away.

The C-130 Hercules was the workhorse of intratheater air cargo movement, or tactical airlift. The Air Force owned 500 C-130s; most were used for missions similar to the one carrying Adams to Ubon.

Tonight's mission carried a mixed load of cargo and passengers. Adams mixed in with the sergeants as the loadmaster handed out ear plugs to everyone. As the number one engine wound up, the ride was hot, humid, noisy, and very uncomfortable. But it was also free.

2000 hours
Gia Lam Airport, 10 kilometers east of downtown Hanoi
Tomb's quarters

Nguyen Tomb rubbed his temples as he mulled over the rumpled papers before him. He had spent the past two hours tending to a critical report he must submit to the Defense Ministry. Brushing away the bothersome moth competing with him for the desk light, Tomb pushed himself to finish the last of the recommendations he wanted to make to his superiors. They must understand the progress his modest fighter force had made, he thought. The gains of the past three months were impressive indeed: a 54 percent increase in combat sorties; a 33 percent improvement in enemy aircraft destroyed; and a 20 percent jump in aircraft available for combat. His pilots and maintenance men were making excellent progress. In his conclusion, Tomb recommended that the number of Russian advisers working on the MiG-17 be reduced to a token four-man team. He ended his work on the report by predicting that he would be able to do the same with the MiG-21 advisers in six months.

Tomb threw down the pencil and rubbed his eyes, strained by the dim light of the only lamp, a Chinese model not up to its task. His return flight from Kep late this afternoon was routine, part of his pattern of moving from base to base, visiting each of his three air companies. He scheduled these flights during periods of low American bombing activity.

He enjoyed these solitary periods after dinner in his private apartment at Gia Lam Airport. He lit a second Dunhill. Gia Lam, the country's only civil airfield, was located just east of downtown Hanoi across the Red River. It was the diplomatic umbilical cord that always remained open, and Tomb considered it a sanctuary. He didn't think the Americans would ever bomb Gia Lam because the International Control Commission (ICC) used the airport to fly its scheduled missions from the Laotian capital of Vientiane to Hanoi twice a week.

Gia Lam was an old French airport, with a short runway more tailored to propeller-driven planes like the ICC's overworked DC-3 and DC-6. His apartment was in the main building, just above the small restaurant that served the few passengers transiting Gia Lam. Each night one of the waiters brought Tomb his meal, which he ate in private.

The apartment was austere by Western standards, more like a studio with a full bathroom. The main room had a comfortable bed, three stuffed chairs, and a desk. Tomb had a wooden console radio that sat on the floor in one corner. One wall was almost all glass and afforded an excellent view of the airfield, and, in the distance, the Red River and downtown Hanoi. On peaceful nights, he sat for hours relishing the moonlight and the few lights that outlined the city. When America brought the war to Hanoi, he would stand and watch the pyrotechnics of the battle: streams of tracers leaping into the air; an occasional SAM, and even the American photo flares popping off in a line of six, like giant flashbulbs in the sky.

Tonight he was distracted and still troubled by the earlier exchange with Colonel Arkov. This whole business with the Russians was uncomfortable. The North Vietnamese preferred self-reliance in all things. That was what independence was all about. The Russians had a different agenda.

Nguyen Tomb remembered the day ten months ago when the Russians formally presented #4326 to him. The fat General Borin had even deigned to make one of his rare trips out of Hanoi. It had been Borin's only visit to Kep Airfield. Two dozen Russian technicians had sweated in the noon heat waiting for Borin to arrive. They had put together the partially assembled MiG in just two days following its ocean voyage by Soviet freighter from Vladivostok.

The transfer ceremony was the closest thing to a media event Tomb had seen. On the previous day, a Soviet test pilot had flown #4326, finding only a few minor discrepancies. About forty-five minutes before the ceremony itself, a tall Russian colonel arrived from the Soviet Embassy, suited himself up, preflighted the fully fueled plane, started its engine, taxied, and took off. Colonel Ivan Arkov was in the air on his first sortie over North Vietnam. Minutes later, a dozen European and Oriental newspaper correspondents and photographers arrived under tight control of the usual Communist party officials.

Almost everybody assigned to Kep Airfield was there. The honored dignitaries were the much-acclaimed, diminutive General Giap and the ponderous, sweaty General Borin, a big chunk of a man. At the appointed hour, a North Vietnamese party official from Hanoi made the customary introductions, and General Borin came to the podium. He read a prepared statement in Russian with little enthusiasm, which was translated to the audience with much more fervor. Everyone clapped politely.

The people came for only two reasons: General Giap and the MiG-21. They all craned their necks to get a look at Giap, the military hero of Dien Bien Phu. Giap was revered by the North Vietnamese, a humble man who always sported a disarming, warm smile. While serving with Ho Chi Minh and current Premier Pham Van Dong in southern China in May 1941, Giap helped them establish the Indochinese Communist party. At the same time, the three men announced the Vietnam liberation movement, the Viet Minh. By North Vietnamese standards, this made General Giap a bona fide founding father.

And, of course, the people had come to see the MiG-21. It came upon them quickly, streaking down the runway in full afterburner at 100 feet and 450 knots with Colonel Ivan Arkov at the controls. At the end of the runway, he pulled the fighter straight up until the relatively small plane was only visible when the sun bounced off its metal skin 10,000 feet up.

Watching the magnificent silver plane, Tomb had thought about how far his air force had come in so short a time. And that he had been with it all the way. He swelled with pride as the MiG-21 went through a series of rolls and turning maneuvers to the oohs and aahs of the crowd. Tomb thought the aircraft would make a substantial improvement in the NVAF's ability to attack and destroy the American fighter-bombers. As the aircraft taxied into its parking spot in front of the reviewing stand, Tomb knew he had a formidable task ahead of him. He alone was responsible for integrating the MiG-21 into the NVAF.

Three months earlier he had sent his six best pilots to the Soviet Union for MiG-21 training. Only four returned. One pilot was killed when he did not eject after his MiG's engine failed shortly after takeoff. And the second NVAF pilot rode his plane to impact in a violent spin. Each pilot had one American kill to his credit. They knew how to fly, yet the Soviets cited the pilots' inexperience as the prime cause of both accidents. The other four NVAF pilots who returned on the freighter with the first four MiG-21Fs told Tomb that the new planes were highly powered, some-what unstable, and very unforgiving.

The returning pilots were part of the acceptance ceremony. They took their assigned places in front of the crowd. Each wore the standard Soviet-made MiG-21 white helmet and rubberized pressure suit. They looked impressive, like cosmonauts about to enter their spacecraft. The crowd cheered when the narrator introduced them as the first MiG-21 pilots in the NVAF.

But Tomb saw things differently. If the ceremony did not end soon his pilots would pass out from heat stroke. Their flying gear was designed for the Russian climate and the Soviet high-altitude, point-intercept mission. The large helmets made the small-framed Vietnamese look like creatures from another planet. The tight-fitting pressure suits accentuated the head distortion by clinging tightly to the pilots' torsos. Tomb realized then he would have to make some adjustments.

The ceremony had gone well up to this point. But in Tomb's judgment, shared by many Vietnamese in the audience, the transfer ended on a down note, one that unalterably set the character of the relationship between Tomb and Arkov. When the Russian pilot opened his canopy by propping it up on its forward hinge, the narrator introduced Colonel Arkov to the audience's applause. Then the speaker announced that Arkov would remain at Kep to train the NVAF pilots in the new MiG-21s. This public statement gave too much ascendancy to Arkov and the Russians, while the NVAF pilots lost face in front of their own friends and families. Tomb had not been given the opportunity to clear the ceremonial remarks, which had been written in Hanoi by administrators and Russians. If he had, he would have stricken this last part.

The NVAF had been flying their fourteen MiG-21s for ten months now. Tomb was not pleased by the transition program's slow progress. His twenty MiG-21 pilots still did not have confidence in their new, very modern fighting weapon. Tomb blamed this more on the plane than on the pilots he'd handpicked for the MiG-21 program.

29 September 1966 0330 hours
Eastern Thailand, 340 miles northwest of Saigon
Ubon Royal Thai Air Force Base, Thailand

The C-130 on final approach for landing at Ubon lumbered out of the bottom of a nighttime tropical rain shower that doused the airfield. The C-130 pilot guided the straight-winged, four-engine transport down to a controlled roundout and slick touchdown. The plane easily plowed through the standing puddles on the smooth, wet concrete surface. The single runway was a relatively narrow 105 feet, 45 feet tighter than the standard U.S. Air Force runway. The Hercules's wingtips overhung well into the 4-foot-high elephant grass bordering the runway.

The airlift pilot put his plane into much tighter Army fields than this almost every night. Still, he shut down the outboard engines as he turned left onto the even narrower taxiway. Two minutes later, he turned into the cargo ramp on the remote southeast side of the field. The C-130 swung around for the final turn into parking. While taxiing to the cargo ramp, the pilot opened the rear cargo doors to keep the interior of the plane a little cooler. The price was increased noise.

Adams caught an initial glimpse of the F-4 flight line on the opposite side of the runway at Ubon. He couldn't see much, just the silhouettes of some Phantoms bathed in floodlights about 300 yards away. Clint Adams felt at home. He was comfortable going into combat at Ubon and with flying the McDonnell F-4C Phantom II.

The C-130 pilot jolted the plane to an unanticipated early full stop in the chocks. This rudely reminded Adams that a four-hop ride on a C-130A was like riding in an electric blender for seven hours. He'd never been so happy to get off an airplane in his life. Except for maybe one time earlier this week.

As the airlift pilot shut down the C-130's last two engines, the load-master lowered the aft ramp so the Ubon passengers could deplane. Adams grabbed his bulging B-4 bag and followed two sleepy enlisted men off into the night.

So this was Ubon. His first combat command. He couldn't see much of it, but he could feel it. The night air was just as steamy as it was in Saigon, made worse by the recent shower. Even 100 miles and three countries deep into the Southeast Asian peninsula, the field was a mere 405 feet above sea level. Ubon's cargo ramp occupied a remote corner of the base, away from the fighter ramp and the main base proper with all its sleeping quarters. Cargo movement was a noisy, round-the-clock operation best left to itself when possible.

Adams hadn't called ahead, but he expected to be met anyway. He consciously chose to arrive this way at this time. It was really a test. He knew that the C-130 aircraft commander called the Ubon command post to pass the required arrival information: aircraft block-in time, breakdown of the cargo off-load, number of passengers off-load, and any special requirements. Any arriving colonel was one such special requirement.

In Air Force jargon, Adams was a DV Code 7F, meaning "distinguished visitor, Air Force colonel." The Ubon command post duty controller should've dispatched a protocol duty officer, nicknamed "Peter the Greeter." Peter would welcome all DVs and provide any desired assistance. A wing that didn't track and help transiting DVs meant poor command and control and wing leaders who didn't pay attention to necessary details and procedures.

Although Adams had assumed that Turbo Woodside would arrange a pickup on this end, he now realized that he had probably scared the young aide-de-camp from making *any* calls to Ubon. While he contemplated matters, Clint saw that the two young noncommissioned officers (NCOs) with whom he had deplaned were in good hands. Two sergeants from one of the 8th TFW's maintenance squadrons greeted the arrivals, piled into a blue van, and departed for the main side of the base. That was good. Ubon maintenance had a program that took care of its own.

Adams picked up his bag and started hoofing over to the perimeter road, some 30 yards away. He hoped to hitch a ride on one of the vehicles using this main artery around the base. Just as he reached the roadside, a speeding pickup truck approaching from the main base pulled off the road toward the C-130. Adams tried waving it down, but the captain at the wheel didn't notice Adams.

Adams threw his B-4 bag onto the roadside gravel. "Goddammit!" When a colonel waved at a captain, the captain was supposed to stop. That was the rule. Adams had no choice but to march back to the cargo ramp. He found the captain signing for a piece of "special handling" cargo, probably a high-priority part of some kind. The younger officer was obviously a pilot. He was wearing the standard-issue, lightweight, green cotton flight suit. Like Adams, he sported black, jungle flying boots with breathable, green canvas sidings.

Adams reached the captain just as the C-130 loadmaster turned back to his other duties. No salute. The younger aviator barely noticed. He obviously didn't expect to see a colonel floating around out here. The young pilot carefully placed the small cardboard package into the back of the pickup.

"Excuse me, Captain. Did you see me waving at you back there?"

Captain Randall James Starbuck was intent on his duties. The 6-foot, sandy-haired bachelor mumbled in a southern drawl without looking up. "Wait a minute, I'm doin' something important here."

"Hey, Bub, I'm talking to you."

The remark caught young Starbuck by surprise, and he turned to see the towering figure of an unknown full-bird colonel standing in the night. Adams's silhouette almost blocked out the C-130. The silver eagle on Adams's flight cap twinkled as the cargo ramp's perimeter light bounced off it. Starbuck saluted. Adams, his fists clenched on his hips, slowly returned the salute. Now he had control of the situation.

"Uh, sir, I wasn't payin' that much attention. I had a part here to get before this trash hauler took off. Been waitin' for this part all week." Randy Starbuck talked with the slow drawl of his childhood days. It always worked well when the teacher sent him down to the principal's office.

"Do you have time now to give me a ride to the wing command post?"

"Oh, yes, sir. But I guess you mean the Tactical Operations Center? The TOC?"

"Yeah, that's right."

Both men piled into the cab. Starbuck drove over to pick up Adams's B-4 bag at roadside, then embarked on the 3-mile trip around the base perimeter road to the command post.

"Sir, are you gonna be stationed here?"

"I'm the new wing commander." Adams held out his hand. Starbuck shook it passively. "Name's Adams. Clint Adams."

"The new. . .," Starbuck started his recovery operation. "Sir, my name's Randy Starbuck. I didn't—"

"That's okay, Randy. What's that part you were so hell-bent to pick up?"

"That's our first RHAW gear logic board. You know, radar homing and warning. Designed to tell us what radars are lookin' at us and what's shootin' at us when we're flyin'. Electronically, that is." Starbuck referred to the new black box receiver that recognized and displayed electronic signals that washed over the aircraft. The APR-25 display panel for the RHAW gear would be located in the upper right corner of the F-4's front seat main instrument panel.

"Why's a fighter jock like you picking it up?"

"I'm the chief of wing tactics. We do everything that's new first. Operationally, that is." Starbuck stopped the pickup in front of the wing headquarters building. "Sir, I'll get your B-4 bag over to the commander's, er, your trailer. The TOC's in there. Can I do anything else for you, sir?"

"No. Thanks, Randy. Look forward to flying with you."

0400 hours
8th TFW Headquarters
Ubon RTAFB

Clint Adams got out of the pickup and walked inside to the 8th Wing TOC at the end of the hall. The air policeman posted as security guard at the single entry door to the TOC was slow to come out of his slouch as Adams approached. Sleepily, he nodded to the colonel expecting to see a routine flash of a restricted-area badge. But that didn't happen. For Adams, it was another test. Strike one. He said nothing to the airman first class, waiting to see what would happen next.

"Can I help you, sir?" The air policeman was still groggy. Strike two.

"Yes, I'm Colonel Adams, the new 8th Wing commander. I want to enter the TOC. I just arrived, so I don't have a restricted-area badge yet, and I'm not on your access roster." He showed his green identification card to the air policeman as he talked.

"I'm sorry, sir, I'll have to check with the senior duty controller." The guard was doing better now. He just wasn't real sharp. The young two-striper picked up the hot line to the TOC duty officer and explained the situation. Then he told Adams that the duty officer was on his way out.

Ten seconds later, Major Roscoe Stewart arrived at the secure entry door, looked through the one-way glass at Adams, and swung the door open.

"Hey, sir, welcome to the war zone! It's me, Roscoe. Haven't seen you since the purple water fountain!"

"Roscoe, is that you behind that beaver? It's good to, ah, see you."

The short, bald, wiry little major in his mid-thirties with an obscene handlebar mustache thrust his hand out to Clint Adams. "Your 'stache looks like you've been here a month!"

"Started it ten days ago when I got my orders," replied Adams. "Still itches like hell."

Roscoe Stewart had been one of Adams's action officers in the Pentagon in the Directorate of Operations Fighter Division in the early 1960s. Anyone who had ever walked the maze of hallways in the Pentagon's basement knew that *the* most prominent landmark was a tiny purple water fountain. All directions were given in relation to the curious little landmark.

"I'll vouch for the colonel, airman." Roscoe hit a four-number code and reopened the entry door. Adams looked coldly at the young security guard, who saluted crisply, knowing he should have been more alert from the beginning. He suspected the security watch sergeant would get the word and chew his ass in the morning.

In Air Force command posts, no one interrupts activity to call the facility to attention for visiting VIPs. This one was no different as nobody in the TOC took special note of their duty officer and the new colonel he had in tow. The two men stood just inside the door. Roscoe Stewart described the TOC's layout to Adams. The officers and enlisted men on this shift were busy coordinating the necessary arrival procedures for the three two-ship F-4 flights currently returning to Ubon after working targets on the Ho Chi Minh Trail.

The TOC was a telephone, status-board, and grease-pencil environment. As a former wing commander, Adams was very familiar with the general layout of a tactical fighter-wing TOC. He was already focusing on the differences evident in this particular one.

When Stewart finished his cursory explanations, Adams asked, "What's that grease board in the far left corner?" Stewart tried to downplay it and change the subject, but Adams asked again.

"That's the board that tracks the missions of our attached pilots, those not directly assigned to our, er, *your* three flying squadrons. You know, the wing staff, really."

Adams moved closer to study the board in detail; the data were quite revealing. Colonel Goodman's numbers were still posted. He finished a full tour of 100 missions over North Vietnam, but he never flew to Route Package Six—the Hanoi area. Adams also noted that the 8th Wing DCO, Colonel Slim Danforth, had been at Ubon four months but had flown only seventeen counters, or missions, over the North. Again, none to Pack Six. The wing assistant DCO, Colonel George "Happy" Parker, had only fifteen counters in five months, none to Pack Six. The board showed Colonel Parker had been off-station on temporary duty (TDY) for six days. He was logged out to "CCK" and due back the next day.

"What's going on at CCK, Roscoe?"

"That's Ching Chuang Kang Air Base on the southern tip of Formosa. We send our worn-out Phantoms there for depot maintenance, and we use it as a good deal for our crews. You know, take up one plane, stay a few days, then fly back a refurbished F-4 by way of Clark in the Philippines."

Adams didn't say it directly, but he thought that these interludes should be more for the line pilots than the senior wing staff. Happy Parker should have been here helping Slim Danforth run the wing, since the wing commander and vice commander positions were temporarily vacant. And Danforth ought to have the good sense to have known that. Worse yet, Parker had taken the usual three-day pad and doubled it.

"Not too red hot, Roscoe."

Stewart shrugged as if caught in some illicit act. "Colonel, it's been like this ever since I got here, sir."

"How come you didn't send out the protocol duty officer to meet the C-130?"

"Just fucked up, sir. Sorry." Adams could see that there was no penalty for poor performance because the DCO and assistant DCO weren't watching the farm. Even good people like Roscoe were letting things slide.

"I'm gonna get some sleep, Roscoe. Ask Colonel Danforth to stop by my quarters at 0730."

"Yessir. It'll be my last official act as a TOC duty officer. Tomorrow I go back to the squadron full time."

"Good. That's where you belong."

Stewart laughed at the remark. Adams left the TOC. He planned on spending lots of time there later.

0730 hours
Colonel Adams's trailer
Ubon RTAFB

Colonel Sylvester "Slim" Danforth pulled up in the wing commander's blue staff car. Danforth looked as if he'd accidentally dropped out of the sky into the wrong war. He was the executive-type colonel, direct from central casting: lean, naturally tan, and neatly groomed to a fault, every close-cut, salt-and-pepper hair was in place. The 6-foot-1-inch, forty-year-old career staff officer was out of place at Ubon. Like his feelings, Danforth's brown eyes remained concealed behind his gold-rimmed RayBan sunglasses. But today was a little different. Slim dabbed away the light perspiration from his forehead as he walked to meet his new boss.

Danforth was more appropriately dressed for a day of staff work at a major headquarters stateside, wearing his 1505 uniform, a short-sleeve, open-collar tan shirt and matching cuffless trousers broken only by a blue belt with a chrome buckle. Danforth's "low-quarter" black street shoes were spit shined to inspection quality. He was wearing his service cap, a dressy, round blue hat with a hard black brim, embroidered with silver clouds and lightning bolts. His appearance matched his approach to life—strong on appearance.

Danforth hadn't changed much since his college days at Stanford. He was very thin, almost gaunt, ramrod straight, and had a stern visage and coldness that made people uncomfortable. He was not a people person and he was not at ease commanding operational units. He coveted the job of 8th TFW commander but only as a quick stepping stone to his brigadier general's star and a series of senior executive assignments in Washington.

Slim Danforth remembered Adams from the Pentagon. He knew Adams was a "fighter-mafia type" who worked in the Operations Directorate in the Pentagon's basement, about as far away from Danforth's fourth-floor office in the under secretary's executive suite as was possible. He remembered Adams as having fighter experience, as being outspoken, and as frequently getting in hot water for his views. Danforth had hoped to draw someone easier to work with; he was not looking forward to Clint Adams.

He knocked on the new wing commander's trailer door. Adams was ready for the day's activities; he was wearing a fresh flight suit, highly polished jungle flying boots, and a thin blue flight cap. He didn't ask Danforth inside the trailer. Rather, Adams stepped out into the already irritating morning sun. His eyes were still red from the C-130 flight and too little sleep. Self-consciously, Adams popped on his gold-rimmed Air Force flying glasses. He tightened his stomach muscles, erasing the small gut he still carried from the States. He didn't want to show Danforth any weakness at the outset.

"Welcome to Ubon, sir. I'm Slim Danforth." Danforth shuffled backward as Adams pumped his hand.

"Thanks. Glad to be here, Slim. Looking forward to a full day."

"Sorry I missed you last night, Colonel, but we weren't sure when you were coming. Couldn't get any info out of General Morgan's office."

"Yeah, kind of looked that way."

"Sir, there's a great deal happening right now. I recommend a windshield tour for openers so you can get your bearings straight away."

"Sounds good to me," replied Adams.

As they drove down the flight line to the headquarters building, Adams watched the activity outside the car. The enlisted men were walking from place to place with their hands in their pockets and their heads down, mostly looking at their shoes.

Danforth filled the silence with small comments, trying to impress upon Adams that good order and discipline were just as important in

Thailand as in CONUS (continental United States). "I got the base commander working on an installation upgrade program. You know, sprucing the place up. We've added fifty Thai workers for cutting the grass and edging, that sort of thing." Most of this chatter was harmless. But not Danforth's last comment, "It's taken me several months to get the squadron commanders to make their pilots toe the line." Adams looked at him, irritated that Danforth seemed more interested in peacetime norms of conformity than in combat operations.

The two men completed the traditional driving tour of the base and pulled up in front of the 8th TFW's Headquarters building. It housed the wing HQ staff, the operations staff, and the TOC. As Danforth stopped the car, Adams noticed the 6-foot-high emblem above the front entrance, the official 8th TFW crest. Like all Air Force unit crests, a Latin inscription was emblazoned in the scroll along its bottom border. It read, "Attaquez et Conquerez." Even the least literate pilot could translate its meaning.

Beneath the official crest hung a second sign, originally conceived during the Korean War, when the 8th Fighter-Bomber Wing flew F-86F Sabres at Suwon Air Base. This sign read, "Through these portals walk the best fighter pilots in the world."

Clint Adams didn't notice the motivators last night and craned his neck to look up at the crest and the motto.

Danforth noted, "Pretty good stuff, isn't it? The 8th has a proud heritage that began in Australia during World War II. Good Korean War record too. Now here in Vietnam, it's building an enviable performance again. Three wars in just over twenty years. Good accounting of itself out here in the Far East."

"Well, I hope the sign painters are right."

"Right, sir?"

"About the pilots."

Adams then chose to outline his agenda to Danforth. "Get rid of this staff car."

"Say again, sir?"

"Turn in this car. It's too blue. It's a sign of the peacetime, stateside Air Force. Get rid of it today."

"What will you drive?"

"This is a war zone. I'll drive a jeep. Let everyone know it's the wing CO's jeep. And get some lights on these signs so people can see them at night.

"One more thing. My personal call sign's Ragtop 21. Everyone should know that too, especially the men in the control tower. The Army Air Forces issued me that call sign during primary pilot training at Stewart Field in 1942. I kinda like it." Adams moved up the steps of wing HQ with Danforth trailing along.

Danforth acknowledged Adams's desires as he followed his new CO into the building: jeep, lights, call sign. Danforth realized there wouldn't be any quiet transition period. Clint Adams had hit the ground running. Things would be different.

Adams grabbed the handle of the front door, then stopped, and turned to Danforth. Looking his DCO straight in the eye, he said, "I'm going to command this wing differently than you would, Slim. Will you back me on all this?"

This was the test question. Danforth said, "Of course, Colonel. You're the boss." But his voice had a hollow, insincere tone. Adams heard it clearly as he opened the door and proceeded inside.

"I stopped by the TOC last night, Slim. Do you spend much time there?"

"Not lately. Acting as wing commander for the past week—"

Adams cut him short. "I plan to spend lots of my time there. It's the heart of the wing's operations. Hope to see you there too, you being the DCO and all." Danforth clammed up, clenching the muscles in his jaw.

Adams continued, "I took a look at your flight progress. Yours and Happy Parker's, that is. Now that I'm here, you'll both have more time to fly on some tough missions. Get the message?"

"Yes, sir." Danforth's voice had a tone of resignation to it.

The Wing

Adams pulled back the blackout curtains blocking the view of the Ubon flight line and the runway beyond it. He scanned his new world just as the last four F-4 Phantoms in the morning launch sequence took to the air, one at a time, thirty seconds apart.

He could see the maintenance men scurrying to police the support equipment they used to launch the planes from their revetments. The din and ground vibration burned through the bug-stained window as each mission-loaded, 50,000-pound F-4 rolled down the runway. Adams felt right at home.

Two minutes later and several miles away, the Phantoms were still visible as they joined up and turned to the north. Four telltale black contrails, characteristic of the F-4's engines, continued to pinpoint the formation long after the planes themselves were too distant to see.

The intercom on Adams's desk buzzed. His executive officer, Captain Rob "Boomer" Wright, asked, "Colonel, are you busy?"

"Come on in." Adams put down the status reports he was thumbing through.

Boomer Wright was a square-jawed, twenty-nine-year-old fighter pilot of the first water: academy grad, captain of the USAFA wrestling team, and on his second operational fighter tour, first as a GIB (guy in back) at Eglin, now as AC (aircraft commander) at Ubon. "Sir, I guess you'll want to interview some of the pilots to pick a new exec."

"What?" Adams pretended to be preoccupied, shuffling some of the papers on his desk.

"Sir, I just thought you'd want to choose your own man in the front office."

"You're my man, Boomer. You know the ropes, and you can teach me a lot." Boomer was pleasantly surprised and swelled with pride. Then Adams added, "But I expect you to carry your load flying combat missions. Understood?"

"*Yes, sir!*" This was great news to Boomer. The previous wing commander had tapped him for the exec job right after Boomer reached ten counters, three months ago. Then Colonel Goodman had kept him chained to the desk, taking all the fun out of the job. With little flight time, he had since fallen far behind his peers in missions North or anywhere else. His three frontseat classmates from Davis-Monthan now had twice his twenty-two counters. Boomer had come here to fly combat, not a gray metal desk.

0820 hours
Thirty miles south of Ubon

Colonel Happy Parker and his GIB, Captain Todd Benning, were in-bound to Ubon after a week outside the war zone. Benning was the DCO's exec, doing double duty by supporting both the DCO and the assistant DCO.

Happy Parker had taken Todd Benning with him to CCK. Both men were roughly halfway through their tour, and Parker knew the exec's job included discretion. Benning kept things to himself as a good exec should. That gave Parker more latitude to let loose without it getting back to the wrong people. The young guys in the flying squadrons thought Danforth and Parker had pulled up Benning to the front office for one reason—to keep Danforth and Parker from killing themselves out of poor judgment in the air. Benning was having a hell of a time meeting that goal, and today was no exception.

Parker thought he saw the airfield in the distance. He glanced back to the instrument panel at the tactical air navigation (TACAN) control head on his side console. Channel 93 showed in the indicator window. That was Ubon's TACAN station. Parker pulled up the audio monitor button marked TACAN and heard the Morse code for the letters UBL, which confirmed he was receiving bearing and distance information from the TACAN station located northeast of the runway at Ubon. Parker looked at the horizontal situation indicator (HSI), the F-4C's state-of-the-art heading and course indicator, on his main instrument panel. He glanced at the miles indicator where the white-on-black tumblers were running down through 27 at the rate of 8 miles per minute.

The Ubon RTAFB itself looked like a patch of dirt scratched in the lush green countryside of easternmost Thailand. From 25 miles out, the base looked compact, bordered on three sides by rice paddies separated by small groves of trees. The airfield itself sat 2 miles north of Ubon Ratchathani, a provincial city of 30,000 on the northern bank of the Lam Nam Chi River, a major tributary of the Mekong, the largest river in Southeast Asia. The Mekong formed the Thai-Laotian border, 30 miles to the east.

Ubon RTAFB was laid out in a standard single fighter-wing air base configuration. The fighter ramp lay along the northwest side of Runway 05/23. A line of eight maintenance hangars bordered the ramp. Beyond these primary mission facilities lay more mission support buildings, including the wing headquarters, clubs, officers' quarters, enlisted barracks, and the fuel and ammo dumps. Five thousand people went about their business at Ubon. And they all answered to one man as of this morning—Colonel Clinton Radford Adams. Unity of command was what was so neat and clean about a tactical fighter base.

Benning expected a routine arrival at Ubon, especially after this TDY. The last two nights had been the worst, watching Happy Parker regale group after group with war stories at the Clark Officers' Club main bar. Benning should have known better. Nothing about Happy Parker was routine. Parker contacted the Ubon control tower. "Ubon Tower, Bolt 22, 2.0 miles south. Request a tactical arrival if the pattern's clear."

After a short pause, the Ubon tower controller answered coldly, "Negative, Bolt 22. Report 5-mile initial for Runway 05."

Without hesitating, Happy Parker slammed both throttles to full power short of afterburners, rolled his powerful F-4 on its back, and pulled the nose down into a 50-degree dive. As the airspeed hit 0.92 Mach, Parker rolled the newly refurbished Phantom upright in a classic, no-notice, "Cuban Eight" maneuver. Bolt 22 hurtled toward the ground, accelerating to 500 knots. The plane bounced uncomfortably as it encountered the thermals closer to the ground, already rising past 4,000 feet in the tropical heat.

All GIBs tend to hunker down when the AC starts getting cute. Todd wondered what this simpleton colonel was going to do next as he grabbed hold of the two hand bars astride the rear cockpit radar scope and commented into the intercom system between the two pilots, "Colonel Danforth ain't gonna like this."

"Screw that tight-assed bastard. We'll show him how to arrive at Ubon." Parker didn't think much of Danforth and his pissant peacetime management style. He considered Danforth a complete suckhole and actively worked against him when away from the DCO office.

Benning tried again to infuse some sanity into what was about to happen. "I'll just check in with the TOC on 370.5."

"Negative. Let's surprise Ubon this morning. We'll see if Danforth has any hair on his ass."

Happy Parker was the fighter pilot who never grew up. He always had good hands in the cockpit—but poor judgment—and he knew how to throw a party better than anyone on base. He was the proverbial life of the party, which took considerable doing in a world of fighter pilots. Enough Happy Parker stories floated through Air Force bars to fill a book. He should be dead, having killed himself in a plane or some dark alley years earlier. Happy Parker did have good qualities too, which always confused his commanders whose inclination was to hammer him. He'd work long and hard for the squadron and always volunteered for the duty away from the family. As a result, he got the support he needed for promotion. Now a full colonel with a responsible position in a combat wing, he simply wasn't up to the task.

0825 hours
Clint Adams's office
Ubon RTAFB

Clint Adams stopped reading his predecessor's end-of-tour report in midsentence when the shrill ring of his command phone broke the momentary quiet of his office. He put the call on his desktop speaker.

"Adams here. Go ahead."

"Sir, this is the TOC. Tower just called. There's a lone F-4, call sign Bolt 22, on a flight plan from Clark, 15 miles out. He wants a tactical arrival."

"Who's flying it?"

"We guess it's Colonel Parker, but we can't raise him on command post frequency to confirm."

"If it's a Ubon bird, shouldn't he automatically check in with the TOC 'bout twenty-five minutes out?" Adams applied some logic to the mystery.

But the TOC duty officer didn't answer right away. "You still with me, Lieutenant?"

"Ah, yessir, but that still doesn't mean it isn't Colonel Parker, sir."

"Thanks. Keep me advised." Adams knocked off the speaker phone, then called out to Boomer, "Is my jeep outside yet?"

"Just pullin' up now, Colonel."

0827 hours
Five miles east of Ubon

Parker didn't hear any radio chatter on Ubon tower frequency, 236.6. He took a chance that the flight pattern was clear and leveled off at 50 feet above the ground. Instinctively, Benning tightened his grip on the two hand holds. At times like these, he hated being an instructor pilot for higher-ranking officers, especially when they wrote his efficiency report. The whole concept tended to break down.

"Ah, Colonel, I recommend you knock this off."

"Sit back and watch the show, Todd." Parker's voice had the tone that let Benning know that inaction was the best course for the young exec—if he knew what was good for him.

Bolt 22 streaked across the northeast airfield boundary and tracked right down the Runway 23 centerline. Once over the runway, Parker eased his plane down to 30 feet and continued toward the southwest airfield boundary at the departure end. This high-performance flyby got the attention of everyone working on the flight line. The streaking Phantom made a different sound, something out of the ordinary. It got the attention of pilots working in their offices and lounging in their rooms; and some of them moved outside to check out the air show.

It enraged the Ubon control tower supervisor. "Bolt 22, break it off! Repeat. Break it off, and full stop immediately."

0828 hours
The Ubon flight line

Captain Boomer Wright drove his new wing commander briskly down the main flight line road toward the base of the control tower, exceeding the 15-miles-per-hour speed limit by at least a factor of two. Adams didn't say anything about it. He was focusing on bigger things right now.

Adams's handheld Motorola radio, tucked in between the two bucket seats, chirped loudly.

"Honcho One, go."

"Sir, Ubon Tower. Some hotshot's beating up the field."

The men in the control tower could see Bolt 22 clearly. Parker's experience as a member of the U.S. Air Force/Europe all-jet aerobatic demonstration team was quite evident. Passing the southwest airfield boundary outbound, he racked his F-4C into a six-G left turn, still skimming the rice paddies. The moisture-laden air condensed off the Phantom's upper wing surfaces each time Happy Parker loaded up his Phantom with the slightest G-force. He made three square-corner turns to line up again on Runway 23. Plumes of water kicked up behind Bolt 22 as it passed over the shallow paddies. As Parker crossed the northeast airfield boundary again, the control tower supervisor fired a red flare in a futile effort to divert Parker from his next maneuver.

"Copy, got him in sight. Tell him the new wing commander wants a full stop ASAP." Adams put the brick-sized radio back into the seat hole next to his exec. "It's good to have a command brick again, Boomer."

The tower supervisor passed on Adams's message. Parker misinterpreted it and mumbled over the intercom to poor Benning, "That pompous ass Danforth is calling himself the new wing commander now."

At the approach end of the runway, the forty-five-year-old colonel retarded his engine throttles to idle power. The two J-79 engines wound back as Bolt 22 decelerated along the entire length of the runway. Parker instinctively trimmed up the F-4's stabilator to keep the plane's nose from plowing into the runway as he let the air drag the Phantom toward normal traffic pattern speed.

At the far end of the airfield, still above 350 knots, Parker pulled the plane up and to the left, establishing a downward leg opposite to his landing direction. He set up for a normal landing, extending the wheels and flaps. After touching down on the runway at 110 knots, deploying his drag chute, and slowing to taxi speed, Parker turned off the runway to his right and changed the radio channel, "Ubon Ground. Bolt 22, parking instructions please." To Todd Benning in the back seat he said, "Nice pattern, eh?"

"Bolt 22, just trail in behind the 'Follow Me.'" A blue pickup truck with a large white "Follow Me" sign raced out to meet the F-4. After dropping the drag chute in the arming area, Parker obediently fell in line behind the pickup truck, now moving along at 10 miles per hour on the main taxiway.

Parker hadn't suspected anything when the tower mentioned the new wing CO. But now with more time to think, he became a little concerned that the "Follow Me" was turning him into "Spot One," the traditional arrival spot reserved for VIPs directly in front of base operations.

Benning saw the reception committee and uttered a low, guttural, "Oh shit. That ain't Danforth!"

Bolt 22 pulled in and stopped. Adams, Boomer Wright, and a nonrated major in 1505s were waiting. Parker and Benning saluted Adams while still in the cockpit. Adams crisply returned their salute.

Parker removed his helmet as he smiled at Adams. Adams didn't smile back. Thirty seconds later Parker had separated all the mechanical connections that bound him to the British-made Martin-Baker ejection seat. He climbed backward down the ladder of his green-brown-black-camouflaged plane. Benning followed him and moved off out of view, hoping that the new colonel understood that he had not conceived of or recommended the arrival profile.

Parker tried to make the best of a rapidly deteriorating situation, just like always. He held out his hand, "Welcome to Ubon, sir. I'm Happy Parker."

Adams didn't take Parker's outstretched hand. Instead, he said, "You might think about changing your nickname, Colonel."

"Sir?"

"You're not going to be *Happy* Parker much longer. You know Major Conroy from the Base Personnel Office, don't you?" Conroy, caught up in the swirl of events, nodded at Parker.

"Uh, yes, sir."

"Go with Conroy back to his office. He'll help you process out. Your tour's over." With that, Adams got in his jeep, and Boomer drove him away.

Parker just stood there, watching Adams drive off. Finally he mumbled, "You goddamn son of a bitch."

1130 hours
Gia Lam District
North Vietnam

Nguyen Tomb pedaled his bicycle toward the eastern approach to the Long Bien Bridge. He preferred living at Gia Lam because it was near Hanoi, and he enjoyed the diversions of the old French city. Nguyen

Tomb occasionally needed the ambiance of Hanoi to pace himself. This war might never end.

Once a month, Tomb treated himself to the luxury of a half-day off—his Sunday outing. He justified this indulgence by tying it to the lifelong fight for independence he shared with the North Vietnamese people. He planned to visit the Museum of the Revolution today.

Like most people in North Vietnam, Tomb owned a bicycle, and it seemed as if every bicyclist in North Vietnam was trying to cross the Mekong into the capital. The Long Bien Bridge, called the Paul Doumer Bridge by the French, was the great bottleneck of North Vietnam. Tomb didn't understand why the Americans hadn't bombed this vital link in the supply chain from Haiphong to Hanoi.

The war didn't stop this day or any day, so Tomb had to mix with the supply movements across the bridge. Surrounded by bicycles, almost all of them camouflaged with tree limbs, he waited as usual for everyone ahead of him to squeeze into a single-file line moving toward downtown Hanoi. Bicycles were the most prized possessions of the North Vietnamese; in a country with very little crime, the bicycle was the most-stolen item. Tomb carried a sturdy lock wherever he traveled, as well as a hefty bicycle chain.

Tomb was surrounded by women, old people, and children. Women played an important role in the war supply train, and it was common in North Vietnam to see dozens of young women pushing bicycles over-loaded with 200 kilograms of rice or other supplies. Tomb watched other women carrying poles across their small shoulders, balancing loads greater than their own body weight. These working women all wore black sateen pants, white cotton shirtwaists, and Ho Chi Minh sandals.

Once on the west end of the Long Bien Bridge and into Hanoi itself, Tomb soaked up the French colonial character of this city of 600,000. The war had taken its toll on Hanoi. Once well-manicured, it now needed a fresh coat of paint. The wide, tree-lined boulevards remained, but every 3 meters there was a small, one-person bomb shelter. The 1-meter-wide cylinders lay open to the citizens, who crawled in several times each day and pulled the nearby manhole covers over the top when the air raid siren wailed.

Tomb thought that the North Vietnamese leaders had written off Hanoi and that they believed the Americans would inevitably pulverize their capital. Prime Minister Pham Van Dong told the people that the United States could only help by removing this symbol of French oppres-

sion. Consequently, the resources once earmarked for urban maintenance, including sanitary services, were diverted to the war in the South.

Hanoi was on a fully mobilized, war-oriented economy. All vehicles
with any weight-bearing capacity supported the supply effort. Tomb had
to pedal around the numerous convoys of Soviet-built, 2.5-ton Likhachev
trucks parked along the boulevards, waiting until the evening to move
across the Long Bien Bridge and farther south. Except for a handful of
official staff cars, all autos and taxis had been long ago confiscated for
the convoys. Even the venerable three-wheeled pedicabs supported the
supply effort. All vehicles carried some form of camouflage. The noisy,
dilapidated streetcars, always jammed to the limit, provided the only
public transportation.

Pedaling onward, Tomb saw small shop owners getting ready to close
for the afternoon air raids. Most storekeepers opened their doors from
0500 to 0800. They buttoned up as the American fighter-bombers attacked targets in the Hanoi area in midmorning. They would close again
for the afternoon raids, then expose their wares in the early evening.

Tomb also saw wooden rail ties stacked high near the tracks, readily
available for rapid repair by local militia. Every 100 meters were dozens
of oil drums, which held petroleum, oil, and lubricants. These decen-
tralized stockpiles were rarely pilfered by the people, who took great
pride in carrying out their roles in this latest war of liberation.

Turning into the embassy district, Tomb observed that the Chinese
and Rumanian embassies had incurred moderate bomb damage. The
trees along the colonnade had taken the main impact of the weapons.
Work crews were removing the remnants of the ripped and splintered
foliage. Tomb did not believe the Radio Hanoi reports that American
pilots indiscriminately dropped antipersonnel bombs on the city. He
thought that some of this civilian damage resulted from SA-2s falling
back into populated areas. Nonetheless, Tomb blamed the Americans
indirectly for deaths and injuries caused by the burned-out SAMs. No
American bombers would mean no SAMs in the air.

Even here, as in all parts of the city, posters tacked to the trees exhorted
the people to new sacrifices for the cause. The most plentiful poster
glorified Nguyen Van Troi, the fifteen-year-old hero who died trying to
assassinate U.S. Secretary of Defense Robert McNamara in Saigon. Almost everyone in North Vietnam revered the young martyr because this
was, above all else, a war fought and supported by teenagers. You either
were one or had a teenage sibling in the war.

As Tomb moved through the city's better parts, he took pictures with his most valuable possession, a 35mm Leica. Like the other few photographers in North Vietnam, he used only black-and-white film. Color film was not available.

Tomb slipped his bicycle into a crammed rack in front of the Museum of the Revolution, the cultural center of North Vietnam. He came here to recharge his revolutionary batteries. By Western standards, the Museum of the Revolution was a veritable chamber of horrors chronicling the atrocities perpetrated on the Vietnamese over the past 2,200 years. Graphic descriptions, paintings, and paraphernalia of torture lined the walls. But to the millions of patriotic Vietnamese, the museum was a cathedral of nationalism, a hall of famous heroes, and a testimonial to the centuries of struggle that they understood and related to their everyday lives.

The government went to great lengths in using propaganda to build upon innate Vietnamese nationalism. This, not communism, was the main theme of the struggle against the Americans and their South Vietnamese puppets. The Americans were merely the latest of the Caucasian colonialists who had first descended on the Vietnamese people in the 1870s. First had come the British, then the Dutch, the French, the Japanese, and now the Americans.

Nguyen Tomb believed he had the solemn duty to drive out these Americans, as other Vietnamese patriots before him had driven out earlier invaders.

1600 hours
Fifty miles northeast of Ubon

Buick and Ford flights were returning from their MiGCAP mission in the Hanoi area. No MiG activity today. Lieutenant Colonel Rod Wells, commander of the 555th TFS, was Buick 01 and led this afternoon's MiGCAP.

Wells took his four-ship formation on a descent through the high undercast and broke out under the cloud deck at 15,000 feet. Like all good flight leaders, he always looked for pop-up air traffic, especially when dropping under a cloud deck. His wingmen flew off his lead, content not to look around much.

"Invert, you got any traffic for Buick flight?" Wells asks the GCI site, on UHF frequency 265.5.

The controller sitting in his air-conditioned radar unit at Nhakon Phanom, handling all air traffic in northeast Thailand, responded, "Negative, Buick. We have you radar contact. Squawk 3100." Wells reached down to the right-hand side console and cranked the new code into his IFF/SIF code box, which electronically sent out the radar code that separated the good guys from the bad for the air defense controllers in the radar vans throughout Thailand and Vietnam.

Wells scanned the flat countryside and the hazy atmosphere. Visibility was only 3 miles. In the fall, Thai farmers made the haze worse by burning off the waste vegetation in their rice paddies. And the northeast corner of Thailand was almost all rice paddies.

Suddenly, he spotted a single F-4 passing directly under Buick flight at high speed in the opposite direction. Wells tried to find out what was up. "Invert. Buick 01. Do you have opposite traffic passing below us now?"

"Buick, this is Ragtop 21. Remember me?" Adams preempted the GCI controller. He had recruited Randy Starbuck as his IP for this afternoon's sortie and coordinated a little surprise with Invert's cooperation, discretely working on another radio frequency.

Wells exclaimed, "Well, I'll be damned!" For a split second Rod Wells recalled his salad days at Nellis AFB, Nevada, and his idol of that time, Clint Adams.

"Hang on, Bubba, it's gonna get bumpy. Find that F-4."

"Say again, boss?" Wells's GIB, Lieutenant Bubba Brown, was confused by the radio and intercom chatter.

Then Wells transmitted to his formation, "Buick, go tactical." Immediately, Buick 02 moved out to the right-side fighting wing position—four o'clock and 500 feet from Buick Lead. Buick 03 put his own wingman in fighting wing position then slid left, moving out 2,000 feet at ten o'clock. Rod Wells broke hard left and up in an attempt to spot Adams, who should have been turning in behind his four-ship.

Wells was set up to do mock battle with his former squadron commander. He vainly searched for Ragtop 21 in the haze.

Then Adams challenged Wells, "Show us your stuff, Buick." Wells clicked his radio button twice, the fighter pilot's unspoken response signifying he accepted Adams's challenge.

The mock dogfight was taking shape. Buick flight's backseaters feverishly cranked the controls of their APG-100 radars, looking for Ragtop 21. It was four on one. Adams easily moved toward the rear-quarter firing position he wanted. He thought of this attack as one-on-four.

Inside of a minute, he'd achieved a tracking solution on Buick 03 and 04, who were slow to pick up on the game of surprise and didn't maneuver their Phantoms well.

Wells saw Adams closing on his second element and shouted over the radio, "Buick 03, break left. Left!" But Buick 03 only put on a mild three-G level turn, a sign that he was mentally out of the battle.

"Tracking, tracking, 04." Everyone in the mock flight knew what that meant. Adams had achieved a simulated heat-seeking missile shot—and assumed kill—on Buick 04.

Buick 03's frontseater asked his GIB over the intercom, "Do you have him? Do you have him?" No response. Then both 03 pilots turned to see Adams locked into a missile offset position seven o'clock low, 3 miles back, at the limits of the haze. They both groaned in unison over their intercom, "Shit!"

Then again, five seconds later, they heard, "Tracking, tracking, 03." Buick 03 was Adams's second victim—an easier kill than the first because the element leader was only 500 feet ahead of 04. The two inexperienced crews flew the standard WWII fighting-wing position technically well. But when the leader didn't fly aggressively, this position only served to bunch up the victims for the attacker.

Buick 04's GIB had had Adams's Phantom in sight for the past ten seconds. "Damn, why didn't 03 break?" Things always looked easier when you could see.

For Adams it was a standard shoot-pull-shoot combination just like the one Hub Zempke taught him back at RAF Wattisham. The pilots in Buick 03 and 04 watched Ragtop 21 in their five o'clock position, tracking them with ease. Resolutely, both the ACs in Buick 03 and 04 followed custom by responding in turn, "Roger, tallyho." All four "dead" pilots felt the sting of the simulated missile kills almost as much as if they had been real.

Meanwhile, Rod Wells in Buick 01 worked his aircraft halfway into firing position on Ragtop 21. "Almost got him, Bubba," Wells said as his six-G turning maneuver drew the skin down off his cheek bones, distorting the sound of his voice. But now Adams turned his full attention to Buick's lead element.

"Damn, we're slipping." Wells snorted between short breaths as he worked hard to yank his F-4 through the sky and keep his GIB informed. Wells actually had a longer, more vulnerable "tail," as he had to drag his wingman with him. In these dogfights, most wingmen slowly slipped farther behind. If the fight lasted long enough, Adams would probably pick off Buick 02.

After two minutes of near-vertical high-G maneuvering, a long time in an aerial dogfight, Adams thought Wells would be smart enough to beat him. After all, Wells still outnumbered him two to one. Yet neither Adams nor Wells gained missile-firing parameters on the other. This turning stalemate, a "Lufberry," ended the day's excitement.

Wells radioed, "Buick 01, Bingo," signifying he had reached the minimum fuel level he needed for a safe return to base. Wells rocked his wings, and his three wingmen joined him.

After landing and taxiing to their respective revetments, Adams and Wells renewed their twelve-year friendship.

"What a way to say hello to your old wing weapons officer," Wells remarked. This was their third flying assignment together. They both had flown F-86s in the mid-fifties back at Nellis AFB, just outside of Las Vegas. And Rod Wells had been Adams's wing weapons officer at RAF Lakenheath. The bond between a wing CO and his wing weapons officer was one of special trust and respect.

Adams peppered his friend, "I thought you were a total fighter pilot. You were carrying some dead wood around the sky today. Even after I killed 03 and 04, you should've used your wingman to sandwich me. That sticking together in pairs is bullshit against a single attacker. Too rigid. Fighting wing formation should be for offense as well as defense. And those weak-dick wingmen are gonna get you zapped, Rodney."

Wells hated being called Rodney. He remembered in one instant all the times Clint Adams had chewed him out for screwing something up at Lakenheath. But he *was* the loser today.

Rod Wells was a total fighter pilot, never had had a desk job, and didn't know or care about politics, only his pilots. Three things excited Rod Wells: flying, his family (now living back home in Billings, Montana), and fixing cars. Rod wasn't the movie-star type, just average in almost all respects: height, weight, and looks. He was the type of guy who would have owned the corner gas station in Billings if the Korean War hadn't given him the chance to fly jet fighters. Even now, he looked like he had grease under his fingernails.

Adams and Wells walked down the flight line together, carrying their helmets, and catching up on old times. Aircraft maintenance activity bustled all around them. Crew chiefs and their assistants worked over nearby F-4s, readying them for the afternoon missions.

"The pilots in Buick 03 and 04 don't look ready for MiGCAP, Rod."

"Yes sir, they're pretty green. This was their first mission to Pack Six. They've got about two weeks of easier missions into Route Pack One and Laos under their belts. This was the first air-to-air they've seen since F-4 school. Ain't good out here, Boss."

"Why the hell not?"

Rod was not proud of his flight's performance. Good squadron commanders took it personally when their pilots lost at anything. He didn't want to sound like he was making excuses, but he decided that he'd better tell his new CO what was happening here at Ubon. "We don't get any air-to-air work in Pack One. And we don't get any on the way back home to Ubon either. Before you arrived, I would have gotten fired for what we did today. All that Stateside flying safety bullshit.

"Frankly, sir, there's no way to know how good anyone really is in air-to-air. Not with the local flying rules we're operatin' under. The way things are now, all flights coming back from combat missions must return directly to Ubon. Local inflight training is against the rules.

"We lost a Phantom doing mock dogfights four months ago, so the Wing King and his DCO put the clamps on. You know, 'safety-is-paramount' bullcrap. Me and the other squadron COs, we argued against it. Winning is paramount in the war zone, not safety. But the bird colonels told us to pipe down or they'd issue us desk jobs at Seventh AF in Saigon. No sir, it's not like the freewheeling stuff we used to do at Nellis. Here we got lots of jungle, but no jungle rules."

"And we're launching MiGCAP from this environment? Hell, that's criminal."

"Not too red hot, Boss. The 'Phantoms' up at wing don't have a clue about what they're doing. And by Phantoms I don't mean F-4s."

"You mean Danforth?"

"Yes sir. And the others. Don't see them much, except for the daily staff meetings. The DCO's a fish out of water. But he didn't get much guidance from the wing commander, either. Everyone wants to look good in the shower when it comes to noncombat losses." Wells stopped running off at the mouth and changed his tone, "Boss, it's great to have you here."

Adams said nothing at first, just grabbed his friend's shoulder momentarily as they continued down the flight line. Then Adams spoke.

"Rod, the rules are gonna be different when you get up tomorrow."

Rod Wells's two vanquished aircrews were gathering near their aircraft just as Adams and Wells arrived. The four younger pilots saluted, meekly.

Wells introduced each of them. "I'd like you to meet the new wing commander." With that announcement, they looked liked they felt worse. "Colonel, this is Buick 03—Captain Mike Nelson and First Lieutenant Knute Peterson; and Buick 04—Captain Vic Sansone and First Lieutenant Pete Cummings." The four pilots took turns shaking hands with Adams. All four wanted to be on another planet right then.

Adams looked over the four pilots. Was I ever that young? he wondered. He could tell easily that Nelson and Sansone were the frontseaters. They stood a few steps in front of Peterson and Cummings. It was always that way with F-4 aircraft commanders and their GIBs.

The square-jawed Mike Nelson was the foursome's informal leader. Standing 6 feet tall with brown hair, matching eyes, and muscular shoulders and upper arms that drew his flight suit taut, he displayed a quiet confidence even in this professionally uncomfortable situation. The Air Force recruiters would have liked to have gotten hold of him for an advertisement for prospective pilots.

Vic Sansone was a fireplug at 5-foot-6, and his rounded shoulders made him look even shorter. Physiologically, he was a near-perfect fighter pilot with almost no neck. His distinctive brown eyes—seemingly pushed out of his head by naturally high blood pressure—darted everywhere and displayed the range of his emotions. Curly black hair and a dark complexion easily gave away his Mediterranean ancestry.

Knute Peterson, nicknamed "Moose" by his Stanford football teammates, stood an inch taller than Clint Adams and pushed 250 pounds. The hulking, crew-cut blond stood motionless behind Nelson, looking like a large sweat-soaked Scandinavian gorilla.

Pete Cummings was thin and wiry, with no excess weight. He stood at Sansone's shoulder, nervously tugging on his ear lobe, waiting for the inevitable hit from Adams. Sansone nicknamed Cummings "Snake" after losing a bet to him back at F-4 school. The spontaneous, 5-foot-8 Cummings had crawled under five consecutive tables at Milo's Cowboy Bar in Tucson one Friday night without getting pasted by any of the local good ole boys.

"How long have you been at Ubon?" asked Adams.

"Three weeks, Colonel," answered Nelson.

"Have you flown together before today, as wingmen or as crews?" probed Adams.

"Not here, only in training back at Tucson, sir. We were looking forward to this, our first flight together, I mean," added Cummings.

Wells interjected, "Managing counters has higher priority than aircrew and flight integrity, Colonel. Keeping pilots equal drives the schedule."

Adams came down hard. "Christ, you four were easy pickings up there today. Don't you know there's a war on? Work on it, dammit. Starting this afternoon."

"Yes, sir," they responded together, hoping their humiliation would end soon.

Adams started to walk away, but he had an idea and turned back. "You four just got married. As crews and as wingmen. For the rest of your tour."

"Yes, sir," the four chirped again. They perked up a little, recognizing Adams's decree as both a challenge and an opportunity.

Randy Starbuck drove up to the group in Adams's newly acquired command jeep. Adams jumped in. Starbuck ground the jeep's gear shifter into first gear and jerked the unfamiliar vehicle into motion with some poor clutch work.

The four young pilots stood there for a few seconds. Wells was smiling because he knew he was out from under Danforth's yoke. Now he'd get to command his squadron the way he wanted.

Pete Cummings said, "Who was that masked man, anyway?"

"He's the man who's gonna save your butts," Wells said. "And he's bad news for the Gomer pilots up North." Wells used the American slang "Gomer" for Vietnamese bad guy.

The "newlyweds" slowly followed their boss to the first stop for all crews returning from a mission: the debriefing shack, where the maintenance and intelligence teams waited. They couldn't know how right Clint Adams had been in warning them, or that Rod Wells was a prophet.

1730 hours
Main briefing room
8th TFW HQ

All U.S. Air Force wing briefing rooms looked pretty much the same. A long conference table took up most of the room, along with the seven chairs down each side of the table, one each for the key members of the wing staff. Less important attendees usually sat in the chairs along both side walls. Everyone was here. Operators, including all three flying squadron commanders, filled half the room. Support people, the nonfliers, made up the rest: base commander, security police, flight surgeon, intelligence, information, comptroller, even the chaplain.

The large, backlit screen for visual aids dominated the front of this rectangular executive minitheater, with a single podium for briefers to the left side. At the other end of the table was the wing commander's chair, taller and more padded than the rest. The only wall mounting was the 4-foot-high 8th TFW coat of arms. Like the one above the main entrance, the motto read, "Attaquez et Conquerez."

The afternoon wing staff meeting, normally held at 1600 hours, was 90 minutes late today because of Colonel Adams's afternoon sortie. The senior staff stood informally in place. They were anxious. A few already knew their new commander, but most didn't know what to expect. Those who did know him entertained themselves by handing out words of wisdom about Adams:

"Take-charge leader."

"You better do your homework on the basics."

"Colonels don't get much sleep on his staff."

"Don't try to snow him."

"Don't ever lie to him."

Some of the staff was mildly irritated at missing happy hour at the Officers' Club bar. Cold beer for a quarter was hard to beat. Others wondered if the dining room would run out of steaks and apple pie before they got there.

Then someone at the door said Adams was back in the building and coming down the hall. There was a feeling of expectation. As he entered, Boomer Wright called the room to attention.

"Stand at ease." Adams made the rounds, shaking hands with everyone and exchanging a few comments with the men who had worked with him before.

Then it was down to business. He was in his flight suit, with sweat rings under the armpits and one large one that covered his back. No one else was wearing a flight suit, not even the fighter squadron commanders. He saw a roomful of tan 1505 uniforms. Only his chief of maintenance, Colonel Hal "Pop" Brewer, wore green fatigues. Adams smiled; maintenance people always wore fatigues.

Adams ran his fingers over the handlebar mustache he'd started back at Shaw, gave a warm smile to everyone, and then motioned for the briefing to proceed. The ops briefer led off as usual, detailing the day's activities, the night's missions, targets, and bomb loads. He concluded by outlining the next day's schedule. The ops briefing was superficial—nothing on intelligence, tactics, and exactly who was leading and flying the missions—but Adams said nothing.

Next came the maintenance briefer. Although this area appeared very solid, Adams grew more uncomfortable as the other briefings proceeded because the emphasis was clearly on meaningless numbers, not quality performance. As the final briefer concluded, the lights came to full bright. Everyone turned to Adams for his first official remarks.

"Thanks, Major." Then he turned to his senior staff. "I've always wanted to lead a fighter wing in combat, so I'm pleased to be here. This wing's entire energy must focus on one thing: achieving air superiority over North Vietnam. I hear the 8th TFW is effective in the air-to-ground role but not very effective air-to-air. We're gonna turn that around.

"Put another way, we're going to start knocking down lots of MiGs and beating up the enemy. Starting right now. If anything we do isn't focused on that, then change it." The headwind was picking up for the staff. Some feverishly wrote down Adams's comments. Others sat transfixed.

He targeted intelligence first. "Let's get these briefings pointed at our basic meat and potatoes. Give me current intelligence. Not eyewash, real gumshoe intell. Expand this point-specific tripe affecting our primary and backup targets into something more meaningful. Tell me what's happening all over North Vietnam. And tell me who's making it happen, how they're doing it, and why. Both sides, red and blue. Don't forget the Navy."

Adams's face flushed, and the veins pulsed out of his graying temples and thick neck as he turned to Danforth and the rest of his ops staff. "Tell me what tactics we're using, Slim. Tell me which ones work and which ones don't. And tell me who's leading the missions, who's flying wing, and who's not flying at all. And don't just tell me what we did today. Tell me how well or poorly we did it. Who are the winners and who are the losers? Let's get it all out in the open so we can make the right decisions."

The staff remained locked on Adams as he moved on to general remarks for everybody. "I think we may be too peacetime ops oriented.

You have to help me change that. For openers, everyone wears fatigues or flight suits—starting immediately.

"Right now, I'm still learning about our wing and how it operates. I challenge everyone to teach me all that you know. I need to get up to speed as fast as possible." Adams then called a meeting for all officers at the Officers' Club, 1600 hours tomorrow. That was it. His first staff meeting was over. Adams stood. So did everyone else.

As he departed, Adams walked over to a square-jawed, heavily mustached pilot in a Royal Australian Air Force (RAAF) uniform. "If you have the time, I'd like to see you in my office, Group Captain."

"Only if you call me Harley like everyone else 'round here, Colonel." Informality helped Group Captain Harley Stockman get things done in a world of Yanks.

"Harley it is then. I want to make you an offer."

Stockman picked at his black mustache, pondering the possibilities as he followed the taller Adams to his office.

The members of the senior staff exchanged glances as they gathered their things to leave. The policies that Adams outlined in the last ten minutes reversed Slim Danforth's edicts. Danforth himself hurriedly shuffled his papers together and quickly left the room.

As the staff filed out the door, Colonel Pop Brewer said to Rod Wells, "I always thought you golden-zippered sun gods looked stupid in 1505s anyway. Makes you all look queer."

"Yeah, kinda makes a pilot feel like a staff puke."

1810 hours
Wing commander's office
8th TFW HQ

Clint Adams didn't offer the heavy-set, thirty-eight-year-old Aussie a chair. Instead he moved to the window and looked at something of interest in the distance.

"Want a cigarette, Harley?"

"Only if it's a Dunhill or one of your American Camels."

"Then I guess you're out of luck." Adams popped the last Lucky Strike from the semisquashed pack he drew from his flight suit pocket.

Stockman was the CO of RAAF Squadron 78, detached from Butterworth, Malaysia. Seventy-eight Squadron was tasked with the air defense of Ubon. The Aussies came to Thailand in 1961, first flying out of Don Muang near Bangkok, and now Ubon.

The Aussies flew a modified F-86 and called it the CAC Mk.82 Sabre. They altered the Korean War Sabre into a lethal machine that sported two AIM-9B Sidewinders and two 30mm Aden cannons.

"How many Sabres do you have?"

"Twelve, Colonel. And what magnificent aircraft they are, sir."

Clint Adams liked the Sabre and wanted Stockman to know he spoke from experience, "The F-86 is still my favorite jet. Got about 900 hours flying Sabres in Europe and Nevada. How many planes do you keep on alert?"

"Four. We can get airborne in five minutes. I make our pilots prove it every day."

"Harley, I'd like you to bounce some of our returning missions. I think we need the work."

Harley started to grin widely, but gained control, "Just what do you have in mind, Colonel?"

"DACT—dissimilar air combat training. American pilots don't get it. When the Air Force sentenced me to the Pentagon, I got together with some other fighter pilots on the Air Staff, and we tried to push through a DACT program. But we couldn't make any headway with the bomber generals and civilian scientists that run the Air Force."

"We call them 'flatheads' in Canberra. Are these the same fellas that took the nose guns out of most of your fighters?"

"Those and some others in Washington. Fighters aren't supposed to mix it up close in dogfights anymore. But someone forgot to tell the bad guys. Hell, it's been hard enough to keep some minimum air combat maneuvers in our fighter training programs. But it's basic stuff. And it's all based on flying against the same kind of planes. You know, F-4 against F-4. Now look at us. We're fighting vastly dissimilar fighters. And we fight them four-versus-one or two."

Harley got ahead of Adams. "Colonel, I'll put two Sabres in the air anytime you want them."

"That's gonna cost you some gas and spare parts."

"No worries."

"Good. But I want to do this right. So we maintain complete control. If we lose a pilot or a plane, either one of yours or one of mine, we'll both be out of a job."

"What's it you Yanks say? Something about breaking eggs to make omelets?"

"Let's try to make this omelet *without* breaking the eggs. I'll speak to Colonel Danforth. Then you work out the detailed rules with 8th Wing Tactics Shop."

"Happy to be on your team, Colonel. Mixing the F-4 with the Sabre should be *very* interesting." Stockman slowly brought his right hand to his forehead in an open-palmed salute as he finished his sentence.

Adams dabbed out the remains of his Lucky Strike in the ashtray on the corner of his desk. He returned the salute and shook hands with the Aussie. "Help us kick some ass up North, Group Captain."

Stockman stopped as he grabbed the edge of the door to leave. "Right you are, Colonel. But call me Harley."

1830 hours

Clint Adams picked up the red phone, his direct line to Blue Chip at Tan Son Nhut, and asked for General Morgan. The duty sergeant put him through. Like Adams, the general was still in his office.

"Adams, you peckerwood, what's up?" Morgan jabbed.

"Nothing we can't handle, General. But I'd like to cash in that raincheck you gave me on a new vice wing commander."

"Who do you want?"

"Sir, when I checked out in the F-4 earlier this month at Davis-Monthan, I found just the right man for this job, Colonel Curtis J. Robinson. He's the DCO there now."

Morgan instinctively turned to a framed photograph hanging on the wall behind his desk. It was a group shot of the F-51 squadron he'd skippered in Korea. On the end of the back row stood a massive young black captain, towering over his squadron mates.

Morgan said, "Damn, Clint, he's even bigger than you are. Well, if you ever run out of bombs, you can drop 'Bear' Robinson on the Gomers. They'll sue for peace the next day."

"Even if we miss, sir, it will cause an earthquake registering 7.4 on the Richter scale." U.S. Air Force fighter pilots had been trading Bear Robinson jokes for years.

"Wasn't Bear your DCO at Lakenheath?"

"Yessir. We worked well together. With him as vice, I can concentrate on hammering the North Vietnamese and Bear can carry the day-to-day activities of the wing. He's already checked out in the F-4; I'd trust him with my life; and he's good at working the details."

"Okay, Clint, I'll get personnel working on Robinson's move to Ubon as fast as possible. How's Danforth handling all this?"

"I've still got some work just to make him a DCO. I'd like to keep him in that role for now."

30 September 1966 0600 hours
8th TFW Operations Center
Ubon RTAFB

Ten pilots from the 555th TFS—nicknamed Triple Nickel—gathered for the 0610 mission briefing for Rambler flight, four F-4s going to Route Pack Six this morning. Rod Wells was Rambler 01.

The newlyweds—Nelson, Peterson, Sansone, and Cummings—were there. The four had become good friends in eight months. During that time they had gone through the entire sequence of combat crew training together: Basic Survival School at Stead AFB in the Sierra Nevadas, initial F-4 school at Davis-Monthan, and Jungle Survival School at Clark.

The newlyweds would fly Rambler 03 and 04 this morning. Rod Wells had taken their shotgun marriage seriously. He knew they needed the work. They, too, were taking it seriously, spending three hours the evening before "hangar flying," going over flying tactics and procedures on the ground. Then they "what if-ed" each other for another ninety minutes.

"When you gonna nail that USO Donut Dolly from San Jose, Snake?" Moose Peterson asked.

"Eat me, you big Swede. At least *I* was trolling," Cummings fired back, tugging his earlobe. Moose had worked beer cans last night, not "roundeyes." Nelson and Sansone, the closest friends among the four, had struck out too, but not in front of everyone in the O Club.

The duty operations officer started his briefing as the door in the back of the room abruptly opened. Since the briefing was classified, the duty officer stopped to identify the new colonel entering with Randy Starbuck.

Randy preempted him. "I'll vouch for the new wing commander."

The duty officer called the room to attention. Adams said nothing but moved to the front row of seats. "Sit down, fellas, please."

As the pilots retook their seats, they got a better view of their new boss. He was very tall, solid, and fit for any age. His olive-green flight suit looked as if it were made specially for him, though it wasn't.

Adams asked, "Where we goin' today?" Actually, he already knew, having spent the last hour in the TOC.

"MiGCAP escort for the F-105 strike force targeted against the Trung Quang Railyard northeast of Hanoi, sir."

Adams then asked, "How's the weather in the target area?"

"It's good, sir," said the lieutenant from the weather shop, due up next in the briefing sequence. Adams looked for someone else. He saw the nonrated career intell officer waiting in the wings.

"What do you expect in the target area?"

Major Tom Cardwell wasn't shy. A short, stocky Texan in green fatigues, he took one step forward and answered his new boss, "We should always expect MiGs, SAMs, and AAA."

"Not good enough. Too general. Be more specific."

Without hesitation, Cardwell spun around, grabbed a long hook, and dragged down a rolled-up map suspended from the ceiling. As the map of North Vietnam unfurled, the aircrews saw that the area around Hanoi was a seemingly solid red mass of red dots. Cardwell said nothing; the map spoke for itself.

At first, Adams merely stared at the intell major, who stared back. Adams liked that kind of answer. He nodded in agreement, then turned around and asked, "Who's leading the flight today?" Rod Wells identified himself.

"Mind if Randy and I come along as Rambler 02, Rod?"

"Glad to have you along, Colonel." Wells turned to the Rambler 02 crew and said, "You two fly spare." Motioning toward the rear door, he added, "Fuzzy, you and Slick go back to bed."

Snake Cummings nudged Moose Peterson in the ribs, and they exchanged an expectant glance. They'd see their new skipper in action. He'd get to see them, too.

0720 hours
Aircraft parking area
Ubon RTAFB flight line

The breadtruck-like crew bus stopped in front of the topless metal aircraft revetment housing F-4C #63–7680. Adams and Starbuck slid out the back of the blue van, which drove off down the flight line to unload other crews.

"I'll do the walkaround for us, Colonel," Starbuck volunteered, treating Adams like a VIP on a courtesy flight.

"Bullshit. I'm flyin' the front seat and you're in the back. Let's get that straight from the start." All frontseaters new to Ubon flew their initial three combat missions with an experienced IP in the back seat. Normally, these early missions were easy runs to Route Pack One in North Vietnam's southern panhandle. But Clint Adams was starting his checkout going Downtown to Hanoi.

By choice, Adams had Starbuck for his IP today. As wing commander, he had to have confidence in his chief of wing tactics. Besides, Adams needed all the help he could get. Today's mission was no milk run to the Panhandle.

Adams took a good nose-on look at #63–7680. He thought #680 looked like a fine machine—clean and no leaks.

He had liked the F-4C Phantom II right from his first flight at the Davis-Monthan AFB schoolhouse. It was the most powerful and versatile fighter in the world. And it was an honest airplane; an experienced fighter pilot like Adams could get in it and move rapidly to the head of the class, using all the skills he had mastered over the past twenty-four years. As he looked at #680, Adams already felt comfortable with the Phantom. He remembered the fighter pilot's favorite semibiblical verse: "Yea, though I walk through the valley of death, I shall fear no evil, for I am the toughest mother in the valley."

Adams started his walkaround, the exterior inspection of the aircraft, starting at the F-4's nose and working counterclockwise. His nostrils filled with the familiar kerosene odor of JP-4 jet fuel.

Starbuck, meanwhile, crawled up into the backseat and started his interior preflight duties. Before engine start, the Phantom #680 got its electricity from a yellow power cart through an umbilical cord attached to its underbelly. Starbuck started to program the F-4's navigation computer, the heart of which was the inertial navigation system, the INS, an accurate and self-contained black box that gave the F-4 crews a critical technological advantage over enemy territory. Phantom crews knew where they were all the time thanks to this totally internal system. The INS couldn't be jammed or fooled by external signals.

The young airplane crew chief, Staff Sergeant Christopher C. Cole, joined Adams as the colonel rounded the left wingtip. Cole, never shy, was unaware that Adams was the new wing commander.

"Morning, Colonel. I wasn't expectin' such a high-ranking pilot. Not with #680 goin' Downtown on MiGCAP. Are you up from Saigon on some kinda test?"

Adams took it all in without comment, concentrating on his inspection.

"Come to think of it, you're the highest ranking pilot that ever flew my plane."

Adams looked over at Cole's green embroidered name tag. "What's your full name, Sergeant Cole?"

"Chris Cole, sir."

Then it dawned on Cole. "Are you the new wing commander everybody's been expecting?" Adams nodded, still intent on inspecting the plane. Now Cole was all business, no more small talk. The twenty-year-old wiry, blond Floridian stuck close to Adams for the rest of the walk-around.

Rounding the right wingtip, Cole moved into Adams's blind spot then motioned to his even younger apprentice. He wanted his assistant to load the pilot's helmet onto the front canopy rail and then stow the rest of Adams's gear on the instrument visor. At first, the airman second class didn't understand; it wasn't standard procedure. So Cole repeated his hand signals, and the one-striper got the message.

Cole followed Adams up the crew ladder and helped him connect his parachute torso harness to the Martin-Baker ejection seat. Then he handed Adams his green-camouflaged helmet, its oxygen mask dangling from its left connector. At this point Adams realized that Cole was doing everything he could for him and responded, "Thank you, Sergeant."

Adams looked at Cole closely for the first time and asked, "Is this a good air machine, Sergeant?"

"Best one I've ever seen."

"What breaks most often on #680?"

"Pardon my French, sir, but it's the damned UHF radio. And nothin' makes the pilots madder. But it's not #680's fault; the UHFs are bad on all these planes. It's just a poor black box. Mean time between failure must be three hours." Cole was referring to the only radio in the F-4. He was frustrated because they bench checked okay, but when put in the F-4, the UHFs rarely lasted more than two missions before failing. The engineers called these "interface" problems.

Adams started to don his helmet. "Well, I'll do my best to bring #680 back in good shape."

Cole always seemed to get in the last word. "I hope so, sir. It's the only F-4 I got."

Adams smiled. "Get outta here, Sergeant. I got work to do."

Cole's apprentice cranked up the pneumatic side of the power cart, ready to provide air pressure for engine start. The power cart's rumble built to a steady high-pitched whine, and both pilots and crew chiefs knew that engine start was only minutes away. Everyone involved in launching #680 quickened their pace and sharpened their focus.

Cole backed down the ladder, removed it, and positioned himself in front of the aircraft on the tarmac for the engine starting sequence.

Alone with the craft for the first time, Adams and Starbuck began to merge with their machine. A modern fighter cockpit was a unique place, and few men ever got to sit in one under operational conditions, let alone combat. The singular combination of smells, sounds, and vibrations separated it from all other environments. Adams enjoyed the smell, much like the back room of a gun shop, but with a kerosene overlay.

Adams connected himself to the plane's oxygen system, latched his face mask, pulled down his sun visor, cinched down all his safety straps, snapped in his anti-G suit hose, and plugged in his radio/intercom plug. All at once, the Phantom provided him with life support. He heard both himself and Randy drawing oxygen. And he heard the radio chatter— the audio inputs that gave him the situational awareness he needed. He and #680 had just become a weapon system.

Rod Wells and the other members of Rambler flight started their J-79 engines and taxied out of the revetment area toward the end of Runway 05. Adams pushed his throttles forward to fall in to second position, right behind Rod Wells. Cole flipped Adams a crisp salute, and Clint returned it.

For perhaps the four thousandth time in his life, he joined the slow procession toward takeoff. Starbuck asked him, "Doin' okay up there, Colonel?"

"Yeah, how 'bout the before-takeoff check for us?" Starbuck already had the page face open on his knee board and launched into it.

"Stab aug?" challenged Starbuck.

"Engaged," responded Adams.

"Flight controls?"

"Watch your knees, Randy," warned Adams as he put the control stick first full left, then full right, full forward, full aft, and finished by swirling it around the entire field of motion sensing for restrictions. "Unrestricted."

"Stab trim?"

"Set for takeoff."

"Canopies?"

"Let's hold it there 'til we get through the armament area," Adams said, knowing there was no reason to cook under Plexiglas for an extra five minutes.

As chief of maintenance, Colonel Pop Brewer watched from a distance. Pop was pleased by what he saw as he watched every facet of this launch, his new CO's first combat mission. Brewer would talk to Chris Cole after Rambler was airborne, learn about the UHF radio comment, and work harder to fix the problem before Adams told him to do it.

Pop Brewer hopped into his staff car and followed Rambler flight down the taxiway to the aircraft arming area at the approach end of the runway. He watched a team of four munitions maintenance men scurry under the Phantoms. Each man wore "Mickey Mouse" ear protectors against the deafening blare of the engines. The arming crew moved deliberately, removing the safety pins and long red warning flags from the four Sparrow and four Sidewinder missiles. This was dangerous work, done on the remote end of the airfield.

Brewer recalled that last week, when one of these young munitions men had pulled out an AIM-9 Sidewinder pin, he had lost both of his hands as the AIM-9 fired off the rail. The tail fin sliced through his wrists, and the rocket exhaust cauterized the stubs before he hit the ground. Then the rogue missile accelerated across the ramp and smashed into four other munitions men standing in the grass, cutting two men in half and killing the other two when the detonation riddled their bodies with hot metal fragments. With disgust, Brewer remembered reading what the accident investigators had said—that the missile was accidentally hot-wired into the launch mode back at the factory. Someone had missed that problem during the missile's final quality-control check back in the States.

This morning, the munitions team chief gave Rod Wells the thumbs-up signal.

Adams saw the signal and prompted Starbuck, "Continue the before-takeoff check."

"Canopies?"

Both men ran their own down using the paddle switch under the left canopy rail. The loud engine noise and the wisps of kerosene from the spent fuel exhaust disappeared as Adams and Starbuck were enclosed in their technology bubble. "Closed and checked."

"Lower ejection handle guard?"

Both men flipped down the red metal guard, exposing the most rapid form of ejecting from the plane. They hoped they wouldn't need it on takeoff or later over Hanoi. "Clear."

"IFF/SIF?"

Adams turned the knob on the black box that identified him as an American Phantom to all the radar controllers on today's routing. Only the friendlies could read the Identification Friend or Foe code. Or so he hoped. "On."

"Pitot heat?"

"On," said Adams as he flipped the toggle switch to the electrical heater that assured his airspeed probe and other sensors wouldn't freeze up in the clouds.

"Engines?"

Adams scanned the two vertical rows of small round dials on the right front instrument panel. "Check."

"Variable ramp?"

Craning left and right, Adams saw the engine intakes were clear for takeoff. "Check full open."

"Flaps?"

"Half down." The most efficient combination of lift and drag for takeoff.

"Anti-skid?"

"On." For better stopping a heavy plane on an aborted takeoff.

"Warning lights?"

"Out." Everything looked normal.

"Shoulder harness?"

Both men checked their straps. "Checked." The inertial locks would take care of the rest if needed.

Rod Wells had finished his takeoff check too. "Rambler, let's go to tower." After his three wingmen checked in, Wells advised, "Rambler, flight of four, ready for takeoff."

"Roger, Rambler. Wind calm. Cleared for takeoff."

Rambler 01 and 02 taxied onto Runway 05. Exactly at the time planned for takeoff, Rod Wells lit both afterburners and rolled for takeoff. In two seconds Rambler 01 was accelerating rapidly through 60 knots 500 feet down the runway.

Clint Adams felt #680 shudder and heard the muffled roar as Wells's burners kicked in. Now it was his turn to go to war. He could hardly wait the required thirty seconds. To hell with it! At the fifteen-second point Adams slapped his two throttles into full military power, the engine setting just short of afterburner. He scanned his engine instruments; all were stable. "Let's do it, Randy." Twenty seconds after Wells, Adams's left hand thrust the two throttles the full 6 inches of travel into maximum afterburner as he let off the brakes. Both men felt the double thud as the J-79s accelerated. Simultaneously, Rambler 03 and 04 moved onto the runway. They would follow the standard takeoff sequence at thirty-second intervals.

Even at a takeoff weight of 48,000 pounds with a standard MiGCAP weapons and fuel load, Adams's F-4 moved quickly down the washboard runway. At 110 knots, he pulled the joystick full aft and waited for the laws of physics to run their course. At 135 knots, #680's black nose rose to 10 degrees nose high, and Adams let off a little on the control stick to hold that takeoff attitude. Just that fast, the plane leaped into the already-humid morning air at 155 knots. Sensing the initial ascent Adams slapped up the landing gear and flaps. He didn't bother checking the cockpit instruments; the plane felt good. Instead, his eyes were outside, looking for Rod Wells. There he was!

He accelerated through 300 knots, cleared the field boundary, and rolled into a 45-degree left bank. Rod Wells was at ten o'clock and 4 miles, in a standard 30-degree bank at 300 knots, out of afterburner, and waiting for the rest of his formation to join.

Adams closed on his leader by flying inside Wells's circle. Just as he had done countless times before, Clint put himself on a collision course with Rambler 01 by freezing the leader in one spot on his canopy. Adams varied his engine power and adjusted his flight controls to keep Rambler 01 frozen on his merging course. Adams moved in on Rambler 01's left rear quarter, pulled back the throttles to idle, and glided almost under the leader's tail to his right-wing position.

"Nice, Colonel," said Starbuck as Adams added the power to maintain position.

Once Vic Sansone in Rambler 04 took his place in the left fingertip formation, Rod Wells accelerated the flight to 400 knots, and moved on to rendezvous for inflight refueling.

0830 hours
Along the Thai-Laotian border
On the Orange Refueling Track, 25,000 feet

Rod Wells led the Rambler flight rendezvous with the KC-135, call sign Oboe 57. The entire refueling process would take place in radio silence, allowing one less cue for the enemy.

Rambler moved in behind Oboe 57 for the actual fuel transfer, the process of topping off the F-4's tanks. Over North Vietnam, JP-4 jet fuel meant fighting capability and life itself. Fuel converted to power, speed, altitude, and distance and gave a pilot options.

Bubba Brown called out the closure rates and distances to his front-seater: "Five miles and 150 knots overtake; 3 miles, 100 knots; 1 mile, 50 knots. Looks good, Colonel Wells." At 500 feet, Wells offset a little right of Oboe 57 and parked his wingman.

Brown used challenge and response to run two important checklists for Wells, who kept his eyes outside the cockpit, on the tanker growing larger every second. The first check ensured that all missiles were safe and that the high-power radar and electronic emitters were in the standby mode. The second checklist configured the Phantom to receive gas.

"Internal wing dump switch?"

"Normal."

"Refueling selector switch?"

"Normal." Wells heard a slight change in the sound of the air blast moving across the upper surface of his plane, caused by the opening of the door, exposing the refueling receptacle just behind Bubba Brown's aft cockpit.

He saw the amber light mounted on the canopy rail in front of him. Everything was ready for the onload. "On." Wells slid in 30 feet aft and 30 feet low on the boom, then he drove in. "Here we go, Bubba." The KC-135 filled his canopy, and he lost the tanker's wingtips as they passed beyond his peripheral vision. To Wells, each air refueling seemed like flying into the tanker's womb.

Wells guided his F-4 into the precontact position: just aft of an imaginary 3-foot cube of air below the refueling boom extending from the rear underside of Oboe 57. The boom operator lay on his stomach, watching Wells from his panoramic chin station, aft under the KC-135's tail. The wary boomer sized up Wells by how smoothly and quickly he stabilized in the precontact position. It was the first check of a fighter pilot's abilities.

Wells felt the sweat beading on his eyebrows, and his heart beating faster, but he passed this first hurdle easily.

Using signal lights on the underbelly of his tanker, the boomer silently directed the seasoned fighter pilot into the critical contact position, the 3-foot air cube closer to the boom.

Wells didn't look at the underbelly lights. He knew where the cube was. He moved forward quickly, and the boomer extended the 15-foot-long probe, plugging it into the F-4's refueling receptacle behind Bubba Brown, as Wells pulled his throttles back a tad to stabilize his position.

"You got flow, Boss?" asked Bubba.

"Yep," said Wells, seeing the green light on his canopy rail.

Adams admired the precise maneuver of both fighter pilot and boom operator. Rod Wells and the experienced SAC boomer made it look easy. The fuel flowed under great pressure into the waiting tanks. For the next five minutes, Wells held his position in the 3-foot cube. He worked extra hard because his fellow pilots were watching. It was a matter of pride not to disconnect—whether in turbulence, at night, in a 30-degree bank turn, in the weather, or in all these conditions together.

Five minutes didn't seem very long to hang on the boom, but Rod Wells thought it might be easier to hold his breath for that long. Wells watched the underbelly director lights. One foot up, one foot aft, and so on. Adjusting his position based on these lights might not avert a disconnect, but they helped Wells confirm his other visual cues.

Clint Adams and the other F-4 crews waited their turn, flying loose formation, right and slightly aft of the KC-135 tanker. He looked at his two 370-gallon external fuel wing tanks, one on each outer wing station. "Do we always fly in this tank configuration, Randy?"

"Yessir. We'll jettison these tanks as we move into the Downtown area. Mean and clean over Hanoi."

Adams used this waiting time to relax as much as he could. Everything looked so peaceful from 25,000 feet. It didn't look much different than taking gas over Georgia or Tennessee. His thoughts turned to Laura and Amy. He wondered what they'd do later today. Church? School?

"What day is it, Randy?"

"Huh, ah, beats me, Colonel. Saturday, I think." In this solar system— the one between Ubon and Hanoi—it didn't matter much.

Wells slid off the boom with all his fuel, and Clint Adams in Rambler 02 moved silently toward the 3-foot cube.

Rambler flight finished the aerial refueling in twenty minutes, and Oboe 57 turned south as it reached the northern limit of Orange Refueling Track. Rambler flight slid off to the northeast. Joining up with the main strike force, coming off other refueling tracks, was the next order of business for Rod Wells. Again, in radio silence.

Adams started thinking about his weapons, mentally going over the switch positions and sequence for changing from one missile to another. "Randy, how do you like the Sparrow and the Sidewinder?" Adams was referring to the four AIM-7 radar-guided Sparrows, each semi-imbedded in missile coves in the underside of his F-4's fuselage, and the four AIM-9 heat-seeking Sidewinder missiles, hanging in pairs on #680's inboard wing pylons.

"The medium-range Sparrow's great. I like being able to shoot an inbound target 20 miles away, but it don't work that way over Hanoi. Too many targets. Got to get a visual ID first so we don't shoot a Navy A-4 or an RF-4C. So we end up firing the Sparrow in beam attacks and stern shots. Less than ideal for a Doppler-logic missile, so we get lots of Sparrow failures. Give yourself a 20 percent chance with a Sparrow."

"What about the Sidewinder?" Adams asked.

"A super short-range speedster. We can plug a MiG up to 5 miles out front, as long as he keeps his hot engine pointed at the AIM-9's seeker head. It starts to lose effectiveness in angle-off beam shots. No head-on capability. Give yourself a 60 percent chance, if you're in the rear half of the MiG's world."

"What's your best advice on using these missiles in combination?"

"Simple. Visual ID early. Shoot 'em with a Sparrow ASAP and convert to a stern Sidewinder attack." Adams listened and, again, wished he had a gun to finish off the MiGs at close quarters from *any* angle.

Still 60 miles west-northwest of Hanoi at 25,000 feet, Rambler joined up with Packard and Ford flights, eight F-105s from Korat, scheduled to bomb supply depots at a junction on the Northwest Railway, 30 miles from the capital. The other support elements were already with the main force, four F-105 SAM suppression aircraft, called Wild Weasels, and the other four MiGCAP F-4s from Da Nang.

Rambler took up its position in the formation—nine o'clock on the left of Ford flight, the trailing F-105 strike section. Rambler would be the screening force between the MiG airfields and the Thuds. All the pilots in the strike force started their descent into the target area, knowing the North Vietnamese GCI radars were tracking them with ease.

0907 hours
Kep Airfield
Forty kilometers northeast of Hanoi

Four MiG-17s rolled down the runway for takeoff in pairs. But today two of the MiGs carried something out of the ordinary.

The second two were each equipped with two heat-seeking Atoll air-to-air missiles, not normal weapons for the MiG-17s. One minute later, a lone fifth MiG-17 took off and followed the others in trail. This one had ten red stars painted on its fuselage. Nguyen Tomb, the Dragon, was at the controls.

At the base of the Kep control tower, a frustrated Ivan Arkov drew in the last centimeter of his Turkish cigarette, slammed the butt to the ground, and briskly walked off to the camouflaged radar control center, 100 meters away.

0909 hours

Rod Wells was keeping Rambler flight between the strike force and the MiGs at Kep. His external fuel tank read zero. As pre-briefed, Wells rocked his wings, the preparatory signal for Rambler to shed its 370-gallon external fuel tanks. One second later, Wells distinctly nodded his head forward, the execution signal for all his frontseaters to flip up their red-guarded wing tank jettison switches. Eight green-and-white tanks tumbled backward end over end into the North Vietnamese jungle below. The external tanks restricted the F-4s to subsonic speed. Shedding the unnecessary tanks was the last barrier to the supersonic speed the F-4s might need.

Next, Wells gave the silent missile arming signal, a rotating fist. He looked at his wingmen: each one nodded his acknowledgment. "Bubba, read out the arming check."

Each GIB read the first seven items on the checklist, but stopped short of reading item number eight—Trigger switch—Depress. Any Phantom crew inadvertently launching a missile this early on a MiGCAP would be buying beer at the Ubon O Club for the rest of their tour.

Rambler was then armed for a medium-range attack using radar-guided missiles. All the while, the GIBs intently searched their assigned sectors of the sky with their APG-100 fire-control radars.

"You know, Boss, that's a helluva checklist just to ready a goddamned missile! What the hell are those engineers thinkin' about?" complained Brown from Rambler 01's backseat.

"Yeah, well, can't change the world from here. Just keep your corneas peeled, Bubba." Wells looked over quickly at Rambler 02. He'd had Adams on his wing several times before—in F-86s over the Nevada desert and in F-100s over the unforgiving North Sea. Adams flew steady, as if in suspended animation 500 feet at eight o'clock. "You know, Bubba, it's comforting to have a double ace locked in one's fighting wing position, even if it is his first combat mission in the F-4."

"If he flies like he did yesterday, we'll do just fine, Boss."

The F-105 strike force was moving off Thud Ridge and out over the flat Red River Valley. Everyone felt exposed. The Thuds encountered some 57mm flak, but it was light and inaccurate.

The strike force leveled off at 15,000 feet, all the while "jinking"—making short, random, sharp turns and altitude changes—but holding relative position on the strike force leader. The MiGCAP was a little higher, at 18,000 feet, and jinking too.

Bubba Brown was getting slightly airsick from the jinking. It often happened to GIBs. "Sir, all this jackin' around better fool the flak radar computers because it's makin' me want to puke."

"Okay, Bubba, concentrate on the bad guys. Now's when the MiGs usually come up to get the F-105s to salvo their bombs early. Keep your eyes peeled."

Later, and closer to the terminal caldron of SAMs and flak, the MiGs faded out of the picture. They would perhaps appear to bounce the exiting fighter-bombers as they headed for the KC-135 tankers, twenty minutes to the southwest.

Mike Nelson in Rambler 03 saw something. Blinking lights—No! It was flashing from the wing roots of MiGs as they closed on the second flight of F-105s. Cannon fire!

"MiGs! MiGs! Nine o'clock!" Not the correct alert call. Not specific enough. Every pilot on this radio frequency looked to his left, vainly searching for MiGs.

Nelson saw now that the attackers were MiG-17s. They had opened fire about 3 miles from the Thuds. Too far out for accurate hits, a common mistake of the inexperienced.

Wells and Adams saw the MiGs immediately, two bogies slicing in fast on the trailing F-105s, nine o'clock low, a classic GCI radar-controlled beam attack. "Rambler 01, tally. We've got 'em, Packard." Wells said this evenly, reassuring the anxious strike force leader that the MiGCAP F-4s had matters well in hand.

Hearing this, Packard 01, the strike force leader, pressed on to the primary target. He, too, saw the MiGs and decided that the 90-degree, ground-controlled enemy attack by the MiGs was ineffectual, several seconds too late for an attack from the flank.

Still, Packard and Ford F-105 flights started climbing left turns to throw off the MiGs' attack angle even more. Packard 01 knew he could continue on to the supply depots with the Da Nang MiGCAP F-4s, while Rambler flight dealt with these MiGs maneuvering behind him.

The MiGs should have seen the Rambler flight F-4s, but they pressed their attack on the F-105s anyway. Going behind the two F-105s, the two MiG-17s passed directly under Rambler 01 and 02. The geometry meant that, as the MiGs blew through on the right side of the strike force, the Ubon F-4s could simply roll in behind the NVAF planes in very good missile firing position. Indeed, that was what happened, with a slight modification. Wells and Adams rolled off their high perch, went to full afterburner power and pulled into a hard, descending right turn, pursuing the two MiGs.

Wells reminded Nelson, "Watch for the trailers, Rambler 03."

"Copy." As briefed, Rambler 03 and 04 momentarily continued straight ahead, then pulled up high and to the right, all the while looking for the trailers, a second pair of MiGs that so often used the lead element as decoys to sucker in the American F-4s. The NVAF exploited the American pilots' hunger for kills.

From the backseat of Rambler 04, Snake Cummings saw a second pair of MiGs about 5 miles behind the first. Snake called out his sighting on the UHF. "Rambler 03. Two more MiGs. Five miles in trail."

Rambler 03 and 04 were now upside down at the apex of their lazy barrel roll over the top. This tallyho crystallized the battle. Wells had the first MiG pair, and Nelson had the second. Rod Wells had no time now to instruct Rambler 03 and 04, the two crews that Adams waxed easily the day before. The newlyweds were on their own.

The first two MiGs followed a standard postattack profile. "They blew straight through, Bubba," Wells observed. Then the MiGs banked into a slight left turn and headed for very low altitude, below 300 meters, where U.S. missile attacks were much less effective because of ground interference.

Wells was anxious to drive home his attack, but he knew the second MiG element was pursuing him. He kept his eyes on the lead MiGs, but told his GIB to look behind him and into the radar scope. "Can we hose the first two with a radar missile?"

"No way, Boss. Too much ground clutter."

Besides, a tail-chase shot was a low payoff opportunity for the AIM-7 Sparrow missile because it used Doppler radar logic. Instead, Wells switched to a Sidewinder heat-seeking missile, a much better choice in a rear-quarter attack. He had a few precious seconds, so he got his GIB's help. "Let's go heat, Bubba."

Bubba Brown called out the AIM-9 launch checklist all by himself, not waiting for Wells to acknowledge each challenge. "Missile select switch—Heat. Sw light—On. Sight mode—Air-to-air. Aural tone—Check. Missile arm switch—Arm. Ready light—On. Trigger switch—"

"Okay, got it. Thanks." Wells rechecked everything. He did it correctly on his own without looking down into the cockpit, but it was best to check. He would hate to lose this one because of a bad switch position or poor crew coordination.

This tail-chase heat shot meant Wells must drive in closer, to about 9,000 feet in trail. The morning sun ahead was keeping the AIM-9 seeker head from locking onto the MiG's engine exhaust heat signature.

Meanwhile, Adams easily maintained his position on his element leader. He was learning that the MiG pilots had this tactic down pat.

"Damn, I don't have a good growl yet," Wells lamented, referring to the poor tracking sound in his earphones from the missile's seeker head. Then he said, "I'm in boresight."

Wells used the radar's preset spotlight mode, which beamed like a laser right through the center of his gunsight pipper, a round circle projected electronically onto a glass plate directly in front of his forward windscreen. Being in the boresight mode gave Wells another option. If he wanted to shift back to radar missiles all he had to do now was put the pipper on the target, throw one switch on his armament panel with his left hand while Bubba locked the radar onto the MiG, then squeeze the trigger on the joystick to launch a Sparrow. But right now he was sticking with the heat-seeking Sidewinders.

Clint Adams, riding the fighting wing, wished for an internally mounted cannon right now, just like he'd once had in his World War II fighters, the P-38 and the P-51. Then this battle would be over, and Rod would have two MiG kills, he thought.

Wells pushed over the nose of his F-4 and moved his throttles into full afterburner. His dive unloaded the F-4 to zero-G so he could accelerate more quickly. He was trying to get to tree-top altitude faster than the MiGs so he could pop up and take the ground clutter out of play for his Sidewinder's seeker head.

He had the lead MiG in his sights now, but he was not hearing the clear audio growl from the Sidewinder's optical guidance logic, signifying that the seeker head had good tracking. The MiG-17 was still below the horizon, and the sun burned brightly out front, hiding the MiG-17's hot tailpipe from the Sidewinder's seeker head.

Wells ate up precious time, and he himself was becoming more vulnerable to attack by the trailing MiG element. His MiG targets entered their defensive circle. They were moving farther left now, away from the sun. Wells told Bubba, "Keep me posted on those trailing MiGs." Adams and Starbuck, too, watched the trailers. The wingman's job was to keep MiGs off his leader's tail.

Randy Starbuck, in Adams's rear seat, contorted himself to get a view left and aft. This slow turn by the lead MiGs helped the trailing MiG-17s to close on Rambler 01 and 02. The trailers were cutting the corner on Wells and Adams. Sometimes the laws of physics helped you, sometimes they helped your enemy. Starbuck, his voice straining against the G-force, said, "They're gaining on us, Boss, but still beyond gun range. 'Bout 3 miles."

Adams grunted, "Let me know if they start shootin'," and then calmly assured his leader, "Rambler Lead, trailers 3 miles." Wells double-clicked the UHF button on his throttle to acknowledge his wingman's update, knowing he had a few more seconds to nail his targets.

But the lead MiG leader reversed to the right, back into the sun, and both MiGs settled into a low-altitude defensive circle. That last turn destroyed Wells's immediate chance for a heat-seeking missile launch. Then came the surprise of the day.

Mike Nelson in Rambler 03 hadn't yet gotten into Sidewinder firing position on the trailing MiGs. Suddenly, he saw something totally unexpected.

"Rambler Lead, break left! Break left! Missile shot! Missile shot!" The leader of the second MiG element had launched two Atoll heat-seeking missiles.

Without thinking, Wells and Adams broke hard in a gut-wrenching left descending turn. Bubba Brown, caught in a rearward-looking contortion, was reduced to a useless lump for the duration of this maneuver, with his head pulled down between his legs by the force of the buckling high-G turn. The Atoll missiles passed harmlessly behind Rambler 02, because the Soviet-made copies of the AIM-9 Sidewinder were unable to negotiate much more than a two-G turn. Ironically, the same sun angle that foiled Rod Wells earlier contributed to his—and his wingman's—narrow escape.

Only now, after surviving his last-ditch maneuver, did Wells allow himself to assess the tactical surprise of a MiG-17 firing Russian-made Atolls. "Shit, Bubba, MiG-17s don't carry Atolls!"

Other aspects of this engagement were clear now. The first two MiGs were decoys. Yet, because the American pilots had reacted quickly, the NVAF tactic failed.

Tactical surprise was over in this dogfight, and the Americans were onto the enemy's game. Wells called out on the radio, "Where are you, Rambler 03 and 04?"

Right where they should be, rolling in behind the second MiG element. "We got the trailers, Lead."

"Better late than never. Any time now, 03."

Wells saw Nelson and Sansone and decided that Rambler 01 and 02 would be the decoys this time. He stayed just beyond reach of the trailing MiGs, while Rambler 03 and 04 closed for the kill. Wells advised his GIB over the intercom, "Let's be the quail now, Bubba. We'll try to sucker these Gomers."

"Aw, Boss."

The trailing MiG element should have disengaged from the fight. The MiG pilots were trained to keep up their speed, break away, head for low altitude, and attempt to join the other MiGs in a defensive wheel—four MiGs flying around in a horizontal wagon wheel.

Wells did his job well, and the MiGs took the bait. They did *not* disengage; instead, they pressed their attack on Rambler 01 and 02. Big mistake number one. The NVAF element leader turned after Wells, converting to a close-quarters gun attack. But Rambler 01 and 02 had plenty of airspeed. Pilots call it "Mach." In a dogfight, Mach meant energy. Good pilots translated energy into any number of advantages, and Wells was a very good pilot.

With his momentum, Wells pulled the nose of his F-4 straight up, climbing rapidly through 10,000 feet at 600 knots and took the MiG-17s into the vertical. This was the F-4 Phantom's backyard, where the American pilots had all the leverage. Wells climbed into the late morning sun, and the MiGs were now at the wrong angle to fire any more heat-seeking missiles. They slipped back beyond range for a gun attack. Worse, the MiGs were losing airspeed faster than the more powerful F-4s and began to fall even farther behind. Rambler 01 and 02 passed 22,000 feet, still climbing at 440 knots.

The MiG leader finally realized things were going against him, and he broke off the attack, rolling to the right. Wells's job was done. He rolled on his back to watch the action and to cover Rambler 03 and 04.

Mike Nelson had his element in good position for a stern Sidewinder missile attack on the fleeing MiGs. Wells had handed a rare opportunity to his fledgling second element, a pair of vulnerable MiG-17s fresh out of airspeed, altitude, and options.

With each passing moment, the geometry improved for Rambler 03. Nelson told his GIB, "Looking good, Moose. Range and angle are great. No growl."

"Go to heat. Heat!" Moose Peterson finally realized what was wrong.

"Dammit." Nelson maneuvered his F-4 to put his gunsight pipper exactly on the lead MiG. He struggled against the G-forces to select his Sidewinder heat-seeking missiles by flipping the missile toggle switch to the "heat" position on the armament panel. Fumbling clumsily, he sought the switch by feel. Nelson and Peterson hadn't had the time Rambler 01 had had for the checklist. They didn't have the crew co-ordination experience either. Mike Nelson realized that he should have set the heat switch much earlier in the pursuit. But he did do one thing right. He never took his eyes off the MiG.

Beginner's luck. "I got it, Moose." Mike Nelson heard the loud growl from the Sidewinder seeker head. More luck. This missile shot was going to be "down sun." He squeezed the trigger. The AIM-9 leaped off its launch rail and tracked straight for the MiG leader. The rocket propellant of the accelerating missile momentarily obscured Nelson's forward vision.

His voice straining, Mike grunted to Moose Peterson over the intercom, "Fox Two." Fox Ones were AIM-7 radar-guided Sparrows. Fox

Twos were AIM-9 Sidewinders. The first Sidewinder missile was on its way.

Even as the AIM-9 tracked toward the lead MiG, Nelson turned his attention to the second MiG. He could do this when working with heat-seeking missiles, because they were launch-and-leave weapons. Nelson was acquiring a keener sense of anticipating events. Nothing breeds success like success.

Vic Sansone stayed right with Nelson by maintaining a good fighting wing position. The two GIBs, Moose Peterson and Snake Cummings, kept checking for other MiGs rolling in behind them. They saw no threats closing on their formation. Both GIBs worked hard, continually transitioning from assisting the attack to protecting the formation. These two GIBs had talent, and it showed. Snake Cummings was rapidly developing a reputation as a real eagle eye, something a man was born with. You couldn't acquire this gift.

"Goin' for two, Moose." Nelson kicked his right rudder and put his pipper on the second MiG. Again, he heard the growl, almost as strongly as before. And again, he squeezed the trigger. The second of his four AIM-9s leaped off the rail and drove straight for the MiG. This time Nelson stated more calmly over the intercom, "Fox Two." The second Sidewinder closed on its target, 1 mile ahead.

Now it was time to cash in on all the investment in time, effort, and hardware. The first missile detonated in the tailpipe of the lead MiG. The plane exploded, and the pilot did not survive. Six seconds later, the remaining MiG's tail section caught fire as the second AIM-9 detonated just under the fuselage. The fatally wounded MiG flopped first to the right, then to the left. It became uncontrollable as it pitched straight up. The pilot ejected before the MiG disintegrated. Both Nelson and Peterson forgot the customary radio call for when a missile destroyed its target. Nelson shouted to Moose, "Got 'em! Got 'em both!"

Rod Wells, observing from above, remembered it. "Splash One! Splash Two!"

Rambler 03 and 04 passed to the right of the surviving enemy pilot, drifting to earth in his green-canopied parachute.

"Okay, Rambler, join it up." Wells gathered his four-ship formation by rocking his wings as he rode in the ten o'clock position to Rambler 03, now crewed by the Air Force's newest MiG killers. Rambler resumed its tactical formation, and Rod Wells took up the proper compass heading to join with the main body of the strike force, now exiting the target area. Bubba Brown made radar contact with the strike force, 10 miles slightly right. Wells spotted it and advised his wingmen, "Rambler, tally on Pontiac and company 10 miles, one o'clock level."

Rambler flight was back again in MiGCAP position, abeam and higher than the strike force F-105s. Naturally, all the pilots in Rambler flight were winding down on the emotional backside of a dogfight. But Snake Cummings was on the UHF again. "Rambler 04, bogey eight o'clock high." Suddenly, everyone tensed up.

Everyone looked, but only the few with eyes the caliber of Snake Cummings's saw the single MiG-17 almost 10 miles away, somewhat up sun from the strike force. Then the rays of the mid-morning sun bounced off the canopy of the distant MiG, making it visible to all the pilots in the strike force. The MiG was definitely beyond range.

Seeing the elusive MiG prompted Adams to think back to the start of the dogfight, just ten minutes earlier. He remembered seeing a single MiG then, too, but just for an instant. It was beyond range then also. For some reason that MiG did not engage. Was he an observer? A mother hen? A battle director? But then, Adams was too busy to think about it further.

0921 hours
Twenty-five kilometers south of the strike force

Colonel Nguyen Tomb was enraged by the turn of events. His anger pushed him beyond his normal stoicism. He banged his left fist on the instrument panel. He had had the Americans right where he wanted them. He had had the tactical surprise. But his pilots had not converted the attack to a kill. Good plan. Bad execution.

The loss of tactical surprise was bad enough. But why did one of his best element leaders choose to stay and fight? It had been a costly error for the NVAF. The price was two planes and, more important, one combat-experienced pilot. Tomb wondered why young men didn't have the necessary discipline in the air. He resolved to drive this lesson home very hard with his remaining pilots. He mustn't let them forget that the Americans were very good.

Tomb had wanted to be in the air battle from the beginning. He had planned to strike like a dagger near the end, but only if conditions were favorable.

He knew he could not engage. Right now, North Vietnam could not afford to lose him to a lucky American missile shot. His primary value to the People's Republic was as a leader. He had to build his air force to inflict severe pain on the Americans. He must not forget that. Above all else.

Unknowingly, two special air commanders had met in the skies over North Vietnam that day. One had surprise on his side. The other, in a subordinate role, had experience and discipline. The Dragon and the Eagle had had their first encounter. It would not be their last.

0922 hours
Moving out of the Red River Valley

The MiG attacks were over. Now the SAMs went into action against the American strike force. And the F-105 Wild Weasels escorting the strike force started their attacks against the active SAM sites. Lots of radio chatter. Lots of verbal confusion.

The strike force leader, Packard 01, observed a dust plume on the ground, in line just beyond Rambler flight. A Soviet-built SA-2 Guideline—as large as a telephone pole and packing a 240-pound high fragmentation warhead—accelerated off its launcher toward the F-105s.

Packard 01 called it out. "Packard, SAM launch. Nine o'clock."

"Hammer 01's in. Two's in." Simultaneously, two Wild Weasels rolled in from different directions for a 20mm Vulcan cannon attack on the radar vans in that SAM site. The pilots knew that these Fan Song radar vans, bristling with antennae, formed the nerve center providing electronic steering to the SA-2. The Wild Weasels wanted to shut down the guidance commands, because without guidance, the SA-2's homing seeker head could not track its American target. Destroying the SAM site itself would be a nice bonus.

A third F-105 Wild Weasel rolled in toward the waning dust plume. The pilot fired an AGM-45 Shrike missile at the SAM site. The Shrike seeker head homed on the electronic guidance signal being sent from the Fan Song control van to the SA-2. This duel became a game of electronic "chicken." Did the North Vietnamese SAM controller have the guts to keep transmitting the target tracking signal, and risk destruction of the radar van and the people inside it? A high price just to shoot down one American plane. Or would he shut down and make haste for the nearest bunker?

The SAM kept coming. It was moving at Mach 3, and it had reached the horizon. Packard and Ford flights pushed hard nose down. The SAM also pushed nose down, moving near Mach 4 now. Then the strike force F-105s pulled nose up, executing a barrel roll into and over the SAM. The missile was moving five times faster than the F-105s, and it could not turn tight enough to compensate for the F-105s' last maneuver.

The distance between the F-105s and the SA-2 had closed to 3,000 feet, but it now began to widen rapidly. Suddenly, the SAM exploded, sensing it was moving away from its target. The detonation occurred 2,000 feet below and 4,000 feet behind the strike force, yet the SA-2's concussion wave bounced the Thuds.

"Packard, Hammer 01. That SAM site's no longer operational." The SAM site commander had gambled and lost in a game of seconds.

The strike force left the target area. Bombs on target. No casualties.

0937 hours
The Plain of Jars
Over central Laos

The American strike formation passed over the first friendly electronic lighthouse, a TACAN station called Channel 51. The recurring ground battles for this electronic lighthouse cost many lives. Now each element of the strike force broke off, heading for its own refueling rendezvous and subsequent return to its own home base.

The F-105s and F-4s drifted apart while cruising at 25,000 feet. Packard 01 transmitted, "Well done, Rambler." That short message said it all to Rod Wells and the other Rambler pilots.

"Nice job, Packard." Wells conveyed the respect that everyone felt for the Thud pilots. Adams was very proud of Rod Wells.

1015 hours
Nearing Ubon RTAFB

Spirit was high within Rambler flight, yet everyone remained alert for a "bounce" by either F-4s or Sabres. Harley Stockman's pilots had leaked the new relationship after too many beers at the O Club last night. Each GIB in Rambler flight worked his radar just as hard as he did over Hanoi. All for naught. No bounce today.

"Ubon Tower, Rambler. Permission for two controlled victory rolls. Rambler 03 inbound with two Splash Ones." Wells looked to the right at Rambler 02 as Clint Adams gave him a thumbs up.

Tower responded after a short pause. "Rambler, you're cleared for a tactical arrival. Understand Ragtop 21's with you. Congratulations." Tower had changed its operating mode just this morning, and the tower controllers were carefully tracking the whereabouts of their new wing commander.

Wells looked to his left. "Okay, Rambler 03. You're cleared. Pick us up when you're done. We'll hold to the northeast."

"Wilco." Mike Nelson eagerly complied. He proceeded down the initial approach to Runway 23 at 500 feet. Just over the large white stripes painted on the approach end of the runway, Nelson pulled up the nose and did two slow aileron rolls. He completed the maneuver at the departure end of the runway, then turned left to the northeast for a rapid rejoin on the rest of Rambler flight.

The people on the ground watched their first victory roll sequence at Ubon, but they all knew what it meant. Some of the maintenance and munitions personnel let out a cheer as they strained to see which F-4 had bagged the MiGs. Some of the medical staff exiting the Clinic also caught the short air show. Slim Danforth saw it too. Very quickly the whole base knew what was going on, and everyone shared the moment. It was the mission-oriented focus that Adams had been talking about at yesterday's staff meeting. There was a message in all this—new commander, new spirit—and everyone in the wing shared the MiG kills.

Nelson slid his jet back into the number three position, left of Rambler 01. Then Wells led all four F-4s in a routine overhead pattern approach, pitch out, and individual landings.

After Adams parked, Chris Cole was up the ladder of #680 in a flash. "Those our victory rolls, Colonel?"

"You'll have to watch more carefully next time. No, that was Rambler 03." Adams stuffed his helmet and sweat-soaked leather flying gloves into his green helmet bag.

Cole was only momentarily disappointed and said, "I've got a full can of red paint, Colonel. Sure hope I get to use it." Adams liked Cole's resilience.

"How's the airplane, sir?"

"No write-ups." Aside from getting a MiG, this was the best news a crew chief could get.

Adams paused for a moment, then found a way to tell Cole he liked his airplane. "Paint Ragtop 21 on it."

"What's Ragtop 21 for?"

"That's my call sign."

"But, sir. . . ." Cole was about to tell Adams that nose art was not authorized.

"And paint some names on the canopy rails too. Yours included." Cole smiled from ear to ear as he saluted his new boss.

A crowd of well-wishers greeted Adams as he stepped off the ladder. Todd Benning came down to the flight line with Slim Danforth. He eagerly asked Starbuck, "What happened?"

"U.S., 2; North Vietnam, 0." Starbuck and Adams purposely moved through this group toward the larger crowd gathering in the revetment two spaces away.

Adams distracted the attention of this second crowd as he approached Nelson and Peterson. Adams congratulated them. "What a difference a day makes. You newlyweds look like real horses to me. Looks like a good marriage." Then Adams added, "So far."

Together, these four joined the rest of Rambler flight in the crew bus. Next stop: maintenance and intell debriefing. Right now, almost everyone standing on that ramp was proud to be in the 8th TFW—and to be working for their new wing commander. Except Colonel Slim Danforth. He didn't care for the victory rolls. Not standard operating procedure.

1145 hours
Debriefing shack
Ubon RTAFB

Rambler flight's pilots finished their spirited debriefing, and ambled back to the squadron's life support section to stow the helmets, anti-G suits, and survival gear. Important business often got done in the pilots' locker room before and after a mission, but today, the younger pilots quickly parked their gear, picked up the wallets they'd left behind this morning, and headed for a hearty lunch at the O Club.

Adams hung back. "Rod. Good work today."

Wells was a little uncomfortable with the praise. A compliment from one's idol was a very big thing. "Thanks, Boss. You did okay yourself."

"Rod, how would you assess the fighting mood of this wing?" A heavy question for a man still winding down from a stressful mission. Adams sat on the bench, signaling Wells that he was looking for a thoughtful answer that might take some time.

"Well, sir, from where I sit, it's not a wing. It's a bunch of squadrons that rotate in and out of this location, but it ain't a wing. Not like you and I have known." Rod Wells pulled out a pack of Camels and offered one to Adams. Both men lit up off Wells's Zippo. Wells continued, "We really haven't had the leadership to pull the 8th together. No cohesion."

Adams listened thoughtfully. "Hell of a thing, Rod. Common enemy, men facing death every day, and we're not pullin' together. Frankly, I think you have to work at it *not* to bind as a team in a situation like this."

"Sir, you know I'm an optimist, but I think things started changing today over Hanoi."

Adams looked at his friend. They each smiled a little, both understanding what was happening. Adams stood up and put his hand on Wells's shoulder, swinging him toward the door in the process. "Let's go get a greaseburger, Rambler 01."

1255 hours
Wing commander's office
8th TFW Headquarters

Word of the day's MiG kills spread through the base as Adams returned to his office. Adams's exec, Captain Boomer Wright, approached his new boss. He wanted to propose rotating exec officer duties with another captain so he could fly more.

But Boomer stowed it when he saw that Adams was preoccupied. "What's eating you, Boss?"

"I'm still learning, but today's mission showed me clearly why we aren't doing very well up North." Adams picked up a model of the MiG-17 that his predecessor left behind. He examined its features as he talked. "It's sickening to watch the MiGs take off from airfields we're not allowed to attack and close. And then to see these same MiGs vectored to the Thuds by GCI operators using radars that remain on the White House restricted target list. No other Air Force ever had to engage and defeat an enemy air force operating over its home turf, while hamstrung by such restrictions." Adams paused, "But I've got to find a way."

Boomer offered, "Captain Starbuck, who runs the Wing Tactics Shop, might be able to help." Adams, still deep in thought, nodded. He wasn't really listening.

Boomer pressed on, "Sir, Starbuck and his pals have some good ideas, but nobody listens to them much. Starbuck's been here since May. One of the veterans. Sir, you really ought to talk with Starbuck about this."

Adams dropped out of his deep thought for a moment. "Randy's a good man. We've flown together twice now."

"Oh, I didn't know Randy was checking you out." Then Boomer changed his approach. "I know you've heard of GIBs. But have you heard of BIBs?"

"BIBs?"

"Yes sir, boys in the back—the Wing Tactics Shop."

"Boomer, get outta here. I'm thinking."

THE FOUR HORSEMEN

1555 hours
Main dining room, Officers' Club
Ubon RTAFB

The single-story Ubon Officers' Club, a teakwood building, was the social center for all 8th TFW officers, but especially the pilots. The O Club was adjacent to the officers' sleeping quarters, and they ate their meals in the main dining room. The main bar was the place where accomplishments, rumors, tactics, and love affairs were distorted beyond all recognition. A smaller, informal bar in the back supplemented the main one and yielded drinks and burgers round the clock.

Besides the movie theater, the O Club was the only facility large enough to host a wing officers' call—the traditional meeting of all officers in an Air Force wing. All of the 8th TFW's 250 officers not involved in that afternoon's missions were gathering in the main dining room.

Today's two MiG kills were the news as everyone waited for Colonel Clint Adams to arrive. But it wasn't just the MiG kills that had everyone talking. It was the legendary Adams himself.

Most of the officers had liked the recently departed wing commander, even though he hadn't flown the hard ones. Colonel Goodman was truly the Old Man. But Clint Adams, the new 8th Wing CO, sent a charge of excitement through Ubon's fighter squadrons. Many of the senior pilots knew him personally; some had served under his command at Nellis or Lakenheath. He had taught many of the 8th TFW's "old heads" the very skills that kept them alive over Hanoi today.

Some knew Adams was both a double ace and an experienced overseas tactical fighter wing commander. They wouldn't have to break him in on either count.

These facts alone would pique anyone's interest. But his behavior in the first thirty-six hours as 8th TFW commander had confirmed Adams's reputation. These accounts spread quickly among the younger pilots. His low-key arrival. His bouncing of the returning MiGCAP yesterday afternoon. The Happy Parker ream job. His instructions at yesterday's wing staff meeting had even spread somewhat—but with the natural distortion that occurred as information was passed through the wing's informal communications network. But his unannounced decision to fly as a wingman in the first possible MiGCAP north to Pack Six this morning had had the most impact on the pilots.

They approved of Adams's behavior over Hanoi today. It confirmed that he wasn't a fool. Trying to lead a MiGCAP mission Downtown without experience would endanger the strike force. Going North as Rambler 02 showed that he wanted to learn fast. And it also demonstrated that he was not afraid to hang it out. He'd let the experienced Rod Wells call the shots—including the one where Squadron Commander Wells used the wing commander as a decoy, while trusting younger and less-experienced pilots to shoot down their pursuers. To fighter pilots, this was true courage, true leadership.

What a position to be in. He had yet to walk in the room, and most—not all—of the pilots had already decided that they *wanted* to follow Colonel Clint Adams. They didn't see leadership by example very often. This just might be the real thing.

Still, it was a big and rapidly changing Air Force. This war was infusing lots of youth into the fighter force, and the junior pilots didn't really know Adams. Many of these younger officers were not career oriented, and they had a sour view of the air war in Southeast Asia. And young fighter pilots almost always had a dim view of their senior leaders because they strongly believed that they were hanging it out every day, while the old farts up the chain of command sat behind their desks, got promoted, and didn't do much to help the jocks do the tough jobs. Adams had sent them a message today that he might be different. But some would wait and see.

The young pilots believed that this was *their* war. Some of them figured Adams was just another touch-and-go colonel on his way to his brigadier general's star, and they would lay back and not commit to him too early.

He'd have to show that he cared about more than just his own advancement and beating the enemy by expending their blood. He'd have to show he cared about them too. Clint Adams would get lots of scrutiny this afternoon.

Then, from the back of the room, Boomer Wright called out, "Wing, Ten-Shun!" All 250 officers stood at attention as Adams moved quickly to the front of the room.

"Take your seats." Adams faced them and scanned the assembly. Like any of the F-4 wing commanders in Southeast Asia, Adams knew his pilots fell into four basic categories, based almost solely on their time in the Air Force: old heads, diehards, Young Turks, and GIBs.

The old heads, like Rod Wells and Randy Starbuck, were in the fighter business before the Vietnam War. These men had earned their spurs in the single-seat fighter force. They knew how to use the high-tech weapons they were issued to maximum advantage, and they'd go to hell and back for you without batting an eye. But not all old heads were progressive.

Some old heads were diehards and much less valuable. Before the F-4 Phantom came along, all Air Force fighters were one-seat airplanes. Some of the experienced fighter pilots were slow to capitalize on the F-4's new technology. These diehards still said an aircraft wasn't really a fighter if it had more than one seat; they resented flying with the younger, less-experienced backseat pilots. They didn't even like listening to their GIBs breathe through the Phantom's hot-wired intercom. It was easy to tell a diehard from a more progressive old head. When flying, the diehard would use the cold-mike switch on his intercom panel, isolating the front and backseat pilots from each other. In cold mike, the two pilots could only talk to each other by holding down the intercom switch on the throttle while speaking.

Worse yet, diehards didn't use their GIBs to maximum advantage. They consciously encouraged a divisive environment on the basis that backseaters weren't really fighter pilots. Such behavior undermined the F-4's major strength in the complex skies over North Vietnam: its two-man teamwork.

Then there were the Young Turks, commissioned after 1960 and brought into the fighter business as part of the Vietnam War expansion. A few Young Turks earned assignments to single-seat fighters, like the F-100, F-104, and the F-105, by finishing at the top of their pilot training classes. But the vast majority started as F-4 GIBs. Several dozen ex-GIBs, like Mike Nelson and Vic Sansone, had been Phantom pilots long enough to become F-4 aircraft commanders. Along with the progressive members of the old heads, these younger F-4 ACs knew exactly how to get the most out of their GIBs. Naturally, the GIBs wanted to fly with these fighter jocks.

And last were the GIBs themselves. They only had one goal in life, upgrade to the front seat—by noon. They were impatient, talented, and outspoken. They were the best-trained, best-educated pilots America had ever had in its Air Force. And they were flying in another fighter pilot's backseat. They wanted respect. For the most part, they deserved it.

As Adams scanned the officer corps seated before him, he noted that the senior officers occupied the first two rows. The nonflying officers, about forty in all, took up the next five rows. They stood out because they wore fatigues instead of flight suits.

The back half of the room was a sea of black-and-green flight suits. Fighter pilots hated wing meetings like these, and they preferred pilot meetings that discussed ops stuff. Any meeting involving nonfliers probably had too much general bullshit in it. They always took back pews first, then filled the forward seats only when absolutely necessary.

Adams saw that almost everyone was sitting up straight. Only a few pilots near the back were slouching, letting Adams know they would prefer to be somewhere else. To Adams, everything looked normal.

This short pause also allowed the Ubon officers a long look at their new CO—a striking figure in his flight suit and white scarf. Adams's handlebar mustache seemed important to the young pilots. Snake Cummings leaned over toward Moose Peterson and whispered, "Nice 'stache, eh, Moose?"

At 6-feet-4 inches and 235 pounds, he looked as fit as when he had played varsity football at West Point. Standing there with his fists planted on his narrow hips and flight suit sleeves rolled up to his elbows, exposing massive, sinewy forearms, it was as if he had prepared his whole life for this moment—the handpicked air combat leader of a critically important fighter wing right in the middle of a war that was not going well.

Adams got right to the point. "My name's Clint Adams. I've been in the fighter business since 1943. But that doesn't mean I know everything. I've got a lot to learn about flying fighters in Southeast Asia, and I'm going to work real hard and learn it as fast as I can. I need your help.

Pretty soon, though, I'm gonna know a lot. But I'll always expect you to know more than I do about your job.

"And you should always know more about your role in this wing's mission than I do. Otherwise you're in trouble." Some of the pilots in the back rows stirred a bit.

Adams continued, "We're all here for one purpose—to establish air superiority over North Vietnam. Everyone has a critical role to play on the team.

"Now listen up. This wing's gonna pull together as a team and take American air power to the enemy like never before. We will live, eat, and sleep with one objective—taking the war to the enemy up North. We're gonna hit the targets, and we're gonna keep knocking down MiGs." The room started a low buzz. The response was good.

Then Adams got to specifics. Drawing on what worked for him in World War II, he was direct. "I want maximum combat readiness in the air. I'm looking for a total team effort. Hear me, I mean *total*. I want maximum honing of both teamwork and individual skills. Pilots will marry up into two-man crews, then small teams, then bigger teams. And you'll work together. It worked for us in World War II and Korea. And it worked for Nelson, Peterson, Sansone, and Cummings today." The room buzzed again. More heads nodded.

"Every combat flight crew will have a designated airplane and a crew chief. Paint your names on the planes. Own the iron together—as a team.

"I want combat readiness all the time. Expect the Aussies and other 8th TFW pilots to bounce you on return to Ubon. Mix it up with these bouncers if you've got the gas and your airplane's sound." The Royal Australian Sabre pilots smiled over in the corner. They'd been itching to prove what they could do. The competition was on.

"This is a war zone, not a stateside base, so put away those tan uniforms until you get home. And do something about those damned blue staff cars." This remark drew hoots. He paused. Scanning the room, he saw many familiar faces.

"Any questions?"

A young lieutenant, one of the slouchers near the back of the room, asked without standing, "How can we kill MiGs with all the restrictions we face flying over the North?"

Adams knew that this was a critical question. He just hadn't thought he'd get it so soon.

He answered quickly. He couldn't blink now. "Stand up, Lieutenant. State your name, and repeat your question." In unison all slouchers sat up straight.

First Lieutenant Joseph "Taco" Martinez was Clint Adams's target. A streetwise young Hispanic-American, who grew up in East Los Angeles, he was scrappy and aggressive, and he tested authority, especially when it didn't pass his logic test.

The lieutenant rose, uncomfortable in the spotlight. "Ah, sir, Lieutenant Martinez. How can we whip the bad guys while shackled by the current restrictions?" Martinez sat down as he completed his question, as if ducking back into a foxhole.

But Adams wouldn't let him off the stage until he converted the situation to his total advantage. "What's your first name, Lieutenant?"

Martinez slinked into the vertical a second time. "Joseph, sir, but people call me Taco." Adams had made a crucial point—maintain the standards of discipline all the time. Ask a question like an Air Force officer, not a high school boy in the back row. Now on to the substance of Martinez's challenge.

"Thanks for your question, Taco. It's the most important one we face. You're right. Our leaders back home are spotting the enemy two touchdowns and granting him a helluva home field advantage.

"We're not politicians, and we're not grand strategists. But I'm looking at the best fighter pilots in the world right now. And the smartest. And the best educated. And we're flying the most sophisticated fighter planes in history.

"How are we gonna do it? We'll do it just like we did it today—with quick thinking, solid air discipline, superior skill, and American creativeness. And we'll do it together as a team." A lot of heads were nodding agreement and support. They accepted the answer. Can't knock today's results.

There were no other questions.

Adams concluded in a more relaxed manner. "You probably don't believe this, but I'm happy to be here. This is where all fighter pilots ought to be. Okay, the bar's open. That's where I expect to meet all our best officers."

Boomer Wright again called the room to attention. Almost everyone followed Adams into the bar. Some turned right out the O Club's main doors to duties on the flight line and in the Clinic to get ready for night missions.

Adams's old friends quickly engulfed him. Others pushed forward to introduce themselves for the first time. The bar was shoulder-to-shoulder thick. And you could walk on the blue-gray cigar smoke that already hung at eye level.

For the new 8th Wing CO, this was a special kind of homecoming—fighter-pilot style, with sharp verbal jabs and counterthrusts. Anything that one fighter pilot knew about another was fair game in this free-wheeling banter.

Meanwhile, Mike Nelson and Vic Sansone eagerly re-created the events of the day for the immediate crowd of inquisitive pilots, doctors, and maintenance officers. They were inseparable on the ground, fast friends since their days as roommates at the Air Force Academy.

In the background, behind the bar, a young Thai barmaid kept watching Vic Sansone. She seemed different from the other Thai women working at the O Club, and she was obviously interested in Vic Sansone. Inexplicably, Vic turned and saw the girl looking at him just before she averted her eyes. Somewhat distracted, he turned back to the conversation buzzing around him.

The bar at the Ubon O Club was a lively place, especially after a day of good action over the North. The wing's fighter pilots formed the core of activity, but many other crew members from all over the Southeast Asian combat theater wandered in and out all the time.

A pilot reached over the bar and rang the big brass bell hanging near the center of the 30-foot-long mahogany bar. Someone had made a big mistake. A hapless second lieutenant had wandered into the bar with his hat on, an expensive error for the young maintenance officer, fresh from the flight line with a heavy thirst. Now he had to buy a drink for everyone in the main bar; he wouldn't make that mistake again.

1710 hours

Mike Nelson, Moose, and Snake were tiring of repeating their deeds to all comers and had had enough of the limelight. Snake's eagle eye spotted a rare set of targets, three decent-looking American females. "Hey, Mike, Moose, let's try our luck with the roundeyes." Armed with long-necked Budweisers, the three aviators broke the circle surrounding the young women.

A squadron mate did the rest. "Hey, look who's here! The four horses! Ladies, let me introduce the Air Force's newest MiG killers!"

An Air Force Officers' Club was a relatively safe place for these ladies. Privately, they were impressed by the approach of Mike, Moose, and Snake—although they didn't reveal this at first. The pilots sensed that more work was needed. They planned to tell these women some war stories to break the ice. But first, the introductions.

"Ladies, I'm Mike. Mike Nelson. And this is Moose, and that's Snake."

The eldest and tallest of the girls, a blonde in her early thirties spoke first, although cautiously, "Those are unusual nicknames, fellas. I'm Lisa Davis. This is Angie Gross, and that's Carol Kuszinski."

Angie, a slim brunette in her mid-twenties, moved toward Moose. She liked hunks. And Moose Peterson was the largest guy in the room—larger even than Whale Wharton, and besides, Whale was drunk already.

Carol, a chunky, athletic blonde looked longest at the 5-foot-8 Snake. He stared back at the shortest and youngest of the girls. Radar contact for the Snake. And for Carol. In deference to the three pilots' accomplishments earlier that day, the other male pursuers melted away.

Introductions past, Nelson broke the ice by shouting his first question over the din. "What are you doing in Thailand?" The competition from the jukebox didn't make it any easier. Someone loaded the machine with a handful of quarters, all earmarked for one of the most frequently played songs at the O Club, "Snoopy and the Red Baron."

"Oh, we're the vocal trio with the Majestics." Lisa Davis saw her explanation was insufficient for these pilots. "You know, the band playing at the Airmen's Club. We're touring most of the U.S. clubs in Thailand."

"How long will you be at Ubon?"

"This is our last night here. We have shows at nine and eleven tonight. Then we go to a place called—what was it, Carol?"

"Udorn. Then on to the other bases around Thailand."

"Ladies, how about a few drinks, then dinner before you have to do your show?" suggested Nelson. That was exactly why the girls came to the O Club. O Clubs had the best food, and free dinners were always nice. Nelson, Peterson, Cummings, and the three Majestics moved off toward a quieter table in the corner.

1730 hours

Lots of business got done in the Ubon main bar. Rod Wells talked with his operations people about ways to comply with Colonel Adams's new aircrew instructions. The squadron's flight surgeon, Captain Steve Kramer, sat with Wells. Doc Kramer hung out with the Triple Nickel pilots whenever he could. As a kid in Chicago, Kramer had wanted to be a fighter pilot, but because of his 20-50 eyesight, being a flight surgeon was the best he could do. Still, he was in hog heaven.

Kramer scrounged every mission he could get in the backseat of the F-4. He'd been the Triple Nickel's flight surgeon for six months and had twenty-four missions, including seventeen counters to Route Pack One. His next goal was to break out of the milk-run circuit and into Route Pack Six. Steve Kramer heard all the talk about Downtown and wanted a piece of it for himself. Wells tried to keep a lid on Doc, but he privately admired the young flight surgeon's guts.

"Colonel, when you gonna take me up North?"

"Doc, I'm stretching the rules now just to get your ass over Dong Hoi in the panhandle."

"Dammit, sir, I'm one of your best GIBs." Wells nodded agreement, conceding that Kramer had taken the time to learn the Phantom's radar fire-control system and inertial nav duties better than some of the Nickel's full-time GIBs.

Kramer decided to pull out all stops. He saw Wells as most pliable now, having had a good day and two beers behind him. "Look, don't you want me to be the best surgeon in the wing? Don't you want me to do my job right for the pilots?"

"Ye-e-s-s." Wells said, playing the straight man for now. He was aware that the doctor was trying to set some logic hook to make his case. And he wanted Kramer to know he was on to his game.

Kramer pursued, "You see, sir, there's a discrete combination of anxiety and stress that affects the pilots flying to Pack Six. I need to experience that myself. Firsthand. Only then can I know how best to advise you and treat them."

"Not now, Doc, I'm havin' a brewski. You're makin' my head hurt with all this logic. Put a lid on it." Wells believed that Steve Kramer had just made a very good case, but he wouldn't let the young physician know it.

Kramer was openly disappointed and wandered off into the crowd.

1800 hours

Lisa Davis and Mike Nelson were into heavy-duty bar talk, trading their personal details at a rapid rate. Growing noise at the far end of the room distracted Lisa. "Is it always like this, Mike?"

"No, this is one of those special nights. This is party night for the 497th TFS. Each fighter squadron flies sixty straight days, then earns a one-day squadron stand-down. The night before the stand-down is always party night."

The pilots assigned to the 497th TFS, the Night Owls, were massing in the corner. Something was about to happen.

It was a "MiG sweep," a spontaneous rush on the patrons sitting and standing at the bar. A dozen 497th pilots locked their arms at the elbows, then whipped outward, picking up speed along the way. The biggest guy was always at the outward end of the whip, and Major Warren "Whale" Wharton liked being point man on the end of the 497th's human chain. Whale considered this one of his additional squadron duties. The sweep hit maximum speed as Wharton reached the first bar stool. In seconds, the 497th had cleared the bar. Bodies and beer were all over the floor.

Clint Adams was among the casualties. He didn't see Whale's approach. Both men found themselves in the human furball on the beer-soaked floor. Adams spoke first. "I take it you're in the 497th."

"Uh, yes sir. I didn't see you at the bar, Colonel."

Adams wasn't looking for excuses. He shook his beer can and showered Wharton and the other 497th pilots still on the floor.

The other squadrons started putting together their own schemes. Slim Danforth stayed near the door, out of harm's way as he watched the assembled mass with a detachment uncommon for a fighter wing DCO. Kids' games.

The evening progressed. It was easy to identify almost everyone by their flight suits, patches, and scarves. Three helicopter pilots entered the bar. These rotorheads flew the HH-3 Jolly Greens and rescued downed crew members, even deep in North Vietnam. To fighter pilots, Jolly Green crews were heroes and couldn't pay for a drink in any fighter bar in Southeast Asia. Tonight was no different.

In the middle of the room, a dozen pilots from the 433rd TFS, wearing distinctive black flight suits, gathered together. Known as the Satan's Angels, they started a "carrier landing" competition. Quickly, the starting three-man team slapped together six tables, cleared an approach zone, and wet down the landing area on the tables with beer. Each contestant took his turn running, then launching himself into a swan dive, hoping to stop on the last table. The 433rd squadron commander and his operations officer joined in. This infusion of executive leadership yielded mixed results.

Soon the challenge went out to the 555th TFS pilots. Moose and Snake heard the call. Both of them still enjoyed the euphoria of the day and a growing buzz caused by several Budweisers. The beer clouded their judgment. Despite their progress with three rarely seen American women, the call to squadron duty was stronger.

Snake saw this chance to represent Triple Nickel as an opportunity to impress their dates, to show them what it was like to be a *real* fighter pilot. To the surprise of both Mike Nelson and the female trio, Snake sprung up and shouted, "Moose, to the tables!"

Peterson, against his waning better judgment, slowly rose to the challenge. He excused himself with an awkward smile as he departed.

Doc Kramer jumped forward to round out the 555th team. As the impromptu Nickel squad huddled to decide who would go airborne first, Mike Nelson made his move. "Ladies, it's time for dinner. Ready to eat in the dining room?"

"We're ready," Lisa Davis answered, and Nelson and the three women got up and left the bar. Mike had fallen into a target-rich environment and didn't mind taking three beautiful women to dinner.

Back at the carrier landings, Doc had started his approach first. He charged, head down, perhaps a bit too fast. He slipped on the beer in the takeoff area and plowed full force into the leading edge of the first table, which didn't give. The spectators let out a collective groan. A few onlookers hustled off the wounded Doc to the Clinic. He was complaining of two broken ribs and wouldn't be flying for a while. But the competition continued.

Snake recovered the 555th's honor with a near-perfect flight, landing astride the crack between the fifth and sixth table. Now all eyes turned to Moose. The ex-Stanford tackle lumbered toward the launch area. He leaped. The third and fourth table gave way immediately on contact under Moose's massive form. The splintered remains crashed through to the floor amid a surge of applause. Snake helped a somewhat-stunned Moose to his feet. The two gladiators turned to their ladies for approval, but found no ladies. Only a small Thai barmaid wiping down the table as Aussie pilots picked up the empty chairs. Snake was crestfallen. Moose nodded in commiseration. Definitely a bad deal for these two "carrier-qualified" fighter pilots. But they weren't quitters.

"Stick with me, Moose. We'll recover our quarry after the late show at the Airmen's Club." With that, Snake pushed Moose into the crowd for the rest of the evening.

2355 hours

The bar was much quieter. Almost everyone who had attended the earlier officers' call had long since left for a good night's sleep in preparation for the next day's missions. The 497th pilots, who could all sleep late tomorrow, continued their party to the very end. Their group had pushed into the adjacent casual bar, and their squadron songs, in a loud falsetto chorus, wafted into the main bar where only a few customers remained. By Ubon standards, things were winding down to normal tempo. The O Club was open around the clock, matching the flying schedule, but only a few hangers-on remained.

For tonight, the war stories were over. Vic Sansone told his share of them, but he'd had something else on his mind all evening, ever since he'd caught sight of the attractive Thai barmaid eyeing him. He had not noticed her before tonight. He really hadn't looked at the barmaids before. But now, for reasons he couldn't explain to himself, he was waiting in the lobby for her to finish her shift. He had to talk to this young woman, learn more about her, and perhaps escort her home.

A few 8th TFW pilots hustled the local Thai girls. Some even had live-in companions. Others bought one-night, or one-hour, stands with the hotsie bath girls downtown in Ubon Ratchathani. Sansone hadn't yet had enough interest or free time to experience these rites of passage.

Until tonight, he hadn't even considered the Thai women his type. But this girl was beautiful. She was taller and thinner than most Thais. She looked about twenty. And she had the most stunning brown eyes he had ever seen.

Vic Sansone jolted back to reality when the girl walked out of the kitchen. She saw Sansone and instinctively knew what was going to happen. She appeared very self-conscious and tried to ignore him, but Sansone intercepted her before she reached the front doors.

"Hello, my name's Vic. May I ask your name?"

She bowed politely and murmured something. He sensed she was nervous over this encounter. There was one set of rules for action inside the bar and a far different set out here. This dilemma frustrated Vic Sansone. He didn't want to cause this woman any difficulties. Sansone, the self-assured fighter pilot, did not know what to do. "I'm sorry, I didn't get your name."

Just then, a Vespa motor scooter pulled up outside. The rider beeped the Vespa's horn twice, as if he'd done this many times before. After a few seconds, the scooter's horn beeped again, this time longer and more stridently.

The second appeal of the Vespa's horn distracted the young woman, shattering the atmosphere in the O Club lobby. Both Sansone and the girl knew that this encounter was over. She averted her eyes, pushed past him quickly, and walked out the door.

"Wait, just tell me your name. Please."

She turned at the door. "Lin May." Vic Sansone stood frozen in place. He didn't have the courage to move outside until he heard the scooter drive off. Reflecting on this one-sided rendezvous, he knew that Lin May was attracted to him. Yet when he had moved to cross the cultural barrier in a serious way, something went wrong, very wrong.

Moving down the walkway to the road, Sansone watched the Vespa's red tail light move off into the night. There was a piece of paper fluttering in the vortex created by the departing scooter. Almost absentmindedly, he picked up the paper as it settled on the grass. What he found jolted him. It was yesterday's 497th TFS flying schedule, the one usually posted in the squadron "hootch" area the evening before: call signs, pilots' names, takeoff times. Did it fall from Lin's handbag? Or the driver's pocket? Or was it already in the gutter, dropped earlier by the 497th squadron scheduling officer leaving the O Club after dinner?

Just then, two Triple Nickel pilots recognized their squadron mate as they came out of the club and swept Sansone into their group. He protested mildly, relented, and stuffed the crumpled paper into his flight suit pocket. They headed off to their hootches together.

Midnight
The Visiting Officers' Quarters (VOQ)
Ubon RTAFB

Mike Nelson and the three Majestics arrived at the VOQ, a quonset hut reserved for transient officers and selected civilians. The evening had gone well for all of them. Nelson had become their protector, running interference when the numerous passes came along. Having an 8th TFW pilot in a flight suit as an escort screened out the young enlisted guys who usually came on extra strong with the three girls. At first, the three ladies had enjoyed all the male attention they had received at the initial stops of their Thailand tour. But they had soon tired of horny men trying to seduce them all the time. That's when Lisa hit on the idea of corraling an officer, sort of a Jack Armstrong–type chaperone, early in the evening at each stop.

Mike Nelson was a real find, especially for Lisa. His dark straight hair, brown eyes, and solid, athletic build were usually found in men much more stuck on themselves. But this Mike Nelson was a gentleman, Lisa thought, with the confidence to be himself and care about her. Earlier, at dinner, she had decided this man had possibilities. She'd invited him to watch the show from backstage at the Airmen's Club. Naturally, he'd accepted. And Mike had enjoyed their act. The girls' singing, at least. He hadn't cared for the four male hippies that formed the band and rounded out the Majestics. They were the long-haired variety. They had that strung-out look—what you could see of them underneath all that hair. After the second and last performance of the night, the three girls had slid off directly backstage. The faithful Nelson had still been there, so Lisa asked him to escort them back to the VOQ. Again, Mike had accepted.

Carol and Angie knew the score. They'd seen how much Lisa was attracted to Nelson. The two younger girls quickly thanked him for their dinner and the escort. Then they headed down the long hallway to the room they were sharing, leaving Lisa and her pilot alone in front of her door.

Mike and Lisa said nothing to each other at first. Mike simply took her in his arms, and they shared a long, very comfortable kiss.

"Is that what they teach you at the Air Force Academy?" asked Lisa, letting out a deep sigh.

"No, I learned that back in high school in Hawthorne, California," teased Nelson, tightening the grip he had around Lisa's very small waist.

"I hope you're not kissing me good night," she said.

"No, that was hello."

Lisa dropped her hands from the small of his muscular back, passing his narrow hips, and clutched his hands with an inviting firmness.

"Come inside, Mike, and tell me your life history. But hurry up."

0010 hours
Rear of the VOQ
Ubon RTAFB

Snake and Moose edged up to the back of the VOQ, after having spent the entire evening at the O Club main bar. The VOQ was ringed by sandbags stacked 6 feet high about 1 foot from the hut. Cummings had a plan, and he shared it now with his large and equally inebriated friend, "Look, Moose, if the Majestics are staying anywhere on base, it's got to be here." Snake aimed to reestablish contact with Carol and Angie.

They moved to the back of the hut. Snake knew how to get the attention of the two girls, and he was positive he could lure them outside. "Moose, pick me up and drop me between the sandbags and the hut."

Snake's plan came apart almost immediately. Moose exclaimed, "Shit," as he lost his grip on Snake, who slipped off balance into the narrow space, banging up against a window. It was not the window Snake had in mind. The Army lieutenant colonel alone in his room was startled by the thump outside his window, sat up in bed, and spotted Snake's form. Snake was trying to regain the balance he'd lost three hours ago in the Ubon main bar. No matter how hard he held it, Snake couldn't get the hut to stop moving. The roused Army officer pulled out both his .38-caliber Smith & Wesson revolver and his ever-present flashlight. Moving to the window, he flung it open in a rapid outward motion, striking Snake in the head and knocking him to the ground.

"Hey, dammit. That hurt." Snake couldn't imagine why anyone would do that.

"What the hell's goin' on out there?" The Army defender was irritated but relieved that this intruder was no enemy sapper. He leaned out the window and shined his flashlight into Snake's eyes. The lieutenant had been woozy before this all started; now he was wounded and night-blind to boot.

Snake, hearing a man's voice, said while rubbing his head wound, "I'm lookin' for somebody. Are Carol and Angie in there?"

"Not here, buddy. Beat it!"

It dawned on Snake that he was losing control of the operation, so he looked for a way to disengage. The space was too tight for him to turn around and climb out the way he'd dropped in. He called for Moose but figured Peterson's arms weren't long enough to pull him out. Besides, Moose didn't answer. Snake looked to his left. Nothing. He looked to his right. The space was wider at the far corner of the hut, and the sandbags were lower there too. Now Snake had a new plan—shuffle to the corner and depart the local area.

The girls' room, by chance, was at that same far corner. They were undressing and getting ready for bed when they heard the commotion through their half-open window. And they heard their names too. Angie looked at Carol with a grin. Carol raced to fill a wastebasket with water from the bathroom sink.

Meanwhile Snake was making progress. Only one more window to go. This window was slightly ajar, and there was a light inside. He had enough bumps swelling out of his skull now, so Snake ducked below the open window and moved by it quickly. He compressed his body even lower into the confining slot. Then he heard, "Oh Snake, that you out there?"

Pay dirt! Snake was encouraged by the woman's voice. This woman knew his name. He straightened up to look in the open window. "Carol, is that you?"

His reward was a wastebasket full of cold water squarely in the face. Snake had had enough. He moved off amid the guffaws coming from the girls' room. Carol struggled to regain her composure. She was still peeved that Snake had wandered off earlier, but now she was worried because he was nowhere in sight. She moved to the window and leaned out at the waist.

"Snake, where are you? I think you're kinda cute."

Snake heard Carol's words just as he reached his escape corner. He decided a bucket of water was a small price to pay for the opportunities that lay back at the open window. He started back, while calling for Moose to join him. As Snake took his first step toward Carol, two meaty hands attached themselves to his shoulders. Snake froze, stunned by the force of the vise-like grip. "No, Moose, come on. I found 'em."

"Come this way, Lieutenant." The giant hands yanked Snake upward and over the lower sandbags by the shoulders. He thought that Moose had misread his signal. Wrong. Slowly, his eyes focused on an Air Policeman who was as big as Moose but who was not smiling. Neither was his air police partner. As for Moose—he was already passed out in the rear seat of their open jeep.

THE PLAN

1 October 1966 0730 hours
Wing HQ
Ubon RTAFB

Clint Adams was taking a tour on his own of his new staff. He didn't like to be guided by a briefed escort officer because then he would only get an ideal picture. Moving about in the DCO's ops staff area, he came upon a small room in the far corner of the building. When he entered, three captains in flight suits popped to attention, startled momentarily by his appearance. At least one cup of coffee spilled onto the cheap tile floor. Wing commanders weren't supposed to wander about unannounced. Adams was the first 8th Wing CO to ever enter this room.

Adams recognized Randy Starbuck. The room looked like hell. "Good morning, Starbuck. What do you fellas do back here, aside from being superb interior decorators?"

Starbuck looked around the cramped 8-by-10-foot room, seemingly for the first time. It was crammed with three gray metal desks, each with a matching file cabinet that Starbuck had reclaimed from Base Salvage last week. Starbuck responded, "This is the Wing Tactics Shop, sir. We think it's the only one in Southeast Asia. At least on the American side."

Adams remembered Boomer Wright's words from yesterday. "Ah, yes, the boys in the back." This remark broke the tension among the three junior officers.

"Sit down, gents," Adams added, dropping into the nearest chair himself. He propped up his feet on the corner of a desk littered with too much paper, most of it topped by red-bordered white cover sheets stamped "Secret."

He directed his next question to one of the other captains, "What are you working on?"

"Right now we're cranking out the first wing tactics manual in this combat theater," answered Captain Turner "Knob" Westcott, the only navigator in the 8th TFW.

"You're the first 'nav' I've seen here, Westcott. Any others?"

"Nossir. I'm here for the electronic warfare stuff, attached to the 497th. But, Colonel, I'm not a navigator. I'm a fighter-gator. There's a big difference." The little fireplug of a man with a clean Yul Brynner skull stood his ground for the comeback.

He didn't get one, because Adams was privately impressed. But he was also learning more about why USAF crews weren't doing so well up North. He could see that these men were very valuable. They also looked overworked but undervalued. He'd change that. As Adams got up to leave, the BIBs rose too.

He stopped at the door and turned back to them. "I want you three to teach me everything you know. Everything." The BIBs looked at each other, then nodded back at Adams.

3 October 1966 0830 hours
The Main Gate
Ubon RTAFB

Lin May stepped off the pink-and-green Baht bus and moved into line with the rest of the local Thai workers queuing up to enter Ubon RTAFB. She flashed her identification card to the Air Policeman guarding the main gate. He took a long look at her. "You're a real fox, honey. Where do you work?"

"At the O Club," she answered.

"Well, if you ever get tired of those college boys, and you want a real man, remember that I work here every day."

Lin May giggled with the other girls in line, put her ID card back into her wallet, then moved through the checkpoint.

"Lin May!" It was an American voice. She looked across the street and saw Vic Sansone coming her way. The other Thai women moved ahead, watching over their shoulders and talking to each other about the American officer, no doubt.

"Lin May, remember me? Vic Sansone?"

"Yes. I remember."

With relief, Vic continued, "Lin May, I've got to see you. I didn't sleep a wink last night. I'm sorry if I upset or offended you in any way. Well, it's just that I saw you looking at me all evening, and I, you know, I thought, well, what I mean is . . . darn it, I want to see you again. Can I meet you after work tonight?"

"Well, Captain, I think it will be all right. No one is picking me up." She spoke slowly with a soft voice, barely audible above the street traffic. She already had arranged for her motor scooter companion to steer clear of her tonight.

"Please, call me Vic."

"Yes, Vic. I will see you tonight? Yes?"

"You bet. I mean, of course. Yes. What time?"

"I finish at six o'clock." She started to move off.

"Six o'clock it is then." Vic called to her, somewhat surprised by this turn of events in his social life.

"Oh, Vic," Lin May called as she hurried toward the O Club, "I didn't sleep last night either."

1030 hours
Outside the village of An Hoa on Highway 1A
One hundred five kilometers southeast of Hanoi

Route Pack Six was subdivided into 6A and 6B, with the dividing line dissecting Hanoi from southwest to northeast. "Six A," the northwest half, was the U.S. Air Force's area. "Six B" was the Navy's domain. Haiphong was in 6B. So was the modest-sized town of An Hoa, now a ghost town, repeatedly bombed into oblivion by U.S. Navy attacks off the carriers in the Gulf of Tonkin. Once a village of 1,500 people who worked the rice paddies in the Phatdiem agricultural district, the richest area of the Red River delta, An Hoa now lay abandoned for the transients of war.

Americans considered An Hoa a military target. Sitting astride the major highway funneling troops and supplies into the war zones to the south, it also lay on one of the few pieces of dry land in this region of North Vietnam. This dry ground made An Hoa valuable to the North's war effort because the French-built railway ran parallel to Highway 1A as it passed through An Hoa. And there was a railway siding in the village too, right next to the town's only industry: a small textile factory, employing about 150 women.

American intelligence experts called this confluence "the An Hoa transshipment point." U.S. Navy attack planes had raided this target twenty-nine times this year alone. The buildings, population, and the pastoral way of life that had existed in An Hoa for centuries were too fragile to survive these attacks. The ancillary damage from long, inaccurate strings of American bombs had leveled the village. A few hundred residents had died in the early bombing raids. But the villagers had stayed on until, finally, a 500-pound bomb had destroyed the Church of Saint Dominique one morning the previous May. The townspeople, Catholics and Buddhists alike, viewed the loss of this prominent landmark, which dominated the landscape for miles, as a bad omen. Most survivors moved to nearby hamlets. A few moved into Hanoi itself.

The An Hoa railway siding rarely contained any rolling stock these days, but the Navy still bombed it once per week just to keep it that way. The attackers came directly off the sea, out of the coastal fog and morning sun. Compared with the Hanoi area, An Hoa was lightly defended. Only one SA-2 site and a handful of AAA sites lined the road to the north, mainly to defend the convoys moving down Highway 1A at night.

This morning, one of the 57mm flak gunners got lucky and shot down Roscoe 202, a Navy F-4B flying through the area on the way back to the Seventh Fleet. Both crew members ejected several thousand feet above the ground when their Phantom gave out on them, 10 miles from the Gulf of Tonkin and relative safety. Once clear of their dying plane, the American aviators saw the gulf's emerald blue water, two minutes flying time away.

The frontseat pilot landed near Highway 1A, 500 meters north of An Hoa, and was surrounded by local farmers almost immediately. At first, the North Vietnamese peasants did nothing. He was probably the first American, and the tallest human, they had ever seen. Then a small boy yanked off the pilot's Swiss Glycine watch before the American could react.

That started it. Two older boys, armed with small machetes, dispatched the pilot's shoe laces and forcibly yanked off the American's canvas-sided flying boots in a few seconds. The Vietnamese children were following what they had been taught in school. Americans could not run in their bare feet. Then the other villagers pulled off the pilot's flight suit and survival gear, scurrying off with their booty in all directions. The women cut up his highly valued silk parachute and nylon risers.

The crowd grew larger by the minute, pushing in on the American, who now looked pasty white and feeble in his underwear and black socks. The people in the countryside were constantly told to turn over all captured Americans to the local militia. But that was not what was happening here. A small boy picked up a handful of mud and threw it at the American. Other children rallied behind the first, pelting their captive with small stones. Then an old man hit the pilot in the back of the head with the handle of his rake. The American dropped to his knees in a daze.

The crowd would have surely beat the pilot to death in minutes, the result of their pent-up hatred for all the death and destruction that the American aviators had brought to their villages. But a platoon of North Vietnamese Army (NVA) regulars managed to rescue the Navy pilot, after firing warning shots into the air and forcing their way through the angry mob. Even as the NVA marched the American off at gunpoint, the crowd fell in line behind the prisoner detail, shouting angry words and still throwing an occasional rock at the hated Caucasian.

Lieutenant JG Harry Harding, the radar intercept officer who rode the backseat of Roscoe 202, drifted down 3 kilometers west of An Hoa. He evaded his pursuers, all regular NVA troops, for about an hour. When discovered hiding in the reeds along the river bank, the young lieutenant resisted arrest, fired his .38-caliber Smith & Wesson handgun, and killed one of the NVA soldiers. Harding was cut down by two teenage troops firing AK-47s into the foliage. The NVA wrapped the American's body in his parachute, placed it in the back of their Likhachev truck, and headed north on Route One.

The real news of the morning revolved around the pilotless Phantom. Inexplicably, Roscoe 202 flew into the rain-sodden rice paddies at a very shallow angle. The soft mud under the paddy water and the benign impact attitude combined to deliver the F-4B to the North Vietnamese virtually intact.

The same unit of NVA regulars who saved the American pilot from his encounter with the ugly mob was bivouacked in An Hoa for the day, awaiting darkness to start moving south again. They watched the ejections, and they observed Roscoe 202 glide across Highway 1A and embed itself in a mud dike 1 kilometer east of the village. The troops kept the locals from stripping the plane of everything they could carry away.

Roscoe 202 crashed at 1015. An hour later, a staff officer at the Defense Ministry in Hanoi called Colonel Tomb at Gia Lam, alerting him to the opportunity. The ministry dispatched a black Volga staff car to pick up Tomb and transport him to the crash site.

Arriving in An Hoa at 1330 hours, even the battle-hardened Tomb was saddened by the extent of the devastation. This total destruction was not the result of an SA-2 falling into the village or from one errant American bomb. No, this was caused by repeated, deliberate raids. The roofless, three-wall shell of Saint Dominique Church was the only recognizable structure. Destroying the American fighter-bombers must remain the top priority for his pilots.

The short hike out the narrow footpath on top of the dike took ten minutes. A crowd of fifty villagers stood on the high and dry right side of the American plane. Tomb had waited a long time for this chance. Making the most of it now would pay large dividends for both him and his pilots.

The F-4 rested in 2 feet of muddy water but exhibited almost no external damage. The huge black radome on its nose had buried itself in the levy. Since the plane had not burned, Tomb concluded that the F-4 was nearly out of fuel. Something had made the crew leave the plane, perhaps a total hydraulic failure, but without a "hard over" reaction in the flight controls. Too soon to know.

Tomb had been this close to American fighters before, but only when they were buttoned up and capable of shooting him down. Screaming by an F-105 or an F-4 afforded only a split-second glimpse. No, this was quite different, a gift of grand value.

He was struck by the Phantom's size. It was huge. Americans liked large, powerful, multipurpose fighters. They possessed the engine technology to pursue this course. The Soviets, however, built small, single-purpose fighters. Whether this was by choice was hard to say. The Russians did not have the engine technology to do anything else.

The Phantom's underbelly was obscured by water. The upper wing surface was massive and allowed the Phantom to carry extensive amounts of weapons and fuel tanks on its four underwing pylons. Tomb stepped onto the right wing.

He was first interested in the F-4B's exterior. The thick gray paint required for sea duty must be an extra burden. The massive black tailhook, protruding from under the empennage, must weigh at least 1,000 pounds. Tomb recalled the superb vertical performance of the Phantom. The engines must have amazing power. The Phantom's skin was peppered with warning and rescue instruction placards. These signs meant that the plane's construction must be quite sophisticated, and that the Americans valued life too much, a weakness the North Vietnamese exploited in countless ways.

The skin, the fittings, and the rivets all mystified Tomb. Everything was so smooth. American engineering and production must be superior to their Soviet counterparts. Even the new MiG-21s were crudely assembled compared with this remarkably tooled machine. Some of the metal used in the engine and tail section was foreign to him, perhaps the titanium he had heard about. The Americans must have gone to great expense to reduce weight and aerodynamic drag at supersonic speeds and to field engines that tolerated the very high temperatures needed for massive thrust.

The large-diameter nose radome held a 1-meter dish antenna for the F-4's powerful radar fire-control system. According to Soviet intelligence shared with the NVAF, the Phantom had the most versatile and longest-range fighter radar in the air. And that led Tomb to what he wanted to see most, the cockpits.

He crawled over the backbone of the plane and dropped onto the left engine intake housing. He looked into a Phantom rear cockpit for the first time. The interior was slick with a pinkish-red fluid. Even the instruments were completely coated. His earlier suspicions were confirmed: a massive hydraulic failure had caused a catastrophic high pressure mist, which had filled the rear cockpit. Fear of imminent explosion probably hastened the crew to eject.

Tomb was fascinated by the rear cockpit. The ejection seat was gone, leaving a cavernous, charred hole that distorted the interior's size and proportion. There was no control stick in the backseat of the Navy F-4. The rear crew member was a radar intercept officer, not a pilot. The flight instruments were rudimentary in function but technologically advanced in design and presentation, used to monitor the pilot's actions. The two main subsystems controlled by the radar intercept officer, the radar and the inertial navigation system, greatly interested Tomb. The radar had a switch to select search ranges from 10 to 200 miles! Could the American pilots detect MiGs at that range? The backseater had controls on the right console that allowed him to highlight and lock onto airborne targets, thus freeing the pilot of this task.

The other major system, the inertial navigation computer, was truly state of the art. Tomb had never seen anything like the navigation control panel. It was a maze of buttons and internal self-test indicators. The operator could feed degrees, minutes, and even seconds into the self-contained system. No wonder American crews could operate on top of cloud decks and know their location. Americans rarely seemed to hunt for their targets, yet Tomb's own pilots often lost their bearings over their own homeland.

Tomb moved to the forward cockpit. This was what he really wanted to see. This was where his main adversary sat. And these were the wondrous tools and gadgets his opponent had at his disposal. Tomb climbed onto the left canopy rail and shuffled forward into the front cockpit. Amazing! As large as the rear seemed, the front seemed twice as large. Tomb squatted where the Martin-Baker ejection seat had been only hours before. He spread his arms fully, and could just touch the outer cockpit walls under the canopy rails. Astonishing!

The number and quality of instruments and indicator lights over-whelmed Tomb at first. Everything was so advanced. Tomb felt as if he had leaped twenty-five years into the future. He was in awe of the cockpit. How could American pilots keep track of everything, yet still pay attention to what was going on outside the aircraft?

His MiG-17 cockpit was ancient by comparison. He marveled at the Phantom's sealed black-box instruments, the forward radar scope and the optical sight in the forward windscreen. After reviewing the group-ings, he concluded that everything was laid out quite logically.

Forward and side visibility were excellent, not accounting for the extra set of eyes in the rear. The mechanical, electrical, hydraulic, and pneu-matic indicators were all clearly readable. The F-4 must have a superb heater, defogger, and air conditioner.

But it was the weapons control panel that intrigued Tomb the most. By reading the wafer selectors and toggle switch positions, he came to understand the F-4's versatility. It could carry air and ground missiles, rockets, gun pods, cannisters, and bomb shapes of all kinds. What a wonder of technology!

A perfect fighter? A magnificent one to be sure. But not perfect by Tomb's measure. And he was here to identify weaknesses. The Phantom was too complex for him. Too many systems to monitor. Far too many switches, knobs, and indicator lights. It must be hard for the pilot to switch weapon modes. Tomb would tell his pilots to change their relative range from Phantoms quickly in order to oversaturate the F-4 crew's ability to handle its weapon systems.

Tomb already knew the F-4 had no internal aerial cannon. Tomb would tell his pilots to attack close up and nose-on with guns blazing. One pass, then disengage.

And the Phantom's rearward visibility was limited. The rear cockpit blocked the frontseat pilot's view. The humpback fuselage blocked the backseater's view. MiG attacks at high speed from the Phantom's deep six o'clock were still worthwhile, as long as the MiG pilot remained undetected until after firing a missile or his cannons.

Nguyen Tomb did not notice the European correspondent over his shoulder. "What do you think of the American fighter plane, Colonel?"

Tomb jerked to his left with a start, but did not answer. He did not like the foreign press corps. They were like vultures, showing up where there was some sort of tragedy, a bombed-out village or a downed aircraft.

"Colonel, I am Mario Contero. I'm the Hanoi correspondent for *L'Unita*, the Italian newspaper. I remember you from the MiG-21 dedication ceremony at Kep field."

Tomb merely nodded. Had he known any newsmen were in the area, he would have requested that the soldiers keep them away until he had completed his evaluation. He noticed that two other Europeans and a Chinese photographer were on the right wing, making their way to the cockpit. Tomb didn't know why the Information Ministry would grant access to foreign correspondents. He started to leave.

The Italian tried again. "Colonel, how would you rate the MiG-21 against this plane? It's a Phantom, isn't it?"

"Please excuse me, I must return to my duties." With that, Tomb slipped onto the right canopy rail and was off the plane quickly, moving down the muddy footpath to the black Volga, a full kilometer away.

1955 hours
The restaurant in the Hotel Thani
Ubon Ratchathani, Thailand

Vic Sansone and Lin May ignored their tender Kobe beef fondue. Vic was finishing his third Japanese Kirin beer; Lin still nursed her first and said, "Did you know that the Kirin is the mythical Japanese unicorn?"

"No, how do you know that?" replied Vic, not really caring as he remained transfixed by Lin's uncommon beauty.

"One learns a great deal in an American bar. A MAC pilot told me." A small slip, but the MAC pilot remark should have covered it well enough. She regretted saying it immediately. Change the subject, she told herself. "Tell me about yourself, your friends."

"No, you're the mysterious one. Tell me about you," Vic answered, but wanting instead to tell her how he felt. "You are so beautiful, but your features are different from those of the other Thai women."

She would tell him just a little. "Because I am not from here. I was born in northernmost Thailand. A place high in the mountains called Chiang Mai. My ethnic background spans Thailand and western Laos. I came here for the work and the money. I hope to attend the university in Bangkok when I earn enough."

"Lin, may I ask you a question?"

"Only one, Vic, then you must tell me all about yourself and your friends I saw you with at the O Club. You all looked so close to each other."

"Fair enough," Vic said, starting into his fourth Kirin. "Who picked you up on the motor scooter?"

Lin May giggled. "Oh, now I see. You think he is my boyfriend." Vic flushed. "That is Nan, my cousin. My parents would not let me come to Ubon alone. Nan and his sister came, too. We all live in a flat together. They work at the NCO Club."

"You don't think Nan's doing anything, well, illegal?"

Lin May's stomach tightened. Why would he say that? "Not Nan. He is an innocent young man. But why do you ask?"

"No reason." He was drawn closer by her enormous brown eyes. He leaned forward to kiss Lin May.

"No, please, Vic. Not here. Besides you must tell about yourself now. You promised."

"I'm from Bayonne, New Jersey. It's across the harbor from New York City."

"It sounds very exciting."

"Not really. I grew up in an Italian neighborhood. My dad owned a pizza parlor. The whole family worked there from the time we could walk."

"Pizza! I like pizza," Lin May giggled. "I had some at the club one night."

"Someday, I'll make you fresh pizza. The best. Sansone-style."

"How did you become such a good pilot, Vic?"

"Went to the U.S. Air Force Academy, finished high in my class. Mike Nelson—the tall guy you saw me with in the bar—he was my roommate. We went to pilot school together, served in Europe for three years. Now we're here. Been roomies the whole time. He's gonna be a general some day. He's got it all—talent, brains, drive."

She tried to keep Vic talking. "I know you are very close. You are always together in the club."

"Lin May, let's get a room upstairs."

"I would like that very much, my Vic."

Vic fumbled for his wallet and flipped 150 baht on the table. He was glad he was not on tomorrow morning's flying schedule.

8 October 1966 1500 hours
Camp John Hay, near Baguio City
Republic of the Philippines

Two light-gray USAF UH-1 Huey helicopters touched down at the landing pad in the middle of the old World War II parade ground. The choppers kicked up very little dust during the rainy season. At 3,500 feet above sea level, the old Army post, now converted to an Air Force recreation center, was literally in the clouds. The temperature was a cool 76 degrees.

Most people would be pleased to spend two days at Baguio. It was a chance to get away from the war for a few days. Almost all of the wing commanders exiting the Hueys were happy to come and bid farewell to General Hartford Stevens, the retiring commander in chief of the Pacific Air Forces (CINCPACAF). The old warhorse was making his last swing through his units in the western Pacific.

Clint Adams did not want to be here and resented being summoned to this gathering of senior Air Force commanders from Thailand, South Vietnam, Korea, and the Philippines. He'd been at Ubon only nine days. Being yanked out to attend this two-day cocktail party was the last thing on his priority list. If he had had a vice commander on station, Clint would have found a way to send him to Baguio instead.

1730 hours
Clint Adams's VOQ room
Camp John Hay

Clint lay in bed staring at the Bombay ceiling fan as it turned slowly above him. The hot shower had rinsed the travel fatigue from his body.

He felt tight. Hard, in fact. That's one thing this war had done for him—reversed his slowly growing gut. Back at Shaw he had had to fight the emerging belly tire with frequent exercise and noontime salads. Here in Southeast Asia, the heavy flying regimen and the hot weather had melted off all the extra pounds. And he ate like a horse.

Inevitably, when it was quiet like this, he thought of Laura. He still regretted how callously he had handled things back at Shaw. She had had every right to slam him as hard as she did, he thought. He sent her five letters for every one she mailed him. Her latest letter was typical. It was shallow, with a little news about the kids and the postings of longtime friends. No emotion, no softening. And she ignored his repeated apologies. She hadn't forgiven him yet.

He mentally went over his pitch to General Morgan for tonight. Adams had an idea. It could drop the NVAF to its knees. And it could crystallize the entire American fighter force in Southeast Asia—not just the 8th TFW.

The blades of the ceiling fan reminded him of propellers and of World War II, his other combat tour. He had seen that war from the other end of the tube as a lieutenant.

Red Blaik had taught Clint Adams about leadership, but it was Colonel Hub Zemke who'd taught him about air combat leadership.

The 479th Fighter Group was the last to join the mighty Eighth Air Force only weeks before D-Day. Flying P-38Js, the 479th set records by getting operationally ready in eleven days, in time to support the big invasion. The correlation between the 479th and Ubon's 8th TFW were not lost on Adams. The 479th was not working as a fighting unit. In the seventy-five days since arriving at RAF Wattisham in Cambridgeshire, the 479th had shot down only ten German planes while losing thirty-five P-38s. While other fighter groups were cleaning up, the 479th was losing. The pilots were down on themselves and on their aircraft. When the 479th lost its commander to enemy fire in August, Headquarters Ajax assigned the legendary commander of the 56th Fighter Group, Hub Zemke, to the relatively green 479th.

Things started to change immediately. Zemke brought powerful credentials. His was a leading ace, flying P-47 Thunderbolts. More important, he was the best air combat leader in the Army Air Forces. He could make things happen.

Measuring his new fighter group, he put together a plan to maximize the strengths and minimize the weaknesses. He petitioned Ajax for a big mission aimed at infusing the 479th's pilots with badly needed confidence and aggressive spirit. He gambled that he could exploit the twin-engine P-38's superior low-altitude performance and heavy firepower. Ajax agreed, assigning the 479th escort duty to a large B-24 bomber mission against the Luftwaffe airfield at Nancy/Essay in France.

After the B-24 Liberators dropped their bombs on the airdrome from high altitude with good results, Zemke took his group down and tore up the airfield with multiple strafing passes. The 497th's score: 43 Luftwaffe planes destroyed, 28 damaged. The Nancy/Essay airfield attack electrified the 479th's spirit, and a new aggressiveness manifested itself in the pilots.

One week later, Zemke let loose his pilots' newfound confidence on 50 ME-109s near Rostock on the Baltic coast. One young tiger, Lieutenant Clint Adams, knocked down three Germans to become an ace. From then on, the 479th proved an eager match for anyone. Zemke had lit the fire in the hearts of his pilots and mixed it with the brainpower on how best to use the P-38 Lightning.

When the 479th converted to P-51 Mustangs in September, Clint Adams was the leading P-38 ace in the European theater, with eight kills. He finished the war with thirteen aerial victories and eleven and one-half planes destroyed on the ground. But Hub Zemke gave him something more valuable than a sexy war record. Zemke showed Adams how to lead pilots to victory in the air.

Adams thought, back then it was Zemke, the 479th pilots, and the P-38 against the Luftwaffe. Now it was him, the 8th TFW pilots, and the F-4 against the NVAF leader, his three air companies, and the MiGs. Clint Adams's current plan was his Nancy/Essay.

1930 hours
Bell House
Camp John Hay

The VIP bus moved slowly up the long driveway to the most prominent house on the camp. Bell House was the senior, most prestigious quarters, reserved the next two days for General Stevens. The two-story, Georgian-style white structure with four large white columns on the front porch was set among giant coconut palms that swayed in this evening's light breeze. All the WestPac Air Force commanders had been invited to the hilltop house for cocktails and a Mongolian barbecue buffet. Adams felt awkward in his barong tagalog, the white embroidered short-sleeve shirt he and all the other attendees were wearing. It was the national dress shirt of the Philippines and the traditional evening wear. The protocol staff had a shirt hanging in every commander's room on arrival.

This was the first time Adams had been out of a flight suit in almost two weeks. Right now, he would rather have had the green bag on and be at the Ubon bar listening to the complaints of his pilots.

As the evening progressed, Adams stayed to himself, with the exception of a few conversations with some of the other fighter wing commanders. He steered clear of the generals. He just did not have the stomach for the cocktail circuit. Never had. He'd catch General Morgan when things died down a bit.

He gathered up as much oriental beef as his plate could hold and moved outside on the veranda to eat in peace. It was cool and quiet, and the view of the camp and Baguio City in the distance soothed his irritation. For a few days now he'd been mulling over his idea—a way to take on the North Vietnamese MiGs as never before. Again, he mentally worked through the concept as he ate his meal and washed it down with a glass of scotch.

"Feeling antisocial tonight, Clint?" It was General Morgan, who had wandered out into the evening air with several other guests for his after-dinner cigar. Breaking away from the main group, he came over to talk to his newest field commander.

"No, sir. As a matter of fact, I was just getting ready to talk to you about something important."

"Ah, classic Clint Adams, all business. Even here." Adams conceded that Morgan had him pegged.

"Tom! Are you out here conducting business with your colonels again?" General Stevens bellowed. He had a few drinks under his belt and was looking for some old friends so he could trade war stories. "Come with me, you old fool, I need you to settle an argument inside." With that, Stevens took Morgan by the arm, and the two four-star generals disappeared inside.

Adams was frustrated by the irony. He was here at another Air Force social engagement by direct order, another command performance. This particular command performance was keeping him from the war, probably his last. He'd worked hard to get into the fight. And there was much to do just to get the Air Force on the right course. Isn't that what General Morgan had told him to do? Shit.

Adams couldn't understand why his commanders didn't have his twenty-four-hour-a-day focus and determination to get things moving in the right direction. He realized he was probably being too hasty in judging General Morgan, but his boss did appear to be shutting out the war tonight. Maybe a man's batteries ran down more quickly as he got older. But it was certainly Morgan's last war too. Why didn't he have the same resolve to work at it?

War stories. Why would the generals want to talk about other wars tonight? There would be more than enough time for that later. Adams downed the last of his double scotch, put down his glass, flicked his cigarette over the balcony, and walked down the back stairs toward his quarters at the bottom of the hill 300 yards away.

9 October 1966 0930 hours
Ninety miles northeast of Ubon RTAFB

Randy Starbuck was leading Plymouth flight, currently spread out in mutually supporting tactical formation. Plymouth was cruising at 35,000 feet, 350 knots, heading for Ubon, after flying MiGCAP up North. There had been no action.

Randy's GIB, Taco Martinez, offered some solace. "Well, Randy, at least we might get to duel the Aussies back here at Ubon."

"Just keep your nose in that radar scope, Taco. I don't want to get waxed by those Aussie Sabres." Plymouth flight was primed. Starbuck couldn't help thinking about the interesting turn of events and having to fight his way into home base. He'd pushed for this kind of training since arriving at Ubon five months ago.

Martinez wanted to wax a Sabre today. "I'd love to rag the boys from Canberra at the bar tonight."

Starbuck knew Taco Martinez was right about tangling with RAAF Sabres today. He and Harley Stockman had agreed to phase in the program personally and would be the first players in such an engagement. Each had agreed that this first DACT battle should be somewhat benign. Just a few turns to get a sense of each other's capabilities. Totally professional.

Bullshit, Starbuck thought as he started to weigh the realities. Stockman had something to prove. His boys had to sit on the ramp while the Americans went for the MiG kills up North. That was all a true fighter pilot saw. Things like that were black and white. Also, there was the element of national pride and bar talk. Taking on the Americans and cleaning their clock would mean a lot to the Aussies.

The rules for this dissimilar air combat were simple. The TOC duty officer would evaluate the status of the returning Phantoms for possible DACT. If anything was out of the ordinary, he would go no further. Hung bombs or missiles, battle damage or mechanical trouble, and real MiG engagements up North meant no DACT on return to the Ubon area. But if the MiGCAP flight had seen no action, or if a strike flight had dropped all its ordnance, then they would be candidates for DACT.

The TOC duty officer would then assess the weather. Visibility had to be 5 miles or better above 10,000 feet with no thunderstorms in the area. If all conditions met these criteria, the duty officer would advise Colonel Danforth, who made the final decision. If he gave the go-ahead, the duty officer would give the launch option to Harley Stockman, who would control it from that point. If the Aussies had backup alert crews and two extra mission-ready Sabres, Stockman would launch his two primary alert fighters.

All the 8th TFW pilots had been briefed on the parameters for launch, as well as the specific rules for them. The floor for all engagements was 10,000 feet. No one jettisoned any fuel tanks or ordnance. All engagements must take place in daylight visual conditions. All DACT ceased if any pilot called Bingo fuel status or had any mechanical troubles. Engagements ended when one pilot attained a tracking solution for five seconds and called it out on the radio. The Phantom flight leader had control of the encounter. At any time, he could terminate the DACT by calling, "Break it off." Safety was paramount in these training exercises.

Starbuck mentally reviewed the DACT rules, then he checked in with radar control. "Brigham Control, Plymouth, flight of four Fox Fours. Flight level 350. RTB Ubon." Randy didn't ask Brigham for reports on any bogies. He knew he wouldn't get any help. The Tactics Shop had set up that procedure with the major who ran Brigham.

"Roger, Plymouth. Radar contact. Descend at pilot's discretion to 15,000 feet."

Then Plymouth 04 called out, "Plymouth 04 has two radar contacts, eleven o'clock high, 20 miles." Starbuck started a climbing left turn and accelerated the four-ship to 500 knots, about 0.9 Mach at this altitude, the F-4's best maneuvering speed. Still, Plymouth flight would fight at a disadvantage. No action up North earlier today meant that each F-4 brought back three external fuel tanks. In one way, carrying the external tanks would enhance the training by making the F-4 crews more aware that they could not turn tightly with the RAAF Sabres. This would drive the Phantom pilots to choose different fighting maneuvers—the same tactics they needed against the MiGs. The F-4 couldn't turn as well as a MiG, even after the F-4 pilot jettisoned his external fuel bags. With limited fuel remaining, the F-4s wouldn't use their afterburner power as much as they would up North. This too made the training more like fighting MiGs.

Fifteen seconds later, Plymouth 03's aircraft commander got a visual ID on the bogies. "Two bogies, twelve o'clock level."

"Plymouth Lead, tally." It was the RAAF, 10 miles away and closing. The simulated fight for national pride began with great vigor. At this geometry, the first move for Plymouth flight was an AIM-7 Sparrow head-on firing, or "face shot," but the real training started after that. Starbuck called out, "Simulated Fox One." He held his heading for several seconds for effect. His radar had to continue to spotlight the target for the semi-active seeker head of the AIM-7. But Plymouth 03 and 04 had no such limitation.

"Plymouth 03 in the break." The second element split off almost straight up to gain early altitude advantage on the Sabres.

As Starbuck streaked by the two Sabres, he saw Stockman's bright red helmet and the red kangaroo logo painted on the Aussie's aft fuselage.

The Australian loaded up his Sabre with all the Gs he could stand as he sucked his craft nose low into a max reverse turn, trying to reverse quickly without losing his airspeed. Twenty seconds later and 50 knots slower, he and his wingman had done just that, but he hadn't anticipated Randy Starbuck's tactics.

Starbuck blew straight through after passing the Sabres. Knowing that Phantoms couldn't turn with the Sabres, he unloaded his Phantom to zero G and put both throttles past the military power limit all the way forward, opening full power on his two J-79 afterburners. He and his wingman started a maximum acceleration to 0.95 Mach. They would have been well past the sound barrier if not encumbered by their three fuel bags. Nonetheless, Randy had put 4 miles between his element and Stockman's. The Aussies had no shot.

Meanwhile, Plymouth 03 reversed over the top in a high-G barrel roll and dropped in behind Stockman and his wingman. In three seconds Stockman decided he couldn't catch Starbuck—the Aussie was caught in a classic squeeze. Then he heard it.

"Plymouth 03. Tracking. Tracking. Simulate Fox Two."

"And Plymouth 04. Bingo."

"Okay, Plymouth, let's break it off." Starbuck radioed. "See you at the bar, 'mates.'" Starbuck rolled into a leisurely right 360-degree turn so that his tailing element could close on him.

Stockman was gracious. "Right, mates; we'll buy—this time."

"Zero Three has a tally, Lead."

Starbuck didn't head the Tactics Shop for nothing. He had briefed his flight on the best way to deal with the Aussies if they bounced Plymouth flight. As planned, the lead Phantom element had taken a radar missile shot, then blown through the bogies. The second Phantom element had split high early to gain quick advantage and to sandwich the Sabres. Above all else, the rule had been: don't turn with the Aussies.

This was the first time Stockman's Sabres had dueled in mock battle with the F-4s. And it had been two-versus-four, to boot. The Aussies would go back to the hangar and work out their tactics. They'd be better prepared next time.

Plymouth flight continued its return to Ubon. The pilots on both sides relished the encounter, with one exception. "You know, Randy, all we got was good practice flying against the Aussie Sabres," Taco Martinez said in a disgruntled tone.

Starbuck responded on the intercom. "Yeah. But it was fun, wasn't it?"

"That's not good enough, Boss. We'd get even more out of this if the Aussies used NVAF tactics. Not just trying to beat us using their own strengths."

"Martinez, that's probably the best brain cramp you ever had. We'll work it on the ground. You fly us home."

Shaking the control stick between his legs in the back seat, the eager Martinez responded, "Rog, I've got it."

11 October 1966 0700 hours
Wing commander's office
Ubon RTAFB

Adams was in his office early, digging out from the paperwork that had backed up while he was gone on temporary duty to the Philippines.

The red phone rang. "Colonel Adams," he answered.

"This is Blue Chip. Stand by for General Morgan, sir."

"Clint?"

"Good morning, sir."

"Sorry for the interruption out on the veranda at Baguio. What's your idea?"

A feeling of excitement swept over Adams, and all the cynicism of the past few days washed away. "I have a concept for squaring up the odds in Pack Six."

"Well, we can't discuss it over these open telephone lines. Come down here and brief me on it."

"Thank you, General. I'll get there inside of a week." The two men said their goodbyes, and Adams put down the phone. Then he called out to his exec, "Boomer, tell Randy Starbuck to get in here." Adams wadded up a piece of paper and vigorously fired it into the wastebasket in the corner 15 feet away. Too agitated to sit, he'd moved to the window to watch the morning launches. When Starbuck appeared, Adams said, "Randy, I want you to flesh out an idea for me. Turn it into a plan, then we'll sell it to the big boys. After they approve it, we'll convert it to a military operation and carry it off. Are you with me?"

"From the git-go, sir."

"Good." Adams said, then gave him the main points.

"Yessir. That's absolutely frippin' brilliant."

"O.K. Get to it. Brief me in twenty-four hours." Starbuck swallowed hard, saluted, and departed. The game was on.

12 October 1966 0655 hours
Wing conference room
Ubon RTAFB

Clint Adams and Slim Danforth sat at the 20-feet-long main table, arms folded and waiting for the show to start. Both colonels had arrived five minutes early for the 0700 briefing. Randy Starbuck was shuffling some charts at the business end of the room. Adams could already tell that briefing was not the strong suit of this boyish, thin Mississippian. By the look of all the briefing materials taped up on the walls, Adams also could tell that Starbuck had put some extra time in on this one. In this role, Randy looked awkward, not the confident instructor pilot Adams had come to know. He even looked a little bookish this morning. Not at all the classic, confident, steely-eyed fighter pilot he was at the controls of a Phantom. But this was common among the younger pilots. They eventually grew accustomed to briefing senior officers.

"Any time you're ready, Starbuck," Danforth said. Starbuck glanced nervously at Danforth, who glared back steadily. Randy knew that Danforth opposed the idea. It wasn't Danforth's style. Too risky. And Danforth had had nothing positive to say when the Wing Tactics Shop had briefed him at 1900 hours the evening before. Instead, Danforth had questioned Starbuck intensely on a number of points. At the end, the DCO had given him no thanks, no "nice effort," nothing. Starbuck and his two assistants had worked until after midnight smoothing out the rough spots.

Starbuck believed Danforth would shelve the briefing if he could. But he couldn't. Starbuck also knew that Danforth suspected that he and the other BIBs had planted this idea with Adams over a few beers at the bar. And Starbuck was keenly aware that Danforth wrote the effectiveness report of each officer in the Tactics Shop. Danforth had a reputation for getting even. None of this helped Starbuck's composure as he stood in front of the wing commander.

"Ah, morning, sir. Uh, you asked me, uh, us, to ah. . . ."

"Relax, Randy. If it's a good concept, it'll sell itself."

Adams's philosophy seemed to buttress Starbuck, who proceeded more confidently to unveil the fleshed-out plan. Adams leaned forward. He was impressed with the younger men's work and the promise of the concept. American targets too tempting to ignore. Simplicity itself. Of most importance, it was a daring plan that could be executed within the restrictions imposed by Washington. It was a tactical scheme that might finally draw out the enemy in sufficient numbers for the 8th TFW to seriously hurt the NVAF. This could reverse the current negative trend in a very big way, and perhaps give the Air Force time until the leaders in Washington lifted the restrictions on bombing the NVAF's airfields and other key installations.

Starbuck finished. Danforth turned to Adams. "Sir, this plan's very risky."

"In what way, Slim?"

"It puts too many Phantoms in the sky over Hanoi. If the North Vietnamese figure it out, they'll have a field day shooting SAMs and flak at us."

"How do you propose that we shoot down more MiGs?"

"Well, I'm not sure."

Adams cut Danforth short. "Well, until you come up with a better, less risky plan, I'll stick with this one. Good work, Randy. Polish up the details—numbers, intervals, Thud call signs, radio calls, missile-free zones—and let me see it again tomorrow."

"Yes, sir."

"We'll fly down to Tan Son Nhut together and show it to General Morgan on Saturday. What will we call it?"

Starbuck already had a name in mind. "I recommend we call it Operation Bolo."

"Why Bolo?"

"It's named after a Philippine machete that just might cut the bastards' heads off!"

"Sounds okay to me."

1100 hours
Wing commander's office
Ubon RTAFB

Adams rummaged through his center desk drawer, looking for the book of matches he'd thrown in there yesterday. He sensed he was being watched, and looked up toward his open door. For an instant the door seemed closed. No light came through it. And for good reason—Colonel Bear Robinson virtually filled up the hole. Quietly, without breaking eye contact, the two men moved toward each other. In the middle of the room, they shook hands warmly, each man grabbing the other's arm with his free hand. Adams and Robinson had known each other for more than twenty years.

Robinson was one of the famous Tuskegee Airmen who'd trained at the rural all-black Alabama university and later distinguished themselves in air combat over Europe in World War II. Physically, Robinson was more imposing than Adams himself. His stature was matched by his fanatical patriotism and enthusiastic strong feelings about military service.

At 6-foot-5 and 245 pounds, he was perhaps the biggest pilot in the U.S. Air Force, hence the nickname "Bear." A man of great courage, he had "dead sticked" three planes after their engines quit, hence his other nickname, "Crash." Robinson was as famous a fighter pilot as Adams, but for different reasons. While Adams was known for his aerial combat skills, Robinson was noted for ground-attack combat experience.

"Good to have you here, Bear. I can use your talents."

"Name it, Boss. What do you want me to do first?"

Adams answered quickly, "It's real simple. I'll run the air war over the North. You handle the details of running the wing."

"What about flying?"

"I'll fly mostly daylight missions, since that's when the MiGs are up. I'd like you to fly a heavy night schedule. Attach yourself to the 497th Night Owls. This will match your role in running the wing's details."

"Got it. Good to see you, Clint. I thought they'd finished you off after the shouting match you had with that SAC two-star." Robinson referred to Adams's behavior during a briefing he'd given at Ninth Air Force Headquarters to the Air Staff's director of the budget.

"The man was giving away the heart of our fighter force just to balance the budget and make a few Defense Department civilian analysts happy."

"Yeah, well, I heard you were farmed out to Bien Hoa as the DCO in Huns. I almost shit a brick when you showed up at Davis-Monthan for a Phantom checkout."

"Well, my friend, somehow you and me got hold of the brass ring now."

"You mean this war saved your ass."

"Something like that. Do me a personal favor, Bear, don't tell anyone about how we trashed the O Club at Wheelus in '62. I'm tryin' to keep a lid on these fellas."

"Anything you say. What do I do first?"

"Get a combat flying checkout, then help me lead."

Robinson nodded.

"Boss, I'm gonna like workin' for you this time. Know why?"

"No. Why?"

"Because you got to be the luckiest SOB in the world to get this wing right now."

"Yeah, well, you just get ready to take over in case I get killed."

13 October 1966 1500 hours
Phuc Yen Airfield
Fifteen kilometers north of Hanoi

Colonel Tomb hated conducting this flight line tour for the visiting Warsaw Pact delegation. The MiG-17s and MiG-21s of the Second North Vietnamese Air Company that Tomb was so proud of were nothing new to the East Europeans. They were more interested in the total picture and how the NVAF was integrating all of the equipment that the Soviets were supplying. Tomb showed them the measures he was taking to harden the airfield's defenses against American bombing attacks.

"The Americans will attack our airfields soon," Tomb predicted.

One portly Hungarian official, most likely a political officer, smugly asked, "Comrade Colonel, what makes you so sure that the Americans will bomb your air bases?"

Tomb smiled. He was hoping he would get that exact question. "Because we are more effective in the air every day. The Americans will have no choice."

Tomb gave the visitors a few examples of how he was hurting the highly vaunted U.S. pilots. He told them the story of Black September, as the American press corps called it. "During September," Tomb told the VIPs, "our MiGs downed eleven American planes."

The visitors expressed their pleasure over this success. But then Tomb cautioned, "We also lost six MiGs and four pilots in September." Characteristic honesty. The propagandists wouldn't like this little speech. The 2nd Air Company's political officer noted Tomb's statement and promised himself to mildly lecture him on this brashness later.

Tomb continued. He called the delegation's attention to the Russian colonel assisting some junior maintenance officers nearby. "Colonel Arkov takes the necessary steps to order replacement MiGs. But there is a problem. The Soviets insist on shipping replacement planes over rail lines through China. And the Chinese delay the new MiGs for months at the border, then they divert some of our cargo for their own use. The same is true for SAMs, Atolls, and high-value radar parts. The Soviets should not tolerate this behavior from the Chinese. Instead, they should send the supplies by ship to Haiphong.

"Our primary difficulty is the pilots. It takes eighteen months to train a MiG pilot who can survive. Right now, we graduate only five new pilots each month. Then it takes another six months to qualify them for combat missions in the older MiG-17 over North Vietnam. Our pilot force is barely holding its own. The Americans can afford to lose many planes and pilots from their inventories. The question with the Americans is how long their pride can tolerate their losses."

Tomb led his guests over to two of his pilots standing near a MiG. They were fully dressed for flight, although they would not fly today.

One of them, Captain Nguyen Van Bay, had become an ace last week by downing his fifth American plane, a reconnaissance RF-4C taking photos of Kep Airfield. The visitors recognized Van from the pictures in the French newspaper *Le Monde*. The guests were pleased to meet the famous flier.

15 October 1966 1100 hours
Squadron commander's office, 555th TFS
Ubon RTAFB

Captain Vic Sansone hurriedly shined his flying boots before reporting to Rod Wells's office as ordered.

"Vic, I want you to meet Agent Thompson," Wells said as he settled back. "Thompson will take it from here."

"Agent?" Vic shook the hand of a thin, long-haired man in his early thirties.

Thompson extended his ID card for Sansone's perusal. "Captain, I'm with the Office of Special Investigations, the OSI."

Like most pilots, Vic Sansone didn't know much about the OSI, except that it was the Air Force agency that investigated crimes and espionage. Vic asked, "You want to talk to me about that flying schedule I found in the street two weeks ago?"

"That and something more."

"More?"

"Yes, you did the right thing turning that flying schedule into the Air Police and making a detailed statement. It dovetailed with a broader investigation we have under way."

"Broader?"

"You've been seeing a barmaid from the O Club for the past two weeks—"

"Lin May? Is she involved?" Vic was afraid of this. That flying schedule the first night. He had turned it in, but he had also satisfied himself that Lin had had nothing to do with it. She was so honest, so beautiful, so gentle. She was so naive about politics and the world.

"We can't say too much, or we'll have to take you off the flying schedule for security reasons. What will it be, Captain?"

Wells interrupted. "Tell him what you can, then let him decide if he wants more."

"We think she's a courier, maybe more. We think she passes flight schedules, you know, call signs and crew names. We believe she picks up talk at the bar as to which pilots are weak flight leaders, that kind of thing."

"Well, what happens now?"

"That's up to you, Captain. We'd like you to keep seeing her and to debrief us after each meeting. If you break it off now, she'll get suspicious, and we'll lose our chance at nailing the whole network. But you have to act like you know nothing. Don't even think about probing her for information. She's trained to pick that up."

"I already did. Just asked her if the guy on the scooter was into anything illegal. He's her cousin. She said he wasn't and that was the end of it."

"How long ago?"

"Two weeks ago. On our first date."

"You can bet it's not the end of it from her viewpoint. Try to act natural with her. If she probes you on that, tell her you heard some people were running opium on the base. Has she tried to get information from you on the flying operation or related subjects?"

"No, but I've told her my life history. One more thing. I think I'm in love with her."

"Yeah, Captain, that's what they all say." Thompson closed his notebook. "She and her scooter pal are probably card-carrying Pathet Lao, the Laotian equivalent of the Viet Cong and the Khmer Rouge."

1630 hours
Blue Chip conference room
Seventh Air Force HQ
Tan Son Nhut Air Base

Adams and Starbuck had flown down to Seventh AF Headquarters this morning in an F-4 to brief General Morgan and his staff on Operation Bolo. Adams was just finishing his pitch.

General Morgan asked his staff for comments, "Any questions? Speak up now." He got mostly positive nods.

But his deputy for Thirteenth Air Force operations in Thailand, Brigadier Max Crandall, cautioned, "The masquerade could come up dry unless we do something special beforehand to draw out more MiGs than normal. I'll work with intelligence on it. My staff has been thinking about something like this for a few months. The time's right for this type of operation. You can expect our full support on the planning effort."

Sensing he was on a roll, Adams decided to press the bigger issue with General Morgan. "Sir, when can we hit the enemy on their airfields so we don't have to resort to operations like Bolo?"

To a man, the staff looked to their general, who fielded the question without hesitating. "Colonel Adams, that's my department. I'll let you know."

Adams's probe broke the atmosphere of positive teamwork. The Byzantine nature of the Seventh AF staff emerged more fully now. Max Crandall turned the discussion to the events of the past few weeks. "Granted, the 8th has brought down two MiGs in the past two weeks, but little else has happened." Crandall added, "We're hearing reports of sweeping changes in daily activities on the ground up at Ubon, but we're not seeing any dramatic changes in the air war over the North."

Adams had tangled with Crandall before, back in the States, when they'd both worked in the Pentagon. Adams worked hard to keep his composure. A man behaved differently as a commander than he did as a staff officer, and Adams needed support for Bolo. He wouldn't get that by boiling over on another issue, no matter how personal it got. He knew he'd screwed up again by pressing for airfield attacks.

In the most objective tone he could muster, Adams responded to Crandall's statements. "We can't kill MiGs if they won't engage. That's what Bolo's all about." Crandall said nothing.

Adams continued, "Destroying MiGs is not an end in itself. We've tightened up our preparation and our air discipline, and we've refocused our mission-support operations. In the past two weeks, we've done our mission well. Not a single strike force aircraft—be it an F-105 or an F-4—has been lost to MiG action under Ubon's MiGCAP. We're getting fighter-bombers in and out of the combat zone. That translates to bombs on target. Now Bolo will take us beyond that."

Crandall started to fire back, but General Morgan took over. "Gentlemen, gentlemen, that's enough discord for the day."

Morgan saw the meeting going beyond its original agenda. He was learning that his staff was not fully behind the changes that Adams was making at Ubon. Personally, he had no objections and felt that Adams was off to a good start, getting results. Morgan thought this Bolo thing looked like a good plan. He ended the debate succinctly, "Frankly, Max,

I wish all my commanders were making such good progress. Why don't you work on them?''

The general concluded the meeting with a decision—sort of. "Bolo has promise, but I want my staff to study the details." Turning to General Crandall he added, "Max, scrub this concept down and give me your recommendation when I get back from Hawaii next week."

Adams stared at his feet. More delays.

As the meeting broke up, General Morgan asked Adams into his office. He started by telling his acolyte that he was pleased with the turnaround at Ubon. "Things seem to be moving in the right direction."

Adams suspected that General Morgan hadn't called him in just to tell him that, but he took the bait. "Thank you, sir."

"My staff's all abuzz with the unorthodox changes you're making. Rumor has it that you're consciously breaking a few standing regulations."

Adams started to explain why he felt this was necessary, but the Seventh AF commander interrupted him almost immediately. "Don't worry, Clint. I've got no intention of telling you how to run your wing. Anyway, it's time to challenge some of the stateside crap we've been carrying around. But that's not what I want to talk to you about.

"Look. I share your frustration with the restricted target list. But remember, Clint, we're both soldiers. And soldiers don't make policy. You know what I like most about this Bolo idea? I'm proud of you and your people for being creative enough to dream it up. It demonstrates that you can work inside the limits imposed by Washington.

"Clint, as the wing commander, you live in a glass house. Everyone watches what you wing commanders do. And also what you say. As one of those select few, you set the example. If you bitch as the leader, then so do your men. If a leader thinks about breaking the rules, so do his men."

"Sir, I know that. I would never—"

Morgan interrupted him, "I had to remove an F-105 vice wing commander this morning for his involvement in strafing a target on the restricted list, a Soviet supply ship in Haiphong harbor. That's a clear violation. I didn't hesitate to do it. That colonel's action has made it tougher for you and my other commanders. The news breaks tomorrow in the *Washington Post*. In a few days, everyone in your wing will be watching you to see what kind of attitude you have toward the White House restrictions.

"Today in the briefing room you sensed a little of what I'm getting at, Clint. Some of my key people think you're the most outspoken commander on the White House restrictions. When you brought it up at the end of the briefing, you only reinforced their concerns. If that same reading exists among your aircrews, one of your frustrated pilots might go too far. Dammit, Clint, you've got to watch what the hell you say!" Morgan walked up to his friend and put his hand on Adams's shoulder. "You're too valuable to the war effort now."

Adams nodded, but said, "Sir, we need to get on with Bolo as soon as possible."

With a smile, Morgan replied, "Get the hell out of my office, Colonel, I've got a war to run." Adams saluted and left.

16 October 1966 1610 hours
Thud Ridge
Forty miles northwest of Hanoi

Chevy flight, at the front of the F-105 strike formation, was eight minutes from bomb release. Their target was familiar, the Yen Vien Railroad Yard, northeast of Hanoi.

Pontiac flight was providing MiGCAP on the left side of the main force, holding position at eight o'clock, 3 miles away. Vic Sansone and Snake Cummings were in Pontiac 03. Nelson and Moose Peterson were on their wing today as Pontiac 04. This was the third MiGCAP in as many days for the pilots in Pontiac flight.

For the past week, the MiGs had been airborne. Lots of long-distance sightings but no engagements. The American strike force started to get AAA flak near the outskirts of Hanoi. The SA-2's Fan Song radars began to track the bomb-laden F-105s, all the while playing cat and mouse with the two F-105F Wild Weasel defense-suppression aircraft accompanying the main force. Five seconds on, ten seconds off in the erratic radar pattern. Snake Cummings watched as the familiar threat environment developed, "Looks like the same stuff again today, Vic. This RHAW gear really lets you hear the Gomer's search pattern."

"Yeah," Sansone replied, concentrating on maintaining his two-ship element's position on the MiGCAP leader.

"Pontiac, tanks," called the flight leader, pausing so each wingman could position his left hand on the red-guarded toggle switch. "Now." All eight empty green-and-white tanks fell off and behind the rapidly moving Phantoms.

The strike force was moving along at 520 knots and 18,000 feet. The flak today was not accurate. And there weren't any SAMs yet, just SAM radar scannings. The pilots of Pontiac flight had grown accustomed to watching for SAMs at this point in the mission, and their eyes were trained on the ground, looking for telltale launch plumes.

Then the unusual occurred. Snake Cummings in Pontiac 03 radioed, "Chevy flight, two MiG-21s, two o'clock high, 10 miles out." The MiGs were flying parallel to the strike force, down sun in clear view.

Pontiac 01 was caught off balance. For a few critical seconds the pilots in the strike force were surprised that the MiGs might mix it up with the SAM and flak activity. For the next five seconds, Pontiac 01 failed to stay up with emerging events, and his MiGCAP flight ended up on the defensive, just when it was supposed to be screening the F-105s.

In the confusion, Pontiac 01 allowed his flight to drift out of position, just as the main strike force F-105s accelerated into the target area. Now Pontiac was in a 5-mile tail chase with the very strike force it should have been protecting.

Sansone tried to determine why his leader was not turning into the two silver bogies. "Ah, Pontiac Lead, 03. Do you tally the MiG-21s?" A radar lock-on and a Sparrow shot were just the order right now.

"Rog, 03. I got 'em." Not very aggressive. Sansone and his GIB, Snake, didn't like the way things were shaping up.

"Hey, Vic, I got a full radar lock-on. A 30-degree turn to the right and you're in the heart of the firing envelope. Steering dot's just right of center circle." Sansone already knew this from stealing a glance every second at the MiGs' two-o'clock-high position.

A third MiG-21 dashed up from behind Pontiac flight at 18,000 feet and Mach 1.2, 800 knots. The NVAF GCI controller vectored him in a wide box pattern to this position, well outside the search angles of the American strike flight's radars. The lone MiG pilot had Pontiac flight 8 kilometers dead ahead on his Spin Scan air intercept radar. But the MiG pilot didn't need the Spin Scan today. For a change, inflight visibility was great.

The two MiG decoys had done their job, and the NVAF pilots broke away toward safety, leaving Pontiac 01 undecided on whether to pursue the MiGs or stay with the 105s. He elected to stay with the strike force. The American pilots still didn't realize that the enemy flak was inaccurate for a specific reason. No SA-2s would be launched today either.

The NVAF plan was working very well as the lone MiG pilot reached firing position behind Pontiac flight. The Russian-made heat-seeking

Atoll slid off the MiG-21's launcher rail and tracked for the lead element in Pontiac flight.

Snake Cummings, in the back seat of Pontiac 03, sensed trouble. Then he saw it—a MiG-21 was breaking up and away from his seven o'clock and an Atoll missile was guiding on Pontiac flight.

"Pontiac! Break! Break hard now!"

Pontiac 01 rolled his F-4 into a seven-G descending left turn. Pontiac 03, flying 2,000 feet to the leader's right in tactical formation, rolled up and over the lead element in an effort to stay in position and avoid flying right through the Atoll's track.

Yet the heat-seeking Atoll continued to close in on the lead element. It exploded just under Pontiac 02. Miraculously, the sturdy F-4 absorbed the shock and the missile fragments with no noticeable effect.

The MiG-21 rose up into the late afternoon sun, rolled over, nose down, and pointed directly at Pontiac flight. He was converting to a front-quarter cannon attack on Pontiac flight from out of the sun.

Pontiac 01 didn't pick up the MiG-21 in the glaring sunlight. He hesitated, rolled wing level, and pulled the nose of his plane 5 degrees above the horizon. Vic Sansone in Pontiac 03 had joined up again loosely on 01's right side and had selected a short-range, heat-seeking attack missile. Sansone had a loud growl in his headset, but he knew the AIM-9 Sidewinder was picking up the sun, not the MiG. The Sidewinder wouldn't work in a head-on shot anyway.

"Lead, watch out for a face shot." Sansone knew a nose-mounted air-to-air cannon would be priceless right now as the two enemies closed on each other at 1,000 knots. The MiG pilot had just such a cannon, and in this geometry, the F-4s were defenseless. The MiG pilot was the total master of the engagement for the next five seconds—an eternity in a close-quarters dogfight.

"Pontiac, bogie, twelve o'clock high!" Snake Cummings called out the target. There was only one last-ditch maneuver left now.

"Pontiac 03 in the break." The two Pontiac elements split, hoping to complicate the MiG pilot's relatively easy, down-sun shot. But the experienced MiG-21 pilot merely picked the easiest quarry by tapping his left rudder ever so slightly. Pontiac 03 was now belly up to the MiG and took the full brunt of a two-second cannon burst. Then the MiG-21 pilot split-S'd away from the F-4s, disengaging in the opposite direction. For him, it was over. Textbook surprise and tactics.

It was over for Pontiac 03 too. Sansone and Cummings felt the three heavy thuds pound into their Phantom's underbelly, an area filled with rapidly rotating engines and accessory turbines. Immediately, Snake Cummings called out, "Pontiac 03. *Mayday! Mayday!*"

In the front cockpit, Vic Sansone was staring at two bright-red engine fire lights on the right side of his main instrument panel. He felt the engine thrust drain away, and black smoke started to fill his cockpit, burning his eyes through his visor. He caught a glimpse of the altimeter before the smoke blocked it out—passing 10,000 feet. Seconds earlier, the cockpit had been a chilly place, soaked by the cold of altitude, but now the temperature was rising rapidly. Sansone and Cummings could feel the dramatic change in their Phantom. Instinctively, they knew their plane was mortally wounded.

The ominous warbling tone in Sansone's earphones that accompanied the fire warning lights drowned out all other chatter on the radio and the intercom. Sansone quickly pulled both throttles to idle, hoping that one or both engine fires would extinguish themselves but to no effect.

Mike Nelson in Pontiac 04 radioed his friend, "Vic, you're on fire. Trailing smoke and flames."

Meanwhile, Pontiac 01 and 02 fruitlessly pursued the lone MiG. But Pontiac 01 broke off the chase when he heard the "*Mayday*" call. Now he and his wingman climbed to higher altitude to initiate a possible SAR effort. The rescue wheels were already in motion.

Sansone, Cummings, and the other pilots in Pontiac flight were taught that the Phantom was a tough bird that wouldn't explode in midair. The McDonnell Aircraft Company's technical representatives said so. The IPs back at Davis-Monthan also said so. Would it explode? Was this the exception to the rule?

Vic Sansone was making for Thud Ridge. Minutes ago, while inbound to the Red River Valley, Thud Ridge seemed very hostile; now it looked like a haven. All things were relative. Just a few precious minutes—that was all Vic and Snake needed.

But it was not to be. Acrid smoke completely filled both cockpits. Then it seemed to grow more concentrated, obscuring even the flight instruments.

"Vic, can you see well enough to fly? I'm WOXOF!" Snake's eyes burned from the acrid smoke as he used pilot's jargon for totally obscured vision.

Sansone leaned forward trying to read the plane's attitude. No luck. "Can't see anything."

Cummings drew on his emergency training and the checklist burned in his memory from hours of rote study, "Go Ram Air." Sansone responded by flipping the air-conditioning system's vent switch. The outside air thinned out the black smoke momentarily. Fumbling along the right forward side console, he selected the 100 percent oxygen lever.

"Go 100 percent, Pete." Sansone didn't tell Cummings that he was leaning forward to barely see the F-4's attitude indicator (ADI)—passing 8,000 feet. He was trying to keep the plane upright, in a semblance of control. Despite all the stress and distractions, Cummings noticed how calm Sansone's voice sounded.

Sansone struggled to remember all he knew about the F-4's internal systems. The bird had two hydraulic systems totally devoted to operating the flight-control systems. If one system failed, the backup could save the day. He remembered that the lines of the two hydraulic systems ran right next to each other throughout the plane. And the MiG pilot's cannon fire cut deeply into both hydraulic flight-control systems. The wounded F-4 began a slow roll to the left despite Sansone's efforts to keep it upright. Seconds later, the nose pitched almost straight down, and the aircraft began to shudder violently. The engine-driven hydraulic pumps did their job well. All the hydraulic fluid was gone, forced under pressure into the skies over the rice paddies below.

The dying aircraft passed 6,000 feet at 400 knots, although Sansone and Cummings didn't know their exact position. Through the confusion, noise, and acrid smoke, Sansone called out over the intercom, "Eject now, Pete. Get out."

This small but supremely unselfish act gave Snake Cummings the warning he needed to eject. The GIB straightened up in his seat so the force of the ejection wouldn't crack the vertebrae in his backbone. He jammed his head into the headrest behind him, closed his stinging eyes, tucked in his elbows, grabbed his right wrist with his left hand, reached between his legs with his right hand, and pulled the yellow-striped metal ring just forward of his crotch. One-half second later, the ballistic-assisted Martin-Baker ejection seat fired in sequence after the rear canopy left the plane. Cummings and his seat cleared the plummeting F-4 in a blast of noise. Immediately, the mechanical butt-kicker snapped Cummings clear of the ejection seat, and the automatic sequence of parachute deployment did the rest, blossoming out Snake's chute about 2,000 feet above the jungle below.

Sansone ejected. But he was much lower, about 1,500 feet above the ground, and his downward momentum carried him and his separated ejection seat into the jungle canopy, 100 feet above the ground. Sansone's unopened parachute streamed behind him. He entered the treetops close to the aircraft fireball and smoke immediately obscured his location.

1640 hours
The NCO Club
Ubon RTAFB

Clint Adams could hear his handheld brick chirping in the back of the main dining room of the Noncommissioned Officers Open Mess. He had given it to Boomer Wright before moving to the front of the audience for his opening remarks. The NCO Club doubled as a meeting hall when needed.

Adams was finishing up a ceremonial function that was one of his favorites. He was elevating twenty-eight airmen first class to the rank of staff sergeant, making them full-fledged noncommissioned officers in the U.S. Air Force.

Adams knew that crossing the line from airman to NCO was a big step for a USAF enlisted man. He thought that the Air Force's field commanders should take the time to drive the point home. Adams started doing these NCO ceremonies when he was the wing commander at RAF Lakenheath in England. He wanted to look each new staff sergeant in the eye and let that young man know that his wing commander expected him to shoulder more responsibility.

NCOs played an important role in a technology-based military arm like the U.S. Air Force, where technical training and operational experience were essential to generate combat air power. Clint Adams knew how important his NCOs were to the 8th TFW's daily operations, so he took the time to preside over this event once each month.

Adams finished reading the noncommissioned officer's creed to the twenty-eight men standing before him. They remained at attention as a supportive gathering of 150 people—commanders, supervisors, and cohorts—looked on admiringly. The crowd was growing by the minute as the dinner hour approached. Hungry onlookers jammed into the back of the room where it was already standing room only.

Each new NCO came forward to receive both a copy of the NCO creed and a fourth chevron from his wing commander. The ceremony looked like a small college graduation, with slight variations, as each new staff sergeant moved through the sequence. Shake, take, salute— twenty-eight times. After the final applause by the audience, the 8th

TFW's senior chief master sergeant serving as master of ceremonies announced the end of the event.

Clint Adams normally stayed on to talk more casually with his new staff sergeants. Today was no different, and he knew that Boomer would advise him if the call on the handheld brick required his attention. It looked as if Boomer had elected to split the difference based on what he knew so far. The young executive officer did not interrupt the ceremony, but now he was moving forward to speak with his colonel.

"Excuse me, sir."

Adams took the cue and politely excused himself from a group of four new NCOs.

"The TOC duty officer called. We lost an F-4 to a MiG about twenty minutes ago near Thud Ridge."

The words cut into Clint Adams like a knife. "Got a call sign and some names?"

"Pontiac 03. The TOC wouldn't give me the names in the clear, so I called them on a land line. It's Sansone and Cummings." Boomer saw Adams pull back a little as the names registered. Adams had grown attached to the Four Horsemen in the short time he had known them. He'd quickly developed a parental sense of ownership over the eager young officers. He knew that that was wrong, but it had happened anyway.

"Any status on the pilots?"

"They're working an SAR on Cummings. Nothing on Sansone. Looks like he rode it in."

Adams nodded resolutely. An SAR on Thud Ridge? Not much chance of getting Cummings either, unless the rescue boys got there fast.

1645 hours
The foothills of Thud Ridge
Twenty miles northwest of Hanoi

Mike Nelson saw the first good chute, but not the second. He knew that Vic Sansone had stayed with the F-4 too long. Nelson also knew he shouldn't be flying under 4,500 feet in the Red River Delta, even moving along at 500 knots. Phuc Yen Airfield was only 6 miles to the southeast. Hanging around here could earn a lone F-4 a handful of swarming MiGs.

"Don't you think we ought to climb up a bit?" Moose Peterson suggested as he kept his eyes on the NVAF main operating base. But all Mike Nelson knew was that he must find his friend.

Ten seconds later, he and Moose streaked dangerously low over the crash site. Nelson could not explain it. It was as if he were trying to draw his friend out of the jungle.

After a second low pass, Moose tried again to bring his frontseater back to reality. "Hey, Boss, how about we go to a top cover station and work 243.0?" Peterson set the UHF radio frequency to 243.0, the Guard channel, used for all aircraft emergency operations. If Vic or Snake were alive and able to use their handheld survival radios, they would be transmitting and receiving on 243.0.

Nelson reluctantly resigned himself. "Rog." He pulled back on the stick and climbed to 10,000 feet, where he set up a racetrack pattern with two-minute legs. Moose set his UHF radio to transmit and receive on 243.0.

Nelson called specifically for Sansone, "Pontiac 03 Alpha, how do you read?" A "bravo" suffix meant the GIB.

"Pontiac 03 Alpha, Pontiac 04, over." Still nothing.

With only air-to-air missiles on board, Nelson and Moose could do little to defend the downed crewmen against any threat on the ground. But at least at this altitude Pontiac 04 was safe from automatic-weapons fire, the leading cause of U.S. aircraft shootdowns. The AAA sites fired at Pontiac 04 only sporadically.

"Zero Four, Pontiac Lead. SAR's in progress. Let's transition to 03 Bravo." This advisory did nothing to buoy Nelson's spirits. Pontiac 01 had also seen the final seconds in the life of Pontiac 03 and its crew.

All energies turned to rescuing 03 Bravo, Snake Cummings. With good reason. Snake was chattering on his emergency radio. He'd told the world he was uninjured and concealed among the thick trees along the foothills of Thud Ridge. He'd relayed that he heard only the noise of American fighters overhead. So far, so good. The bad news was that his location was on the outer limits of USAF SAR capability. Two more things worked against Snake Cummings's successful rescue today: time and the remaining daylight hours.

1650 hours
Seventy miles west of Thud Ridge

The odds were low for a clean rescue of Cummings, but the two A-1E Skyraiders and two Jolly Green rescue helicopters made their way toward his position. The A-1s were cruising in from their orbit over northern Laos at 180 knots. The choppers were moving at 120 knots.

"Zero Four, Lead. Choppers thirty minutes out. Any movement or contact with 03 Alpha?"

"Negative."

"Roger. We'll go for 03 Bravo first."

"Zero Four, copy. I'm near 'Bingo' on gas, Lead. Zero Four outbound to Orange Track to top off."

"Pontiac 01, understand. We'll stay on station as long as we can. About fifteen minutes."

The two A-1E Sandy aircraft were twenty minutes out. Sandy 01 would be the on-scene commander for the rescue operation. These single-engine, prop-driven aircraft would pinpoint Cummings's location for the lead Jolly Green chopper when it arrived. Just as important, the Sandies would suppress enemy ground fire if it occurred. The Air Force lost many Sandies, and their pilots couldn't buy a beer at a fighter base, either.

1655 hours
Thud Ridge

Time passed slowly for Snake Cummings. The ejection sequence had been a blur of tumbling noise. Before he could get his bearings, he had been in a fully deployed chute watching the treetops between his dangling feet. The opening shock had driven one of the crotch straps directly into his right testicle. The pain had almost made Snake pass out and distracted him from the fast-moving events around him. Snake had lost all sense of height or time at that point. A few seconds later, he had found himself crashing through the upper limbs of some very tall trees.

Cummings was thankful he had fastened his helmet chin strap back at Ubon. That had kept his helmet from separating on ejection due to wind blast. It had probably saved his life too. The helmet had kept his head from slapping against the thick branches like a melon and had protected his eyes. Nonetheless, the impact with the tree had left him dizzy. His normally perfect vision was now blurry.

Snake had never had a chance to position his legs, arms, and torso for the classic parachute landing fall he had practiced so often back in Undergraduate Pilot Training and at Survival School. He'd just hurtled into the oncoming foliage like a rag doll flipped into the bushes. He'd crashed into a stand of thick bamboo as he neared the ground. This bit of luck had probably kept him from breaking a leg or an arm.

After Snake landed, he'd just sat amid the thick bamboo, listening. He could hear only one thing above the ringing in his ears: fighters overhead. No voices, no shooting. Then he started to remember his training. He shut off the beeper that automatically activated on parachute deployment. That one signal on 243.0 would let his searchers know he'd had a good, fully deployed chute. That signal alone had too often been the last electronic message that a downed pilot might just still be alive—albeit wounded, captured, or both.

Snake continued to get on with the actions that would improve his chances for rescue. He pulled out his ARC-21 emergency radio, stretched out the antenna, slid the selector to transmit, and attempted to let the world know he was alive on the ground. Only a muffled sound resulted. Snake shook his head, disconnected his oxygen mask, and tried again. "This is Pontiac 03 Bravo. Anyone read me?"

"Roger, Pontiac 01 here. Read you loud and clear. State your location and condition."

"Ah, Lead, I'm okay I think. I'm in a stand of tall trees. That's all I can see. Trees." Snake swatted at a handful of mosquitoes that had discovered him.

"Rog. Sit tight. SAR in progress. ETA thirty minutes."

"Zero Three Bravo, wilco." Snake stood up and started to pick his way out of the thickness of the bamboo stand. One step later he pitched forward, his feet entangled in a mass of parachute risers and survival gear. It dawned on him that he was still connected to everything that followed him into the jungle. He disconnected himself from his parachute harness and pulled the last few snags to the ground. He was having trouble seeing things; he didn't know it would be so dark in the jungle. Then he realized that he still had on his helmet, with the sun visor down. Let there be light.

After what seemed an eternity to Snake, the Sandies arrived at the crash site. Pontiac 01 had hung on, endangering his element to identify Cummings's position for the A-1Es. Pontiac 01 and 02 departed for the KC-135 tanker that had finished refueling Pontiac 03 and was now moving north of its normal refueling track to catch the other two fuel-starved Phantoms over northern Laos before they flamed out.

Sandy 01 established contact with Snake. "Ah, 03 Bravo, Sandy 01. How copy?" The sound of another southern drawl put Snake measurably more at ease.

"Loud and clear, Sandy. I hear your propeller west of my position. But I don't have you in sight."

"That's good, little buddy. You won't see us until we clear up a little business first." Sandy 01 was referring to an authentication procedure designed to prevent the North Vietnamese from trapping rescue choppers. They, too, monitored 243.0 with dozens of captured ARC-21 radios, picked off the bodies of dead and captured American pilots. The likelihood of a deception happening here was slight because the crash had occurred only forty minutes earlier. But stranger things had happened. For now, the Americans had a slim advantage. Quick action this deep into North Vietnam was the best hope for a downed pilot's rescue. The probability of a successful operation decreased with every passing minute.

The SAR force started working the authentication procedure while the two Sandys were moving to the target. Using secure communications, the Rescue Coordination Center, located at Nhakon Phanom Air Base on the Thai-Laotian border, had obtained Snake Cummings's passport to one free Air Force rescue. All American pilots provided their wing intelligence officers with the answers to three questions that only they could answer.

"Hillsboro, go ahead with your data." The on-scene commander for the rescue piloting Sandy 01 translated and scribbled down the coded answers to these questions on his knee pad.

"Okay, 03 Bravo, put your thinking cap on. Got a question for you."

"Question?" Cummings vaguely remembered that he'd had to provide some such info during in-processing at Ubon five weeks ago. He was luckier than most evading crew members on the ground in North Vietnam. He was uninjured. He was not in shock. And he didn't have any enemy search parties breathing down his neck. He just hoped he didn't clank up on the most important test he would ever face.

"Roger, Sandy. Go ahead."

"Who did you take to the senior prom?"

A wave of relief washed over the backseater because he would never forget the first love of his life. His brain flashed back to Central High in Wichita on that warm May night in 1960.

"Becky Collins. Becky Collins."

"One Becky Collins is good enough. You hit the jackpot, 03 Bravo. Now pay attention. Any bad guys in the area?"

"Negative."

"Call me when you see me, little buddy." With that, Sandy 01 popped up over the last ridge line of the mountainous spine that had protected the A-1Es. Even this veteran of two dozen SARs swallowed hard as the expanse of the Red River Valley in the distance loomed into view through his forward windscreen. He'd never been this far into North Vietnam. And he'd never felt so exposed.

The Sandy pilots pinpointed the smoking crash site on the upslope of the last densely foliated rise before the endless stretch of rice paddies in the distance.

"Sandy, I hear you getting much closer. I'm under a high canopy of trees. I only have visibility straight up. I can't see you yet."

Sandy 01 started to work out an exact location for the Jolly Green choppers, still a good six minutes from the crash site, but didn't want to expose the downed pilot position to enemy search parties that were surely moving up the slopes. "You got a compass, little buddy? Get it out and orient north."

"Roger." Snake reached into the left leg pocket of his G-suit and pulled out his olive-green military compass.

"Are you near the crash site, 03 Bravo? Do you smell any smoke?" Black smoke was moving off the slope northeast into the valley below. Sandy 01 flew directly over the remains of the burning F-4. He had two purposes in mind.

"Negative, I don't smell smoke. But I do hear some shooting now. Rifles. Maybe a mile away. As best I can figure you are northeast of me now, inside of a mile I think."

Sandy 02 interjected, "You're taking fire, Sandy Lead." Sandy 01 banked sharply and moved away from the crash site. Meanwhile, 02 rolled in and strafed the area just downhill from the smoking hole in the jungle canopy.

Sandy 01 had risked his life to get two important bits of information. He now knew about where Cummings was. And he knew the area was getting hot. He would decoy the main search party. The enemy moved for the crash site first. He would try to get them to think Cummings was northeast from there.

"Copy. Sit tight, friend. Pop a smoke flare on my command." Both A-1s banked steeply and disappeared northeast to the protective ridge line. The goal now was to buy time until the choppers, still 10 miles away, got there.

"Roger." Snake was not sure what was going on. He felt more alone now as the propeller sound moved off into the distance. But he was reassured as he again heard F-4s overhead.

"Pontiac 03 Bravo, Pontiac 04. We're back with company." Mike Nelson in Pontiac 04 was back on top cover, accompanied by two F-105s from the exiting main strike force. The rescue armada was growing, lacking only the two choppers now. The Jolly Greens were three minutes out, still flying at 2 miles per minute.

Actually, the rescue was proceeding like clockwork. No MiGs, no SAMs, and no flak, although Sandy 01 had picked up some additional small arms fire about 1 mile down the slope toward the flatlands. That was to be expected this deep in North Vietnam. Sandy 01 would work this search party with some Vulcan metal.

"Hammer 01, you're cleared in hot on the tracers."

"Rog, Hammer 01 in from the west." Big Jim Kuszinski dragged around the nose of his Thud, pointing it down out of the setting sun. Hammer 01 and 02 were invaluable in this role as high-speed strafers with their nose-mounted M-61 cannons walking their incendiary shells down the slope. After each F-105 made three strafing runs, peppering the slope below Cummings's position with more than 2,000 rounds of 20mm cannon shells, all enemy fire stopped. Further movement up the slope seemed to stop as well.

"Thanks, Hammer. Good pattern. Hold high 'til you Bingo." The experienced Sandy pilot elected to keep the Thuds in reserve.

"Glad to oblige, Sandy. Just call the Polish Warrior when things get rough," Kuszinski rattled as he climbed up to orbit at 10,000 feet in case he was needed again. The North Vietnamese GCI controllers listened, knowing that the Polish Pig had just snuffed out the lives of their countrymen.

Sandy 01 then directed Cummings to pop his orange smoke flare. The choppers were now only two minutes out. "Zero Three Bravo, Wilco." Cummings held up a small canister about the size of a frozen orange juice can and pulled the small ring on top of it. A 6-inch lanyard released. Another yank and the dense orange chemical erupted from the flare. Cummings stood in the "Statue of Liberty" position. Forty seconds later, the acrid-smelling colored smoke drifted straight up through the primary jungle canopy, 75 feet above Cummings.

Then a new voice chimed in on Guard channel. "Jolly 01 has the smoke." In perfect coordination, the two Sandies moved to straddle the lead HH-3 Jolly Green helicopter as it made its final approach toward Cummings.

The lead chopper quickly broke into a hover over Snake's position and lowered the jungle penetrator rescue device suspended on a steel cable into the trees. It was here that the Jolly Green and the entire SAR operation was most exposed—much like being tied by an umbilical cord to the earth below.

Cummings saw the yellow metal jungle penetrator move slowly down to him. It was halfway down now, only 40 feet to go. The primary jungle canopy still seemed so high that Snake only saw shadowy glimpses of the largest chopper in the Air Force inventory. He saw the treetops fluttering, but he barely felt the residual of the wind blast from the chopper's blades. Even its sound, normally a din, was somewhat muffled.

Then Snake heard the crack of rifle fire coming from the slope below him. The sound nearly paralyzed him because it seemed very close. He forced himself to concentrate on the yellow penetrator, only 10 feet above him now. The sporadic rifle fire continued. He'd been shot at before, but that was in an F-4. This was different; this was personal.

Snake could hear a pinking sound but didn't know what it was. He focused entirely on the 3-feet-long jungle penetrator approaching him on the end of the cable. He jumped for it, but it was still beyond reach. Then he remembered to wait until the penetrator hit the ground. His survival training kicked in again, and he avoided the nasty static discharge he would get by touching the penetrator before it grounded itself on the earth. The helicopter's rotating blades built up a powerful dose of static electricity in flight. The charge would pass through the first thing it touched.

Snake quickly pulled down one of the three sitting bars attached to the side of the jungle penetrator. He fumbled with and eventually buckled the safety strap around his sweaty torso and gave a thumbs-up while tugging on the cable. Immediately, he felt the upward force as the chopper's hydraulic winch reeled in the penetrator cable. In a minute, he was through the canopy and into the late afternoon sunlight, just a few feet away from the chopper. Snake reminded himself that now was not the time to panic by reaching for the entry door. No, it was time to hold on for dear life. Let the pararescueman do his job.

Then Snake Cummings heard the pinking sound again, just as he saw a spark on the chopper's bottom. He realized that bullets were zinging past him and bouncing off the underside armor plate of the helicopter!

Suddenly the tree canopy off to the chopper's right erupted with tracers. Then a bone-shuddering whoosh shocked Snake. He lost all sense of what was happening. The incredible noise completely confused him. He instinctively huddled his body in the fetal position and put a death grip on the jungle penetrator. When he opened his eyes, he saw an American F-105 moving away in a right high-G turn barely above treetop level, and the chopper was moving across the jungle canopy, 50 feet below. The pinking stopped. To Snake's astonishment, the Polish Warrior had struck again.

Seconds later, the pararescueman at the door spun Snake face out to the world and pulled him inside. The Jolly Green moved away quickly over the ridge and out of harm's way.

The Jolly Green's inbound flight had seemed excruciatingly slow to Snake while he was on the ground. But now, the ride felt very fast as they streaked only yards above the upward sloping jungle treetops. Snake understood now why the rescue pilots were the most decorated combatants of the Vietnam War. It took guts to hover for three minutes over the treetops while staring at the Red River Valley in the distance and taking small-arms fire the entire time.

The lead chopper and his backup exited the area as fast as possible. Pontiac 04 and the Wild Weasels hung back to cover the choppers' rear against a MiG attack.

"You're bleeding, Lieutenant." The grease-painted sergeant slapped a gauze pad and some tape over a flesh wound across Snake's left cheekbone. "Those Gomers almost took your face off, sir. You're pretty lucky."

"No shit!"

Next stop for Snake was Nhakon Phanom Air Base. Once on the chopper, Snake asked about Vic Sansone. He was told that the SAR force was transitioning to Sansone's location now. Snake leaned forward to peer out the chopper's side door. His thoughts were with Vic.

The Sandies remained exposed, continuing the SAR. They were hunting for any sign of life at the crash site. No radio calls. No automatic emergency beeper that would signify Vic Sansone had a good chute and descent into the jungle, just sporadic automatic-weapons fire. After ten more minutes, the enemy ground fire intensified. Still nothing from Sansone. Sandy 01 wisely called off the SAR operation, and the A-1Es slowly moved off to the northwest along Thud Ridge.

Pontiac 04 and the F-105s stayed on orbit for another twenty-five minutes until they exhausted their fuel. Then they left the area too. Nelson was hoarse from trying to raise his best friend on the radio, but he didn't care about his throat.

Colonel Tomb had shot down Pontiac 03 only eighty minutes earlier.

1805 hours
The Orange Refueling Track
On the Thai-Laotian border

After inflight refueling from the same tanker that had supported the entire operation, Mike Nelson and Moose Peterson started the last leg of today's odyssey, the thirty-five-minute flight back to Ubon. They were silent all the way home, except for the necessary radio calls and crew coordination.

Moose took the controls; it was routine on the way home from a mission. It was still daylight bright at 28,500 feet, but dusk had enveloped the ground below in a charcoal-gray haze.

Mike Nelson thought about that MiG pilot. He was very good. He knew exactly what he was doing. He was like a spider who'd wrapped Pontiac flight in a web of confusion. Then he simply went in and selected his prey at random. Vic Sansone and Snake Cummings hadn't had much of a chance.

THE CONSPIRACY

Adams and Robinson entered the O Club and moved to the bar. The 8th TFW had lost a pilot today, so there wouldn't be any MiG sweeps or carrier landings in the bar tonight. Squadrons pulled together in these times. Squadron lines melted away. Pilots got together and talked. The mood was somber, subdued. Someone selected Tony Bennett's "San Francisco" on the jukebox. The haunting song only underscored how everyone felt.

Some of the pilots were sitting at the bar, talking about how Vic Sansone had bought the farm. Nelson and Moose had finished their intell debrief thirty minutes ago. They didn't need to relive the events of the day in such naked detail. No, they needed to sit somewhere and reflect on those events in the company of their fellows instead. They were flanked by Adam's exec, Boomer Wright, and two pilots from the 497th Night Owls, the bulky Whale Wharton and his GIB.

All pilots engaged in postmission discussions as a necessary cleansing action. Combat pilots had to rationalize that they would have behaved differently, that they would have survived where Vic Sansone had not. Only then would they let it go. Without this process, some pilots would lose their edge, their nerve. To all pilots at war, the most feared event was the "golden BB," the bullet that you could not avoid because it had your name on it.

Whale Wharton put it simply. "I would've broken off and chased the first two MiGs. They were probably weak dicks anyway."

Taco Martinez added, "I definitely would have done a hard break and a total split right when I saw the missile. No use runnin' around in a tight group of four targets." Tonight, without fully understanding the details of the day's air engagement, they convinced themselves that they would have reversed on the attacking MiG and carried the day.

"Did he shave his mustache or something?"

"Nope. Didn't have one. 'Course maybe that was the problem." Like baseball players on a winning streak, pilots behaved illogically to preserve their winning streaks, or return from their combat missions alive. All pilots had irrefutable proof that being superstitious worked. Each could recount a half-dozen instances where a pilot got shot down immediately after varying his behavior.

And each war had its particular superstitions. By far the most prevalent one of this war among fighter pilots was the mustache. Growing a 'stache was optional, a personal choice. But should a pilot start growing one he had to keep it for his entire tour. If the itching got so bad that he couldn't sleep—tough! If he shaved it off, he incurred the worst of luck.

Yet another ominous superstition kicked in this afternoon with the death of Vic Sansone. The pilots, and commanders, strongly believed that aviation tragedies happened in threes. If that were true, two more would occur soon.

"Well, gents, one down and two to go. Besides, the problem today was a piss-poor flight leader." No one at the bar took issue with Whale Wharton's pronouncement.

Lin May was listening intently to the pilots as she rinsed used drink glasses. She did not understand much of the special language of pilots. But she did pick up that they were talking about her American. Her American. She never thought she would ever feel that way about one of these arrogant killers. But Vic was different—more human, softer. Since her encounter with him at the Officers' Club two weeks ago, Lin May had learned much more than his name. But he was not here tonight, and that worried Lin May. She liked him very much.

Boomer Wright raised his beer mug and proposed a toast, "To Vic Sansone, may he return to the Nickel soon." The customary "hear, hear" affirmation followed from the others.

Whale Wharton cynically concluded the true feelings of those present, "No such luck, but at least Pete Cummings made it out okay."

As the pilots moved on to another subject, Lin May dropped a glass and ran into the kitchen in tears. The pilots at the bar noticed Lin's emotional exit, and one of them said, "What the hell was that all about?"

Lin hurried out the rear of the O Club and stopped to gather herself. She was alone among the clatter of the air conditioning unit and the dogs rummaging through the garbage cans. She ignored the rotting smell kicked up by the dogs' hunt for discarded food.

She wondered if the flight schedule she'd passed yesterday had anything to do with Vic's death. After all, she did pass on that the Pontiac flight leader was considered weak and indecisive by his fellow pilots.

For a few more minutes she mourned for her lost pilot. But she knew that in a few hours, like an unthinking machine, she would tell Nan that the pilot shot down today was Captain Vic Sansone of the 555th TFS. He was Pontiac 03. In twenty-four hours, that information would be briefed to key leaders in the North Vietnamese military, and it would be passed to the intelligence officers in the NVAF air defense system. Still, it would hurt her heart to do this.

2030 hours

Major Tom Cardwell, the 8th TFW's intell officer, entered and moved to the bar, just as he did every night. He was running about twenty-five minutes late tonight because he had to finish writing up the debrief on the Pontiac 04 shootdown and complete a little extra research. Cardwell loved intell work, especially at the tactical level. For him, this beat the hell out of working in the bowels of some Washington building as a cog in the world of strategic or national intelligence where it was all too impersonal. Still a bachelor at thirty-five, Tom Cardwell planned to extend his tour until America won the war.

A creature of habit, Cardwell started his day at 0600 by reading all the intell dispatches that had rolled in since he'd gone off shift the night before. Then he tweaked the intelligence briefing he'd built the previous night for the morning wing staff meeting. After the meeting, he immersed himself in the routine of briefing crews on their targets and the threats they would face. Then there were the mission debriefings where he tried to glean information from tired, emotionally strung-out crews. Somehow he made sense out of their eyewitness accounts and wrote up the reports for the ops and intell communities to use as they saw fit.

Cardwell normally worked a sixteen-hour day, driving himself to do what he could for the aircrews. By working longer he thought he might uncover some seemingly insignificant fact that just might give the 8th TFW pilots a decisive advantage on their next mission.

He took the loss of a pilot personally. Was there something he had failed to tell Captain Sansone earlier today that might have made a difference? After going over it all again since the Pontiac 04 debrief, Tom Cardwell thought so.

The balding major made his way to his usual seat at the far end of the bar near the barmaids' station. He liked to talk with the Thai girls while they waited for the bartender to fill their drink orders. He never tried to hit on them, so they didn't really mind.

Once he had his usual long-neck Budweiser in hand, he scanned the room to see what was up. As expected, the pilots were gathered in a group near the center of the bar. Their rationalizing was over, and they were polishing off their drinks before heading for their hootches. Nelson and Peterson remained after the others were gone.

Cardwell called out from the end of the bar, "Captain Nelson. Can I see you for a moment?"

Mike and Moose exchanged glances as they made for Cardwell's dark corner of the bar. They didn't want to go over the day's details anymore. "What now, Major? We're about to rack out."

"We can't talk here; can you come outside with me?" Cardwell was as cautious as most intell officers. He threw down a quarter on the bar as he headed for the door. Nelson and Peterson followed; they were heading out anyway.

Once outside, Cardwell spoke. "Something you said during the debrief got me to thinking. You said, 'That MiG pilot was good. Real good.' "

"He was. So what?" Moose carried the pilots' end of the conversation.

"Well, I pulled out the debriefs on all the other 8th TFW pilot shootdowns after I wrote up yours. I found that a single MiG was involved in two others. Same kind of deep six o'clock attack."

"What are you driving at, Major?"

"Well, then I pulled out a file I've been keeping on the MiG pilots. I think it's a good possibility that Colonel Tomb shot down Captain Sansone."

Nelson and Peterson shot glances at each other again. They had heard the bar talk about the infamous Tomb; pilots argued about whether he even existed. Nelson spoke for the pair this time. "What makes you think that?"

"From my evaluations, this kind of profile would be Tomb's style. You know, a single-ship attack where surprise and the other advantages are on his side."

Nelson was skeptical, "What makes you think there really is a Colonel Tomb?"

"Captain, you're not talking to some dildo fighter pilot who's three beers into his cups. I've got a file 2 inches thick that says he not only exists, but he takes out American pilots with startling regularity."

Nelson decided to take the intell officer at his word. Cardwell had an impeccable reputation for doing his homework. "What else can you tell us about this Colonel Tomb?"

"He's elusive in the air. He only fights on his terms. And he is a very good tactician and pilot. But he has other duties that give him somewhat of a routine. That's his weakness. He commands the NVAF fighter forces, three air companies. One report suggests that he moves between his three air companies during the day."

Nelson was interested. "Where are these air companies?"

"Mostly Phuc Yen, Kep, and Yen Bai. My guess is that he spends more time at Phuc Yen right now than anywhere else."

"How come?"

"Because that's one of two bases currently converting to MiG-21s."

"You said two bases."

"Yeah, Phuc Yen and Kep."

"Then why more time at Phuc Yen?"

"Trust me. I can't tell you how I know this. You're not cleared for that. But the MiGs you engaged today recovered at Phuc Yen. Jeez, you guys look like shit. Let me know if you want to talk about this after you get some rest." The major walked away into the evening.

2045 hours
Base Hospital
Nhakon Phanom RTAFB, northeast Thailand

Pete Cummings wouldn't be stuck in this hospital bed overnight if he hadn't told the flight surgeon he'd smacked his head on the tree trunk during his wild descent through the jungle canopy. He had a field-grade headache, but he knew that two cool beers would have dilated his tensed-up blood vessels enough to remedy that. The king-sized dose of aspirin he'd received in a small paper cup would have to do the job.

Snake looked around the twelve-bed ward. He made the rounds of the ward after dinner to pass the time. Nhakon Phanom was on the Mekong River, which separated Thailand from Laos. This was the frontier, and he was in the first hospital with clean sheets on the American side of the secret war in Laos. He figured to see some interesting patients in a place like this. Of the twelve patients in this ward, only seven were American.

The three beds closest to his corner were occupied by Meo soldiers. The young men, teenagers actually, had been convalescing here for a while. Their families, who were camping nearby, had been here earlier in the evening wearing the colorful Meo headbands and matching sashes over their black pajamas. One of the other patients, an Army Green Beret, told Snake that the Meo tribesmen were the mythical mountain fighters of northern Laos, descendants of a migrating clan that had moved down from China more than 1,000 years ago. To the ethnic Lao, the Meo were still outsiders. The Meo had fought the Pathet Lao and North Vietnamese with a vengeance, and they had taken high casualties for years now. In a few years the Meo would be decimated by their alliance with the CIA, Air America, and the "good war" in Laos. The flatland Laotians were considered poor fighters, largely corrupt, and generally didn't care if their country was overrun by Communist forces.

Beyond the three bedridden Meos, Pete saw two Green Berets, two Air Force Special Operations types, an overweight civilian who worked for Air America, and a few Thais, most likely mercenaries fighting with the Meo on the Plain of Jars in northern Laos. Snake figured one could learn a great deal about the war in Laos by hanging around this place.

Then Snake got his last big surprise of the day, this time an unexpectedly pleasant one. Three USO singers walked in to cheer up the troops.

"Carol! Lisa! Angie!"

All three women rushed to surround his bed, covering him with hugs, kisses, and a flurry of questions. They were shaken by the events of the day. They hadn't met Vic Sansone at Ubon, but they were saddened by Snake's loss.

"Is Mike all right?" asked Lisa.

"Yeah, as far as I know, he stayed and capped us until after they picked me up. He and Vic were best friends."

Lisa knew that Mike must be hurting. She had to talk to him, and she asked the ward nurse if she could use a phone to call a pilot at Ubon. The two left for an adjacent office. Angie sensed that three was a crowd, "I better circulate around the ward." She apologized to Snake for the wastebasket full of water, then moved off to visit with the other patients.

Carol was genuinely concerned and asked, "Snake, are you really all right?" She moved closer to him as he sat up on the side of the bed.

"Sure. Please call me Pete." He knew this relationship wasn't going to go anywhere if Carol didn't know his real name.

Carol took the lead from there. "My full name's Carol Kuszinski. And I have to warn you: I know all about fighter pilots. My older brother flies F-105s at Korat. Do you know him?"

"Know him! Hell, I probably saved his ass half a dozen times!"

2115 hours
8th TFW TOC
Ubon RTAFB

Clint Adams was on Ubon's only secure telephone line, and he was shuffling his feet, already frustrated. He was talking to Brigadier General Max Crandall, Morgan's chief of operations in Thailand. General Morgan was back in Hawaii at a commander's conference. Crandall told Adams, "General Morgan has extended his stay in Honolulu. He won't be back for five more days."

Adams knew what this meant for Bolo, but he pressed for a decision anyway. General Crandall threw the impatient Adams a bone. "I'll bring up the subject with General Morgan when he makes his daily call to me in Hawaii tomorrow morning."

"Goddammit, General, that's not good enough! General Morgan said to make things happen. Press him for a decision that will get things done," Clint shouted into the phone. For a few seconds, everyone in the TOC stopped and looked at Adams.

Crandall fired back. "Get hold of yourself, Adams. Who the hell do you think you're shouting at? I'm not one of your staff colonels. If I had my way, you'd still be pushing papers back in South Carolina. You'll get your answer when it's fully staffed and the general gets briefed on all sides of the issue. Not before. And don't end run me on this or you'll regret it! Now get some sleep."

"Yes, sir," Adams signed off, irritated but polite. He already regretted losing his temper on the phone and hoped he hadn't blown the Bolo plan then and there. Robinson, who had since followed him into the TOC, saw Adams hanging up the red command phone. Adams shook his head. Robinson nodded and looked back sympathetically. They both converged on the board showing tomorrow's mission schedule.

Adams needed to distract himself from the impatience that was eating at him. Flying would do that; he scanned the lineup. "Bear, it's time that I led a MiGCAP north. I'll lead Phantom flight in the morning. They're carrying the new air-to-air missiles."

"Yeah, well, I'm goin' up in a little while, too." Curt Robinson was already scheduled to fly the strike mission later that night, against Mu Gia Pass on the North Vietnamese–Laotian border, the hottest section along the Ho Chi Minh Trail.

Adams scanned the VIP board. "Danforth's got twenty-one counters now, six up in Pack Six."

Robinson caught Adams's surprise at Danforth's progress, "I thought you knew he's been pressing hard. You know, goin' for combat credibility with the pilots. Talk at the bar says he's a good stick, a natural talent."

"No shit," noted Adams. Moving on to other things, he said, "I'm going down to the intell shop and read the debrief report from the Pontiac MiGCAP today. Then I'm racking out. Clean out the Mu Gia Pass tonight."

"Boss, you know I hit everything I can see."

"Yeah, just make sure it's their trucks, not ours."

Robinson proceeded to the briefing room where the other pilots in his two-ship night flight were gathering. His day was just beginning.

2245 hours
The flight line
Ubon RTAFB

Robinson and his GIB, Captain Lew "Condor" Byrd, exited the back of the crew bus. Their F-4 was bathed in floodlights for security and safety reasons. The floodlights were a problem for the pilots. Robinson and Byrd looked curiously out of place because both were wearing sunglasses to save their night vision. They each started into their preflight duties. Night flying was often an unorthodox business. Pilots consciously took more time to perform their functions at night. This made for safer flying operations. After his exterior walkaround, Robinson imbed in the front cockpit. Technical Sergeant Joe East, his crew chief, tollowed him up the ladder and commented, "Sir, I still can't get used to seeing pilots wearing shades at night."

"It's only until we taxi clear of the lighted revetment area. Got any more of that tape?" Robinson took the tape roll from East and added another patch to cover up a white light beaming through his first attempt to mask the caution light panel.

"Thanks, Joe." Bear handed back the roll, took his helmet off the forward canopy rail, and slipped it on his head. It still bore the same distinctive tiger he'd worn on his F-51 Korean War helmet.

East was impressed at the sheer size of Robinson and asked, "Colonel, do you have any trouble getting into the F-4?"

This drew Robinson out of his preoccupation with his cockpit duties. With a grin he replied, "I don't get into a plane, son. I strap it on."

Minutes later, Robinson started the engines of his F-4 and taxied off into the night, heading for Mu Gia Pass.

2330 hours
The Triple Nickel Officers' Hootch
Ubon RTAFB

Mike Nelson lay in the top bunk staring into the blackness. He'd had two more beers, but he couldn't shut out what had happened to his friend and roommate of the last seven years.

He felt the loss most when lying here; he could almost sense Vic turning over in his sleep in the bottom bunk. But something unnatural was closing in on Nelson's sense of loss—anger. Why did it have to be Vic? Why not him?

And the man who'd caused Vic Sansone's death. Colonel Tomb. Nelson couldn't stop thinking about Colonel Tomb. Pilots didn't usually know their killers. Air war was impersonal; an anonymous bullet fired from the jungle, or the shrapnel from some flak laid in a general pattern. Even the cannon fire from a MiG slicing through the formation was fired by a faceless pilot.

But this was different. Nelson believed in his heart that Tomb had taken his best friend's life, and that personalized the whole thing. That just about made it murder. And murder required retribution.

Nelson couldn't forget Cardwell's words outside the O Club. Phuc Yen. And Tomb was the fighter commander. Bar talk said he was their top ace. Tomb had to be very valuable to the NVAF. His loss could be a big blow to their air defense effort. And the younger NVAF pilots would feel it too.

Nelson was angry with himself. He was much too professional to personalize this war. But who would atone for Vic? Nelson had his killer's address: Phuc Yen, Phuc Yen, Phuc Yen. Mike Nelson drifted into a restive sleep. The hum of the air conditioner drowned out everything.

THE EAGLE AND THE DRAGON

17 October 1966 0700 hours
8th TFW Operations Center
Ubon RTAFB

The wing staff meeting was very sober this morning, and the talk was full of yesterday afternoon's events. Cummings's rescue had been a textbook snatch, pulled off in the nick of time. Sansone's loss was tragic.

All the premeeting banter stopped abruptly and inconclusively when Adams arrived and said, "Be seated, gentlemen." The briefing sequence started without further comment. Adams reversed the order of the briefings and got the routine ops and maintenance status briefings out of the way, then he turned to his main area of interest. Major Tom Cardwell was already standing at the front of the room with the yardstick pointer in hand. Adams and his intell officer were getting very familiar with each other. "Good morning, Tom," Adams greeted him.

"Morning, sir. Last night we received a significant update to the North Vietnamese air order of battle. I'd like to go over that today, skipping the routine aggregate sortie counts." Cardwell knew that the daily, weekly, and monthly combat mission totals were merely eyewash that no one would miss. Today's information was far more interesting—and valuable.

"Good. Go ahead, Tom." On that cue, Cardwell squeezed the buzzer he held in his left hand. The intell NCO behind the reverse projection screen threw up the first Vu-graph transparency. It was a high-altitude photograph, obviously taken from a U-2 or one of the other supersecret airborne platforms. Like all intelligence visual aids, this one was plastered with an abundance of classification warnings.

"Sir, this briefing's top secret with the additional classification as shown on this slide. This is Phuc Yen Airfield."

All the people in the room had seen similar photos of MiG airfields, but this one was different. Six shiny MiG-21s occupied the half-dozen revetments along the west side of the runway. Cardwell hit the buzzer again. "And this is Kep. The aircraft array speaks for itself." Again, six MiG-21s were stuffed in the bunkered slots near one end of that airfield. In both photos, the usually prominent green MiG-17s had been jammed in pairs into the lower-priority revetments, those farther from the end of the runways. The older MiG-15s, normally grouped in the more remote aircraft bunkers, were no longer visible on the airfield.

"Sir, these photos—taken two days ago—correlate with the message traffic we received oh-dark-thirty this morning." Cardwell hit the buzzer again. Up came a before-and-after numbers chart.

"Note the North Vietnamese fighter air order of battle has increased by 35 percent in the last ninety days. The NVAF now has twelve MiG-15 UTIs, thirty MiG-17Fs, and fourteen MiG-21PFs. Note that the oldest MiG-15s are gone. Most of the rest are relegated to Yen Bai and Gia Lam. But they're still active. We see them being used as trainers and potential decoys, but little else.

"The NVAF have clearly advanced from a MiG-15/17 force to a MiG-17/21 force. The parking priority given to the MiG-21s in the previous photos shows they are fully operational in serious numbers. Squadron strength and growing. Those twelve MiG-21s are on air defense alert this morning. That translates into a big improvement in both quantity and quality.

"That leads to my main point. Either the NVAF's getting combat-qualified pilots into the MiG-21s faster than we thought they could or they're getting some outside help to fly these new machines."

Slim Danforth interrupted, "What kind of help?"

"Russian, Cuban, or Chinese. We believe, however, that the North Vietnamese won't use this kind of help. There hasn't been any propaganda about their Communist volunteers. And it's not Ho Chi Minh's style. The North Vietnamese favor an image of self-reliance."

Rod Wells voiced his frustration, "Don't we have anybody on the ground up there? Don't the South Vietnamese have any operatives after twelve years of confrontation?"

"You're talking HUMINT. We don't get a breakout on any of that. All we get is the product, not an explanation of who supplied the information. But my assessment's that we don't have a good HUMINT effort going up North. Nothing like we had in World War II. It's more like Korea. Closed society. And if HUMINT's operating, it doesn't focus on the air war very much. I can think of a hundred questions I'd like the HUMINT boys to answer on MiGs, SAMs, AAA, command and control, employment tactics, you name it.

"The products we do get on the air war look like they come from three sources: standoff strategic photo and electronic recon, good old penetrating tac recce, and debriefs from any jock who flies up North. Strategic recon's highly classified, and much of it isn't shared directly with combat units."

Cardwell's statement irritated Rod Wells, "Then what the hell good is it?"

Adams interjected, "Okay, we're not gonna solve the world's intelligence problems here. Tom, what more can you tell us about the pilots and their tactics?"

"Not much new, sir. I'd only be repeating myself. But this type of war, one that gives the NVAF total sanctuary on the ground and all the help they want, makes it hard for us to throw them off balance. The NVAF air defense leaders pick when to engage. And that gives them more time to improvise little surprises that are hard to predict. Stuff like the infrared missiles on the MiG-17s two weeks ago, and the low-altitude defensive circles.

"I do have reports that the MiG-21s that hit Pontiac flight yesterday recovered at Phuc Yen."

"Fat lot of good that does us if we can't close the base. Tomorrow they'll be from Kep." Wells was especially cynical today. He didn't like losing pilots. "Someday you're gonna tell me how you know about the Phuc Yen business, aren't you, Tom?"

"Yessir, if we ever get you operators properly cleared for that information."

Adams gave Cardwell some guidance. "Make sure you brief all the missions on this stuff. And watch the dispatches and our own debriefs, Tom, for any changes in MiG tactics. And work closely with the BIBs in the Tactics Shop."

"BIBs, sir?"

"They'll tell you what it means. Let us know how the NVAF's using its MiG-21s—singly, pairs, or other variations. And how they are using the 17s and 21s in mutual support. Then work up a sequel to this briefing in coordination with the Tactics Shop."

"Yes, sir, will do." Cardwell started to move off center stage when Adams stopped him.

"Speaking of debriefs, how did the NVAF take out Pontiac 03?"

Danforth started to field the question, but Adams stopped him with a hand gesture. "I want to know what the pilots told us at the debrief. Specifically, what did Pontiac 01 have to say?"

Cardwell answered, "Pontiac flight got bounced from behind by a MiG-21 in a decoy squeeze. Two turns later, Pontiac 03 took a gun shot in the belly, and the MiG was gone."

Adams turned to his DCO. "Now, Slim, what were you going to say?"

Danforth was more tentative this time. He didn't want to get caught in a vise. He'd been through enough staff meetings to know when the senior officer was taking the staff somewhere. "Our MiGCAPs hadn't seen any action for more than a week. Then some decoys popped up, and our guys focused on them. That's when the stern attack hit the flight."

"Okay, does anybody have anything else?" A few of the colonels at the main table started to gather up their notebooks and hats, anxious to get on with their day's work.

But Clint Adams wasn't going anywhere just yet. "Well, I have something. Actually, I've got a hell of a lot." The impatient colonels settled back into their chairs.

"We lost a damn good officer and an F-4 yesterday, and we're not really doing anything to compensate for that. We're not even scrubbing down what we *are* doing to see if we *ought* to change anything. Take Cardwell, for example. He just briefed us that the bad guys are turning up the wick. Then I asked him if he had seen any changes in tactics centered on the new infusion of operational MiG-21 capability.

"And what did he say, Slim?" Danforth shrugged his shoulders and started into a tortured response.

Adams interrupted his DCO. Everyone in the briefing room now understood that this would be a one-way conversation—a lecture on how to respond to emerging events up North. Adams told everyone what Cardwell had actually said, "He hasn't seen anything new."

"Then what did *you* say, Slim?" Again, Danforth started to respond, and Adams was on him again. "You just superficially described what happened. Gentlemen, that's how we'll lose more pilots and aircraft.

How many do we have to lose before we get our asses in gear? Two? Four?"

Clint Adams paused. Rod Wells piped up, "The answer is we've lost one too many already, sir."

"Shack! You're dead on target, Rodney."

Wells squirmed a little. He didn't like hearing his full given name. That was the price of speaking up.

Adams continued to push. "Now, let me ask you all a question. How many of you read the debrief report on Pontiac flight?" Only Cardwell raised his hand. "Tom can't do this alone, guys. He's not a tactics expert. He's not a DCO or a squadron commander. And he doesn't plan how we're gonna fly tomorrow's MiGCAP. Remember what I said at the officer's call? If I know more about your job in this wing than you do, you're in deep shit!

"Attention to details, that's what it takes. The damned North Vietnamese are fighting for national survival. They're cunning as hell. They devote every waking minute to knocking our asses out of the sky. Just as we would if someone were bombing California or New Jersey.

"We can't beat 'em with the superficial bullshit I heard here this morning. I read the Pontiac debrief report last night. And this is what my experience tells me.

"First, they lulled us into expecting a standard behavior pattern—that MiGs won't fly when SAMs and AAA are active. Like Indians not fighting at night. Bullshit.

"Second, when they surprised us, we got behind the power curve. We were off balance, just when we were supposed to protect the strike force.

"Third, they threw decoys at us when we were mentally behind—and we took the bait. Even though they use decoys all the time. Decoys behave like decoys! That's a hint! Incidentally, Tom, those were MiG-21 decoys. Does that tell you something about evolving tactics?"

Cardwell shuffled his feet and nodded. Mentally, he kicked himself in the ass for having missed that and not integrating it into this morning's briefing.

"That's when a single MiG pilot attacked four fully armed F-4s and missed, somehow. Still, the NVAF pilot converted to a gun attack and shot down one of our best young ACs when our flight leader exposed his entire formation belly up to the MiG attacking out of the sun.

"Slim, who was the flight leader?"

"Uh, I'll have to—"

"Wells, who was it?"

"Major Willis, sir."

"How long has he been a qualified MiGCAP flight leader in Pack Six?"

"This was his third mission as lead."

"When were the other two?"

"Earlier this week."

"No real heavy contact on those, was there? Is he a good stick in air-to-air?"

"He's okay."

"We just learned for the thousandth time that 'okay' doesn't hack it."

Conclusions turned to directives. "Danforth, I want a top-to-bottom scrub of all our MiGCAP flight leaders. Today. Weed out the weak dicks. We're not givin' people an area checkout to fly cross-country gaggles.

"Next, start a MiGCAP flight leader program with some teeth in it. Today. Teach them what they need to know.

"On tactics. Get the BIBs and their squadron tactics counterparts deeply involved in daily operations. And let's *all* read the postmission debriefs. Get any other engagement reports you can scrounge up from other wings. We're not the only Swinging Richards fighting up North.

"Set up a mechanism for reacting rapidly to what we learn. No 8th TFW sortie should go to Pack Six without knowing the kind of detailed tactical response we need to do our mission and stay alive. Details followed by more details.

"Are the MiG pilots getting smarter? Hell yes they are! So we better not fly up North with our heads up our asses!

"When I hear that a single MiG has the balls to attack four of us, it makes my blood boil. When I hear he stays around for a converted gun attack, I'm embarrassed for the whole lot of us.

"Now listen to me carefully." He paused. "We didn't get bounced by a MiG. We got bounced by a MiG *pilot*! Machines don't conceive and execute these interceptions—men do. Cardwell, got any clues into the *men* behind yesterday's operation?"

"Actually, yes, sir. But I wouldn't say 'men,' I'd say 'man.' We studied yesterday's events and correlated them with debriefs from previous 8th TFW aircrew shootdowns. Our assessment's that Colonel Tomb did the attack. And he probably planned it too."

Danforth said, "Major, not that Tomb business again. You have no way of proving that."

"Hold on, Slim. Let Cardwell talk. He's probably read more reports and message traffic than all of us combined. Go ahead, Tom."

Danforth slipped back into his chair, vowing not to open his mouth and get Adams's foot in it again.

"Pontiac 03 was the third 8th TFW shootdown by a fast moving bogey from the deep six o'clock. We haven't had the time to check actual numbers, but there's been other such attacks where the shooter missed. Actually, Tomb missed yesterday on the missile attack. This tactic matches a half-dozen reports we've received on the possible existence of Colonel Tomb."

Adams built on the symbiosis he had with Cardwell, "And it squares with the initial brief I got at Seventh Air Force. Go on."

"Well, sir, there's not much more I can add."

"Okay. It's a good start. Shows you're applying the kind of mental elbow grease we need to beat this Colonel Tomb and his pilots. I believe that when we start working together more closely we'll find other nuggets in some of your reports, Tom. Get the BIBs involved in going over your reports. Share your inclinations and gut feelings with them too."

"Yes sir."

"And let me give you and the ops staff a place to start." Adams held up his index finger. "One. Find a way to counter the 'Tomb Maneuver,' the deep-six attack."

Then Adams held up two fingers. "Two. Devise some means to break up the 'defensive wheel.' There are lots of vulnerable apprentice MiG pilots turning around in those daisy wheels."

Danforth nodded. "Yes sir."

"And work it out in time to brief up tomorrow's MiGCAP flights. It's too late for today's missions."

"And everyone at this table better do everything possible to foster what's needed. Get the message, Slim?" Danforth clenched his jaw and nodded. In the end, he couldn't avoid this spear in the chest. It was inevitable. All the key players—intell, tactics, and Rod Wells—worked directly for him. If they screwed up, he screwed up.

"Now, let's get our damned shit into one sock and keep it there." Adams got up and left for his premission briefing. He was the next MiGCAP flight leader in the barrel.

0755 hours
Wing commander's office

On his way to Operations, Adams popped back into the office for a quick review of the morning message file. He flipped through the inch-thick stack of teletype dispatches, scanning the titles for the most pertinent subjects to Ubon and the wing.

"You don't give a shit about me, do you?"

Adams looked up, momentarily startled to see a red-faced Slim Danforth closing the door behind him. "What did you say?"

"You heard me, dammit," Danforth continued. "You and Robinson are the only fighter pilots with the answers. Trash your DCO in front of the whole wing, what does it matter?"

"I'll chew you out if you don't know your stuff. Out here, it's not who looks good, it's who lives to fight tomorrow," Adams countered.

"You're not the only one who cares about America winning this war and our pilots not getting killed. You think the rest of us are just sleepwalking through the whole damn thing.

"I remember you from the Pentagon. 'Clint the Crusader' they called you, but you weren't very effective," said Danforth angrily. "You never really got anything done. Finally, they had pity on you and sent you back to where you were good—wing operations in the UK.

"You see those Phantoms out there?" Danforth pointed to the revetments. "I did more to get those fighters on the ramp than you ever did. You could be flyin' Navy F-8s instead of F-4s up North today if I hadn't turned around a group of elite eggheads one Friday night on E-Ring. You'd gone home by then, moaning about pushin' papers when you should have been flyin' fighters. Everybody else's an uncaring asshole, right?

"And just in case you didn't know, I'll tell you something else. The secretary liked to see the new wing commander assignments too. When your Lakenheath nomination came across my desk, it had some 'no' votes and negative comments on it from some of those generals you'd tangled with. I pulled the notes, and the secretary concurred in your assignment. I knew you stunk as a staff officer, but I also knew you were effective in the air. Christ, I never thought it would end up like this."

"I'm not not gonna give you an award for doin' your job, Slim," interjected Adams.

"It takes all kinds of colonels to put air power in the air. This isn't my strong suit out here. Operations, I mean. I didn't ask for this job, but I'm doing the best I know how. And Colonel, if that's not good enough, then shove it up your ass." With that, Danforth threw Adams a crisp salute and left.

For a few seconds Adams digested the mixed emotions he felt. Then he came down on the side of wonderment. Damn, he thought. This outburst and flying into Pack Six too. Slim may have a backbone after all. The son of a bitch had possibilities, Adams thought. But the question was whether the war would allow Danforth time to realize them.

One thing was certain, Adams decided. When the war was over, men like Danforth would be back in the Pentagon, doing what they did best.

Then Clint Adams remembered that he had a mission to fly. Maybe he'd been wrong about Danforth. Maybe not.

0815 hours
The aircrew briefing area
8th TFW HQ, Ubon RTAFB

Clint Adams hated being late for anything. It irritated him for his men to see that. Still, he wouldn't apologize outright. "Office business. Let's press on."

The ops duty officer started his briefing to Adams and the other members of Buick flight. Major Roscoe Stewart, freed from TOC duties and back full time in Triple Nickel, was Adams's wingman today. Stewart would give Adams his Pack Six flight lead checkout.

Adams felt good about the lineup. Roscoe was an old hand in Pack Six with thirty-five missions over the Red River Valley. Buick would support an F-105 strike on the Northeast Railway, one of two key umbilical cords connecting Hanoi to China. Their target today was a transshipment point 30 miles northeast of the capital, very near Kep Airfield.

The ops briefer reminded Buick flight that the Northeast Railway was always a tough go. The NVAF protected it with a vengeance. The ops briefer highlighted the weapons loading, "Buick 01 and 03 will carry the Air Force's newest heat-seeking air-to-air missile, the AIM-4D Falcon. Buick 02 and 04 will carry the older AIM-9 Sidewinder heat-seekers. All four planes will have four AIM-7 Sparrow radar missiles."

The 8th TFW pilots had been getting information briefings on the Falcon for the past two weeks. The briefer continued, "Ubon's the first operational base to get the Falcons, produced by Norris Aerospace Corporation. This will be the first combat mission for the AIM-4D. It's being touted as a real improvement over the Sidewinder because it has much better high-G turning capability. And the missile has a supercooled argon gas seeker head, which is much more sensitive to heat sources in the jet engine's infrared frequency range."

The pilots were anxious to try the Falcon in a real MiG engagement. They'd been told all about the Falcon's superior performance during operational tests at the Eglin Missile Test Range in the Gulf of Mexico. The missile was so accurate it actually clipped the flares off the target drones' wingtips, even when the drones were in high-G turns and maneuvering in hazy conditions.

The missile was being rushed into combat service to help in the air war over North Vietnam in an attempt by Air Force leaders to compensate with high technology for the absence of a nose-mounted air-to-air cannon in the F-4. The two element leaders in Buick flight, those most likely to have shots at the enemy, would carry the Falcon into battle today. Clint Adams in Buick 01 and Roscoe Stewart would have the chance to fire the AIM-4D in combat for the first time.

Taco Martinez was Adams's GIB today, but he was skeptical of the AIM-4D Falcon. Taco was wary of anything that he didn't know much about.

1030 hours
Sixty miles northwest of Hanoi

Adams had Buick flight positioned between the strike force and the MiG airfields to the south. After several feints toward lower priority targets, the strike force now moved decisively toward the Northeast Railway. Buick flight jettisoned their external fuel tanks and entered the battle mean and clean.

1031 hours
Kep Airfield
Forty kilometers northeast of Hanoi

The alert klaxon sounded for a scramble. Three younger pilots raced past Colonel Tomb to their MiG-21s. Tomb donned his gloves as he trotted briskly to his own favorite aircraft, a green MiG-17. His crew chief saluted him and quickly removed the ladder after Tomb climbed into the cramped cockpit. In seconds, Tomb signaled for engine start.

1035 hours
Thirty miles northeast of Hanoi

Today's target area was bristling with AAA. Adams watched the lead four-ship in the strike force, Parkhouse flight, start its bomb run right into the teeth of intense 57mm and 85mm flak.

He thought, How can the bad guys miss? The stuff's really thick going down the chute today. The 57s detonated all around the F-105s, leaving a gray residual cloud, while the larger 85s went off with a red-orange fireball.

Because the transshipment point was close to Kep Airfield, Adams expected MiG activity today. He didn't see any on the way in, so he was sure Buick would see MiGs on the way out. Adams looked down on Kep and noted to Taco in the backseat, "What a juicy target. You can see the MiGs in their revetments, but the revetments closest to the runway are empty. That's where the air defense alert birds were, before they scrambled. Shit, what a way to fight a war. Be alert, Taco."

Adams vividly remembered the offensive counterair missions he had flown in World War II, attacking the Luftwaffe airfields. Allied tactical fighters chewed up the German aircraft on the ground much worse than they did in the air. The very last place you wanted to meet a fighter was in the air, when it was buttoned up with a trained pilot at the controls trying to kill you. On the ground, an empty fighter was a piece of inanimate, defenseless junk.

If the MiGs were indeed up, Adams knew they'd have the advantage of attacking out of the morning's sunlight and haze. He could sense it. He wondered why the Saigon mission planners kept scheduling strikes so the sun always favored the enemy.

Parkhouse flight was moving away from the worst of the flak zone, all bombs on target. The F-105s were down sun to Adams and the rest of Buick flight, and he squinted into the sun. The morning haze was especially milky and troublesome today.

Adams finally picked up the eight F-105s climbing out of the soupy haze at his three o'clock position, right where he expected to see them. All the pilots were scanning with no verbal chatter.

Adams saw it first this time. A glint of sunlight off the canopy of an unidentified plane, eight o'clock high. U.S. Navy planes frequented the area, so Adams had to determine if this target were friend or foe before firing.

"Buick, break it up." The four-ship formation quickly split into two two-ship elements. Buick 01 and 02 broke hard left and low, executing a high-speed reversal to change direction as quickly as possible while keeping their Mach up. The second element, 03 and 04, executed a high-speed yo-yo, a more leisurely nose-high reversal that traded some airspeed for increased altitude and a better viewing angle down into the sunlit haze. These two maneuvers changed Buick flight into two very different, widely separated, but mutually supporting, fighter sections.

"Got 'em on the scope, Taco?"

"Roger, sir. Full logic." Taco Martinez locked his radar onto the first of the two bogeys that he had acquired while Adams was racking their F-4 through the five-G maneuver they had just completed. But Buick 01 still required a visual ID before shooting a missile at the target. Frustrating. Critical seconds passed. Unless Adams could ID this bogey as a MiG in the next few seconds, he'd forfeit the Phantom's radar-missile, front-quadrant attack advantage. Buick 01 would be too close for a radar missile shot, and at the wrong angle for a heat-seeker shot. Almost nose on.

"Can't make 'em out yet, Taco. Could be the Navy." The two bogeys advanced far enough off the sun angle for Adams to be almost sure, then gave themselves away by rolling into a hard right turn to attack the F-105s. Adams's experience told him they had to be MiGs.

The MiGs hadn't noticed the maneuvering F-4s yet. "Some days you just get lucky," Adams said out loud.

Based on pure geometry, Buick 03, breaking high, had the best chance for the visual ID. The delta-wing profile of the MiG-21s was unmistakable now to the pilots in Buick 03 and 04. "Buick flight, bogies are MiGs. Bogies are MiG-21s. Copy, Lead?"

Adams didn't wait for 03's transmission to end. He followed the ID by launching one, then a second AIM-7 Sparrow missile. The two radar-homing missiles accelerated off Adams's F-4, which was sitting nicely in the MiGs' eight o'clock position. Both missiles tracked smoothly, barely turning at all on their 4-mile journey to their intended target, the MiG element leader. Adams grunted in the intercom, "The missiles doin' well, Taco."

A classic missile kill was in the making. Beautiful to watch. All Adams needed now was proximate missile detonation. There it was! The first Sparrow exploded just beyond the leading MiG, spraying its lethal pattern of steel flechettes into the belly of the Russian-built jet fighter.

The injured plane immediately belched black smoke. The MiG porpoised through several cycles. Finally, the plane exploded, strewing hot metal fragments onto the countryside below.

"Splash One, Buick Lead."

Adams didn't wait to see if the NVAF pilot ejected. Getting transfixed on a target almost guaranteed the enemy a successful counterpunch. He transitioned immediately to the second MiG-21 and pulled into a nose-high turn to counter the very tight nose-low turn of the remaining MiG.

"Still with me, Taco? We can turn with this puppy." Martinez grunted back under the G-load. Adams knew MiG-21s were incredibly maneuverable above 20,000 feet, but these MiGs came below that threshold to make a high-speed missile attack up the stern of the departing Thuds. This was now a dogfight where the F-4s could turn effectively with the MiG-21, down at 15,000 feet. As long as the remaining MiG maneuvered near the horizontal plane, Adams could use his superior training and experience and the F-4's overwhelming engine power to dogfight with the NVAF pilot.

As Adams worked himself into the rear quadrant of the lone MiG-21, the North Vietnamese pilot had to see that Adams had gained a good missile firing position. The MiG driver tried a last-ditch effort by pulling his delta-winged interceptor very hard back into and underneath Clint Adams.

It was the MiG pilot's top percentage play, providing him the best chance of keeping the pursuing F-4 offset just enough to deny Adams a missile shot. And perhaps Adams would make a mistake.

No chance. Adams had actually gained a better shooting angle throughout the high-G turning maneuver. During this sequence, Adams had selected his heat-seeking missiles by feel. "Don't take your eyes off the target, don't take your eyes off the target," he kept repeating. Losing your target at this critical juncture could mean more than squandering an aerial victory. It could mean that you became the target. Adams was ready to fire the first AIM-4D in actual combat.

He heard a low, soft tone in his headset. "It must take a little longer for the argon gas seeker head to cool itself down to optimum effectiveness," Adams growled to Martinez. So he waited. Why not? The MiG was cooperating. A few more seconds passed. The tone seemed to build up a little, indicating slightly better target tracking by the missile.

"Goddammit." Adams regretted that he hadn't selected AIM-4D seeker-head tracking sooner in the attack. He decided to creep lower in the MiG's rear quadrant to help the missile get a better contrast between the target and its background. It shouldn't be necessary, according to the damn brochures. But what the hell, the MiG pilot was still cooperating. Adams strained to put the MiG above the horizon, but the MiG started turning back into the morning sun. This favorable shooting angle wouldn't last much longer.

Adams fired his first Falcon. "Fox Two, Taco." The Falcon missile frittered off to the right, against the turn. America's first AIM 4-D attack was an unguided dud.

"Son of a bitch!" cried Taco into the intercom.

Adams experienced the same audio pattern with the second missile. He fired it anyway. "Fox Two."

Same result, almost. This Falcon exploded about 3,000 feet after launch. Not very good. By putting the MiG above the horizon, Adams gave the enemy pilot a turning advantage over the pursuing F-4s. The North Vietnamese pilot was using it well as he tightened his turn passing through the sun, a very smart move. Adams went nose-high again and barely regained a shooting angle. He fired his third AIM-4 missile.

The Falcon's performance startled Adams. "Crap!" It, too, failed to guide. The sweat dripping from his forehead was beginning to impair Adams's eyesight. Time to use the backup plan briefed at Ubon.

Buick 02 would fire at the MiG. Major Roscoe Stewart's F-4 carried four AIM-9 Sidewinders.

"Buick 02, he's yours." Roscoe Stewart had had a loud growl in his earphones throughout the whole sequence. He'd been waiting for just such a chance, like a linebacker who saw a pass coming and knew he could grab it and run for a touchdown.

Stewart's finger squeezed the missile trigger, launching an AIM-9 Sidewinder immediately. A second squeeze and a second Sidewinder leaped off the rail one second later. Both missiles tracked. "Fox Two, Fox Two," Stewart called into the intercom.

The first AIM-9 struck the MiGs tailpipe, and the aft end of the MiG exploded. The pilot ejected and popped out safely under a green parachute canopy incredibly fast. The second missile flew right through the debris and detonated just beyond it.

Adams exulted, "Splash One MiG, Buick 02. Thanks for the backup."

Adams quickly looked for other action. He located Buick 03 and 04 flying level near the horizon about 5 miles away, and the strike force, still in formation, about 10 miles beyond the MiGCAP Phantoms. Adams quickly closed on their part of the sky; protecting the F-105s was still top priority.

Then Taco Martinez spotted two more MiG-21s lurking at 10 miles. "Buick 01, two more bogies, eight o'clock level."

Tomb heard this American radio call. He was trying to sneak in on the strike force when the MiGCAP was occupied. But he got caught. He no longer had the leverage of surprise, and an F-105 could turn into an attacker and hose him with his 20mm cannon. So Tomb just tracked parallel to the strike force, 10 miles to the south, much like a hungry hyena waiting for a weak animal to appear so he could pounce on it.

Tomb concluded that all hope of further attack had vanished as the American flight leader rejoined the MiGCAP. Buick 01 would attempt a radar missile attack on him if he continued to parallel the American force. The NVAF ace broke hard left and exited to the south. By leaving now, he knew the F-4s would not pursue him because the Americans were low on fuel and had to leave the area for Thailand.

Again, the Americans had had the best of the day's doings, by killing two MiG-21s and protecting the main strike force so it could bomb the railroad transshipment yard. As he returned to Kep, Tomb thought of the American flight leader today. The American knew exactly how to take out the lead MiGs. If that pilot's missiles had worked properly, the American flight leader would have dispatched both MiGs quite handily. Tomb wondered who the pilot was. "Have I faced him before?"

They didn't know it, but the Dragon and the Eagle had met a second time. Again, the Eagle had won the day.

1115 hours
Kep Airfield
Forty kilometers northeast of Hanoi

Tomb stormed away from his plane. Major Duc Van Do, his chief of maintenance, met him on the airplane ramp and saluted.

"Colonel, will the other two aircraft be returning today?" It was a natural question; NVAF pilots often compensated for the limited range of their MiGs by stretching their fuel, then recovering at the nearest available base.

Tomb stopped and stared at him without saying anything. Major Duc nodded submissively, knowing what this meant. Tomb then caught himself and consoled his key assistant by placing his hand on the major's shoulder.

"The Russians will supply all the aircraft we can use. The pilots, my friend, are another matter entirely." Tomb walked on, hoping he would learn later that both NVAF pilots had ejected safely.

Colonel Arkov met Tomb in front of the modest command building. "Good hunting today, Colonel?"

This irked Tomb because he knew Arkov had more details than he did about this morning's aerial engagements. Arkov usually observed the air battles at the nearby GCI radar site.

A rain shower was passing over the airfield so the two men continued inside. Tomb asked his administrative clerk to summon Lieutenant Vu Ngoc, his intelligence officer.

Arkov had no qualms about telling Tomb the bad news. "One pilot, the wingman, ejected, but he's badly burned." He got a certain satisfaction from this. He knew that Tomb was very attached to his pilots. When one of them was injured or killed, it gave Arkov further justification to push for Soviet pilots in the NVAF attack formations.

"Colonel, I would be honored to be your new element leader." Tomb said nothing but reflected that this was the first time Arkov had ever referred to honor.

"Together, you and I can teach the Americans some bitter lessons. And the Americans will never know."

Tomb had always rejected this idea out of hand in the past. Yet the concept of two high-caliber pilots feeding on the American formations was intriguing. This time he thought about it longer. Tomb had observed Arkov's natural cunning and aviator skills during the training flights. But Tomb dismissed this line of thought. If the Russian ever tasted American blood he would be absolutely insufferable. He was barely tolerable now.

"But I will know, Arkov. No, Colonel, the time is not yet right for such action. Just help me train more pilots for now."

The Russian noted that Tomb did not categorically reject his idea this time. For Arkov, it was an important change.

Lieutenant Ngoc, Tomb's arrogant young intelligence officer, knocked on the door sill.

"Come in, Lieutenant." Tomb's tone was brusque.

Ngoc bowed forward as he saluted. The Russian drifted off into the corner, lighting a Turkish cigarette.

Tomb gave an order. "Lieutenant, I want you to find out who led the American fighter protection flight today."

"The U.S. Air Force pilots call it MiGCAP," said Ngoc. "I believe that will be easy to find out."

"Tell me as soon as you can."

Tomb dismissed Ngoc, but the younger officer lingered. He was anxious to add something. "My pardons, Colonel. The pilot of the Phantom you destroyed yesterday? Your eleventh victory?"

"Yes?"

"His name was Captain Sansone. He had no air victories. A somewhat new arrival in the 555th Squadron at Ubon."

"I see. Thank you, Ngoc."

The intelligence officer bowed and left. Tomb then wandered to the window and looked skyward. He, too, lit a cigarette. Still looking out the window, he remarked to his Soviet adviser, "Today's American flight leader was very capable, a man of considerable experience. But he had very unreliable missiles."

Arkov would report this to General Borin in Hanoi.

1200 hours
Aircraft parking area
Ubon RTAFB

Adams unstrapped from his ejection seat. Sergeant Chris Cole had seen the victory roll, and he leaped up the ladder, anxious to get the news.

"That was our victory roll this time, wasn't it, sir?"

Adams confirmed it.

"Congratulations, Colonel."

Adams removed his helmet, and the two men shook hands. Adams was preoccupied, and he quickly started climbing out of the cockpit. Cole backed out of the way onto the top of the engine intake to let Adams step down the ladder. Adams stopped at the bottom rung and looked up at Cole.

"Sergeant, #680 performed well again." The young man beamed as he climbed down the ladder after Adams, and he pressed for a few more facts.

"Can I paint a red star on the plane?"

"Yeah, go ahead." Adams was unzipping his lower-body G-suit.

"What kind of MiG did we get?"

"MiG-21." Adams started moving off to the waiting crew bus.

"What kind of missile did we use on the shootdown?"

Adams stopped dead in his tracks and turned. Cole knew that he had struck a nerve as Adams said, "The first of two Sparrows got the kill. Those damned AIM-4Ds were just expensive duds."

As Adams got ready to board the dark blue step van, Colonel Pop Brewer pulled up in his jeep to congratulate the boss but saw his boss was tightjawed. After quick congratulations, smiles evaporated as Adams got to the point straight away. "Crate up the AIM-4D Falcons and send them home."

Pop Brewer asked for clarification, not believing what he'd heard. "What's the problem, sir?"

"Today."

So ended the initial combat experience of the AIM-4D.

1400 hours
Wing commander's office
Ubon RTAFB

Adams was clearing out some paperwork, mostly officer efficiency reports and recommendations for combat medals. He heard a commotion in his outer office. "What's going on out there, Boomer?"

Boomer came to the door, "Mr. Byron Watson wants to see you, Colonel." Adams had been expecting this visit from the on-scene technical representative for Norris Aerospace. He was the company man who was supposed to help the Air Force keep Norris equipment working. Today had become his worst nightmare. Adams told Boomer to send in Watson.

Watson brushed past the young exec, and said excitedly, "Colonel, did you really shelve the AIM-4s?"

"That's right."

Watson tried to take the offensive, challenging Adams's decision, "I'm Watson, the Norris tech rep. Colonel, if anyone has a problem with a Norris missile at Ubon, I should be consulted first."

Adams fired back, "I know who you are, and I should've been told the damn things don't work!"

Watson drew a deep breath and used a more reasonable tone. "You know what I mean, Colonel. If something doesn't work as advertised, the Norris team needs to check out the cause. It could be a mechanical, or perhaps even an operator error. After all, the missile performed so well in the tests back in the States."

"It doesn't work here in Thailand. Takes too long to acquire the target. The three missiles I fired never warmed up."

"Perhaps you weren't within parameters. We could set up more training. Operator error is often at the heart of our missile misfires."

Watson's second use of the term "operator error" got Adams up. He walked over to Watson and stood directly in front of the thirty-year-old contractor employee, towering over him. "Look, you little pissant, if it were legal, I'd make you ride in the backseat of every F-4 equipped with the AIM-4D until the son of a bitch worked smoothly. Unfortunately, I can't allow that, but I can decide which missiles our crews carry into battle. The Falcon missile ain't one of them. Not until you and the Air Force testers fix it."

"But, Colonel, those missiles tested out okay this morning."

"They failed the only exam that matters. I suggest that you accompany the remaining missiles back to the Norris factory and personally convey my message to the president of your company. You can tell him to shove those missiles up his ass!"

"That's not very funny."

"No, it's not. It's a shame that the American taxpayer paid good money for those duds. Good afternoon," he said, as he ushered the tech rep into the outer office and closed his door.

Watson looked at Boomer, rearranged his shirt, and stomped out of the office.

2015 hours

Slim Danforth had come into the main bar fifteen minutes ago and worked some informal office business with some of his staff officers. Now he was tiring of the barroom banter, and he wanted nothing to do with Clint Adams, who was holding court at the other end of the bar. Not after this morning. Danforth wandered off to his regular table in the back corner, where some pilots went to have a burger with their cold beer. Danforth sat at the small round table, alone, as usual.

A middle-aged civilian leaned against the bar, waiting for his beer and still perspiring from his walk over from the VOQ. Usually, the only civilians at the bar were the technical representatives that worked for the defense contractors who made the military equipment used by the Air Force at Ubon. But this civilian was not a regular. After sucking in the first satisfying gulp from a fresh Budweiser longneck, he turned and scanned the room. He saw a familiar face at a corner table. "Jeez, Slim Danforth," he mumbled in disbelief.

The newcomer had graying hair, was on the bad side of fifty, and was losing the battle of the waistline. He was wearing a war correspondent's standard issue—olive-drab cotton shirt and matching tan pants, all with too many pockets, that looked like they came from an RAF rummage sale. He picked up his beer and walked over to Danforth's table.

"Well, Sylvester Danforth. You're a long way from the Potomac."

"Massey? Is that you?" Danforth squinted in the dimly lit, smoke-filled corner. "Didn't recognize you without a suit and tie. Still stinking up the Pentagon press corps for the *Post*?"

"No, now it's Tom Massey, war correspondent for the *Washington Monthly*, writing for the capital's elite."

"Give me a break, Massey." Danforth said with a sense of pleasure. "You finally found your niche, wedged in between stories on the charms of downtown Manassas and the Smithsonian's upcoming African art festival."

"Let's just say the *Post* and I had journalistic differences," Massey admitted but quickly went on the offensive. "You look like shit, Slim, and those flying coveralls aren't your style if I remember right. You were always spit and polish." Massey's comments cut Danforth down to size. He was still smarting over the reaming that Adams had given him the day before.

The two men finally got around to shaking hands, although Danforth didn't get up. "Looks like we're both a little out of our element. Mind if I join you?" asked Massey.

"Do I have a choice?" Danforth countered, unimpressed with Massey's feeble attempt at bonding. They had known each other back in Washington, but they weren't friends. Men like Danforth and Massey didn't really have friends; they just knew people.

"This is a long way from E-Ring in the Pentagon. Actually, I'd heard they'd sent you out here to be a wing DCO. How long have you been in country?"

"Since early May."

"My sources say that the Air Force recently changed commanders here. I thought a 'comer' like you would've moved up. You need to start turning this war into your first general's star. How old are you now?" This last remark made Slim uneasy but left him an opening.

"I've got plenty of time. Probably go back to the Pentagon from here, then get promoted," Danforth said, trying to rationalize his current situation in the only way he knew how. But he gave up. "Actually, Tom, you're right, I should have gotten this wing last month." As Danforth spoke, he narrowed his eyes and peered across the room toward the bar, where Adams and Robinson were surrounded by young pilots. Massey wasn't expecting this turn in the conversation, but he decided to see where Danforth was going.

Then, all at once, an idea came to Danforth. Until now, he'd been undermining Adams through his friends on the Seventh Air Force staff at Tan Son Nhut. But he wasn't making much progress that way. Why not work on the home front as well? After all, this was a strange war. Two fronts were better than one, especially the one that he considered his strongest suit. The strings back home stretched across the Pacific, thanks in large part to the news media. Massey might just be a convenient key to those strings.

The two men started talking about the 8th TFW's recent exploits. Slowly, Danforth turned the conversation toward Adams and how he had commanded the wing so far. Massey saw this new direction as a fertile opportunity. This was a rare chance, having a wing DCO open up and give the straight poop about the internal workings of a combat fighter wing. Massey smelled a story.

Danforth said, "Adams's leadership is unorthodox. The wing is close to the brink, right on the edge of doing something extraordinarily stupid. Adams runs the wing like a cowboy; long on splash, short on results. Discipline is declining across the whole base. I'm concerned that lax discipline in the combat zone brings trouble. He also seems more interested in partying with his pilots at the O Club than in flying out the missions as directed by the highest levels in government back in Washington."

This last point was the hook that set in Massey's brain. Danforth saw it and capitalized on it. "Adams sets a bad example for his pilots by questioning the wisdom of his superiors' decisions in Saigon and Washington. And he does it for all to see."

"You know," interjected Massey, "that was a bad thing that happened down at Korat last week. That vice wing commander deserved to get fired and a lot worse."

"Got to live by the rules and regulations, Massey. That's what the military's all about, isn't it?" Danforth said, sipping on a fresh beer.

"That's why I'm moving around the combat wings, Slim. I'm doing a story on the civilian-military line of authority. You know, do our field commanders have the self-discipline to fight these dirty little wars the way Washington wants them fought, regardless of the consequences?"

"I bet you're not real popular when you bring that up."

"Haven't mentioned it to anyone up 'til now, but you know the score, Slim. I'm working a deadline for next month's issue." Massey thought that he might have something here at Ubon—a political incident about to happen. He told Danforth, "It could be big news if a wing commander crosses the line. Something like that could break the whole combat theater wide open and lead to a career purge of all the key commanders in Southeast Asia. I respect your ability to read this kind of situation, with your Pentagon background and all."

Danforth feigned reluctance and discomfort. Lowering his voice and leaning forward, he continued, "There's a close-hold, hush-hush operation in the wind."

"Is it classified?"

"Yes, of course."

"I know you can't tell me much, but just tell me this. Is it aimed at a target on the restricted list?" Massey was buying the whole story. After all, Danforth was the wing DCO. Massey didn't know he had an ax to grind.

Shaking his head and appearing uncomfortable with what he had already said, Danforth pushed further, "Tom, I can't tell you that. But I can tell you one thing. This is Adams's idea. All of the detailed planning is being done right here by one pilot on my staff. Keeps it very limited. Just a few people involved."

"You mean he's taking the lead on something like that at this level of command?"

Danforth looked into his almost empty bottle, then replied, "I can't say anymore. Just observe what's going on around you while you're here. Draw your own conclusion."

At the bar, Adams, Robinson, and some of the younger pilots were again lamenting the personal drawbacks of limited war. Snake Cummings brought up a not-so-old wound. "If we could strike the enemy airfields and radars, Colonel, Vic Sansone and other pilots like him would be alive today."

Whale Wharton let the beer do his talking, "You're goddamned right. When are those pussies gonna let us kick some ass?" Others nodded in agreement. Massey soaked it all in as he looked at Danforth. Danforth only stared back.

A shadowy figure in a sweaty flight suit slammed down his glass beer mug. A geyser of beer shot straight up and splashed down on the bar. It was Mike Nelson. Moose Peterson patted his AC on the back as Nelson turned to Adams and asked, "Colonel, why do we have to fight this lousy air war on the enemy's terms? Why did we have to lose Vic Sansone?"

Adams tried to give them a little something, "Hang in there. We're planning a surprise to address the situation up North."

Massey thought Adams meant something sinister—striking a target on the White House restricted list. Sometimes two plus two equaled five. Danforth watched Massey's eyes follow Adams out of the bar. Game, set, and match.

Lin May was listening too.

DROPPING THE GAUNTLET

Cadillac and Chevy flights gathered for the intell and operations briefings before their MiGCAP this morning. The 555th would fly Cadillac and have the primary CAP duty. Randy Starbuck, in Cadillac 01, would lead. The 433rd would man Chevy flight, the secondary CAP four-ship.

Major Tom Cardwell started his pitch, and Starbuck noted that it had a greater tactical focus than the same briefings had had only four days earlier. It ought to. Colonel Danforth had turned up the wick on countertactics after Sansone got shot down earlier this week.

Cardwell had worked with Randy and his BIBs all day yesterday as part of Danforth's new tiger team. Randy found that Cardwell was a wealth of detailed information. And he knew whom to call throughout Southeast Asia to get more. Starbuck's workload was increasing fast because of planning for Bolo, Tomb maneuvers, and defensive circles. He had asked the DCO to add three more pilots to his Tactics Shop, one from each squadron. To his surprise, Colonel Danforth made it happen immediately. But Randy was getting paranoid, because a full-fledged ops-level division at wing headquarters rated a major as chief, not a captain. His days might be numbered as head of the BIBs.

Starbuck liked the countertactics that the tiger team had worked out, and he thought they'd work. Colonel Adams asked yesterday if the MiGCAP had had a chance to employ them. Not yet. But Seventh Air

Force had to be satisfied: the Thuds had been reaching their targets without being attacked by the MiGs. Bombs on target.

Starbuck and the other 8th TFW pilots wanted more than that. They wanted to take apart the NVAF's growing MiG threat. At any other time, any other Air Force would have been able to do just that.

This morning's lineup looked strong again. The flights going North would be strong from now on. Another outcome of the wing staff meeting of 18 October had been Rod Wells's downgrading of seven flight leaders until he was satisfied that they could lead MiGCAP formations in Route Pack Six. The remaining MiGCAP flight leaders were taking up the slack by leading CAPs more often.

Randy Starbuck preferred it that way for now. He tried out all the new tactics first anyway, and there would be a strong Tactics Shop presence North until the 8th TFW pilots wrung out the new procedures.

Taco Martinez was his GIB today and was the 555th's new pilot in the Wing Tactics Shop. The two men only broke up now when one of them flew with the wing commander.

Mike Nelson and Moose Peterson would lead the second element as Cadillac 03. These two had rapidly come into their own in Pack Six. Boomer Wright, now paired with Snake Cummings, would be Cadillac 04.

0815 hours
The 555th crew briefing room

Randy Starbuck had finished leading Cadillac and Chevy flights through the detailed premission tactics and procedures briefing that always followed the formal intell, weather, and duty ops briefings. As the pilots filed out of the briefing room, Tom Cardwell waited in the main hallway outside the intelligence vault, essentially a large room that could be sealed like a walk-in bank safe used for maximum security. He signaled to Mike Nelson and Moose Peterson. "Can I see you fellas in here?"

They followed Cardwell into the vault, and Mike Nelson said, "We've been talking about what you said the other night and—"

Knowing that the pilots didn't have much time before they had to move out to their aircraft, Cardwell interrupted, "I wanna show you something that just came in. It's unclassified, but it fits with what we were talking about."

Cardwell laid a foreign newspaper clipping on the waist-high counter running along one wall of the vault, and Nelson picked it up. The article had a picture in it of a Navy F-4 lying in a rice paddy surrounded by some Vietnamese.

Nelson recognized the language, but didn't see the connection, and said, "Thanks, sir, but I didn't take Italian at the Academy."

"Our intelligence analysts are all in a lather over this. First, the Gomers have an intelligence windfall. They're going to learn a lot about the F-4 because this plane didn't crash and burn."

Moose interjected. "The Russians will trade the Gomers three squadrons of MiGs for this F-4."

"Probably more than that," Cardwell added. "But don't you eagle-eyed pilots see anything else?"

Nelson and Peterson gave the picture another scan, then shook their heads.

"It's only a guess, but I think that's Colonel Tomb in the front cockpit."

The pilots checked the grainy picture again; the photo was taken about 100 feet away from the plane to get the entire aircraft in the picture. Nelson and Peterson could barely tell that someone was in the front cockpit. Moose couldn't help himself and teased, "I know you intell guys are good, but you're not that good."

"You're right. No, look at the article."

Nelson scanned it. Near the end, he saw the word "Tomb." As he looked at Cardwell, the major handed him the translation.

> *L'Unita*—HANOI, Oct. 5, 1966—The American Air Force lost three more planes today as they attacked the farm villagers in the pastoral countryside south of Hanoi.
>
> A two-man crew was taken prisoner by the North Vietnamese peasant farmers when their Phantom plane splashed into a rice paddy near An Hoa in the Phatdiem agricultural district. The reserve flak gunner, Nguyen Van Than, assigned to the 59th People's Anti-aircraft Battery and a resident of a nearby village brought down the plane this morning as it was strafing unarmed field workers 5 kilometers from here.
>
> The plane is now being studied by military experts for valuable information. Even noted NVAF pilot, Colonel Nguyen Tomb, toured the crash site and studied the airplane's systems before he returned to Hanoi several hours later with valuable information on the American plane.
>
> The North Vietnamese authorities have transported the pilots to a secure area, where they are being treated humanely.

Nelson handed the English version to Peterson after he finished it. As Moose pored over the words, Nelson looked at his watch. They had to hustle over to life support. "Thanks, sir. We needed that motivator before cranking up."

0950 hours
Over the Plain of Jars in central Laos
Approaching the North Vietnam border

Cadillac finished its refueling on Green Track and rendezvoused with the main strike force, led by Spike flight. Spike 01 would take the main force in to hit a fuel depot across the Red River, northeast of Hanoi.

"Spike, Cadillac and Chevy here. Coming up your four o'clock high."

"Tally, Cadillac." The two MiGCAP four-ships drifted apart to flank the main force, but remained stacked up 2,000 feet high.

1007 hours
Above the foothills southeast of Thud Ridge

The strike force moved out over the flat expanses of the Red River Valley, fully exposed to all the usual threats. It was hazy with 10 miles visibility above thinly scattered showers. Looking down toward the ground, the inflight visibility was less than 3 miles.

Taco Martinez scanned the horizon beyond the main strike force when he saw a Sparrow-sized missile boost itself off the right wing of Spike 02. "Hey, Randy, the number two 105 just threw a Shrike at the emitters."

"Good, but keep your eyeballs moving."

The AGM-45 Shrike picked up speed and moved up and well forward of the strike force. Following its preprogrammed flight profile, the Shrike climbed higher, then pitched over and headed for the electronic signal that its seeker head had locked onto. The defense-suppression missile was doing its job just fine, veering off to west Hanoi, an area bristling with SAMs and numerous acquisition radars.

Starbuck saw the Shrike's effect on his RHAW gear. The signal density thinned itself to a level where the APR-25 could actually sort the remaining emitters and display them on both the scope and the indicator light panel. Ninety seconds later, the Shrike hit, and the signals overwhelmed Starbuck's RHAW gear again.

Martinez thought out loud, "Wonder what the Shrike hit?"

"Dammit, Taco! Take your mind off that magnetic arrow. All it bought us was two minutes and 18 miles of safety."

The sixteen F-105s were all off the target intact. To Starbuck, looking down sun, the sight of the last four pointy-nosed fighter-bombers screaming out of the haze was a beautiful, eerie sight. Inaccurate 85mm flak popped off at the top of the haze behind the last F-105s.

1018 hours
Colonel Tomb's office
Phuc Yen Airfield, 15 kilometers north of Hanoi

Lieutenant Ngoc tapped on the door. Tomb asked him in, interrupting his meeting with Colonel Arkov, who moved to the back of the room.

"You have something for me, Ngoc?" An unnecessary salutation. The lieutenant looked very confident.

Ngoc saluted and said, "The pilot who led the American MiGCAP yesterday was Colonel Clint Adams, the new commander of the F-4 Phantom wing at Ubon." Ngoc went on to describe Adams: World War II double ace, charismatic, aggressive, unorthodox, had the total loyalty of his men.

Tomb was intrigued. He asked, "Can you determine when this Adams will fly missions?"

"Normally this information can be obtained, but not in the case of Colonel Adams."

"Oh? Why?"

"Adams lives by another code—unpredictability. This man has no established behavior pattern. He does not schedule himself for missions in advance, like other American commanders. Instead, he decides on impulse where and when to fly. Then he simply replaces the scheduled pilot."

Tomb pondered this information, pacing his office. "This is unfortunate. Do you know why, Ngoc?"

"Because we cannot target him in flight?"

"That and another reason. From what you say, he is so accomplished, so superior an aviator that he can lead their toughest missions on short notice. It appears we must now deal with a competent leader."

Arkov interjected, "Yes, a real American Eagle."

Ngoc added, "Yesterday's mission was his first as a flight leader. We can anticipate he will lead all his missions in the future. Colonel, his pilots consider him fearless and very capable as a fighter pilot."

"This is disturbing information, Ngoc. It will be difficult to gain the advantage on this American flight leader. One lives to be an experienced combat pilot by following certain paths. It would be unwise for our pilots to confront this new American commander directly. Instead, we must use alternate methods to disrupt the formations he commands. Only then will we extract tribute on our terms. And we must punish his formations. This man instills an aggressive fighting spirit in his pilots. It is that spirit we must attack first. I observed this fighting spirit firsthand yesterday."

Ngoc nodded in agreement.

Tomb continued, "Adams himself should be avoided by our pilots."

"My pardon, Colonel, his unpredictable nature may not permit this. I am unable to tell you when he is in the American MiGCAP flights."

"That could be most unfortunate for our young aviators."

"But certainly you are his equal, Colonel."

"That is not the matter at hand. A single battle between two leaders is not possible." Tomb pondered some alternatives.

"Colonel, our basic tactics appear sound. Hit and run, and our decoys draw away the American MiGCAP flights so our main attack can concentrate on the F-105s."

"You are right, Lieutenant. Nothing is more important than the F-105s; they destroy our industries, our villages, our people. We must always concentrate on the F-105s. That is why this new colonel must be dealt with. But to confront so skillful an adversary directly would be unwise."

"Perhaps we can arrange for him to be 'dealt with' in Thailand." Ngoc looked to his superior for approval.

Tomb, who had wandered to the window in thought, turned on his heels and looked squarely at Ngoc. Tomb remembered only too well his days as a Viet Minh terrorist. His victims were French politicians and Vietnamese collaborators.

But like all fliers he had developed that sense of honor that exists between aviators. For Tomb, the battle was in the air now, strapped in the machine. Even over North Vietnam, neither side shot at a man in a parachute. But this situation was different. This was a strategic matter, not a tactical one. Assassinating Colonel Adams would hurt the American air campaign, which was becoming effective. And it was a logical extension to take the war to the enemy. Still, Tomb was uncomfortable that so magnificent an aviator might die so unceremoniously.

Tomb concluded the meeting. "Your suggestion has much promise, but I will have no direct part in such a plan. Meanwhile, try to tell me when this man will fly against us. If something happens to him in Thailand, then our people will be safer."

Ngoc saluted and started to leave, but the Vietnamese fighter commander stopped him near the door with one last question. Tomb dropped his stoicism and let his curiosity finally emerge. "How do you get the American flying schedules?"

"We have operatives at all the American bases. We exploit their weaknesses," Ngoc said smugly. "American officers overlook many important details in their daily lives. They have too many material things, too many complex organizations, and are often too busy to see what happens around them. Security is very lax. They behave as if Thailand is an impenetrable sanctuary where war does not come.

"The Americans hire many maids to clean up after them, and many servants to supply them with their food and drink. No one checks the loyalties of these maids and servants. No one knows what happens to yesterday's flying schedule. And like soldiers everywhere, Americans reveal too much when they drink. Our intelligence operatives do the rest."

1019 hours
Thirty miles north of Hanoi

Randy Starbuck saw Spike 01 and the rest of the strike force 10 miles ahead on his radar scope. They appeared safe and were moving out of the area quickly.

"Cadillac 03 has four bogies, one o'clock level." Mike Nelson called out the MiG-17s about 6 miles ahead. They might be setting up for a stern attack on the exiting F-4 MiGCAP.

Mike Nelson at 18,000 feet easily saw the dark green MiGs as they emerged from the luminescent haze. But the GIBs didn't have them on radar yet. Bad down angle.

Randy Starbuck, 5 miles ahead of Nelson, didn't see the MiGs, but he followed the cardinal rule of the fighter pilot's bible: Don't just stand there, do something, even if it's wrong. He rolled left into a reverse high-G barrel roll. "Tally. Got the lead pair?"

Mike Nelson radioed, "Cadillac 03 taking the two trailers." But the MiG-17s wanted to avoid a vertical turning battle with the stirred-up Phantoms.

Fifteen miles behind the exiting Thuds, Cadillac flight continued twisting through the murky air with the four MiG-17s.

Cadillac 01 and 02 were hopelessly out of position despite having more speed, more power, and more pure-energy maneuverability. It was hard to beat a well-engineered bounce by a tighter-turning opponent. The MiGCAP Phantoms were beautifully jammed.

The lead MiG-17s dove for the surface, falling in behind the second pair that split-S'd away from Mike Nelson in Cadillac 03. All four MiGs seemed headed for Phuc Yen, north of Hanoi.

Two pairs of MiGs were being chased by two pairs of Phantoms, 5 miles behind. No tail-chase missile shot for Cadillac. No radar lock-ons because of the growing ground clutter and no headset growl from a heat-seeker. The MiGs were passing 1,000 feet, headed for the deck.

Then Randy Starbuck's luck changed. The lead MiG peeled off into a defensive circle. Starbuck suspected the second MiG pair would peel off one at a time into the circle, too. He didn't wait.

"Ah, Cadillac, follow me high and hard right to counter the defensive wheel."

"Zero three, copy." Nelson and Wright pulled up their Phantoms and closed on Starbuck and Stewart, moving to a half mile behind them in a right climbing turn. Starbuck had to put pressure on the MiGs, or they would have broken out of their defensive circle as quickly as they had formed it. The tactic was to attack the defensive circle in staggered pairs.

Randy Starbuck had set up this attack superbly. He and Roscoe Stewart passed 1,000 feet, still descending. Starbuck couldn't help thinking that this might be his only chance at a defensive circle. So far, so good— Cadillac 01 and 02 were 4 miles from the turning MiGs, circling at 500 feet. Nelson and Wright were 2 miles in trail.

Back at Ubon earlier this morning, Randy Starbuck had briefed each pilot on the tactics for busting the circle. The lead Phantom took the nearest MiG. The second one took the next closest and so on.

Leveling off at 100 feet above the rice paddies at 480 knots, Randy Starbuck called out, "Cadillac, pick your targets, now." The dark-green MiGs silhouetted nicely in the haze.

Starbuck's attack plan called for Sidewinder-only attacks at this altitude, since it was too close to the ground for radar missiles. And Cadillac was coming out of the morning sun and haze, good for a down-sun Sidewinder shot.

Too good to be true? Maybe not. Randy had his missile switch in heat. He heard the growl in his headset; he had had it ever since he leveled out in this favorable shooting geometry. He put his target reticle on "his" MiG as it moved around to the three o'clock position on the imaginary circle. He had an optimum shot. He took it.

"Fox Two." A one-second delay. "Fox Two." In two seconds, Starbuck's last two AIM-9s were on their way and tracking. Immediately after the missiles were away, Starbuck rolled high and left, over the top of the circle.

On the "freeze target" call, Cadillac 02, 03, and 04 broke left to shift on the circle. Now Roscoe Stewart in 02 rolled back to the right and put his pipper on his designated MiG, the next one in the circle.

In practical terms, the defensive circle was broken right then. Yet the dogfight was really just beginning. When the second MiG pulled around for a shot at Starbuck, he gave Roscoe Stewart's Sidewinder a better shot. Roscoe sent two AIM-9s on the way. "Fox Two."

Starbuck's Sidewinders were closing on the three o'clock MiG, but the NVAF pilot was alerted by his in-trail wingmen. He loaded up five Gs on his nimble Soviet craft, and he drew an extremely tight left circle, virtually swapping ends in seconds.

Starbuck's first Sidewinder couldn't turn with the MiG-17, and it passed wide and behind the escaping MiG, detonating on the far side of it. His second missile cut the corner on the MiG and had the angle. But the MiG pilot had turned his hot tailpipe away from the Sidewinder's seeker head. Without a heat source to home on, the second Sidewinder streaked through the MiG's hot air track. Two optimum shots, two misses.

"Damn!" Starbuck yelled into the intercom. He had had two sure shots and had come up empty.

Starbuck's straight-through flight kept the second MiG's hot tail section pointed squarely at Roscoe Stewart's rapidly approaching AIM-9s. Any second now. . . .

The third MiG should have alerted his exposed comrade by now, but the lure of destroying an American Phantom distracted him. He failed to alert the second MiG pilot to Roscoe Stewart's Sidewinder.

The heat-seeking Sidewinder embedded itself in the second MiG's tailpipe and detonated. The debris, much of it smoking or on fire, splashed into the rice paddies, 1,500 feet below. The pilot never had a chance. Peasants working in the fields watched the incredible dogfight much like spectators at an air show.

The two remaining MiGs abandoned their circling maneuver, rolled wings level, and headed south in the general direction of Hanoi. This heading took them straight at Cadillac 03 and 04. They fired their aerial cannons at the F-4s, much like cowboys shooting their way out of town. But the cannon fire was largely defensive, aimed at scattering the F-4s so they could escape more easily.

It worked. Nelson and Boomer pulled vertical. With a speed advantage and the power of their J-79s, 8th TFW pilots knew to take MiG-17s into the vertical plane, but these NVAF pilots were having none of it. They were already shaken by the loss of their fellow pilot and the breach of their defensive circle. They did not relish a treetop dogfight with American aircrews who knew their business. No Americans had ever tried to break a defensive circle before today. Colonel Tomb had trained them to avoid situations where U.S. pilots could prevail. That was why they had formed a defensive circle in the first place.

Randy Starbuck and Roscoe Stewart in Cadillac 01 and 02 joined up in a climb and turned for Thud Ridge. Mike Nelson and Moose Peterson in Cadillac 03 checked for the MiGs.

On the intercom, Moose said, "The Gomers flew straight through, staying on the deck." He craned his thick neck to keep the fleeing MiGs in sight.

Upon hearing this from his GIB, Mike Nelson should have rolled off on his left wing to the west and caught up with his flight leader, 5 miles ahead. But he didn't. He went for the exiting MiGs.

"Good," said Nelson, as he decisively pulled his Phantom's nose through straight vertical toward the southern horizon, then increased the G forces as gravity combined with the engines to increase his airspeed. In a 45-degree dive and passing 8,000 feet at 400 knots, Nelson rolled wings level and tapped in three-quarter afterburner as he unloaded to zero-G flight for ten seconds—a classic high-performance, half Cuban Eight designed to stay with the fleeing MiGs. Boomer Wright in Cadillac 04 stayed with Mike Nelson, his element leader, and began closing on him. The MiGs were 4 miles ahead on the deck, headed for Phuc Yen 15 miles north of Hanoi.

Moose Peterson was confused. Since he was welded 3 feet aft Nelson's six o'clock, he had a right to be. "What's the plan, Boss? We're runnin' a tad low on gas." By Peterson's accounting, they had 1,500 pounds of JP-4 to burn before they had to head for the tanker, 125 miles to the west.

Nelson pulled both throttles out of burner and quietly said, "How's that?" His voice had an uncharacteristic edge to it. Moose had never heard that tone before, and it scared him more than anything that had happened that day. Mike Nelson had just turned Moose into a passenger for the first time. They were no longer a team. And they were headed straight for Hanoi.

"Cadillac 03, do you have us?" Randy Starbuck tried to gather his flock.

Nelson preempted Moose Peterson. "Don't answer." Another first. Moose said nothing.

Boomer Wright had worked his butt off to maintain his fighting wing position on Mike Nelson. He jumped in on the radio. "Uh, Cadillac Lead, Cadillac 04 here. We're chasing the last two bandits."

"Say your position."

"Ten miles south of the circle. Heading southeast. In a tail chase. Nelson must have radio trouble."

This worried Randy Starbuck. He had two young crews hanging it out all alone and heading the wrong way with radio problems. And they had to be running low on gas. He called to 04, "Get 03's attention, take the lead, 'n break it off. Let's go home."

Boomer tapped his afterburner and moved abeam Cadillac 03, spreading out a few yards for safety as the Phantoms pressed along at 400 feet above the ground. Wright waggled his wings. Moose looked over. Boomer gave the hand signal signifying he was taking formation lead.

Over the intercom, Moose tried to prevail on Nelson's professional fiber. "Mike, what're you doin'? We'll run out of gas chasing those little peckerwoods! Let's get back on the team."

Boomer flew abeam 03, now 300 feet above the paddies at 500 knots. Mike Nelson looked over at him, shook his head no, and gestured with his thumb for Boomer to fall back to fighting wing position.

Wright tweaked back his throttles a fraction of an inch and started to slide rearward. Boomer ordered Snake in his backseat to dial up Guard, 243.0. Snake Cummings spun the UHF frequency selector to the universal emergency frequency that everyone—friend and enemy—always monitored.

"Cadillac 04 on Guard. How copy, 03?"

Nelson looked over and gave a thumbs-up. He tapped the front of his helmet and pointed forward with his index finger, indicating he still had the lead. Boomer decided Mike Nelson knew what he was doing and elected to cooperate, but he didn't have a clue about what was happening.

Moose prodded Nelson again. "Mike, we can't catch those guys before they jump in the Phuc Yen traffic pattern, and I can't get them on radar for a Sparrow shot. Let's get outta here."

Nothing. No response.

The MiG-17s broke hard left into a clearing turn. When they saw the Phantoms, they rolled halfway back to the right, heading now for Haiphong, not Phuc Yen. They were undoubtedly talking on the radio, trying to set up a flak trap somewhere down river for Mike Nelson and his wingman.

Moose wondered why Nelson didn't instinctively cut the corner on the MiG-17s when they cleared left. Instead, he barreled straight ahead and eased down below 100 feet. Moose, totally perplexed, asked, "Hey, Mike, didn't you see the MiGs turn?"

"Trust me." The MiG-17s slowly drifted off to the southeast, now 5 miles at eleven o'clock.

Randy Starbuck broke in on the UHF. "Cadillac 04, you outbound yet?"

"Rog, we're swinging around. Catch you at the tanker." Boomer Wright was now on record as part of this conspiracy—if only he could figure out what it was.

"Lead copies. Hustle it up."

Nelson looked over at Boomer and nodded.

Sporadic tracer rounds worked their way up from the forward quadrants and appeared to roll back over the wingtips of Cadillac 03 and 04. At their speed and altitude, the North Vietnamese ground gunners couldn't compensate with enough lead to hit these F-4s.

Mike Nelson finally saw what he had been looking for—a distinctive elongated mound in the middle of the floodplain north of Hanoi. Then he saw the Phuc Yen Airfield control tower off to the right. He turned right 25 degrees and lined up on his intended target.

Moose summed it up. "Holy shit, Mike! You going mad or what? You're gonna get everybody from us to the Seventh Air Force commander fired for this stunt!" Peterson's voice had never reached this high a pitch in combat before.

"Hang on, Big Swede," said Nelson as he went to half afterburner, sapping more of the precious little fuel he had remaining. Phuc Yen was 5 miles ahead—thirty-five seconds. The added thrust pushed Nelson's

Phantom through the sound barrier. Boomer Wright followed his leader using the extra afterburner margin to make up the few yards he had lost when Nelson made his supersonic decision.

Everyone had the picture now—Cadillac 03 and 04 were going across Phuc Yen supersonic at 100 feet.

Every Air Force Academy graduate was very familiar with the biggest aviation stunt ever pulled at USAFA. In 1961, two F-105 Thunderchiefs screamed across the mile-high campus at supersonic speed and created the largest pile of shattered window glass in the history of the Air Force. Nelson, Boomer, and every other cadet at the time were members of the clean-up detail.

While it's true that in automobiles speed kills, over North Vietnam speed was protection. Nelson was now 3 miles, or fifteen seconds, from Phuc Yen. Mach 1.15. The sonic shock wave was dragging 20 feet behind his Phantom, kicking up a spray that leaped from one rice paddy to the next at a speed of 13 miles per minute. Two miles—ten seconds.

The North Vietnamese in the Phuc Yen control tower saw Cadillac 03 and 04 clearly now. The tower had the best view on the north side of the Red River, only 10 kilometers south of the airfield. But what could the tower people do? Grab their rifles? Dive for cover? No, but they could sound the alert. And they did. But with seconds left, the siren would have little effect. As his assistant turned the hand crank to energize the mechanical air defense siren mounted atop the tower itself, the tower chief reached for the ancient French telephone on the instrument console.

Nguyen Tomb put down the phone, which rang back in protest. The air defense sector control officer called to tell him that the American MiGCAP had shot down a MiG-17 belonging to the First Air Company at Kep. Tomb asked about the tactics. Tomb pounded his fist into the table when the officer told him the U.S. pilots had broken up a defensive circle. Four MiG-17s should have been able to protect themselves against American missile attacks at low altitude. The pilots were experienced enough to employ the correct tactics. How did that happen?

He decided to call Kep and get more details on exactly what had gone wrong. As he reached again for the telephone, it rang again, blocking his progress. Out of habit, he paused to let the second ring begin.

"Yes?"

A panicky, high-pitched voice started jabbering on the other end of the phone line. "Colonel Tomb, this is the control tower! Two American planes are—"

A deafening blast blew out the glass in the window panes opposite Tomb's desk, strewing the shards about the room. Instinctively, Tomb turned away, but three glass slivers smashed into his right shoulder. Another clipped the top of his right ear, then bounced off the wall behind him. The blood spotted his green khaki shirt as Tomb rolled under his desk.

Cadillac 03 burst across the NVAF fighter base from the north, at a 30-degree angle to Runway 11/29, tracking directly over the control tower. Cadillac 04, offset now 300 feet right, screamed over the lower-profile maintenance hangars. The overpressure generated by the Phantoms' supersonic shock wave shattered almost every pane of glass in the path of Cadillac 03 and 04. Hundreds of people on the airfield got the shock of their lives.

Nelson and Wright zoomed over the low ridge and passed out of sight before the unsuspecting gunners on the ground had the time to look skyward. Not a single shot was fired from the airfield at Cadillac 03 and 04.

Nelson hit his UHF transmit button. "Colonel Tomb, Colonel Tomb, Cadillac 03 on U.S. Guard channel. That low pass and the broken glass were for Pontiac 03. The 8th Tac Fighter Wing pilots will be waiting for you tomorrow and every day. We'll be back."

Then Nelson turned around to the west but kept the two-ship low over the paddies to the south for another thirty seconds. When clear of the flak sites that ringed Phuc Yen, the F-4s popped up and headed for Thud Ridge, picking up sporadic flak as they climbed out. No SAMs.

Nelson queried his wingman. "Fuel state, 04?"

"Zero over 2." Two thousand pounds, or a full 1,000 pounds below the fuel level for heading out of North Vietnam. That translated into 150 nautical miles, not accounting for any adverse winds. No margin for error. And the tanker had to be at the northernmost end of the refueling track. Nelson had calculated that he'd be this low on gas. "Hope it's enough," he said to the now-silent Moose.

Nelson checked his own fuel gauge—0 over 2.3—2,300 pounds. No surprise that he had more than Boomer. The wingman always burned more to hold position and to compensate for starting all maneuvers a split-second late.

Once over Thud Ridge, Mike Nelson used all his technical knowledge to "lean out" his fuel consumption. He slowed to a more vulnerable airspeed, but it was a necessary risk at this point.

"Keep an eye out behind us, Moose." Moose complied but said nothing.

"Moose? You hear me?"

"Yeah."

Mike Nelson worked the needed flight coordination, "Cadillac Lead, can you get the tanker to its northern limit for Cadillac 03 and 04?"

"Rog. Cadillac, let's go Button Twelve." Starbuck ordered his flight crew to change their radios to the pre-set tanker rendezvous channel.

"Two."

"Three."

"Four."

"Cadillac, check in."

"Two."

"Three."

"Four."

Randy Starbuck contacted the modified C-130 airborne command-and-control aircraft working all the aircraft in North Vietnam and northern Laos. "Hillsboro, Cadillac, flight of four Fox Fours with two very deep stragglers, about 90 miles behind. Need a tanker way up north."

"Copy, Cadillac. Violin 22's waiting for you on Brown Track. We'll point him north." Another frequency change and the rendezvous was well in hand.

"Cadillac 02 has a single large radar bogie, eleven o'clock low, 3.0 miles." It was the KC-135.

"Violin 22, Cadillac. Keep heading 0-2-0 as long as you can. We have a tally, and we'll roll in behind you." Randy Starbuck picked up the KC-135's contrails as it cruised at flight level 240, 24,000 feet. He could see the converted airliner flying straight ahead at 8 miles per minute, stretching northwest into Laos for Cadillac 03 and 04.

"Ah, Violin, Cadillac needs you to stay north of the track for fuel-hungry stragglers."

"Copy. Can do."

Thirty miles northwest of the regular track, Starbuck decided the tanker guys were hanging it out enough. "Ah, Violin 22, that's plenty. Hold here and we'll do fine."

"Wilco." Violin 22 set up a tight holding pattern with two-minute legs. Cadillac 01 and 02 refueled through the entire maneuver, so they could be out of the way when 03 and 04 caught up.

Then Starbuck turned back to working his stragglers, "Say position, Cadillac 03."

Nelson responded, "We have you radar contact, 2.8 miles. Flight level 370." Nelson had made the maximum stretch by topping out as high as possible, in the most economical profile he could fly. He pushed over now with his throttles barely above idle power setting.

"Fuel state, 03?"

"Zero over point nine."

"Zero four?"

"Zero over point eight." Boomer's gauge was more like 700 pounds. Not much, but hopefully enough to get the job done.

"Violin 22 here. We're turning back to you now." That sealed it. The remainder of the refueling went very quickly. Cadillac 03 and 04 onloaded 1,000 pounds each, then went back in for enough gas to make Ubon. Nelson figured they'd gotten by with three minutes' fuel to spare.

Randy Starbuck knew the debrief was gonna be damn interesting. And he hoped they'd all still have jobs.

1045 hours
Colonel Tomb's office
Phuc Yen Airfield

The old Vietnamese woman picked up the last of the glass from the wooden flooring. Tomb had summoned his key assistants.

Major Duc, the maintenance chief, spoke first. "No serious damage to our planes. Only a punctured fuel tank on #4323 when a supply dolly rolled into it, Colonel."

Tomb's base commander was anxious to get back to his duties and interjected, "Colonel, almost all our windows are broken. Dozens of people were injured by the flying glass. And, sir, I'm very sorry to see you are hurt. I will call a nurse immediately."

"I am of little importance." Tomb's shirt was spattered with his own blood. He had doctored himself, pulling the glass out of his shoulder and using his rice wine as an antiseptic. He had shredded his undershirt for a bandage and replaced his overshirt. Tomb held a piece of cloth to his bleeding ear.

His base commander continued. "At least one person will lose an eye. A small boy. I will pass my findings to the political officer. We need to get the facts to the Information Ministry immediately. I have a photographer taking pictures to accompany the report." Everything in North Vietnam had political overtones. Tomb worried that the base commander, who should be seeing to the needs of victims and cleanup details, was more interested in exploiting the propaganda value of the event. "Colonel, may I be excused to return to my duties?"

Tomb nodded in agreement, and the base commander submissively departed. "Ngoc, how much warning did you have?" Tomb's tone was cold; it made young Ngoc uneasy.

"Air defense provided no warning. We knew there was an air battle 40 kilometers to the north. We always try to observe these maneuvers. One of my sergeants was in the control tower and used binoculars, but the haze was too great to see anything. But five minutes later, my assistant observed three MiG-17s veering away to the northeast. He did not see the American Phantoms at first. When he saw them, he thought the Phantoms were chasing the MiG-17s. The Phantoms were splashing up the water in the paddies. They were moving at very high speed. He thought they would bomb the runway."

Tomb did not change his expression. "It is inevitable that the Americans will attack our air bases. We have our preparations in place. But we must have more warning than this. Perhaps they were testing our terminal defenses." He paused a moment, pondering this possibility, then dismissed it. "No. Somehow this is different."

Ngoc spoke again. "Colonel, there was something else. A radio call. A message."

"What kind of message, Ngoc?"

The wiry young officer handed Tomb the Vietnamese translation. Tomb read it as he moved to his glassless window to get better light. He folded the paper and slowly stuffed it into his pants pocket. Without turning to look back at the others, Tomb closed the meeting. "Leave me now."

1058 hours
With Cadillac flight enroute to Ubon
Over northeastern Thailand

The absence of radio chatter between the members of Cadillac flight was uncharacteristic of a four-ship that had downed a MiG and returned without a loss.

On the positive side of the ledger, Roscoe Stewart was a MiG killer. He had a perfect tour going. Two AIM-9 Sidewinder shots and two MiG kills. And another positive thing: the 8th TFW had broken up an NVAF defensive circle for the first time.

Yet this mission had a few significant negatives. Randy had *almost* bagged a MiG, which would have been even sweeter because his plan to bust the defensive circle would have yielded the prize. And he had to expose his own ass just a bit too much for his liking, turning the tables on the MiG pilots with a decoy tactic. The BIBs would work on that tactic.

However, the most unsettling aspect of the morning was the near loss of two crews and their F-4s to a breach of flight discipline, a stunt by a young, inexperienced pilot. Randy Starbuck had monitored the UHF Guard frequency. He had heard Nelson's radio call.

1059 hours

Moose Peterson was mad. Very mad. "Hey, Mike, have you blown a fuse, or what? You wanna tell me what that was all about back there?"

Nelson knew he was in trouble. He was counting on Peterson's support, but he'd handled Moose badly. He'd blown his close aircrew bond with Moose Peterson over Phuc Yen today.

Professionalism. The USAFA faculty and officers drove home the concept incessantly. Nelson remembered his favorite definition for professionalism: doing it right when no one was looking. He'd failed the course today in some ways, not others. He'd done it for Vic. He quietly said to his backseater, "I thought you'd understand more than the others, Moose."

"Don't 'Moose' me. That was bush league all the way. You almost got us killed. Twice!" Peterson had never been so pissed off. "And thanks a helluva lot for reading me in before you did it."

Mike Nelson understood that this last remark was the deepest cut of all.

1600 hours
Squadron commander's office, 555th TFS
Ubon RTAFB

Rod Wells was on the phone. Wells already had a copy of the Cadillac mission debrief, and he had read it, part of a rapid response system he had set up after Colonel Adams's tasking. Randy Starbuck was on the other end of the phone line. He was filling in some of the more pregnant details of the mission that were not in the debrief report.

"Okay, thanks Randy. Get over to the O Club and get a burger, fries, and a chocolate shake before your grease low-level light comes on."

Mike Nelson knocked on the door sill. Wells motioned with his free hand for Nelson to come in. Nelson saluted his squadron commander as Wells put down the phone. The young captain was ready to take both barrels.

"Sit down, Mike," Wells said, offering a handshake.

Nelson nodded in resignation.

"Randy Starbuck told me about your side trip to Phuc Yen. He said you gave him all the details right after you landed."

"Yessir. And Captain Wright in Cadillac 04 corroborated the facts. Sir, nobody else had any part in the plan. It was all my idea. Not even Lieutenant Peterson. He didn't know what I was up to."

"You braggin' or complainin'?"

Nelson was confused by his commander's question and wondered when Wells was going to lower the boom. Wells propped his feet on the edge of his desk and lit a cigar. "You want one of these, Mike?"

"No, thank you, sir."

"What *were* you up to, son?"

"It all started the night following Captain Sansone's death. That's when I started to conceive the plan."

"You boys were pretty thick. Conceived what?"

"Well, sir, there's a good chance that Colonel Tomb shot him down."

"Oh?"

"I've been talking to Major Cardwell. And frankly, sir, this Colonel Tomb has been controlling the ball game. We play on his field, with his balls and bats, with rules that favor his team. And we only play when he wants. He stacks the odds his way, then he comes at us. And he has tactical surprise on top of everything else."

"Yeah, I know. That's a pretty elegant description of the operation up North. I bet you'd make a crackerjack strategist."

"Sir, I didn't mean it that way. But it's how I got started. I wanted to do something to avenge Vic. And show Colonel Tomb that he's not holding all the cards. And I was looking to do something else."

"What else?"

"I was hoping to goad him into altering his behavior pattern. But I knew I had to operate within the Rules of Engagement, or I would rip it for everybody else. What I mean is, no attacks on NVAF airfields or on aircraft in the traffic pattern. But the rules don't say anything about flybys. I checked."

"Bet you did."

"I wanted to rattle Tomb. Push his patience. Throw a rock through his window with a message on it."

"He probably doesn't have any window left. Is that what the radio call was about?"

"Yessir, I wanted to personalize it for him so he got the message loud and clear."

Wells took a deep draw on his El Producto and puffed it out in three rather equal bluish clouds. He took a moment to respond. "And what do you think of your actions now?"

Nelson paused to gather his thoughts. Taking a deep breath, he knew this was the test question. "Sir, I regret breaching flight discipline. The situation presented itself, and I didn't know when I'd get another chance, so I took it. I regret dragging along three other pilots who risked their lives to stay with me. But, sir, I don't regret the flyby. Colonel Tomb needed his cage rattled—for a lot of reasons."

Again, Wells drew in a full complement of cigar smoke. This time he held it for a while as he mulled over his alternatives for dealing with Mike Nelson. Then, all at once, he exhaled all the smoke, popped his feet to the floor, and came out of his semireclined position. He leaned forward with his right elbow on the edge of his desk. Using his half-smoked cigar as a pointer for emphasis he said, "Right answer, Captain. On all three counts."

Nelson was dumbfounded. No lecture? No riot act? Wells pounded out the cigar in his overloaded ash tray.

"Just a couple things. When you recounted the facts you said 'I' way too much. That oughta tell you something."

"Yessir—"

Wells kept talking. It was his turn now. "And think about why those three pilots stuck with you even though they didn't know what the hell you were up to. They're team players. And they respect you so much that they went to hell and back with you. You can't buy that, Mike."

"Yessir."

"Do you know what a letter of reprimand is?"

Nelson braced himself. "Yes, sir, I do."

"Well, there's two kinds. I can give you a heavy one that goes in your records. But I'm throwin' that one away. That's a sack of rocks you couldn't carry around. Weighs a man's career down. But I'm gonna give you the second kind, called the 'desk drawer reprimand.' If you keep your nose clean for the rest of your tour at Ubon, I'll throw it in the trash when you rotate Stateside."

"I understand, sir." The captain knew he was getting off easy.

Wells handed Nelson a single sheet of paper. "Here, read this."

22 October 1966

FROM: 555 TFS/CC
SUBJECT: Letter of Reprimand
TO: Captain Michael T. Nelson, 088357FR

You are hearby reprimanded for a lapse in flight discipline over Phuc Yen Airfield, North Vietnam, on 18 October 1966.

You shall perform such actions as directed by me as punishment for this error in good judgment.

/signed/
Rodney D. Wells
Lt. Colonel, USAF
Commander

22 October 1966

1st IND.
I acknowledge receipt and understand the contents.

Michael T. Nelson
Captain, USAF

Nelson finished reading the letter and started to return it to Wells. "Do you understand it, son?"

"Yessir."

"Then sign the first endorsement."

Nelson complied.

"And Mike, no combat missions for a week. Fly test hops to stay proficient. And you're gonna pull mobile control duty all week too."

"Yes, sir." Nelson winced. He liked flying but really hated sitting in the mobile box on the end of the runway checking for leaks, wing flaps, and landing gear.

"And for not regretting the flyby itself, well, that shows you got the right-sized flame in your heart."

"Uh, Colonel Wells, I just want to—"

"Get your ass out of here, Nelson, before I kick it."

"Thank you, sir." Nelson saluted, executed an about face any cadet would have been proud of, and made for the partially open door. Mike Nelson felt better about himself right now. Rod Wells had done that.

Wells decided right then that he'd make Mike Nelson his squadron tactics officer in about thirty days, if they both survived that long.

1715 hours
Outside 8th TFW HQ

Todd Benning stopped Danforth's staff car, dropping off his boss for the end-of-day paperwork surge that Danforth seemed to relish. "I'll be back just as soon as I check in the car for servicing at the motor pool, sir."

"Wait a minute, Todd. I want to talk to you."

"Sir?" Todd said, wondering if he had screwed up some correspondence earlier that day.

"You've been doing a bang-up job as my exec. There aren't too many young men who can be an instructor pilot in combat and keep a wing DCO on track like you have, Todd. Most of us can do one or the other."

Nearly struck dumb, Benning managed a "Thank you, sir."

"Todd, when this war's over, we'll be fighting another battle. On the Potomac. Americans always cut back their armed forces after a war. That's when we need talented young officers in key jobs in the Pentagon. People like you, Todd, with the savvy to do what's right and the credibility to be heard. Think it over, son, and we'll talk about it again."

Danforth disappeared into the building to battle his in basket. Todd Benning was stunned.

1730 hours
Clint Adams's trailer
Ubon RTAFB

Rod Wells knocked on the aluminum door. "Sir, it's your best squadron commander."

"C'mon in, Rod. Want some dinner?" Adams ran off a string of six hacking coughs that bent him over, then spit into the sink. "Got to stop smoking one of these days before I die from the damned habit." He sliced up a Genoa salami to go with his cold beer.

"No, sir, but I could use a bottle of brew. How's Laura doing?"

"I'm worried, Rod." Adams ate the salami as quick as he sliced. "She's not coming around like I thought she would."

"Hang in there, Boss. Laura will do the right thing."

"I hear Roscoe Stewart bagged his second Gomer today," said Adams, changing the subject.

"Yep, sure did."

"AIM-9 shot?"

"Yessir. Roscoe's gettin' good at it."

"Help yourself to the beer, good buddy. Some left in the fridge." Adams sized up his best squadron commander as Wells rummaged for the last long-neck stuffed behind the leftovers. Curious about the impromptu visit, Adams asked, "Got something that can't wait 'til tomorrow's staff meeting?"

"One of our flights buzzed Phuc Yen today."

Adams stopped slicing. "Whoa, give it to me straight, Rodney."

"Not much, really. Cadillac 03 took his wingman across the field supersonic after breaking off a fruitless MiG chase. No ground fire. Came in low, caught them by surprise. Must've broken every window on the field."

"Who?"

"Captain Mike Nelson."

"Kid's making a name for himself, isn't he?" Adams resumed slicing the salami.

"Colonel, there's more. Nelson admitted it was a deliberate act. He's been despondent over Captain Sansone's loss, and he heard from Cardwell that this Colonel Tomb fella probably took out Sansone."

Adams stopped slicing again, put down the knife, and took a long swig from his long-neck Bud. He didn't say anything for a long time. He'd been proud of Mike Nelson's performance. Up to now at least. The kid had all it took to be a Vietnam jet ace. Under the right conditions, Nelson could get three more kills in a week, even with the slim pickings up North. Now this brash act over Phuc Yen. He looked up at Wells, "The North Vietnamese might complain about this through diplomatic channels. Shit. Could get serious. What'd you do?"

"Gave him a desk-drawer letter of reprimand an hour ago and took him off the mission schedule. He'll sit mobile control duty, counting full-stop landings for a week and fly check flights. Don't think he'll do it again."

Adams drew another mouthful of Budweiser. "Shit, what the hell are we talking about? Look what Washington's got us doing, Rod—covering our asses instead of kicking their asses. We should've blown those air-fields away long ago."

"Boss, I checked the Rules of Engagement carefully before coming over. Just talks about not strafing and bombing. Doesn't talk about flyovers."

"Maybe we won't get fired, Rodney."

"Nelson mentioned something else, Boss. He, too, checked the rules. Then he chose this stunt specifically because he wanted to piss off this Tomb. You know, goad the little bastard into doing something stupid."

Adams twisted the right end of his mustache. "Well, I'll be damned. The kid does have potential, doesn't he?"

"I think so."

"Go brief Slim Danforth. Tell him I want him to issue a strong written directive to each squadron commander reminding our crews not to push the Rules of Engagement. I'll call General Morgan right away and tell him we disciplined a pilot for sideswiping the rules. Thanks, Rod."

After Wells left, Adams thought back to a young, precocious lieutenant flying P-38 Lightnings in 1944. That frustrated pilot had broken away from his flight leader too, taking his wingman on a hunt for the Luft-waffe. The lieutenant had shot down his first two enemy planes, German FW-190s, that day over France. On return to RAF Wattisham, his group commander, Colonel Hub Zemke, chewed him out but understood why the young man's aggressive spirit had made him do it. Zemke found a way to chastise Lieutenant Clint Adams without snuffing out his spirit. Ten days later, young Adams was an ace.

THE TRAGEDY

---

23 October 1966 2245 hours
Clint Adams's trailer
Ubon RTAFB

Clint Adams played Laura's audiotape for the fifth time, listening for something different. A break in her voice or a sympathetic tone that he had somehow missed before. But it wasn't there.

Laura hadn't come around like he'd hoped. Not when he'd called her from Tucson. Not when he had returned home to Shaw to patch things up. Not since.

Things had remained unchanged since the day he'd left for Tucson. After Amy finished at Central High, Laura was taking her to Connecticut. This would be her last move; he could join her there on *her* terms.

Clint couldn't sleep now, not after listening to Laura's tape. He laced up his flying boots again, then pulled his flying suit back on, and zipped it up.

2330 hours
The J-79 Engine Shop, near the flight line
Ubon RTAFB

The 8th TFW's round-the-clock operation was an endless flow of combat sorties. Good wing commanders took every chance to check the pulse of their operation, any time of day or night. All Clint Adams had to do was decide where and when to plug in.

He followed no particular pattern, but relied on the little voice in his head to signal when he should lead "by wandering around." Commanders who didn't wander about inevitably lost touch with their mission and their people. See and be seen. It never stopped.

Adams came out of the Engine Shop and got into his command jeep. Then the abnormal happened. As he grabbed hold of the ignition key he heard a small explosive report in the distance followed several seconds later by two distinct thuds. The first sound was more substantial than a rifle shot. More like a grenade. The subsequent noises were unique.

Adams's stomach turned a little when he heard shouting coming from the aircraft revetments on the flight line. Through the alley between the airplane hangars, he saw maintenance vehicles racing toward the commotion, disregarding the flight line's 15-miles-per-hour speed limit. Then Adams spotted an Air Police car with flashing lights and wailing sirens zip past.

Simultaneously, his Motorola brick came alive with a half-dozen high-pitched beepings. It was the TOC duty officer.

"Command One, go ahead."

"Sir, request you proceed to Bravo Row. We've had an incident."

"Copy. I'm enroute." Adams knew better than to press for details over the radio. The duty officer would have provided them if he could. As Adams pulled into Bravo Row he saw a crowd of maintenance men parting for an arriving ambulance. A fire truck stopped beside the gathering and the truck's crew rushed into the crowd.

As Clint stopped his jeep, Pop Brewer moved toward him, finishing some instructions to Maintenance Control on his own handheld radio.

"Got a bad accident here, Boss."

"What happened?"

"Looks like an inadvertent ground firing of the rear ejection seat on #640. The GIB's hurt bad. Don't think he's gonna make it."

Adams looked beyond Pop Brewer. Doc Kramer, Triple Nickel's flight surgeon, was bending over the crumpled figure on the ground. Kramer stood, too slowly for it to be good news. The doctor removed the stethoscope from around his neck and stuffed it in his flight suit knee pocket. One of the white-suited medical assistants covered the pilot's body with a green wool blanket taken from the back of the ambulance. A second corpsman backed up the ambulance, guided by two of the maintenance troops.

Kramer noticed Colonel Adams and made his way toward him. The young doctor shook his head sadly and reported, "Broke his neck on impact. Plus a lot of other body and bone trauma. Nothing we could do, sir."

"Who was it, Doc?"

"Lew Byrd."

"Damn." Byrd was Bear Robinson's GIB. Lew Byrd, a full-time line jock, often flew with other aircraft commanders. Tonight was one such night.

"What the hell happened anyway?"

"Not sure exactly, but that's the crew chief over there. People say he saw the whole thing." Kramer pointed to a young airman squatting in the corner of the revetment. Two of his comrades steadied him by the elbows as he tried to control his retching.

Adams made his way to the young airman. His fellows moved away, sensing that this was a one-on-one session.

"Son, how you doin'?"

Staff Sergeant Chris Cole looked up between retchings. "Oh, Colonel, it's you," he said, embarrassed, not wanting Adams to see him this way. "I just can't help it. I saw him hit and his . . . oh, wow." Cole puked all over his boots.

"You're bleeding, Chris. Looks like you took some shattered Plexiglas," said Adams, seeing the fresh blood dripping down Cole's rear skull and onto his khaki tee-shirt between his shoulder blades.

"Huh, oh, yessir. Pieces was flyin' all over when it hit," mumbled Cole, pulling an overused wiper rag from his back pocket and absent-mindedly dabbing his minor wound.

"What were you doing out here this late?"

"Finished up on #680 about two hours ago, then the Maintenance Line chief, well, he put a few of us on this launch because the regular crew chief got the clap and all."

"I understand you saw what happened, Chris. Can you tell me about it?"

Cole's eyes were still red and running tears. He sniffled and swallowed hard. "It was dark, sir, and I was adjusting the lights downward on the power cart. I always wait until the backseater gets up onto the engine nacelle. After pulling down the second light, I looked back to see how Captain Byrd was doing. You know, to see if he had gotten into the cockpit yet. Then it happened. Colonel, it was real bad." Cole lost control again.

"Tell me exactly what happened that was bad, Chris."

The young man took a deep breath, let it out, swallowed hard, and continued. "The pilots have to lean forward to get into the back seat. This plane's skin was still slick from the shower we just had. Captain Byrd grabbed hold of the raised canopy like everyone does, but he slipped a little. His hand dropped to the ejection seat. Then he leaned forward to get in and wham! The seat and the canopy and the captain all went up together." Cole lunged forward into dry heaves.

"Sorry to put you through this, Sergeant. Get in that ambulance, go over to the hospital, and get that head gash sewed up. Six four oh isn't going anywhere tonight." Adams motioned for some of the other crew chiefs to help Cole over to the medics.

Adams had a pretty good picture of what had happened now. The safety officer standing close to Adams was talking to the base fire chief. Adams overheard him, "The safety pin in the actuator of the ejection seat was somehow bypassed, allowing Byrd to put pressure on two small metal bars, called the banana links. The links are located on the top of the ejection seat, just behind the headrest. Pressing hard on these bars is like pulling the trigger of a pistol.

"When the seat actuator fired the ballistic charge at the base of the seat, it slapped that 200-pound slab of metal into the upper half of Byrd's body with more force than a car traveling at 80 miles per hour. The impact probably broke his neck and collapsed his lungs. Without the slip stream to pull it out of the way, the canopy finished the job. The seat smashed Byrd into the canopy's metal edge, which knifed into his back, slicing him open across the shoulder blades. The seat, Byrd, and the canopy continued 50 feet into the air. A few seconds later, Byrd and the seat likely hit the tarmac at the same time. The more aerodynamically designed canopy sideslipped to the ground after that."

Adams walked back to the main group, still gathered around the pool of blood that marked where Byrd had died.

"A hell of a tragedy, sir," Pop Brewer lamented.

"Yeah, it's a damn shame," Adams agreed. "But something set him up. Get your safety people on it. Find out what it was. Fast. Start with that safety pin and check the procedures for ensuring it's in place. Get with Slim Danforth, and make sure all our pilots know what happened and how they can avoid it."

Brewer nodded, saluted as Adams headed for his jeep, and replied, "Yessir. I'll start by checking every red-flagged pin in every F-4 we got."

Clint Adams ground the gears and set off to give Bear Robinson the bad news.

Back in the group of onlookers, two aircrews on their way to their own F-4s moved off to preflight their planes. Whale Wharton, the 497th's main MiG sweeper, and Knob Westcott, the Tactics Shop fighter-gator BIB and Wharton's primary GIB, picked up their helmet bags. Westcott mumbled, "I don't like it, Whale. That's two bad ones: Sansone and now Byrd."

Unfazed, Whale popped back, "Jeez, Knob. It ain't much fun flyin' off into the night with a pessimist."

2340 hours
The senior officers' trailer area
Ubon RTAFB

Lin May slipped in behind the row of long aluminum boxes housing the wing's key colonels. She was nervous, because something unusual was happening. She heard sirens in the distance, and several security vehicles had raced by at full speed with their red lights flashing. Could someone have sounded a security alert? After crouching in the bushes for five minutes, Lin satisfied herself that all the commotion was happening on the flight line, most likely an accident or a fire. Lin saw this distraction as her good fortune, and she moved about her business more confidently.

The trailer area was lit poorly, and she had no difficulty slipping among the shadows. Another local operative, the maid in the 497th hootch area who had supplied Lin May with the flying schedules, briefed her in detail. Lin located Colonel Adams's trailer and Adams's bedroom at the far end.

Earlier today, "cousin" Nan had smuggled in the plastique explosive, detonator, and the timer in his Vespa's seat cushion. He had entered the base at the peak of the morning rush hour, when the gate guards were more interested in reducing the traffic jam than in checking out local Thais who already had valid ID cards. Nan had passed Lin the bread-sized package as she left the O Club after finishing her shift ten minutes ago. The two blocks to the trailer seemed like 2 miles.

She and Nan had planned everything. They had watched the trailer for three nights, learning the movements of the officers and security patrols. They knew when Colonel Adams normally went to sleep, and they knew he was not on tonight's flying schedule.

Ubon had never had a serious breach of security. Consequently, people of all sorts moved around the base unchallenged around the clock. This made it easier for Lin May to slip into the trailer area. But Lin was frightened nonetheless because this was her first serious act as an operative. She heard her own short breaths as she attached the bomb to the underside of Adams's trailer, directly beneath his bedroom window. Every action was slow and deliberate. Every physical contact was quiet, vibrationless. She did not want to wake Colonel Adams. Nan, a trained explosives expert, had preset the timer for two A.M.

Her work done, Lin worked her way to the end of the trailer row, and blended into the stream of Thais leaving the air base after finishing their work at the three American clubs. She passed uneventfully through the main gate for the final time. This was Lin May's last operation at Ubon as she believed the Americans were suspicious. Even her own Vic Sansone had known something.

2350 hours
Three miles north of Ubon's runway
Outbound to Laos

Whale Wharton yanked the two throttles out of afterburner with his beefy left hand. The two powerful engines forfeited the benefits of nearly 10,000 pounds of thrust, creating a mushing sensation much like driving a car into a shallow lake of water. The moonless night and scarcity of civilization east of Ubon combined to mask the ground and horizon references pilots needed to confirm through their senses that they were still flying, and actually accelerating.

Both Wharton and Westcott momentarily felt the plowing effect as the Phantom coped with reduced thrust. Both men instinctively looked at their airspeed indicators. Reading: 275 knots and increasing, just more slowly than moments before. An aviator's inner ear could fool him when he was denied the normal visual references his brain expected. Only his training and experience could compensate when darkness or bad weather obscured these references.

The F-4 instruments in Whale Wharton's cross-check rounded out the flight geometry: 30-degree right bank to a heading of 100 degrees; climbing through 2,500 feet at 3,000 feet per minute to a precleared altitude of 12,000 feet.

"Poker flight, go Button Six."

"Poker 02."

In the backseat, Knob Westcott automatically changed the Poker 01's UHF radio frequency to 342.2 MHz after Whale's wingman acknowledged the routine command. Brigham Control, the air traffic control agency for eastern Thailand, tracked Poker flight for the next 40 miles until the two F-4s passed into Laos en route to tonight's target—supply trucks moving down the Ho Chi Minh Trail near the provincial town of Tchepone in central Laos.

"Poker 01" was Wharton's initial radio call on the new frequency.

"Poker 02. Lead, go 'dim steady.' " Wharton's wingman closed to within 300 feet of the lead aircraft. The red anticollision beacon and the wingtip position lights on Wharton's F-4, so vital as visual aids during the pitch-black visual rejoin, were now too bright for close night formation flying.

Wharton guarded the control stick with his left hand and dropped his right to the light control panel on the side console. He flipped both toggle switches aft, extinguishing his rotating beacon and dimming his wingtip lights. Poker 02 edged into a close route position, maintaining 20-feet wingtip clearance. Poker 02's lights went "bright steady" about this time as the pilot drew in closer to Wharton's plane. The reflected light bouncing off Poker 01 was enough to fly precise formation. Westcott watched the closure from the backseat and advised, "He's tucked in there pretty good, Whale."

Knob Westcott flew with Whale Wharton whenever he could. Wharton was the 497th's squadron weapons officer. Wharton and Westcott teamed up to evaluate the effectiveness of the wing's tactics and munitions against the most elusive, yet plentiful targets of the air war: trucks operating under a jungle canopy at night.

The night war over the Ho Chi Minh Trail was active and deadly, as usual. Whale could actually see it in the distance.

"Looks like the Fourth of July, Knobby. Fireworks all over the place."

Westcott breathed back, "Problem is, *we* are the hot dogs and the Gomers are the buns."

"You really got the rag on tonight, Knobber. Cheer up. Looks like we're gonna get some serious bombing done on this operation. You watch, lots of secondary explosions as we cook off the ammo in those rice trucks. I can feel it."

Up ahead, Whale saw three distinct battles in progress, one north, one straight ahead, and one south. Parachute flares, dropped by a variety of American aircraft, including the F-4s themselves, drifted slowly to the jungle below and marked the hot engagement areas. Watching the active arena to the south for a few seconds, Wharton saw detonations on the ground, most likely bombs exploding into a truck park or a convoy caught by one of the low, slow American aircraft working the trail.

Whale knew that a new kind of air force, one that did not exist three years ago, had sprung up to interdict the Ho Chi Minh Trail. This ungainly combination of specially modified C-47s, C-130s, B-26s, B-57s, light planes, and high-performance fighters worked together to constrict the movement of supplies that started their journey in the Haiphong harbor and ended in South Vietnam. The United States selected central Laos as center stage for the American interdiction effort, forgoing naval blockades, direct attacks on the North Vietnamese harbors, and large-scale ground operations on the trail itself.

Whale Wharton saw more action in Mu Gia Pass, the circus arena to the north. A stream of AAA tracers flowed up from the ground. The shell pattern was so thick it resembled a giant flamethrower belching a rope of fire into the sky. But flak offered a special bonus at the end, each shell exploding at a preset altitude, truly resembling Independence Day fireworks. These beautiful pyrotechnics masked the real danger of the flak, which was laying down a carpet of deadly hot metal shards designed to penetrate the outer skins of both the airplanes and the men who flew them.

Wharton called Westcott's attention to the most deadly and visually frightening weapon that the North Vietnamese used on the trail, the Soviet-made ZSU-23-4 anti-aircraft gun system. "Hey, Knob, look at that Quad-23 barrage in Mu Gia. The Gomers are really hosin' down some poor sonuvabitch." Westcott already knew that the Quad 23 was a vehicle-mounted set of four 23mm flak guns that fired such a high volume that it put ten times more AAA shells into the air than the older, single-gun 37mm and 57mm AAA systems. Some Quad 23s were guided by radars mounted on the same vehicle; the Quad 23 was almost impossible to destroy unless attacked directly and quickly. Quad-23 crews were elusive, employing shoot-and-move tactics.

Pilots called Mu Gia "The Pass," and it erupted into a violent battle zone every night. The Pass was the most prominent constriction in the trail, a narrow corridor hemmed in to the east and west by 3,000-feet ridge lines. The trail passed here from North Vietnam into Laos, and it was the northernmost target on the American air interdiction campaign. It was fiercely defended by the North Vietnamese.

Whale kept ragging his GIB, "See, Knob, Lady Luck's been good to you tonight. You coulda got fragged to Mu Gia. All we got to do tonight is beat up on some hapless movers around Tchepone."

But Westcott knew Wharton was only half kidding. A night mission to Mu Gia Pass was never a milk run. U.S. pilots could always expect accurate ground fire from the hundreds of flak guns on the valley floor and on the ridge lines. American aircrews often encountered a deadly crossfire from 23mm, 37mm, 57mm, even 85mm AAA, much of it radar guided.

"Yeah, what a deal. I must've stepped in some good shit today." Knob Westcott lived up to his reputation as the 497th's Sad Sack even when he was alone with Whale.

Actually, the circus arena near Tchepone appeared the least active tonight. Whale saw only routine flare drops in progress. As the older, lower flares approached the jungle canopy, an ancient AC-47 gunship exposed itself to ground fire as it dropped the next round of flares 10,000 feet above the ground. Flare droppers flew above the burning phosphorus flares that dangled from the flare's parachute.

The burning flares helped screen the AC-47 somewhat; there were almost no winds aloft to blow the flares off the target area tonight. No moon to expose the silhouette of the gunship. And for a change, the haze favored the flare dropper. Most important, there was no sign of radar-guided AAA in the area yet. It was all a game of cat and mouse, a game of action, counteraction, and counter-counteraction.

Wharton saw that tonight's operation was a standard flare operation for sure. He and Knob were experienced hands at night attack. Both had more than 100 night combat missions, 44 over North Vietnam, most to Mu Gia. They'd been to Tchepone several dozen times. Sometimes Tchepone was a cold target; other times it could burst into a boiling cauldron of ground fire.

Brigham Control radioed, "Poker, contact Alley Cat on 316.0." It handed over Poker flight to the C-130 airborne command-and-control aircraft that worked the night operations in central Laos and the North Vietnam panhandle. Alley Cat had a copy of the daily Frag—the Seventh Air Force Fragmentary Order that tasked the operational flying wing with targets and weapon loads. The weapons controllers aboard this flying command post, operating from radio panels in the back of the black-camouflaged, heavily modified C-130, handed off incoming strike flights to the forward air controllers (FACs). The FACs worked the individual circus rings on the trail, usually as preplanned in the daily Frag. But if things got hot, Alley Cat redirected strike aircraft where most needed.

"Poker, go Button Ten." Wharton then switched his flight over to the pre-set strike frequency.

"Poker 02."

"Poker, check in."

"Two."

"Alley Cat, Poker, flight of two Fox Fours, each with six LAU-3s and six CBU-24s. Good evening."

"Roger, Poker, take up standard orbit over Tchepone at base plus ten." Alley Cat already knew Poker flight's loaded weapons from the daily Frag. This radio call confirmed it. Alley Cat passed this validated information to the FAC flying low over the trail near Tchepone.

The FAC was Covey 22, assigned to the 20th Tactical Air Support Squadron at Da Nang, flying a twin-engine light Cessna loaded with radios that allowed him to talk with Alley Cat, the fighters, and a variety of friendlies on the ground on or near the trail.

Covey 22 was the vital link in the whole operation. Like most Covey pilots, this one was a young Air Force captain who repeatedly worked this same area both day and night.

Whale Wharton rolled into a holding pattern over Tchepone at 18,000 feet and 230 knots and mused, "You know, Knobber, I don't think there is any place called Tchepone. I've never seen it, even in the daylight. It's just a point in the sky that we home on so the bad guys can shoot at us."

Things moved quickly tonight as the standoff control plane made the handoff, "Poker, Alley Cat. Contact Covey 22 on 331.5. He's got some business."

24 October 1966 0010 hours
8th TFW TOC
Ubon RTAFB

Clint Adams watched as the TOC duty officer, one of the GIBs from the 497th TFS, relayed the details of Condor Byrd's accident to his counterpart at Blue Chip. The duty NCO was typing up the SitRep (situation report). All the key people who needed to know about the accident would have the information by teletype by morning. "Blue Chip says they'll advise General Morgan in the morning, Colonel," summarized the duty officer.

"Thanks, Lieutenant. You always seem to be on duty when there's action."

"Well, sir. . . ," stammered the duty officer, not wanting to be labeled a jinx.

"Don't take it personally. You handle yourself well. I'm turning in," said Adams in a tired voice, his eighteen-hour day catching up to his forty-four-year-old body. "But wake me if you get anything else."

0015 hours
Above Ho Chi Minh Trail, near Tchepone
South central Laos

"Poker flight, let's go 331.5."

"Zero two, copy." Wharton and his wingman switched UHF radio frequencies.

"Poker."

"Zero two." The radio calls got shorter and more focused.

"Covey 22, Poker, base plus ten. You got our load?" Pilots didn't like to repeat their weapons load. It gave the Gomers another chance to get it right. Wharton and Westcott were anxious to try out tonight's hardware on the enemy movers and bring their experience back to the other crews. Each of the LAU-3 pods contained nineteen 2.75-inch rockets with high-explosive, incendiary warheads, which could penetrate vehicles with medium armor. The rockets also worked well against flak sites. The tactics tonight called for ripple-firing two pods of rockets per pass—three passes' worth of rockets each for Wharton and his wingman.

Knob Westcott was especially interested in Poker flight's other weapon tonight, twelve CBU-24s, new cluster bombs designed for the target set most often found on the trail, dispersed soft targets supported by lightly fortified flak and legions of workers firing automatic weapons into the air. Westcott wanted to gauge the effect of the CBU-24 canister, which released more than 400 tennis-ball-sized high-fragmentation explosives. These bomblets dispersed into a lethal donut-ring pattern that spanned 300 feet, tearing apart any soft target, like a truck, in the killing zone.

The North Vietnamese already feared the weapon, calling the CBU-24 bomb cannisters "Bee Hive Bombs" or "Lazy Dogs."

Everyone turned off his exterior lights when he crossed into Laos, so the Covey 22 FAC carefully coordinated his location with Whale Wharton in the ink-black sky. He was on the radio again, "Roger, Poker, I got your weapons info. I'm at base, north of Tchepone. Got about fifty movers backed up north of a road cut made late this afternoon. The Gomers are workin' like hell to fill it under the flares."

"Copy, Covey. Taking any ground fire?" Wharton knew the North Vietnamese gunners would strongly defend the road repair teams.

"Usual small arms and AW. Expect mobile triple-A soon. Here's the layout. See the dirt area just north of the river ford illuminated by the flares?"

"Affirmative. Tally. Viz is pretty poor." The nocturnal haze over the Laotian jungle was a serious problem for pilots as the latent water vapor that burned out of the dense foliage all day settled into a moisture-laden band in the 5,000 feet of air above the jungle canopy. Adding to the problem, the burning of rice fields just to the west of the trail created persistent smoke that mixed with the natural moisture over the trail, making the haze thicker. Worse yet, the phosphorus flares created a heavy smoke residue as they burned. The longer a flare operation continued over the trail, the worse the haze got. As more flares dropped into the moist, smoky soup, the burning phosphorus turned the haze into a milky liquid.

"Crap, Knobby, the milk bowl effect's bad tonight," Wharton lamented because he couldn't see the horizon in the moonless night. These were the ingredients for inducing pilot vertigo, spatial disorientation. Wharton kept his head out of the cockpit to acquire the target in the milk bowl. Westcott kept his head *in* the cockpit and monitored the instruments, ensuring that Wharton didn't lose control of the plane. A good GIB talked to his aircraft commander all the time during this phase of a night mission. The quiet Westcott usually became a motor mouth about now. Tonight was no different.

But things didn't always work out as planned. If the frontseater had to bank his F-4 to acquire the target, the sensitive hairs in his inner ear could get distorted and he would slowly lose his sense of which end was up. If he rolled in on the target while in this condition, he never established a nose-low, wings-level reference for his body. Pilots broke off bombing runs because of vertigo.

Others made more violent recoveries from unusual attitudes. Occasionally, an F-4 crew would literally—and inadvertently—do a split-S maneuver over the target area and through the flares. Some GIBs told about being inverted over the target while *under* the flares. A fighter pilot could lose his nerve when hosed by AAA tracers that seemed to come from above him. It could spook a pilot permanently.

Covey 22 was waiting for the next flare ship and told Whale Wharton, "Poker, if you see the contrast between the road cut and the foliage to the north, run your CBUs 500 yards north of there. I'll be watching that the convoy doesn't sneak back up the road as soon as I can get another slow mover in here."

"Wilco, Covey. Are we cleared in hot?"

"Uh, Roger, Poker, cleared in hot. Best run-in headings are northeast and southwest." Before every mission, each 8th TFW pilot had to sign off that he had read and understood the Rules of Engagement. In Laos, the prime rule required that a FAC had to clear a pilot in on every target.

Wharton continued around his high roll-in circle for another fifteen seconds, then he transmitted, "Poker 01, off the perch from base plus four."

He wouldn't say from which direction, but it was from the northeast toward the southwest. The Gomers were always listening. Whale rolled his plane into a 90-degree bank and pulled the nose of his F-4 well below the artificial horizon of his attitude indicator. Now looking inside, then outside, he rolled wings level in a 35-degree dive angle, with the target reticle about 1,000 yards short of the target. He started to walk his pipper up toward the edge of the tree line north of the road cut. Whale and Knob were using their experience to reach the perfect release point in the night sky: 7,500 feet above the ground, at 450 knots, in a 30-degree dive, just as the target pipper passed through the target.

The Phantom accelerated down the chute. Whale tried for 35 degrees of dive because he usually shallowed out a little as he tracked down to the pickle point.

Knob called out what he saw on his rapidly changing instruments, "Ten point five, 375 knots."

"Nine point five, 410, 5 degrees right bank. Straighten up."

"Yeah, just correctin' the track." Whale assured Knob that he wasn't getting vertigo.

"Eight point five, 440." Whale pulled the throttles back to catch the airspeed at 450 knots.

On Westcott's cue, "Ready, pickle," Whale pressed the red button on the top of the joystick with his thumb. Both pilots felt a small double thump as the explosive charge on the ejector rack propelled two CBU cannisters free of the Phantom. Immediately, Wharton pulled back on the control stick. Loading up four Gs in less than a second, the Phantom shuddered as the nose came up through the horizon. Only then did Wharton roll into a 45-degree right climbing turn.

"Lead's off to the west, climbing to base plus four."

Poker 02 continued around the perch circle so he now was ready to roll in from the opposite direction, the southwest. Had Wharton taken any ground fire in this sequence, his wingman was poised to roll off the perch and jam thirty-eight 2.75-inch rockets down the flak gunner's throat. But Whale took no fire on his first pass.

"Poker Two's in." Wharton heard his wingman's call, then looked back, seeing two distinct flashes about 2,000 feet above the jungle. The flashes looked like ground fire, but Wharton knew they meant that his two CBU cannisters had peeled open on schedule.

Seconds later, Wharton's 800 bomblets hit the target area in two overlapping donut patterns. Five hundred feet of the Ho Chi Minh Trail came alive with violent twinkling for six seconds. A half-dozen secondary explosions erupted as the flammable supplies on the Russian-built trucks began to cook off. Three residual fires billowed up, growing out of control. Whale exhaled, "Hot damn!"

"Two's off to the east."

"Lead's in." The mutually supporting two-plane daisy chain was now in synch. Wharton drove down the same chute on the second of his three CBU-24 passes. Then Whale Wharton saw his worst nightmare. A stream of ZSU-23 tracers belched right up the chute directly at him. For a moment the tracer stream looked like a flamethrower spewing at him at short range. "Knobby, they're hosin' us. I'm aborting the pass." Wharton yanked hard left and nose up. Then he felt the multiple deadening thuds and saw the bright screaming flash. He tried to pull harder and—.

Covey 22 thought he saw Wharton's F-4 take three AAA hits. It was hard to know exactly what happened to Poker 01 without more light, but three distinct burning pieces tumbled into the jungle below. "Poker 01, Covey 22, over."

Nothing.

Covey 22 tried again. "Poker Lead, how do you read?"

No response.

The FAC switched to the emergency frequency. "Poker Lead, Covey 22 on Guard, do you copy?"

Nothing.

"Alley Cat, Covey 22 on Guard. Poker 01 took a direct hit. Radar-guided ZSUs. Recommend you start an SAR. I'll cap the site with Poker 02. No chutes. No beepers."

"Alley Cat, Wilco." Everyone sounded so matter of fact. They'd all been involved in these situations before and knew the odds of recovering downed American pilots anywhere near the trail. The area swarmed with very mad North Vietnamese who considered U.S. pilots devils from the sky.

U.S. intelligence believed that American pilots captured in Laos tended to stay in jungle prison camps, where they received very harsh treatment, if they survived capture. The North Vietnamese had yet to report a U.S. pilot downed in Laos as a prisoner of war in Hanoi's jails. All that seemed meaningless when thirty minutes had elapsed and still no chutes. Still no beepers.

First it was Sansone up North. Next it was Condor in the flight line accident. Then it was Whale and Knob. Tragedies did happen in threes.

0045 hours
The senior officers' trailer area, Ubon RTAFB

Adams's brick chirped at him. Irritated, he stopped the jeep. His battery was running down, and he needed some rack time. Couldn't this place run by itself for a few hours? he thought. His attitude was markedly different from that of the active wing commander moving among his maintenance troops only ninety minutes earlier. Fatigue and adversity could wear anyone down.

"Honcho One, go ahead."

"Sir, this is the TOC. I think you ought to come back over. We've got a problem."

In an instant, the weariness drained from Clint Adams. "Copy. On the way." He cranked up the jeep. The bad news about Poker 01 waited for him at the TOC.

0155 hours
Outside the 8th TFW clinic

Keeping vigil at the TOC for Whale Wharton and Knob Westcott was grinding Clint Adams's stomach into a knot. The three cups of thick, duty-officer coffee smothered all thoughts of sleep. He had to keep busy. Checking on Chris Cole proved a good tonic; at least his crew chief was pulling himself together.

Some nights a wing commander didn't get any respite. Clint decided to let Bear Robinson sleep; he'd have to carry the wing in the morning when the adrenaline stopped and Adams truly burned out.

Heading back to the TOC, Adams swung by the flight line. The base fire chief was still at the accident, surveying the physics of the event with the wing ground safety officer. It all had to go in the report. The chief saw Adams drive up. "Surprised to still see you out here, Colonel. This part's usually left to us technicians."

"We lost a plane over the trail about an hour ago," explained Adams. "Do we have any worries about aircraft #640 itself?"

"Nossir. If it didn't blow when the ejection seat fired, it won't now. Would have cooked off lots of trouble with all those rockets underneath."

Clint started to say something about downloading the damaged plane, when the crack of a small explosion in the distance interrupted him. He asked, "What the hell was *that*, Chief?"

"Beats the crap out of me, sir. This is one busy night. Excuse me, sir."

Adams saw a smoking fireball rolling up out of the trailer area. When Clint turned back, the fire chief was already in his car and driving toward the trailers. Adams followed the fire chief's lead and shouted into his brick, "Ubon TOC, Honcho One. Get fire, medical, and Air Police moving toward the trailers now. Hustle it up."

Coming upon the scene, Adams found half of his trailer gone and the other half being hosed down by the fire department. The base commander saw Adams arrive and exclaimed, "Looks like someone put a bomb under your bed, sir!"

"Most any other night I would be in it." Adams thought that if it hadn't been for Laura's tape and a string of bad events he'd be spread out over the whole trailer area in little pieces.

OSI Agent Thompson moved out of the gathering crowd and introduced himself to Clint Adams. Thompson had a lot to tell him.

1030 hours
The 497th TFS Officers' Quarters
Ubon RTAFB

Randy Starbuck and Taco Martinez stopped their Air Force blue pickup in front of the Night Owl Officers' Hootch, where the squadron's majors, captains, and lieutenants lived. Senior officers lived in nearby trailers. Many of the pilots in the two-story building were still sleeping. There were no windows, but each two-man room was clearly marked by an air conditioning unit protruding from the exterior wall, where the window ought to have been.

Starbuck had checked and knew that Wharton's Phantom didn't carry the new APR-25 RHAW gear on his F-4. Only twenty-one of Ubon's F-4s had been modified. The APR-25 worked very well in a place like Laos where there were very few electronic emitters, and the RHAW receiver would have told Whale that a North Vietnamese gunner was tracking him. Whale would not have continued in a straight track down the chute if he had known radar-guided AAA was onto him. He would have jinked and aborted the bombing pass earlier. Wharton and Westcott would have been alive.

Randy and Taco dragged an 8-by-4 sheet of plywood from the pickup's cargo bed. Each man grabbed one edge and turned the plywood edge up. Starbuck led the way into the Hootch and down to the end of the hall. They stopped at room 14, Condor Byrd's room.

The room to the left was room 12. When the building was first occupied a year ago, some superstitious pilot had renumbered all the rooms 12 through 20. He skipped 13, so that the new numbers were 14 through 21. But fate was not so easily dispatched. Room 13 was *still* room 13, even if it was marked room 14 on the door.

This room had a terrible history. Condor Byrd was the fourth occupant to be killed. The first two residents of room 14, both captains, died on a night-instrument approach to Ubon trying to penetrate a violent thunderstorm. The Accident Investigation Board found the primary cause to be pilot error. Their report called it "poor judgment in the face of adverse weather." Pilots called it "get-homeitis." The aircrew should have diverted to Da Nang, but instead they had pushed to land at Ubon.

Room 14 stayed vacant for two weeks as the training pipeline went dry for a while. Then a single new GIB checked into the 497th. The Night Owl's newest backseater arrived at Ubon alone because his AC had broken a leg in a motorcycle accident at F-4 school at Davis-Monthan. The billeting officer assigned him room 14. Later the next day, a milk run popped up on the 497th's flying schedule, so the new GIB flew his "dollar ride," his first introduction to the easiest part of the combat zone.

But his experienced frontseater was feeling aggressive and dueled with the flak guns on the trail that day. The AAA won when it bracketed the

Phantom pulling off its third pass. No chutes. No beepers. The FAC watched the whole grisly scene all the way to the Phantom's impact into a granite outcropping.

Nobody living in the 497th Hootch even knew the new GIB's name. He'd been on-station for forty-eight hours, and only the squadron commander and the operations officer knew who he was. He hadn't even converted to the night flying schedule yet. Still, the Night Owls suffered his loss.

At the bar the next day, his surviving comrades convinced themselves that they would not have gone nose to nose with the flak guns in daylight. Then someone at the bar room critique mentioned that the new GIB had checked into room 14. Another pilot told how room 14 had gotten its number. All fighter squadrons had a bad luck room. From then on, room 14 was the squadron's unlucky room.

That night, after returning to the Hootch, a few pilots conducted a small ritual. With a magic marker they inscribed the names of the three dead pilots and the dates they had died on the inside of room 14's door. From that day, the billeting officer avoided putting new pilots into room 14.

Wars didn't allow for the even flow of new pilots to combat squadrons. It was feast or famine, and inevitably, the 497th's billeting officer had too many young pilots and too few rooms. Still, he advised each newcomer of room 14's history. No one *had* to take it; the pilot had the option. Dozens turned down room 14 and lived in transient quarters for an extra week or two until another room came available in the Night Owl Hootch.

Four months earlier, Condor Byrd had moved into room 14. For a week he'd stayed in the transient quarters like everyone else. But the transient building had no air conditioning, little privacy, and too much noise. Byrd was a very light sleeper, one of the few pilots who couldn't sleep through Ubon's normal flight line action. Always flying at night made it even worse.

Reluctantly, he moved into room 14, and he slept like a baby as the air conditioner droned on constantly. He had all the privacy he ever wanted because no one would move in with him. No one, that was, until the air conditioner blew a compressor in Knob Westcott's room next door. A windowless room in Thailand with a bum air conditioner immediately became a steam bath.

So Knob Westcott grabbed his pillow and flopped into the extra bed in room 14. One night. Hell, it couldn't hurt. He'd get a new air conditioner in the morning. Besides, nothing had happened to Condor Byrd. . . .

Starbuck had cleaned out Byrd's belongings earlier that morning. He had volunteered to be Condor's summary court officer, that thankless job of inventorying a fallen soldier's possessions, going through a comrade's belongings, and forwarding the appropriate things to the deceased's next of kin—in this case, Byrd's wife.

After adding Condor Byrd and Knob Westcott to the list of names on the back of room 14's door, Starbuck and Martinez nailed the plywood sheet into place. The banging of the hammers woke a few 497th pilots. One miffed captain, unaware of how last night's tragedies related to this morning's noisy intrusion of his valued sleep, stuck his head out into the hall. "Hey, what the hell's goin' on out here?"

Randy Starbuck, in no mood for lengthy explanations, shot back, "Shut the fuck up, asshole."

Room 14 was sealed forever.

THE TOUR EXTENSION

The rule was simple. The combat tour in Southeast Asia for Air Force personnel was one year. For 99.5 percent of blue-suiters, that was it. When arriving in country and processing in at the Base Personnel Office, a new pilot got a projected return date one year from the day he'd arrived. There was only one exception to this iron-clad rule—if an Air Force crew member accumulated 100 combat missions over North Vietnam, he could leave before his one-year tour was up.

This exception was official acknowledgment that flying combat missions over North Vietnam was the most dangerous thing that Air Force people could do in Southeast Asia. Fighter pilots, therefore, and the small number of navigators who flew up North with them, were an elite group. Many other missions got Air Force people killed, but day for day, taking an air machine up North was the toughest game in town. The pilot survivability rate was only sixty-three missions. After that, statistically, he didn't come back. He was much likelier to be killed, missing, or captured. With that possibility, from the pilot's viewpoint, 100 missions over the North didn't look like that good a deal.

The 8th TFW pilot who beat the odds would fly 180 combat missions, 100 over North Vietnam, in eight months. The squadron scheduling officer ensured that pilots arriving together would progress toward the magic 100 number at the same pace. The scheduler got more help than he wanted from every pilot in the squadron. The pilots studied the squadron mission board with more intensity than Wall Street day traders watched the ticker.

Every pilot knew all the other pilots in the squadron who'd arrived thirty days before and after he did. If the scheduling officer allowed one pilot to get more than a few missions ahead of his buddies, the others hounded the scheduler for an explanation. If they weren't satisfied, they complained to the squadron ops officer, even the squadron commander.

When a pilot migrated to a job at wing headquarters, the ground rules changed somewhat. A wing weenie could drop behind the pace of his peers, but he couldn't ever get ahead. The demands of wing-level jobs simply tied up an officer's time and availability. Boomer Wright dropped about two months behind his peers until Adams unchained him from the wing exec's desk and allowed him to fly more missions. The DCO's exec, Todd Benning, hadn't been so lucky. Slim Danforth still kept him on a short leash. Benning would stay a full year and wouldn't get a full 100-mission tour under his belt.

Randy Starbuck had arrived at Ubon in March. After eight months, he had 98 counters over North Vietnam and 151 total combat missions, the difference being his sorties against Laos. He would complete his combat tour by the end of the week. Starbuck could be eating Thanksgiving dinner with his parents in Buckatunna, Mississippi.

But Randy had a different plan. He wanted a second consecutive tour, right here at Ubon. But the wheels of the Air Force personnel process were grinding against him. The sergeant in assignments at Base Personnel had called Starbuck last week with his next assignment: as a B-52 copilot at Loring AFB, Maine, on the Canadian border. Starbuck sloughed it off and asked the assignments NCO about the status of his consecutive tour request. The sergeant's reply hit Starbuck like a ton of bricks, "Oh, that. Colonel Danforth nixed that right away. Enjoy Loring, Captain Starbuck."

Randy was sitting on the edge of the Naugahyde plastic sofa in Danforth's outer office. His brain was tying itself in knots. Why hadn't Danforth advised him that he'd disapproved the second tour when he'd applied three months ago? What reason could he have had? Why hadn't he had the courtesy to tell him?

Starbuck could answer this last question himself. He remembered Danforth's reputation. He got even. This could be Colonel Danforth's way of squaring things with his tactics chief for getting too cozy with the wing commander and working up the Bolo plan.

The intercom on Todd Benning's desk buzzed for a full second. "The boss will see you now, Randy."

Starbuck opened the door to Danforth's office. There was no open-door policy here. Randy closed the door behind him and saluted.

"What's up, Starbuck?" Danforth divided his attention between his tactics chief and the officer efficiency reports (OERs) he was reviewing. Danforth was a born paper pusher. He liked spending an enormous amount of time on the OERs of his subordinates. He mulled over every word and often substituted his own for those that were suggested to him.

"Sir, I've got ninety-eight counters, and I just found out I'm going to fly a SAC B-52. Even worse, I'm going in as a copilot. I probably won't upgrade to left-seat aircraft commander for more than a year."

"We all have to do our part for the war effort, Captain." Danforth had waited for this day. Sooner or later, he knew Starbuck would fall into his net.

"Sir, it's not good for the Air Force to squander away my combat experience." Starbuck's summary didn't begin to capture the totality of what was happening to him. He was a victim of top-level Air Force personnel policy. Six months earlier, Pentagon planners had decided that the air war in Southeast Asia could last for years. If it did, fighter pilots might have to fly two or three combat tours. A fighter pilot's longevity over the next five years would be very poor.

In contrast, some of the other 40,000 pilots in the Air Force might never fly a combat tour. Most bomber, tanker, trainer, transport, and utility pilots didn't fly missions leading to a full-time combat tour.

So the big brass believed that the only practical decision was to tap the existing base of experienced pilots flying the nontactical missions of the U.S. Air Force. It was an incredibly expensive decision because now almost every Air Force pilot got trained in a new aircraft.

Both Danforth and Starbuck were acutely aware of what this meant for career fighter pilots. Some of the Randy Starbucks and Mike Nelsons would fill the seats of the bomber and cargo pilots who had orders to report to F-4 training schools in Florida and Arizona. That's why Starbuck and many other veteran fighter jocks wanted to extend for a second consecutive combat tour. They'd signed up to fly fighters. And they would much rather fly combat F-4s than sit SAC alert in Maine or North Dakota.

Danforth looked up over his black-rimmed reading glasses and almost gloated, "You know the score, Starbuck. You had your fun. Now you gotta go fill some SAC pilot's seat."

"Sir, I'm more valuable to the Air Force here at Ubon, especially now."

"Now?" Danforth already had Starbuck's OER in his out basket. Danforth had weaseled the word picture on the back of Starbuck's end-of-tour efficiency report just enough to question Starbuck's loyalty as a staff officer. When Randy Starbuck's personnel record met the USAF Central Major's Promotion Board the following year, this lukewarm report would be a small cancer in his personnel folder.

"Yessir. Now. With all the Bolo planning I mean." Starbuck knew that he had to play his only trump card—his relative indispensability in planning Bolo's details—early. Danforth was a hard-ass of the first water.

"You just don't want to be a SAC puke. That's it, isn't it? You think you're too good to go where the Air Force needs you, right? So you're tying yourself to something important, something current."

"I've got all the Bolo planning done. But there's a bunch of coordinating that I started. And if I depart in the middle of it, we'll lose weeks of detailed spadework."

Danforth had turned his attention back to his OERs, but he looked up now. "Don't blow smoke up my butt, Captain. No one's indispensable, and Bolo's on indefinite hold. It may never happen. Brief one of your BIBs and press on to SAC, young man. You still have a lot to learn about the Air Force and taking orders. We all have to do what's required."

"Well, I reckon that's it, sir." Starbuck didn't grovel. He was a realist. Dammit! He saluted and left.

Starbuck pounded out into the main hallway and started the long walk down to the Wing Tactics Shop. Halfway there he passed Boomer Wright, who was in his normal upbeat mood. "Hey Randy, what's the problem? You look like Doc Kramer just grounded you for a case of the crabs."

"Worse than that. I've got two counters to go, a B-52 copilot seat at Loring, and Danforth won't back my extension request."

All this caught Boomer cold. Starbuck kept walking down the hall.

1015 hours
Wing commander's office
Ubon RTAFB

Clint Adams's weekly logistics meeting was running fifteen minutes over the scheduled hour. Boomer jammed his black government ball-point pen on the pad of recycled paper to get the ink flowing. He hurriedly scribbled the main points he wanted to tell Colonel Adams on Randy Starbuck's behalf, if he ever got the chance. Adams had a meeting with all the chief master sergeants on base at the NCO Club at 1030. And he flew a mission after that. Come on, guys, logistics couldn't be that interesting.

The door opened, and Adams was the first one out, hat in hand. "Boomer, I'm off to see the chiefs."

Boomer stood, "Colonel, we need to talk."

"Then you better ride with me." Wright grabbed his hat and the keys to the command jeep, just in case.

Outside, Adams was already cranking the jeep as Boomer hopped in the right seat and said, "Sir, Randy Starbuck flies his ninety-ninth counter tomorrow."

"Uh oh." Adams knew what this could mean. It was one of those things that snuck up and bit wing commanders. Adams had to rely on his subordinates to keep all parts of the personnel puzzle on track and consistent with his overall strategy for the wing. He suspected the worst, but he had to ask for the details anyway. "He's a bachelor. Did he put in for an extension?"

"Yessir. But Colonel Danforth denied it."

"Danforth?" Adams didn't believe it. He thought some external force in the personnel system must have put the kebash on Starbuck's request, but not his own DCO.

The short, two-minute drive to the NCO Club was over. "Okay, Boomer. Thanks for the heads up. I'll take it from here. Tell the ops briefer I may be a little late for the mission briefing."

Adams stepped out but paused. "By the way, what assignment did Starbuck pull?"

"B-52 copilot at Loring."

"Christ Almighty." Adams wondered what kind of a personnel system would pull a highly valued national asset like Randy Starbuck out of the fight he wanted to be in, the one the American taxpayer had spent millions to train him to fight. Not to mention the Bolo planning. Without another word, Adams bounded up the NCO Club's four steps two at a time, and he was through the teakwood double doors in a second. Boomer could hear the building called to attention. All was in order.

Boomer Wright got out of Adams's jeep, put on his hat, and started the four-block walk back to wing headquarters. The late morning sun burned the back of his neck. He didn't mind. He had done his job well so far today.

1115 hours
Near the DCO's office, 8th TFW HQ
Ubon RTAFB

Clint Adams's brick chirped at him for the thousandth time. He acknowledged some routine information about rain showers closing in on Ubon from the northwest. But the noise in the hall had tipped off Todd Benning to the wing commander's imminent arrival. He alerted the enlisted clerks and popped up to knock on Colonel Danforth's door.

"Sir, Colonel Adams is on his way down the hall." Adams walked past Benning with a quick smile and closed Danforth's door behind him.

"Good morning, sir. What can I do for you?" Danforth stopped.

"You can get with the program, Slim."

"Sir, I don't know what you—"

"Randy Starbuck gets an extension. Get it worked with Major Conroy at Base Personnel. Today. No ifs, ands, or buts. Got it?"

"Yes, sir."

Adams started to leave but added final instructions. "Fix it by the time I land, or you're going home in his place."

"Yes, sir."

"Slim, I'm disappointed." Adams closed the door on his way out without waiting for a response.

Danforth was quivering with rage. There was a knock at the door. The knob started to turn, but it stopped when Danforth angrily shouted, "Not now!"

Slim flipped through the papers in his in basket until he found what he wanted. He glanced at Starbuck's efficiency report, opened his upper left-hand desk drawer, and slipped the form inside, slamming the drawer behind it. That OER would be ready when Starbuck rotated back to the States. He would just change the dates.

It was Clint Adams that Danforth wanted to get even with right now. And his plan was already in motion.

THE CONTROVERSY

14 November 1966 0530 hours
The senior officers' trailer area
Ubon RTAFB

Boomer ran through the compound on a beeline for Adams's new trailer, surrounded by sandbags like all the others now. He knocked forcefully on the door, listened for movement inside. Nothing. Impatiently, he knocked again, harder this time. His boss was a heavy sleeper, and last night Adams had put away more than a few scotches while presiding over a farewell party for one of his squadron commanders. There was some stirring inside the trailer, and a light came on in the bedroom. Thirty seconds later Adams opened the door slightly and peered outside. "What the hell brings you out this early, Boomer?" He threw open the door for his exec to enter, then shuffled into the toilet to relieve himself, leaving the door ajar as a signal for Boomer to get to the reason he was there. Boomer started to talk, but Adams's morning cigarette cough made it difficult to tell the story.

"You're not gonna like this, Boss." All execs to combat wing commanders brought their bosses bad news now and then. Boomer was no exception. Over the sound of running water, Adams, still hacking and staring at his bloodshot eyes in the bathroom mirror, prompted Boomer, "Dish it out. Straight up."

"Got a heads-up from the public information officer (PIO) at Seventh Air Force about a negative story running in the States."

"So what's new?" Adams flushed the toilet and reentered the outer room, scratching his crotch.

"Uh, Boss, a war correspondent did a story for *Washington Monthly*. The PIO said it's on page one of the Pentagon's *Early Bird*." Boomer knew that mentioning the Pentagon's daily clipping service of defense-related news articles would pique his commander's interest, because every general and civilian bureaucrat in the Pentagon read it from cover to cover.

"People have been bad-mouthing me for years, Boomer, but this is serious shit. What the hell's this all about?" Adams padded away in his bare feet and rummaged through the kitchen for something to eat fast.

Boomer continued. "The *Washington Monthly* article takes dead aim at you for doing a poor job as the wing commander here at Ubon. The reporter questions the quality of our pilots. Sir, he even questions your loyalty to higher headquarters, all the way to President Johnson."

"What?" Adams pressed Boomer. "Do we have a copy yet?"

"Nossir."

"Who wrote it?"

"Some guy named Massey."

"Does Morgan know yet?"

"Nossir, the public information officer at Seventh said he would call General Morgan about 0600 our time."

Adams sent Boomer off with definite instructions. "Get a verbatim transcript over the phone—fast." Adams showered and dressed quickly. Shit! The day was sure off to a poor start. And his head hurt like hell.

0600 hours
8th TFW command section
Ubon RTAFB

Adams walked quickly into his office, motioning Boomer to follow. Curt Robinson came in too. Danforth, by coincidence, was in the outer office browsing through the morning message file. Adams saw him and waved for him to join the group. Boomer was tentative at first, shifting his eyes from one colonel to another in rapid succession. Adams asked, "Do you have the exact words yet?"

"Yessir."

"Read them," Adams said impatiently.

Boomer knew what was ahead. This made him pause, then he read the piece out loud, headline first. "'American Pilots Down More Booze Than MiGs.' It's by a Tom Massey."

The exec stopped reading for a moment, looking at each colonel to gauge his reaction. Adams's expression didn't change. Robinson, new to the event, looked surprised. Danforth raised his eyebrows.

Boomer shrugged his shoulders, then he launched into the text. It was short but hard hitting.

> Ubon, Thailand. The bar at the Officers' Club is an exciting place. It's much like a college fraternity party in full swing. The fighter pilots assigned to the 8th Tactical Fighter Wing involve themselves in a series of ritualistic games that result in broken furniture, personal injuries, and beer all over the place.
>
> Since World War II there has been a disturbing trend. It seems as if the size of the Officers' Clubs and the energies devoted to partying have increased at our fighter wings, while the performance against the enemy in the air has decreased.
>
> In the skies over North Korea, for example, U.S. F-86 pilots racked up an impressive 13-1 kill ratio against the enemy. Over North Vietnam, we are barely earning a 1.5-1 advantage against a badly outnumbered enemy flying antiquated planes. In Korea, we had many aces. But although we've been flying over North Vietnam for 18 months, America does not have a single ace. What kind of leader allows his pilots to behave like adolescents every night when they ought to be figuring out how to gain air superiority?
>
> Enter Colonel Clint Adams, the wing commander at Ubon for two months. His major accomplishments have been to relax discipline and encourage a party atmosphere. When discipline erodes, so does respect for authority. As a result, talk among the 8th TFW pilots often turns to contempt for higher authority. They don't believe the air war over North Vietnam is being run correctly. So they bad-mouth their generals and even LBJ himself.
>
> They even talk about striking restricted targets that would undermine the prosecution of the war. Confidential sources hint that Adams himself, the chief cowboy at this ranch, is planning an unorthodox mission that will cause the people in Washington to sit up and take notice. One month ago, the Pentagon brass relieved a wing commander for breaking the rules. Is Adams next? Time will tell.

Adams was dumbstruck.

Robinson was furious. "I'd love to get my hands on that scumbag," he said.

Danforth looked indignant.

"I better call General Morgan immediately," Adams said, signaling for the meeting to break up.

But Boomer hung back after the others left. "Sir, I think I remember the reporter. You know, this Massey guy."

"What do you recollect? Tell me exactly."

"Well, there was a civilian correspondent here, oh, a few weeks ago. Like most of those reporters, he hung around the O Club most of the time. If you want, I'll check with our own wing PIO about when Massey was here."

"Yeah, check right away."

Boomer popped back in as fast as he left Adams's office. "Excuse me, sir, General Morgan's on the regular phone. Line one." Preempted, Adams picked up the phone and waited for Morgan's secretary to put the general on.

Morgan's voice was cold and very businesslike. He wasn't pleased. "Have you seen the news article, Clint?"

"Yes, sir, just read the transcript."

"Do you have an explanation?"

"No, sir, no explanation. We're checking now, but we believe the reporter was here last month."

"That's all well and good, but what about the allegations made by this Massey fellow?"

"The substance of the article's all wet. Morale's high, it's getting higher, and any plan to bomb targets on the White House restricted list is pure bull crap. The only thing we have in the wind is the plan I briefed you on last month."

"I've always given you your head, Clint. I hope that you've honored my trust in you. For now though, I'm going to get to the bottom of this."

"Sir, you know I wouldn't—"

"Clint, I just got off the line with the Chief. He's on the hot seat back in Washington. He told me that the White House staff and the Pentagon civilians are pressuring him to send you home. Permanently."

"General, I—"

"The Chief doesn't hang people based on news stories. But don't be fooled. This is a funny war. Many of the most important battles are being fought in the news media. And in Washington we're not winning many of them."

"What can I do to set things right, sir?"

"The Chief agrees with me that we need a formal investigation. And fast. Inspector General Brigadier Carl Waters will conduct that investigation. He'll fly up to Ubon this afternoon and inspect the 8th Tac Fighter Wing from head to toe. Give him your full cooperation."

"I will, sir. We'll open up everything to the IG."

"Oh, by the way, I did get a TWX from the Pentagon this morning. The North Vietnamese complained through the Burmese Embassy that Americans caused substantial damage to one of their MiG bases. The Joint Chiefs want to know more about what happened."

"Anything I can add to my debrief to you last night, sir?"

"No, I've already answered that it was an inadvertent flyover after a low-level MiG chase. No ordnance expended. Pilot disciplined immediately. I think that should do it. But I need to tell you, Clint, that if you hadn't called I might have handled things differently, especially based on this morning's news. Remember our last face-to-face talk about this very subject."

Adams knew this would come up. It was the first thing he thought about when Boomer gave him the bad news in the trailer.

"Clint, true or not, Washington and the American public are beginning to think we have a discipline problem in the officer corps over here, thanks to the events of past few months. If anyone at Ubon is bellyaching about the target restrictions, you need to knock heads. And we need to knock down MiGs."

Adams saw his chance. "Yes, sir. Give us the execute order for Operation Bolo. That could yield more MiGs, while firing up the pilots. As well as everyone else."

"No. Right now a failed Bolo would look like a bush-league, grandstand play to recover the confidence of the folks back home. For now, continue on course, tighten discipline, and keep your mouth shut. The war effort is bigger than any one man. Clint," Morgan said, sounding warmer now, "if the reporter's allegations are groundless, someone's gunning for you. And, he's not above dragging the 8th TFW and the whole U.S. Air Force through the mud to get you."

Adams responded quickly, "I don't believe there are people in the weeds obsessed enough to do that kind of thing, sir. These peckerwood reporters make a living stirring up this kind of trouble."

"Well, that newsman must have had some help. Some of my staff are negative toward you and the wing at Ubon, but they wouldn't stoop to this. Someone may be right there at Ubon, particularly if Massey was a recent visitor."

"I can't think of anyone, but I'll give it some thought, sir."

1200 hours
Lake of the Restored Sword
Hanoi

Nguyen Tomb's Sunday outings to Hanoi were never complete without a visit to his favorite place on earth. Before returning to Gia Lam, he always made his way to Hanoi's Lake of the Sword. Unlike other parts of the city, the major lake parks were still maintained and provided the people with an anchor of natural beauty, continuously filled with fresh plantings.

Tomb turned onto the densely treed boulevard that ringed the lake. It was like bicycling into another world. The ever-present bomb shelter manholes were the only signs of war. The atmosphere was festive, and many North Vietnamese strolled along the water. Old women sold fresh bouquets to the young soldiers on military leave about to meet their wives or girlfriends. The lake was well known as a lovers' rendezvous. Tomb noticed many young couples crammed onto the available benches, while others stole away across the stone footbridges leading to the Buddhist pagodas on the small islands that dotted the lake.

The people of Hanoi dressed up when they visited the lake, a difficult task in a country where the annual ration was five yards of cotton cloth. Most men wore newly laundered uniforms. The women wore pre-war classic Vietnamese ao dais, the traditional high-collared silk tunic worn over sateen trousers. Breaking with custom, some women removed their conical straw hats, normally held in place with a matching white scarf tied beneath the chin. This was a clear sign that these women, always traveling with girlfriends, wished to be seen.

As a full colonel in the NVAF, Nguyen Tomb enjoyed one major perk; he was allowed to shop at the Diplomatic Store on the east shore of the lake. This was the only facility in North Vietnam that came close to resembling a Western department store. And for Tomb, it was always a basket of surprises. This was where he had bought his radio and his Leica. The store contained little variety, but it did have large quantities of each item. The export stock were always the same: trinkets made in North Vietnam's cottage industries and coffee, a fallout of the French occupation. But the imported stock changed frequently, depending on what Communist-bloc freighter had docked in Haiphong the previous week. Tomb could choose among jellies from Romania, Russian caviar and vodka, Chinese and English tea, and even Russian dresses in patterns

Vietnamese would not wear. Today, Tomb bought some jelly and tea, paying 40 dong for the lot.

He liked to sit on the shore of the 110-hectare lake. To Nguyen Tomb, this was what paradise must be like. He was at peace here. An ancient myth tied the Lake of the Restored Sword to the fifteenth-century Nguyen Dynasty. Tomb could imagine that he saw the ancient Vietnamese soldier-patriot Le Loi on the lake in a boat just as the legend described him. The fifteenth-century hero had led the charge for Nguyen Trai's army that drove the Chinese Mings from his homeland. In that final battle he used a magic sword that he returned to a golden turtle in the center of this very lake.

Like Le Loi, Tomb saw himself as a soldier-patriot, driving twentieth-century invaders from his homeland. Tomb's magic lay not in a sword but in his favorite MiG-17.

One thing made this small pocket of Nirvana incomplete. Sometimes Nguyen's thoughts wandered to that future time when there would be peace throughout his country. Then he would like to marry, if he were not too old. That was why he'd always returned to this particular spot on the southeast side of the lake.

He remembered the day he'd met the most beautiful young woman he had ever seen. It had been about nine months earlier, on a Sunday afternoon trip to the lake. She had been as tall as he was, with long black hair that shone like silk in the sunlight. She'd walked with her girlfriend along the lake's edge, throwing seeds to the ducks. The two women had passed in front of Tomb's bench several times during one hour. He was quite sure that she'd taken note of him, probably attracted by his uniform. When the girl's younger friend had gone off to buy another bag of seed, Tomb had taken the big step; for the only time in his life, he had had the courage to introduce himself to an unescorted woman.

He'd asked her to join him on the bench. She'd agreed after feigning that she was late and must soon return to her parent's home, above the flower shop they owned, seven blocks away. He'd learned her name, Tran Li, and her age, nineteen. She had been a student at the Peoples' University until the government closed all the schools and evacuated half the city. Now, like her fellow students, she had finished her local militia training and would soon leave for full-time duty in Laos.

Tomb had asked her to join him for a light meal at the Bo-Ho (lakeside) restaurant, and they had enjoyed a modest snack at one of the outdoor tables. This had been a special treat for Tran because all food was rationed. Until she reported for active duty, her rice ration would be only 10 kilos per month, half that of a production worker. There were no overweight people in North Vietnam.

They'd both enjoyed a sweet onion bun, he with a Hanoi beer and she with a café au lait. But thirty minutes into their conversation the air raid siren had sounded. Over the wailing din they'd hastily agreed to meet again the following Sunday. Unfortunately, his duties had kept him from that rendezvous for the next six weeks. When he finally made it back to the lake on a Sunday afternoon, Tran Li was nowhere in sight. After a half dozen such Sunday trips, Tomb found and spoke to Tran Li's younger girlfriend. She told him that Tran Li had been sent to work on the Ho Chi Minh Trail. At the beginning, she had written to her parents, but the letters had stopped about a month ago. He did not want to think that Tran Li was dead, probably in an American air raid.

For now, Nguyen Tomb knew he must forgo thoughts of marriage in this time of national sacrifice. Nearly thirty-eight, he had been waging war since he was twelve. He mounted his bicycle and pedaled toward the Long Bien Bridge. The air raid sirens wailed throughout the city.

1300 hours
Aircraft parking area
Ubon RTAFB

Two staff sergeants loading radar missiles into the underbelly coves of an F-4 saw Clint Adams driving past the front of their revetment. Adams always spent a lot of time on the flight line with the maintenance men. He'd learned a long time ago that this was where a commander found out how well his organization was running. And this was where he found out if morale was high or low.

One missile loader remarked to his buddy, "I hope the colonel and his pilots aren't too hung over to fire these AIM-7s later this afternoon." The other loader grunted, nodding in agreement.

Further down the flight line, Adams stopped in front of F-4 #680. Sergeant Chris Cole was working in the front cockpit. Cole jumped out and scurried down the ladder when he saw Adams. Cole was a positive person by nature, so he put his best face on for his commander.

Adams hoped Cole would give him an honest assessment. "How are the maintenance troops taking it?"

Cole started to give an optimistic response but then stopped. He felt the colonel deserved a straight answer. That's why he was out here. "Crap, sir, they don't know what to think. But they want to believe it's not true."

"Well, that's just it. There's enough truth in it that you can add two and two and get five."

Adams heard the sound of the four-engine C-130 cargo plane on short final approach for landing. "Thanks, Chris," he said. "Tell the troops to hang in there. We're gonna figure out where that lousy rumor came from and fix it." Adams drove off. Cole was pleased that the colonel hadn't tried to give him some lame excuse.

General Carl Waters was the first person off the C-130 Hercules. The other twenty members of the inspector general (IG) team filed off after him.

Adams was courteous, respectful, and resolute, remembering his promise to General Morgan. "Welcome to Ubon, General."

"Clint. Good to see you. Not the best of circumstances though, is it?"

"No, sir."

Carl Waters was an aloof, by-the-book officer. Always had been for the fifteen years Adams had known him. There were no surprises here. Adams loaded Waters in his command jeep, which Waters noted was an unusual staff car, but the two men didn't talk on the way to the VIP trailer. Waters was preoccupied, assessing the passing scene.

Boomer saluted the jeep's occupants as they arrived at Waters's trailer, and then he took the general's bags inside.

Adams asked, "What do you want to look at first, General?"

"I'm okay for now, Clint. But let me lay out the ground rules for this investigation. You can expect me and my team members to move around the base unescorted and unannounced. We won't have any set agenda or any predetermined length of stay. What we find at one place will drive where we look next. My exec will work with yours to set aside some office space for interviews."

"Fine, sir. I'll have a staff car sent over right away."

Waters paused, then said, "A jeep will do just fine." Both men smiled, shook hands, and exchanged salutes. The general's last comment suggested that Waters would give the 8th TFW a fair shake. Adams was less concerned than he had been twenty minutes earlier.

1325 hours
8th TFW HQ
Ubon RTAFB

Adams entered the main entrance to his headquarters, deep in thought as he proceeded down the hall to the wing command section. He didn't notice Randy Starbuck and walked right past him.

"Hello, Colonel."

"Oh, Randy, how's the detailed planning going on Bolo?"

"Got almost all the kinks worked out."

"Almost?"

"Yessir, almost." Starbuck lowered his voice and checked that they were alone in the hallway. "Still havin' some hang-ups with the pods."

"What pods?"

"The jamming pods."

"But we don't carry—" Adams caught himself and stopped.

"The Thuds just started carrying them on every mission."

Adams smiled to indicate that he liked Starbuck's attention to detail in this operation. "Let me know when you get it worked out."

"Oh, and Colonel, thanks for the tour extension."

"Sure thing. But I want you out of here when Bolo is over. Danforth's right, SAC needs talented pilots like you."

Starbuck watched the broad-shouldered colonel walk off toward the wing command section.

1630 hours
The Triple Nickel officers' hootch
Ubon RTAFB

Mike Nelson had had a lousy month. The Phuc Yen incident had cost him a lot more than he'd expected. He really hadn't thought through his actions very well. Most important, he'd stepped out of character and acted on undisciplined impulse. Now he had a lower opinion of himself, despite Rod Wells's efforts.

Nelson was troubled because Moose Peterson hadn't come around either. Before Phuc Yen, Moose was always there, on duty and off. It wasn't like the closeness he'd had with Vic Sansone, but it was solid. Something with which he and Moose had been comfortable. In the air, they had been an effective team, correctly anticipating what each man needed to do next for the other. On the ground, Moose had been the ever-present linebacker, there to support Mike Nelson and Vic Sansone in any endeavor. Moose and Snake both, that is. The four of them had been the Young Turks of the Triple Nickel. They had been the Four Horsemen. And then they'd lost Vic, and the whole thing had fallen apart.

The last month had been quite different. Without Vic Sansone, Nelson had become a loner. So had Moose Peterson. They flew out their missions, but they hardly talked, even in the cockpit. Their aircrew performance, once superior and getting better, had dropped off. Now they were like most other crews—adequate. Nelson and Peterson didn't socialize together, either. Moose even preferred being called Knute now and palled around with the other GIBs, if at all.

And Snake had drifted off. He split his flying between Randy Starbuck and Boomer Wright, depending on their availability.

It's ironic, thought Mike Nelson. He'd broken up Tomb's defensive circle and Tomb's air base. But Tomb had broken up the Four Horsemen.

Nelson rapped his special four-tap knock on Moose Peterson's door. In a few seconds the crew-cut lieutenant swung it half open, then returned to his bunk and the international version of *Time* he'd bought at the Base Exchange earlier that day. Nelson took this as an invitation to come in, although Moose did not offer him a seat.

"Moose, er, Knute, we need to talk."

"Got nothin' to say. Unless it's about flying."

"I know I ripped it bad with you, Knute. The Phuc Yen business, I mean."

"You got that right, Mike." The hulking Swede was dishing out more cynicism than anything else these days. He hadn't taken his eyes out of the magazine yet.

"Pay attention, dammit! We got to talk this out." Nelson swept his GIB's feet off the bed.

Moose Peterson reacted immediately, bouncing to his feet. With both of his massive hands, he grabbed Mike Nelson's flight suit at chest level and pushed him into the back of his door. Even Nelson was surprised by Peterson's strength and catlike speed. Somehow the door held.

Moose looked his aircraft commander square in the eye. "I trusted you, and you let me down." He relaxed his iron grip on Nelson's flight suit and returned to his reading on the bed.

"Knute, look, I know what I did was wrong. I should've read you in on it from the beginning. I could give you a line of bull about us having to work together in the air, but you know that. For me it goes deeper than that. I need you. You're my friend. And it hurts bad to go through all this without your friendship."

Peterson put his magazine down, crossed his arms, and stared at the ceiling. Still, he said nothing.

After about ten seconds of crushing silence, Nelson grabbed the door-knob to leave. "Goodbye, Knute, see you at the briefing tomorrow."

"Hey, wait a minute." Moose called out, catching Nelson at the door, "Wait, Mike!"

"Say again, Knute?"

"Who's Knute? Goddammit, call me 'Moose.'" This declaration hit Mike Nelson right between the shoulder blades. He turned to see Moose Peterson standing in the middle of the room with an outstretched hand to shake—and a smile on his face.

Well, there were Two Horsemen anyway.

1850 hours
The Officers' Club main bar
Ubon RTAFB

The main bar was almost empty. The few people in the bar were all sober. And none of them were 8th TFW pilots.

General Waters was on his way into the main dining room for a Kobe beef steak and a hot buttered baked potato. He looked into the bar. He only saw Aussies, a pair of rotorheads, and a few transient marines. The 8th was showing a cohesiveness that wasn't characteristic of a unit with low morale, Waters thought. This solidarity correlated with the other things he and his team had seen today.

Morale and unit pride were high indeed. The pilots held their wing commander in very high esteem. Not because he let them do what they wanted, but because he didn't. The officers said his standards were extremely tough. Adams didn't tolerate mediocre performance from any-one. And he demanded perfect discipline in the air. Not a single strike aircraft MiGCAPed by the 8th TFW had been lost to a MiG since Clint Adams took command. The strike force was getting in and out safely.

General Waters moved into the main dining room, filled with the wing's officers. A few got up and left when Waters entered; he was used to that.

The Thai hostess approached him, bowed, and escorted him to an empty table. Several tables away, Boomer, Moose, and Snake were finishing their supper and recounting the events of the day. Their discussion turned to the reporter who had stiffed the wing in general and Adams in particular. Boomer Wright, remembering one of his least favorite wing exec experiences, remarked, "I'm sure I remember Massey drinking at the bar one night about three weeks ago."

Moose added, "Yeah, like a lot of those war correspondents, he was probably getting his next story from the bottom of a glass." Pretty caustic stuff, coming from Moose. Then Moose slapped the table with an open palm, startling the others. "Wait a minute. Did you say three weeks ago?"

"Right."

Moose became excited, "Hey, I remember that guy! He was having a beer right next to me at the bar. I remember because that's the day we lost Vic Sansone. I was feelin' real low so I went to the club for a few beers. But the guy didn't stay at the bar. I heard him mumble, 'Well, I'll be damned,' as if he recognized someone, and then he moved off into the corner to sit with—" Moose's eyes grew wide.

Snake couldn't stand it. "Who?" he prompted.

"Colonel Danforth," said Moose.

The other two pilots reached the same conclusion at once. For a few moments, they said nothing. They just stared at each other, wide eyed and mouths agape. Moose summed it up for all of them. "That son of a bitch." And he wasn't referring to Massey this time.

They all looked to Boomer. He moved in the right circles; they didn't.

"Okay, I'll handle it." Boomer stood to leave. Moose and Snake followed. Then Moose came to his senses. Where were his priorities? He swung back to the table and downed the last two bites of his apple pie, then hustled to catch up with the others.

1900 hours
Captain Todd Benning's room
Ubon RTAFB

Boomer Wright knocked on Benning's door, hoping Danforth's executive officer wasn't flying tonight. The others crowded in right behind Boomer as if they all planned to squeeze through the first small crack as the door opened. Todd Benning swung the door full open.

"Hey, guys. What's up?" They interrupted Benning while he was cleaning himself up. He had just returned from a twilight mission over the trail in southern Laos. He was currently on his one-week flying break from his duties as Slim Danforth's exec. Todd was attached to the 497th, so he flew nights almost exclusively. Consequently, Benning hadn't heard about the news article flap.

"C'mon in, you turkeys. What're you doin' in our hootch?" He turned back to the small mirror over the sink, wiping shaving cream off his face with a damp towel.

Boomer confronted Todd. "We need to have a serious talk."

"Sure, what about? You guys wanna transfer out of the Nickel and join the elite Moon Raiders?"

Boomer gave him the news article. "Read this, Todd." Benning read it, shook his head, and handed it back. Then Boomer told him about Massey and Danforth. Todd turned quietly defensive. As Danforth's exec, he had to be loyal. That had been ingrained in him; it was an exec's first imperative.

"Shit, Boomer, what do you want from me? I don't know anything about that reporter."

Boomer fished for corroborating information. "Wouldn't expect you to. You wouldn't sit on that kind of bad poop. Just tell us if Danforth's been acting strange lately."

"No. Just routine idiosyncrasies, like always."

"Has he done anything to indicate that he's not supporting the wing commander?"

Benning hesitated. Then he said, "No."

Snake jumped in. "Hell, Todd, everyone knows Danforth has a hard-on for Adams. He's so bitter about not moving up that he stinks up the base with it. Everyone knows that Adams's leadership style didn't set well with Danforth from the start."

This visit wasn't producing anything. Boomer would have acted the same in Benning's place, at least for now. Boomer motioned for Moose and Snake to leave. Boomer hung back and stopped at the door. "Think it over, Todd." Benning stared back at him and said nothing. "Todd, this will probably cost Colonel Adams his job." Boomer closed the door behind him.

Benning turned back to the sink and the mirror. He knew he had placed an inordinate number of telephone calls to Danforth's friends at Seventh AF Headquarters. And he'd caught bits of those conversations. There'd been negative overtones about Adams, and Danforth referred to Adams as a cowboy. It was the cowboy stuff that was nagging at him. It was just like the news article. It hadn't meant very much—until tonight.

Benning stared at himself in the mirror. He didn't like the black-haired fighter pilot in the reflection. Maybe he was carrying this loyalty shit too far. He was fed up with being an exec to a dandy like Danforth. The man never had had a kind word for him or for anybody, really. Todd Benning had seen senior officer rivalries before, but this was far beyond that. He respected and admired Adams. He kept thinking about Adams getting the hook. The 8th deserved better, so did the Air Force and so did the war. Benning dressed quickly.

1945 hours
The Triple Nickel Hootch
Ubon RTAFB

Todd pushed open Boomer Wright's door. "We need to talk."

"You don't need to tell me anything, Todd. Let's talk on the way over to see General Waters."

Todd wavered. "Wait a minute." But he knew it had to come to this. "Okay," he relented.

2200 hours
8th TFW legal office
Ubon RTAFB

General Waters had commandeered the base legal office for the duration of his inspection. Waters was reviewing his IG team's report from the first day.

"Colonel Danforth's here, General."

"Send him in, please."

Danforth moved through the door, wearing an innocent look. He had worked with Waters when Waters was a colonel in the Pentagon. He had done Waters a number of favors in those days. "Hello, General. Good to see you again. Long way from the battles we fought together in the Pentagon's halls."

"Yes, a very long way. Take a seat, Colonel."

From Waters's coolness, Danforth got the feeling that something wasn't right.

"Danforth, I'll put it to you straight. You were seen in the O Club with Mr. Tom Massey."

"Say, what is this? You don't think that I—"

"There's more. Massey used terms that you, and only you, have used to describe Clint Adams. What do you think of your wing commander, Colonel?"

"What does that mean?"

"It means we have evidence that you have made a habit of undercutting your commander. Both internal to the wing and to Seventh Air Force Headquarters. Now, I could go through the trouble of getting statements from your entire staff and the staff down at Seventh Air Force. And I think you know what I'll uncover. I've interviewed key people here and called enough people down at Seventh to see the pattern clearly."

Danforth thought that somebody close to him had blown the whistle to the IG. But who? Bet it was that damn enlisted clerk, never liked the slimy snake. . . .

Waters continued. "I've talked to General Morgan. We'll give you an option, Danforth. I can read you your rights under the Uniformed Code of Military Justice and proceed with an Article 131 investigation leading to a general court-martial, or you can go quietly. You can start for home on the plane with me tomorrow and retire at your first port in the States."

Danforth stared at the floor. He couldn't let go of his earlier line of thought. Which bastard had squealed? Hell, what did it matter? Look at the alternatives. Either way, he was a goner. He was going no place in this wing. He'd never see that general's star.

"Well, Slim, what will it be?"

Danforth rose stoically. "I'll pack my things."

15 November 1966 0725 hours
Wing commander's office
Ubon RTAFB

Adams had said his goodbyes to General Waters over at the VIP trailer earlier this morning. He still had a few minutes to himself before the staff meeting, and he moved closer to his office window. He watched as his hulking vice commander saw off General Waters and his team. Just before the door closed on the cargo plane, another passenger hurried to board. Slim Danforth was obviously late, and he was loaded down with his bags. It was going to be a long flight home. Danforth stopped at the door of the C-130 and took a long hard look back at wing headquarters, as if he knew Adams was watching him. Adams turned and walked away from the window.

The red phone on Adams's desk rang. He picked it up on the second ring. "Adams."

"Clint, how are you?" It was General Morgan.

"Too trusting, I guess."

"Carl Waters filled me in. I told him to write it up for the Chief. Then the Chief will brief the Chairman of the Joint Chiefs, Secretary of Defense, and the White House. Do you have anyone up there to take Danforth's place?"

"Lieutenant Colonel Rod Wells, the Triple Nickel commander, would be an outstanding DCO, and he's someone the pilots respect."

"I know Rod. A DCO with max credibility would be best. Bad time for some new shiny full colonel from the States. I'll keep the colonel's assignments people off your back on this one." The general, acting as if he had almost forgotten to mention something, added, "Oh, Clint, Bolo is a 'go.' You're cleared in hot. Pick the date and advise me."

"Thank you, sir." With a sense of relief, Adams put the phone down and called to the outer office, "Boomer! Get Rod Wells and Randy Starbuck over here."

As he put down the phone, General Tom Morgan turned his attention to the single brown envelope in the middle of his desk. He licked the gum, carefully pressed it shut, and tossed it into the out basket. The instructions on the envelope were "Eyes Only—to be opened by addressee only." It was addressed to AF/DPG, HQ USAF, Washington, D.C. General Morgan had just submitted his nomination list for the 5 December Brigadier General's Promotion Board. General Jack McKean, now the Air Force vice chief of staff and the newest four-star general, would be president of the board.

Morgan's list had only one name: Clinton Radford Adams.

1830 hours
The officers' club
Ubon RTAFB

The bar was packed. Adams and Robinson walked into a resounding wave of cheers, whoops, howls, applause, and handshakes. The 479th launched a MiG sweep, but they weren't as effective without Whale Wharton. There was an intense carrier landing competition. Doc Kramer served as the umpire out of a sense of self-preservation and to keep his clinic empty. The jukebox blared out "Snoopy and the Red Baron."

OPERATION BOLO

---

26 December 1966 0900 hours
Wing briefing room
Ubon RTAFB

Boomer Wright called the packed room to attention as Clint Adams walked in and moved to the front.

The audience was handpicked for Randy Starbuck's briefing: the 8th TFW wing staff, all three flying squadron commanders and ops officers, specific MiGCAP flight leaders, and the wing's best GIBs. Visitors from out of town also filled the room: key ops people from the 366th TFW at Da Nang, planners from the 388th TFW at Korat. Wild Weasel aircrews from the 355th TFW at Takhli, F-104 drivers from Udorn Air Base, and three Seventh AF staff officers who would set up the other airborne support for the Bolo operation, tankers, standoff jammers, and SAR. The only flight surgeon present—Doc Kramer—sat in the back row.

Clint Adams kicked it off. "Gentlemen, I called you together so we could all start from the same baseline. Captain Randy Starbuck from our Wing Tactics Shop will give the briefing. Go ahead, Randy."

"Thank you, sir." This was a more confident Starbuck than the one who had stammered at his first Bolo briefing. He believed in the plan, and he'd worked the details hard with all the men in the room. "The objective of Operation Bolo is to deliver a knockout punch to North Vietnam's Air Force by finally luring a large number of MiGs into a decisive air battle.

"To prime the pump, Headquarters put out the word in Saigon diplomatic circles that a big American bombing effort will begin immediately after January first. Concurrently, a special intelligence operation, using the American press corps in Saigon, leaked false information about a growing shortage of air-to-air missiles because of aggressive shootings over the North outside the missile firing envelope and problems with getting spare missile parts. Bolo must be a highly coordinated air superiority operation." While speaking, Starbuck kept hitting the beeper cueing Taco Martinez to throw up the next slide. The briefing clicked along without a hitch.

"All the normal support aircraft will fly their regular profiles: refueling tankers, EC-121s, EB-66s, ABCCC C-130s, SAR, and Wild Weasels. The F-104s from Udorn will fly MiGCAP south of the main strike force to screen the exiting F-4 four-ship formations."

Starbuck finished his briefing. "For the first time, the F-4s in this operation will carry ECM jamming pods, called QRC-160s. As you know, the Thud drivers have carried these pods since mid-November. Major Kuszinski, Korat's wing weapons officer, will brief you on the pod now."

Big Jim Kuszinski jumped onto the raised podium and put his beefy hands on his hips, sucking in his gut a little for the pride of Thud pilots everywhere. "The little white pod don't look like much. You can't even tell if it's on because it's hot-wired to the utility electrical bus. But it really garbages up Gomer's EW/GCI scope.

"To him, the goddamn thing glows in the dark. But watch your ass. It works best if you stay in formation. The combined power of four pods really washes out his radar scope, but if you move off alone, about a mile away from the flight, you form your own separate jamming bubble. Then Gomer knows where you are. Right in the middle of the goddamned blob. He'll smoke a few SAMs at you and detonate them by feel. We lost a Thud like that last month. Any questions?"

Nobody pressed Kuszinski to expand on his eloquent explanation, but Big Jim remembered something else. "Oh, yeah. If you want to turn the goddamn thing off, just pull the circuit breaker on the utility panel. Which one of you guys is Cummings?"

Snake Cummings raised his hand. "Over here, Major."

"You owe me a beer, Cummings. Remember Hammer 01?"

"Sure do! See *you* at the bar later!" Lots of whoops filled the room as Kuszinski jumped off the raised stage. Almost everyone assumed

Cummings had dorked up something while "CAPing" a Thud air strike over Pack Six. Wrong!

Taco Martinez leaned over to Moose Peterson and said, "Christ, Moose, we're gonna be goddamned invisible!"

Starbuck popped back up and continued, "The stage is set for Operation Bolo: fourteen four-ships of F-4Cs, four flights of F-105 Wild Weasels, four flights of F-104 fighter-interceptors to screen the exiting F-4s, supporting flights of EB-66 jammers, EC-121 surveillance planes, and the ever-present KC-135 tankers. D-day is 1 January. Big question is, Can we entice the Gomers to challenge us?

"It'll take until 1 January to square away the mechanics of attaching the ECM pods to the F-4s. Even this is a very accelerated procedure. Without the urgency of Bolo, the normal Air Force process would allow another six months of operational testing to satisfy everyone that F-4s could indeed carry the jamming pod into combat." War had a habit of hastening weapons into combat. The failed AIM-4D Falcon missile was a case in point. Clint Adams hoped that the jamming pod would work better than the AIM-4D had on the Phantom. Korat had sent some of its more experienced maintenance troops to Ubon to help with the installation.

After fielding questions for an hour, Randy Starbuck turned the meeting over to Clint Adams for his final comments. Adams stood as all eyes in the room turned toward the double ace. "All right you bastards. Follow me. Watch my smoke. And kick ass."

Everyone left the briefing room to begin an intense week of preparation, since three 8th TFW fighter squadrons would fly in Bolo.

The inevitable began almost immediately. Pilots in each of the squadrons lobbied their ops officers and squadron commanders for a slot in the Bolo sequence, but the crews had already been selected. The next day, they'd start getting operational tactics and intelligence briefings ad nauseam.

As the briefing room emptied, Adams stopped Kuszinski outside. "Thanks for coming up, Jim. How many strikes have you led Downtown?"

"Fifty-six. Why?"

"I was just thinking. If we're supposed to look like you, behave like you, and emit like you, then why not sound like you too?"

"So?"

"Want to ride in the backseat in the lead four-ship and make the radio calls inbound?"

"No fucking way, sir. When I go to Pack Six, I go in a Thud, or I don't go at all."

Clint Adams looked at this master of the air over North Vietnam. He knew Kuszinski was right. And he knew Kuszinski was more valuable in a weapon of his own choosing. Kuszinski would be an asset in any fight. If things got rough, Adams knew Big Jim could handle himself.

"You got a deal. But you're number four. Work it out with Starbuck. And clean up your goddamn language. My guys aren't that crude."

Kuszinski snapped Adams a salute as the two went their separate ways. "I like your fuckin' style, Colonel."

27 December 1966 0930 hours
8th TFW medical clinic
Ubon RTAFB

Doc Kramer scrutinized the medical tests that Rod Wells had taken earlier this morning. Every Air Force pilot hated his annual flight physical. He had to complete it during his birth month or be grounded. If any real problems showed up, he would be grounded. Each succeeding year, the odds increased that this would happen. Too many things happened to pilots during their annual physicals, and they were all bad! No wonder most fighter pilots put off their annual flight physical until the last possible day as they advanced in age. Rob Wells's birth date was 1 December 1923. He waited until after Christmas to see Doc Kramer this time.

Wells was a typical combat leader. He prided himself in leading by example. That meant he did what he expected of his youngest, most robust jock. That included the fighter pilot's dinner: a steak and a handful of beers, every night. It also included the fighter pilot's breakfast: a Coke and a cigarette. There was only one major problem with this way of life. It worked well for the twenty-five-year olds, but it caught up to the forty-three-year olds.

"Colonel, you have high blood pressure. 140 over 110."

"Okay, I'll cut back on the salt tablets and beer, Doc." Everyone in Southeast Asia took two salt tablets every day to reduce the possibility of heat prostration and, even worse, heat stroke. It seemed like there was a salt tablet dispenser in every military john in Southeast Asia.

Doc Kramer's two broken ribs had healed about a month ago. Since then, he'd added eight more counters to Route Pack One in North

Vietnam's southern panhandle. He now had thirty-six counters, not bad for a flight surgeon who'd come to Ubon the previous June, but had to stand down for six weeks because of his inability to make carrier landings at the club. Kramer hadn't forgotten the abortive plea he'd made to Rod Wells almost two months ago. He cleared his throat. "I'm afraid it's not that simple, sir. I've checked it three times. Same every time. And your medical records show it's been creeping up over the past few years."

"What do you mean?" Here it comes, thought Wells.

"I'll have to ground you until we get the blood pressure numbers under control." The G-word cut into Wells like a knife.

"Dammit it, Doc! I'm scheduled to fly in the second flight over Phuc Yen when Bolo goes on the first of January."

"I'm afraid that won't do, sir. We'll have to ground you for three weeks to put you on the prescription. You know the drill."

Yeah, Wells knew the drill. As a squadron commander and now as the wing DCO, Wells had heard many an aging fighter pilot complain about the flight surgeon's decision to put him on the ground until a new diet or a medication did its job. "Doc, don't do this to me. You know how important this is to me as the wing DCO. Shit, it's important to me personally."

The tables were reversed now. Wells had to make his case to Doc. Kramer was enjoying it. Air Force flight surgeons had total power to ground any aviator on medical grounds, even wing commanders. Wells knew his fate was in Doc Kramer's hands.

Kramer faced the wall, still pretending to study the test results. He was standing directly under his academic sheepskins for the most dramatic effect. All military doctors hung their undergraduate internships and medical school degrees on their office walls to impress their patients. Flight surgeons did it to impress the pilots, but it didn't work very well, even though University of Chicago magna cum laude '60 and Harvard Medical School '64 should impress anybody.

Wells broke first. "Okay, Doc, I'll make you a deal. If you let me fly until Bolo, I'll ground myself the next day."

Kramer held out for the brass ring as he replied, "Sorry, sir, that's just not good enough."

Wells knew he was in deep shit, so he relented. "All right, I'll let you be a GIB on one of the ground spares for Bolo."

Kramer went for the throat with his aggressive response, "Make it an airborne spare, or it's no deal."

"Okay, dammit, airborne spare. You know, Doc, you're a son of a bitch."

29 December 1966 1400 hours
The flight line
Ubon RTAFB

Maintenance activity had reached a feverish pitch with round-the-clock tweaking of every plane, as everyone on Ubon's flight line took advantage of the Christmas bombing halt.

Adams had spent most of this week continually cruising the flight line. He knew enthusiasm was very high among the maintenance troops. On this day he spotted Sergeant Chris Cole on crutches shuffling underneath #680. He jumped out of his jeep and asked, "What happened, Cole?"

Cole was evasive but finally came clean. "I just slipped on the wet tarmac last night while installing the new adapters for the ECM pod."

Adams was eager to know about the adapters. "You got them on? How do they work?" But he caught himself. "Did you break your ankle?"

"Nossir. Just a bad sprain."

"What the hell are you doing out here on crutches?"

"Colonel, I'm not gonna miss any of this. This air machine will be ready when you are. The adapters seem to work just fine." Adams was betting a lot that Chris Cole was right.

30 December 1966 1230 hours
Kep Airfield
Forty kilometers northeast of Hanoi

Colonel Tomb was enjoying lunch with his pilots. He was most at ease when with these elite aviators. He considered them the best young men in the People's Democratic Republic. And for a young Vietnamese pilot, dining with Colonel Tomb was like an American pilot sharing a meal with Captain Eddie Rickenbacker and General Hap Arnold all wrapped up in one.

Arkov normally avoided the Vietnamese officers' mess. Fish parts and rice made him gag. In fact, the smell of this food nauseated him. But today he had to speak with Tomb. The Vietnamese pilots always regarded Arkov's entrance as a mild intrusion; it broke the fraternal atmosphere among them. But they knew that some business must be addressed. A working lunch, Communist style.

Tomb said nothing to Arkov when the Russian moved to take a seat but made an acknowledging gesture that the Russian could join them. He continued eating his meal of sticky rice peppered with specks of seasoned fish. Two of the NVAF pilots made room so Arkov could sit next to Tomb.

"The information is valid," Arkov said, while displaying his usual smugness. "The American approach to war. So predictable. They have no concept of the operational art. They are merely capitalist businessmen in uniform. In fact, their whole military system is controlled at the top by men in fancy, single-breasted suits serving only a few years in government before going back to their high-paying jobs in private companies. What an unusual way to fight a war.

"The Americans are losing yet they unilaterally declare a holiday from combat, then attempt to make it all up in one big day. They don't seem to realize that these bombing pauses allow you to strengthen and resupply your fighting units in the South."

Tomb wondered why Arkov never said "we." The North Vietnamese colonel finished his meal and slowly dabbed his face with a napkin. He did everything in a measured way. The younger pilots watched and listened to him carefully. "We should be thankful they do not realize this, Arkov. If what you say about the large attack is true, then we should exploit this weakness in their thinking, shouldn't we?" He rose to leave. All the other NVAF pilots stood.

Tomb's response irritated Arkov. Once again, Arkov learned that he simply could not share his personal opinions with this Oriental. Tomb had twisted this encounter into an arrogant snub! Arkov knew it was his idea to capitalize on the opportunity that this large American raid presented. Arkov would have liked to snap the head off this little snake.

Tomb spoke to the Russian as he moved to leave, "I know you have verified that the Americans are running short on air-to-air missiles, and that could mean limits to their firepower in the air for some time. Well and good. But something is not right. I sense it. You must show me more."

Arkov followed him out the door and into the hall. "Colonel, this is a rare political opportunity to embarrass the Americans. If you mass for one large attack soon, you can gain an ascendancy that could last for months. If you don't believe your own patriotic operatives in Saigon, then perhaps you will believe your enemy." With that, Arkov pulled a handful of American newspaper articles from his pocket and flung them at Tomb's chest.

Tomb did not flinch or stoop to gather up the news clippings. He merely looked at the Russian, put on his cap, and walked away toward the flight line. He wasn't convinced. "And of course, a large attack might allow you to fly one of our MiG-21s. Is that right, Arkov?"

2 January 1967 1245 hours
The flight line
Ubon RTAFB

General Max Crandall at Seventh AF had put Bolo on weather hold forty-five minutes ago. At 1300 hours, he'd decide to launch or scrub for the second day in a row. He'd scrubbed Bolo yesterday because of poor weather in the Hanoi area. Solid overcast. Nothing flew to Pack Six on 1 January 1967.

Clint Adams leaned against his jeep just outside the aircraft revetment housing #680. The weather at Ubon was just fine, 3 miles visibility in a sunny haze, 85 degrees, a light variable breeze. The ever-present microscopic gnats homed in on Adams's ears, and the sweat built on the back of his neck in the afternoon heat. The complete overcast in the Hanoi area was the showstopper right now. Looked like a repeat of yesterday.

This was déjà vu for Clint Adams. The winter weather pattern over Hanoi reminded him of the long periods of solid cloud cover he knew so well in the European theater during winter. As a young fighter pilot in Cambridgeshire, England, he had gone through this same torturous waiting game many times. The 8th TFW was experiencing that frustration now: full preparation right up to engine start only to get the scrub order at the last minute. Adams didn't like it. It took the edge off the entire team effort. The uncertainty turned the whole thing into an unusual production played out in a trance by each member in the cast. People didn't know whether to let the adrenaline flow or not.

Randy Starbuck wandered over from his cocked air machine to Adams and Martinez. "Waitin's the worst part, isn't it, Boss?"

"Randy. Good. Glad you came over," said Adams. "Let's go over the whole sequence again. One more time." Adams had learned long ago that keeping focused on the mission made the waiting easier.

"Okay, sir," Starbuck answered, resigned to go through the Bolo execution sequence with Adams for the umpteenth time. "As we've planned from the start, F-4s from Ubon and Da Nang will masquerade as F-105s ostensibly targeted against the bulk of North Vietnam's steel industry, housed in two plants in the town of Thai Nguyen, 20 miles north of Hanoi.

"For the past three weeks, we've been using disinformation to create the illusion that American bombing strikes into North Vietnam will be lightly defended because of a shortage of air-to-air missile parts.

"The F-4s will electronically 'impersonate' a strung-out, lightly defended F-105 strike force. The bogus main strike cells will use the tactics, profiles, speeds, altitudes, and call signs normally associated with Korat-based F-105s. This means we'll go into the target at medium altitude."

"Yeah, I know all that, Randy. Get to the execution sequence," Adams chided impatiently.

"Well, Colonel, you did say the whole thing," countered Starbuck, getting back at Adams for making him run through Bolo again. "The main strike force of Ubon F-4s will be sequenced in four-ship formations at five-minute intervals, a target so attractive that the NVAF should attack it in force. When the MiGs do attack, they'll realize they've tangled with F-4s ready to battle them directly in air combat."

"Confronted by this tactical surprise, some MiGs should try fleeing north to China. To block their escape, a second force of F-4s, from the 366th TFW's 'Gunfighters' at Da Nang, will be the screening force, waitin' for the MiGs northeast of Hanoi.

"The main Bolo strike force of 'Korat-based F-105s' will seem loaded with special cluster bombs. All the masquerading F-4s have had APR-25 RHAW gear installed. And, for the first time, each F-4 carries the QRC-160 jamming pod, greatly aiding the deception."

Randy turned to more detailed points now. "Bolo will generate fourteen flights of four Phantoms, fifty-six F-4s in all. Ten four-ships come from Ubon, and Da Nang's Gunfighters fly the other four. The Da Nang flights sequence in halfway through the overall flow. Both bases will field all the necessary ground and airborne spare aircraft, ready to fill in at a moment's notice.

"As mission commander, sir, you're leading Olds flight, the first four-ship cell over the real target of the Bolo operation: Phuc Yen Airfield, located just north of Hanoi itself and code-named 'Chicago' for Bolo. Thirteen more four-ships will pass over Phuc Yen at five-minute intervals."

"Good. Thanks, Randy."

"Colonel, I hope we go, just so I don't have to repeat all that again tomorrow."

Clint Adams sensed that Crandall and the Seventh AF ops staff wanted Bolo to go today if at all possible. They wouldn't cancel quite so quickly today, and there was an RF-4C weather recce flight up over Hanoi now. Adams hoped Crandall went with their best guess. If the weather thinned out at all, it would happen in midafternoon, just when Adams had planned his time over target (TOT).

But the prospects of better weather were slim. Adams knew Crandall's drop-dead time for a mission go-ahead was 1300 hours, just a few minutes from now. It was time to fish or cut bait. Adams couldn't do anything about it. If Crandall gave the go-ahead, Clint Adams had control of Bolo as the mission commander; but only General Crandall controlled the whole armada of fighters and support aircraft right now. C'mon Max, have some balls.

Adams's brick chirped. He spoke into it, "Honcho One."

"Sir, this is the TOC. Just got a call. You have Condition Rainbow, repeat, Condition Rainbow." Good, thought Adams, Rainbow means that the KC-135s, EC-121s, and EB-66s, flying from Korat, Takhli, and U-Tapao in southern Thailand had been launched to get the necessary head start. Only the F-105 Wild Weasels at Korat and the F-104s from Udorn remained on the ground with the F-4s. Adams took this initial movement as a positive sign.

Then it happened. Adams's hand-held Motorola radio beeped loudly again. The maintenance men nearby turned toward Adams, looking for some sign to break the uncertainty.

"Honcho One."

"Roger, sir, TOC again. You have Condition Sterling, repeat, Condition Sterling. Engine start, two-zero past the hour. Tango Oscar Tango is 1500 local. Copy?"

Adams thought, Crandall, you peckerhead, you *do* have the balls enough to take a chance on us! Adams would lead the first Bolo four-ship over the Hanoi area at 1500 hours, the new time over target. Now Clint Adams had control of Bolo. He wouldn't turn back. Bolo was going to Hanoi no matter what.

"Honcho One, copy. Thanks much." Adams tossed his radio onto the seat of the jeep and pulled his flying gear out of the back seat, putting it on, one piece at a time, over his flight suit. Anti-G suit, survival vest, and parachute harness—all donned in three minutes. The aircrews and maintenance men watching Adams saw him give the hand signal for a mission launch and saw him suiting up. Adams stuffed his gloves and clipboard, loaded with mission details, into his helmet and started the 20-yard walk to his plane. The external power carts rumbled as they spooled up to deliver electricity and air pressure to their waiting Phantoms. The Ubon flight line came alive in a flurry of orchestrated action.

Taco Martinez, now considered the best GIB in Triple Nickel, was already entering coordinates into the INS computer in #680's rear cockpit. He'd be welded three feet behind Clint Adams over Phuc Yen today.

Chris Cole saw Adams moving briskly in his direction. Free of his crutches now, Cole hobbled out to meet his aircraft commander. He could tell Bolo was a go. Adams tossed Cole his overstuffed helmet bag. "Start engines 1320. Let's cock this bird, Sergeant."

"Yes, *sir*." Cole shuffled ahead of Adams to position the contents of the helmet bag in the proper place—helmet on the front canopy rail, flying gloves on the black instrument visor, and knee clipboard on the right side console, just aft of the lighting panel.

Adams started preflighting his F-4, which had never been configured this way before. It was loaded to the gills with missiles—four Sparrows in the underbelly coves and four Sidewinders, two in each inboard wing pylon. Instead of two balanced fuel tanks under each outboard wing station, #680 had only one 370-gallon wing tank on an outboard pylon and a larger 600-gallon fuel tank on the centerline station. The other wing's outboard pylon held the curious little ECM pod. It looked like a white 100-pound bomb with fish fin antennae sticking out of the bottom.

Adams's call sign was Olds 01. He didn't like the call sign, but it was issued by the Seventh AF fragmentary mission order too late to change. He would have preferred Hammer flight.

Adams had handpicked his element leader today. Mike Nelson and Moose Peterson climbed up the ladder of their plane. Their call sign: Olds 03. Although relatively junior, Mike Nelson had earned the honor of being the element leader in the first flight over the target area.

And he had a unique wingman. The fourth airplane down the line jutted in an ungainly manner out the front of the revetment built to house a Phantom. Kuszinski's Thud, the Polish Warrior, was cocked and ready to go as Olds 04.

Farther down the flight line, Colonel Bear Robinson "strapped on" his Phantom. He was leading the second four-ship with the call sign Ford 01. He donned his tiger helmet. Rod Wells donned his helmet after a thumbs-up to his crew chief. Call sign: Ford 03. Randy Starbuck and Snake Cummings climbed into Rambler 01, while Roscoe Stewart crawled into Rambler 03.

This was the vanguard of Operation Bolo, its leadership: Olds, Ford, and Rambler flights. These eleven Phantoms and one F-105 would taxi first in the sequence for takeoff at Ubon.

Only one F-4 remained unused today, the wing's "hangar queen." That Phantom, now cannibalized for various mission-essential parts needed on the other Phantoms, was unceremoniously stuffed into the back of a dark hangar. All the rest of Ubon's F-4s were part of the strike sequence or served as spares. First, they'd be ground spares. Then they'd transition to airborne spares, filling in for any Ubon F-4 that dropped out after takeoff because of maintenance problems.

Olds flight had its engines running. Clint Adams unhooked the right side of his mask after engine start, allowing the outside air to cool his face as the heat from the dark metal cockpit slowly cooked the rest of his body in the humid, midafternoon heat. No use keeping your face completely covered any longer than necessary. It didn't feel like January, he thought.

"Ubon Tower, Olds 01. Taxi."

"Roger. Olds flight, taxi Runway 17, altimeter 29.97."

Adams and the other pilots in Olds flight automatically synchronized their altimeters by turning the small knob to the current barometric setting. The mission flow began. Each subsequent flight followed the actions of the preceding one in five-minute intervals, but alternated their taxi routes to opposite ends of Ubon's single runway.

1330 hours

Randy Starbuck had a problem back in the revetment area. After engine start he couldn't get his left-hand generator on line. F-4s required two operating generators for launch. If he lost his other generator after takeoff he'd have big problems. He'd have only battery power until he deployed his ram air turbine (RAT) into the slipstream. This six-inch propeller-driven turbine would allow him to power his equipment to land safely but not fly combat.

Randy shut down his left engine while his crew chief and three electricians swarmed under Rambler 01. In sixty seconds, the crew chief reinstalled the aircrew ladder and crawled up to the cockpit with the bad news. "Won't reset manually, sir. Requires a two-hour generator change. Better notify the spare aircraft. Sorry."

"Thanks, Sarge. I'll take it like it is and try to reset it in flight."

"But, Captain, the rules say not to take off in this condition." The crew chief was sticking to his guns. He didn't want to lose his plane to a pilot who wanted to fly it in an unsafe condition.

"Take away the fuckin' ladder, Sarge. I'm goin'."

The crew chief backed down the ladder but didn't remove it. The little pissant, thought Starbuck. Who the hell does he work for anyway? Actually, the crew chief knew exactly who he worked for and what he ought to do in this case. He motioned over the flight line superintendent, who, in turn, radioed Colonel Pop Brewer. Starbuck watched the whole thing. "The little bastard," he mumbled into the intercom. "If I weren't strapped in this Phantom, I'd kick that crew chief's skinny butt right now."

Pop Brewer was up the ladder in a flash. "Captain, this plane's a no-go."

"Colonel, if we argue about this much longer, there's gonna be a hole in the launch. If there's any chance I can get the damn generator on line after takeoff, I want a shot at it. This ain't peacetime. Let's use our judgment. If I can't get it on the line, I'll air abort, and the airborne spare can fill in as Rambler 01." Pop Brewer mulled it over and concluded that this scenario had logic.

"OK, kick some ass for us maintenance hogs, Captain." Brewer jumped off the ladder and took it away. He swirled his left hand at the wrist to signal engine start. Randy Starbuck was back in Bolo.

Clint Adams pulled into the arming area at the end of Runway 05, and his three wingmen parked in echelon with him. As soon as they stopped, a combined team of armorers and maintenance men scurried under each plane, pulling the arming pins on the missiles and making a last-minute maintenance check for leaks.

This time-consuming procedure was the main reason for the alternate-end takeoffs. If anyone had any problems, the arming process might take longer than five minutes. By using both ends of the runway, there was a ten-minute interval between flights on the same end of the runway, a sufficient time to do the arming procedure, troubleshoot any problems, and even plug in a ground spare aircraft if needed without affecting succeeding flights.

The last maintenance checker moved out from under Olds 04. The team chief gave Adams an exuberant thumbs-up and a crisp salute, then turned about and jogged a safe distance into the grass.

Even though some aircraft had yet to start their engines, all pilots were monitoring their UHF radios so they were in direct contact with the mission commander. Adams knew that this was his last chance to motivate his pilots.

"All flights on ground control freq, Olds 01. Let's go get 'em, Wolfpack." Adams felt a surge of adrenaline through his body as he spoke. He hoped everyone on frequency felt it too. "Olds flight, let's go Button One." Adams commanded his four-ship to go to Ubon Tower frequency.

"Two."

"Three."

"Four."

"Olds flight," said Adams on Ubon Tower frequency.

"Two."

"Three."

"Four."

Even the standard procedure for moving fighter planes from one frequency to another, accomplished countless times before, took on special significance today. Big missions did that. Even the details were electrically charged.

"Ubon Tower. Olds 01, flight of four, ready for takeoff."

"Roger, Olds 01. Wind 040, 5 knots. Cleared for takeoff at pilot's discretion." Olds 01 and 02 took their positions on the runway.

Clint Adams pushed both throttles into full afterburner. Eighty minutes to Phuc Yen. Operation Bolo was in full forward motion.

1445 hours
Blue Chip Operations Center
Seventh Air Force HQ
Tan Son Nhut Air Base

"They ought to be off the tanker by now. You got anything down there?" Tom Morgan growled from his glass-enclosed battle staff room through his microphone at the duty officer on the situation floor.

"Just coming in now, sir." The major hustled over to one of his communications NCOs for details.

Morgan swung around impatiently, now taking on his out-country DCO. "Max, this weather's still dogshit. I hope we haven't set Adams up on this one."

"We could issue a recall order if you want to, General."

"Hell, no! Right now Clint would rather take a face full of SAMs than an air abort."

1452 hours
Olds flight inbound
Above Thud Ridge

The lead elements of the Bolo strike force were coming down the familiar mountainous backbone at 20,000 feet, heading directly to Phuc Yen. Adams started descending into the valley. The weather in the Red River Basin was still piss poor—almost totally undercast at 7,000 feet. Adams listened to the chatter on the tactical strike frequency. The radio calls from exiting Navy aircraft indicated moderate SAM activity in the Hanoi area.

"That's bad news, Colonel." Taco Martinez had an opinion on everything. Both pilots knew that SAMs were most effective in this kind of cloud cover because you couldn't see the SAM launch plume. And it was hard to spot the white missile as it broke through the undercast. Not enough contrast. If the missile were targeted on the flight, it would be only a few miles away when it broke out above the clouds. Traveling at Mach 3, the SA-2 was seconds from detonation. The chatter indicated that the Navy had lost an A-4 Skyhawk to SAMs on the way to targets south of Hanoi fifteen minutes ago.

"Yeah, Taco, that's the way I heard it too."

Martinez took the hint and clammed up on the negative stuff. Then Adams got some added bad news from the C-130 command plane orbiting over Laos. "Olds, Hillsboro. East Force Alpha went sour due to weather."

As briefed, Kuszinski gave the commands on the UHF radio from tanker refueling all the way to Phuc Yen. "Olds 01, we copy Hillsboro." The flights from Da Nang wouldn't be there to act as a screening force northeast of Hanoi. The Wolfpack was on its own.

"Damn," said Adams over the intercom. Now he was worried that the basic plan wouldn't play itself out logically. In this kind of weather, the North Vietnamese should throw up a large-scale SAM attack, not MiGs. This wasn't the weather the MiGs preferred. They liked the haze. Their pilots were skittish about bad weather, and they probably wouldn't show up in large numbers. If a lone MiG came up to scan the strike force, Adams worried that Bolo would lose the element of surprise. With the possibility of little payoff, he was taking a helluva risk by dragging his F-4s over Phuc Yen today. "I sure hope the intell boys did the job down in Saigon, Taco. On a better weather day, the MiGs would be on us by now. Damn weather." But with this undercast, thought Adams, the MiGs won't be expecting a big strike today. If the MiGs engaged at all, the NVAF would hesitate and be somewhat slow to react.

"It don't look good, Boss. The RHAW gear shows plenty of radars scanning us."

"Any SAM action?"

"Radar outs; no hard acquisitions."

Adams wagged his wings to get the attention of his three wingmen. He gave a two-finger hand signal followed by a head nod for execution to jettison the 600-gallon centerline tanks, now only an empty burden to the three F-4s. The hand signals were crucial to the deception plan. F-105s would not normally shed their tanks at this point in their strike mission. A radio call would've tipped off the Gomers. Each succeeding flight followed the same procedure. Kuszinski still had fuel in his external tanks. He'd manage his own gas and jettison when ready.

The 500-knot relative wind peeled away the three sharply pointed white belly and three wing tanks from Olds flight. As the tanks tumbled into the solid undercast, #680 and the other two Phantoms lunged forward, more aerodynamically pure and 400 pounds lighter than seconds before. Kuszinski merely pushed his throttle up to a hold position in the formation. Big Jim, armed only with four Sidewinders and his internal nose cannon, was a fighter pilot today. Hell, it was fun being an air-to-air fighter, he thought.

Nothing so far. Adams complained to Taco, "Shit, we may not see any MiGs today."

1454 hours
Kep Airfield flight line

Tomb and his pilots anxiously sat in the cockpits of their MiG-21s. Twenty minutes earlier, the Hanoi air defense sector chief had alerted Tomb that a large American strike force was inbound to the Hanoi area. Could this be the attack that Arkov had spoken about? The attack that the Viet Cong operatives in Saigon had uncovered in November? Perhaps, but the weather was not right. Why would the Americans expose a large formation in such conditions? They were not stupid, thought Tomb. Only a highly valuable target warranted so great a risk.

Tomb was monitoring two radio frequencies. One was the American tactical strike frequency. The other was tuned to the NVAF command-and-control net, which passed launch commands and radar intercept information to the MiG leaders. Tomb was still wary. He was waiting for something—some special signal that would make his decisions more clear.

Tomb scanned the Kep flight line; all sixteen MiG-21s sat in their protected areas at the ready, singly or in pairs. All serviceable MiG-21s were here at Kep today. Tomb would lead the first eight MiG-21s. Colonel Arkov would lead the remaining MiG-21s. Yes. Arkov would fight the Americans today if Tomb scrambled his MiGs. Arkov had not been able to convince Tomb directly, so he had prevailed on the fat Russian pig, General Borin, at the embassy for help. Somehow, Borin and the Soviet ambassador had convinced General Giap to allow one operational flight against the suspected large American strike that the National Liberation Front operatives in Saigon had uncovered some weeks ago. Tomb had spoken against the decision, but the Defense Ministry had overruled him.

Just then, Tomb heard the American radio call he had waited for so patiently. "Olds flight, green 'em up." American F-105s were arming their bombs to drop on his homeland.

There was busy chatter on the NVAF air defense frequency net. "Do you have the bandits, Sector Two? What is their height?"

"Yes, this is Sector One, they burned through on my scope at 20 kilometers range. Height is medium. There is much interference on the radar. The North Vietnamese radar controllers are experiencing trouble in determining the altitude of the strike force, because of radar jamming from the strike formation itself." Medium height inbound and heavy jamming told Tomb he would have to make a medium-altitude attack against the Korat F-105s. He started thinking about the appropriate tactics. Tomb hated the Korat-based F-105s the most and vowed that he would carry out an especially vicious attack.

More radio calls blared into Tomb's headset through the NVAF radio net. A small MiG-17 force was returning to Yen Bai Airfield after failing to engage the Navy attack planes operating earlier northeast of Haiphong.

"Dragon Leader, where are you? Turn left 20 degrees, Dragon 02." These MiGs were almost out of fuel because their recovery took longer in the weather. The pilots sounded anxious and frightened. This disquieted Tomb. He knew Arkov was listening to his fledglings as they floundered about in the clouds above.

Growing impatient, Colonel Arkov prodded Tomb over the radio. "What are you waiting for, Colonel?"

Tomb was very irritated with the arrogant Arkov. The Russian was already hampering the attack and should not be allowed to fly today. Tomb glared at the Russian seated in his cockpit across the wet tarmac but said nothing on the radio. Tomb had complete discretion as to when to launch his force on intercepts. The radar controllers merely advised him of the attack parameters, and they could recommend a timely launch, but Tomb had the final say. If he launched the MiGs, then the radar controllers supported the employment of his planes.

"Tomb, this is Control. The strike leader's voice is a familiar one. We believe it is the Polish Pig."

Tomb acknowledged. He knew of this F-105 strike leader. The American was very experienced and a man who must be punished. Kuszinski had done his job.

Suddenly, a single thought penetrated Nguyen Tomb. His heart began to pound in his chest. If the Americans were indeed short of air-to-air missiles and could not provide sufficient MiGCAP protection for the strike bombers, then they might try to destroy his MiGs on the ground in a preemptive strike. What if Arkov and Russian intelligence were right in saying that the Americans were planning a big strike right after the New Year and that the attack might involve hitting targets on their restricted list? The NVAF airfields!

Tomb thought back to the American supersonic buzzing of Phuc Yen last month. He still wanted to settle the score for that humiliation. What if the Phuc Yen incident had emboldened the Americans? Hadn't they learned that a bold surprise attack would go unchallenged by the NVAF? Tomb had sworn that that must not happen again. American reconnaissance must have shown that he had marshaled all his MiG-21s here at Kep to prepare for this attack. They could destroy Kep itself, where almost all North Vietnam's MiG-21s were sitting on the ground. This airfield was a fixed target and could be carpet bombed from above the clouds using the F-105s' radar systems.

"This is Tomb. Start engines immediately and launch in sequence." Tomb's voice sounded calmer than he felt.

1457 hours

Lieutenant Ngoc, Tomb's intelligence officer, rushed from the ramshackle hootch that served as his office with important information for Colonel Tomb. His superior would be so proud of him. This would make up for the failed assassination attempt on the Ubon wing commander. Ngoc wanted Colonel Tomb to know his latest report from Ubon: that wing commander Adams was piloting Olds 01, leading the American formation of F-4s. All the Phantoms at Ubon had taken off ninety minutes ago. The secret listening station had heard a distinctive call on the Ubon ground control frequency, the call by Olds 01 about a wolfpack going to get "them."

Ngoc started for Tomb's building at the base of the tower, but remembered that his commander was sitting in his cockpit on alert. Ngoc abruptly changed direction toward the center revetment, but his Ho Chi Minh sandals were not up to the task on the muddy foot path. His feet slid out from under him, and he crashed to the ground. A sharp pain shot through his left knee, and he rocked back and forth, trying to gather himself enough to continue.

Then Ngoc heard the MiG-21 engines winding up. He had to get to Colonel Tomb with this report before he took off. Fighting the pain, Ngoc pulled himself to his feet and hobbled toward Tomb's plane, dragging his injured left leg behind him.

Tomb pulled his canopy closed, then advanced the throttle of his R-11F turbojet engine. The Russian-made engine wound up, slowly at first, and then delivered a surge of power as the RPM passed 80 percent. Tomb began to roll out of the bunkered revetment and onto the narrow taxiway leading directly to the runway, only 50 meters ahead.

Something to the left caught Tomb's attention. It was Ngoc, wishing him good hunting no doubt. But why did Ngoc look so distressed and splattered with mud? The young officer was lunging toward the plane, waving in an effort to get his attention. But there wasn't any time to stop for the spindly Ngoc. I must get airborne with the other planes, Tomb concluded. If Kep Airfield is the American target today, the attack is only minutes away. We must disrupt the American formation. If it is important, Ngoc will pass the information through the airborne control radio channel.

Ngoc saw that Colonel Tomb was fully committed now. He knew that his extraordinary effort had been in vain; he had missed his commander by seconds. Ngoc had seen Tomb look directly at him, yet the colonel had elected to continue. All that effort wasted, thought Ngoc. He concluded that perhaps the aloof Colonel Tomb did not really value his information.

Ngoc was a good intelligence officer. He knew that he would have to wait and brief Colonel Tomb on his return. Such sensitive intelligence couldn't be passed over the radio; one must assume that the Americans monitored all NVAF frequencies. Ngoc could not afford to compromise his sources in eastern Thailand.

1500 hours
Overhead Phuc Yen Airfield
Ten miles north of Hanoi

Clint Adams hit his time on target (TOT) right on the money. He crossed directly over Phuc Yen, heading east southeast at 12,000 feet and 530 knots. He bitched over the intercom to Taco, "Still no MiGs, dammit." All eyeballs in the flight were scanning the horizon or checking their fire-control radars.

"Goddamn weather," Adams cursed. He inventoried the situation. These conditions favored the NVAF MiGs, who were under GCI control and could position themselves well for their initial pass out of the undercast. By contrast, the American pilots had limited reaction time. The geometry of the battle gave the MiGs the initial advantage, if they chose to engage. And if the MiGs did battle with the U.S. fighters, the undercast would allow them an easy exit from the fight. "I'm startin' to have second thoughts about driving up here today, Taco. Things are stacking up on the bad side of the ledger. Know what I mean?"

"Yeah, Colonel. I know exactly what you mean." Damned weather.

"Time to alter the plan, Lieutenant Martinez." Adams was supposed to turn and exit the area after passing overhead Phuc Yen if he didn't encounter any MiGs. "Let's continue on. If the Gomers weren't expectin' us, they'll be slow to come up. Besides, it takes longer to do a weather intercept. It's more deliberate. You with me, Taco?"

"Yessir. Didn't know I had a vote."

"You got that right. This ain't no democracy." Adams decided to continue southeast for two more minutes, 17 nautical miles at this airspeed.

Adams had to risk blowing the Kuszinski factor. He had to take control of the radios. But he would fuzz it up a little. Perhaps the Gomers wouldn't catch on. "Ford, Olds. We're pressing ahead for a little longer."

"Roger, copy." Forty-five miles behind, Bear Robinson's voice was steady. He knew Clint wanted a part of the action. And Robinson also realized that things rarely came off as planned.

1501 hours
Blue Chip Operations Center
Seventh Air Force HQ
Tan Son Nhut Air Base

"Well, what's up, Major?" Morgan hadn't been this uptight waiting for his first son to be born.

"Hillsboro has Olds 01 on time over target. All succeeding flights moving through the refueling without incident. No action at Chicago, General."

"Dammit." Morgan lit his third cigar of the last hour when he heard the codename. "Just call it Phuc Yen, Major. We're all friendlies in here."

1502 hours
Ten miles east of Hanoi

Still nothing. Olds flight was 15 miles past Hanoi and halfway to Haiphong. Reluctantly, Adams started a wide 180-degree left turn back to the northwest. To Adams, this was a classic MiG sweep. But to the enemy radar, Adams's four-ship still looked like an F-105 strike cell hunting for a hole in the clouds.

"Ford, Olds. Turning back up track now, comin' at you, we'll pass you on the right."

"Copy. We're painting you." Robinson had four closely grouped targets at twelve o'clock, level elevation, 46 miles in a left turn. Nothing else was showing in the radar's search mode.

As he steadied out on a northwesterly heading, Adams again altered the Bolo tactics. "This is Olds 01. Condition Sierra Sour." Adams notified all the Bolo flights that "missiles free" was canceled. When he'd continued past Phuc Yen and then made a subsequent turn back to the northwest, Adams had put his flight on a parallel but opposite track with Ford flight, five minutes behind. Now the American pilots would paint him as a target on their radar scopes. All radar targets now had to be visually identified before the U.S. pilots could fire their missiles. Adams had forfeited yet another advantage to the enemy because of the evolving situation. Momentarily, he thought that he didn't get paid enough to hang it out this far. But he knew Bolo was a sound plan, and besides, he'd have a tough time trying to fool the NVAF again if Bolo didn't flush them out.

"Pickin' up anything, Taco?"

"Just Ford flight, 30 miles at eleven o'clock."

Clint Adams wondered if he'd outsmarted himself, and if Colonel Tomb would take the bait.

In Olds 03, Mike Nelson's APR-25 RHAW receiver picked up the first indications of SAM activity. "Hear that chirping in the headset, Moose? Damn SA-2 tracking radars again." Normally, the RHAW gear was so noisy that most pilots turned down the audio signal knob on their RHAW gear so they could hear the critical radio transmissions. Pilots had to prioritize. But today, Nelson could hear only the single tracking signal. He diverted his eyes into the cockpit for an instant to look at his RHAW scope. "Textbook stuff. Fan Song acquisition radar, Moose man." A solitary green strobe pulsated. "They're painting us from two o'clock. Hell, Moose, looks like we may get issued some Russian telephone poles."

"Don't worry, Mike. This ECM pod will fake 'em out."

Nelson wasn't so sure. The chirping in his headset stepped up in frequency to the distinctive rattlesnake noise that meant a SAM launch was very likely. He decided to alert Olds 01. Too late, the launch light on his RHAW gear panel went to steady red.

"Olds flight, 03. SAM launch, three o'clock." All eyes strained in that direction, searching for the SA-2. Soon two missiles, one about a half mile behind the first, wandered up through the clouds, but they were not headed for Olds flight. Instead, the SAMs moved off to the rear of the formation. Both missiles harmlessly detonated about 10 miles away at five o'clock. "Damn, Moose. Maybe these American electrons are smarter than the Communist electrons."

1504 hours
Tomb's MiG-21

Airborne now and on a radar vector from the North Vietnamese radar controller, Tomb led his MiGs on a westerly climb from Kep Airfield through the lower clouds. He leveled off his eight MiGs at 2,000 meters, staying below the highest cloud deck.

"Control, Tomb. Where are the attackers?"

"Turn left to 20 degrees. Lead elements are 10 kilometers ahead and almost abeam to your left. They have turned back northwest toward Hanoi." Curious, thought Tomb, as he started his left turn to fly in behind the American leader's track. At least the Americans are not radar bombing Kep Airfield, he thought. Perhaps the lead Americans either had turned for home or were looking for a break in the cloud cover for a visual attack of some kind.

"Tomb, Control. The American flight does not have a fighter escort. Only F-105 defense suppression aircraft are with the strike force, and they are just now entering the area 60 kilometers west."

"Acknowledged." More curious, thought Tomb. I have not seen this kind of formation—only unescorted F-105 strike bombers—since the very early days of the air war. Perhaps Arkov's information was accurate. Perhaps this was what Ngoc wanted to tell me. Why hadn't Ngoc called through Control?

"Tomb, Control. Correction. There is indeed a fighter escort, but it is 75 kilometers southeast. Four aircraft."

"Acknowledged." Tomb was comforted by this call. He could accept a light, malpositioned MiGCAP on the far side of the strike.

"Tomb, Control. Strike force is an endless string of four-ship attack flights spaced 70 kilometers apart. So far, the count is sixty enemy planes. All carry jamming devices." A new American tactic, thought Tomb. Could the Americans believe that electronic devices would protect F-105s well enough to forgo aggressive fighter escort? The Americans loved their technology, but this was exceptional. Perhaps the Americans needed an old-fashioned lesson.

Now Tomb took his first decisive action. "Zero two, go to maximum supersonic speed and dash ahead. Maintain 2,000 meters altitude below the clouds. Fly a right-to-left zigzag." Tomb ordered a single MiG forward at Mach 1.8 on an angle as a decoy, aiming it at the American strike force, but still below the clouds. Tomb was sure this single target would be detected on radar, but not seen, by the Americans. This maneuver might get the F-105 Thuds to jettison their bombs. And it would tell him how nervous the American pilots were. Classic Tomb, waging war on the minds of the Americans.

"Tomb, Control, now turn right 20 degrees," the NVAF ground controller steadied Tomb's remaining seven MiG-21s behind Olds flight. "Targets 10 kilometers ahead. Maintain your speed."

Tomb closed in behind the lead American strike cell, setting up for a supersonic stern attack. This weather brought good fortune, thought

Tomb. His Spin Scan radar showed the four targets ahead and high now, confirming his relative geometry.

Once the NVAF radar controller saw that Tomb had stabilized in pre-attack, he continued his vectoring. "Tomb, Control. Accelerate to 1.1 Mach." Tomb now started to drive up the American leader's tail.

He'd pop up through the clouds and take out the trailing element in Olds flight with Atoll missiles before the Americans knew he was there. He would also outnumber the unsuspecting Americans, seven to four. By making a fist and moving it forward as far as his arm would extend, Tomb signaled for his MiG-21 wingmen to accelerate to supersonic attack speed.

The Americans, just 4,000 meters ahead now, were in for a rude ambush. Tomb had found a way to move in behind the Americans completely undetected. He would have surprise on his side as usual. Perhaps this would teach the Americans not to strike North Vietnam when cloud cover was complete.

1507 hours
Ten miles east of Hanoi

Olds flight was still heading northwest. Taco Martinez in Olds 01 picked up a single, fast-moving bogey—Tomb's decoy—on his fire-control radar. The target was low and coming in from the right, straight at them.

"Sir, bogey, two o'clock low, 5 miles, closing very fast."

"Olds 03, do you have radar contact on the bandit two o'clock low?"

"Affirm."

"You're cleared for VID, but stay above the cloud deck," Adams said, directing Mike Nelson in Olds 03 to lock on and pursue for a visual identification and attack.

Nelson complied, nosing over his F-4. Almost immediately, Adams observed that Nelson and F-105 wingman Kuszinski were skimming the top of the undercast. Eight seconds later, the bogey passed under the American Phantoms, visually undetected, masked by the cloud deck.

"Olds 03, no joy." Nelson replied, meaning he couldn't see the target aircraft. He hit both afterburners and started to rejoin Olds flight at 12,000 feet. And none too soon.

Doubly frustrated now, Adams decided to pack it in for the day. "Let's go home, Taco. We're starting to garbage up the flow." Adams began to exit the area, maintaining a 290-degree heading for Thud Ridge. He was leaving some rare MiG opportunities to Curt Robinson and the other Bolo strike cells. Some MiGs were there. Somewhere.

Clint Adams looked at his APR-25 scope, saturated with green, useless electronic soup. A few strobes stretched out from the center to the edge of the scope. These were the closest, most intense signals—the ones that were tracking him with the greatest interest. All the mode indicator lights were lit up: EW/GCI, AAA, SAM acquisition, even air intercept (AI).

AI light! That grabbed Adams's stomach like a vise. Unless he was getting a false alarm, MiG-21PFs were airborne, nearby, and painting Olds flight.

"Taco, check the RHAW gear. See it?"

Martinez leaned to his right and peered into the front cockpit. The APR-25 scope was angled toward the AC's view and covered with a rubber shroud. But it was the indicator lights that Adams wanted him to look at. "Yeah, Boss. We got AI on the RHAW scope. We may get some action yet!"

"Keep your eyes out when you can. Check six. Check six." Adams gave Taco the fighter pilot's warning to watch his ass.

"Will do, Boss." Martinez set up a scanning routine that split his scan between his radar search and the undercast below. The MiGs were up, and the GCI had vectored them to intercept course on Olds flight. But from which direction? What was their range?

Adams couldn't alert his wingmen without exposing the masquerade, but something would happen soon. He checked his missile switches and mentally reviewed what his initial actions would be if the MiGs popped up from his six o'clock direction.

1508 hours
Tomb's cockpit

Tomb was waiting for the right moment to spring on his target. The NVAF air defense radar operator had kept Tomb's formation below the undercast as long as possible. The ground controller consciously delayed the zoom maneuver so that the MiGs would surprise the Americans at the last minute.

Tomb, however, knew that his less-experienced pilots would be momentarily confused by flying into the weather, then bursting into the clear brightness of the afternoon sunlight. They were poorly trained to fly in actual weather, and the MiG-21 was difficult to fly on instruments. His pilots would be slow to react to the American formation. He had to keep his seven planes with him through the first attack so that they had time to adjust to seeing the first American F-105s explode. That would give them the confidence they needed to drive home their follow-up attacks.

These pilots were nervous, Tomb thought. A good flight leader knew when his wingmen were straining. Tomb watched them bounce around. It was a signal that they were letting their minds wander to troubles ahead, rather than concentrating on maintaining formation. His wingmen had been flying sloppy formation ever since they'd joined up after takeoff. "This is Tomb. Fly steady, my friends." And these MiG-21 pilots were his most experienced aviators.

Tomb wondered if some of his pilots would lose their initiative. Yes. They had never seen an air battle of this size. He had triple-briefed them all this morning, but they would revert to instinct. He told them that if they got confused, they should drop below the clouds and contact the air defense controller for directions to the battle or to Kep. But these instructions wouldn't be enough. The cloud cover would offer the necessary extra security. Perhaps he should call off the attack. So much was at risk. No, he was so close, and he had to teach the Americans a lesson after their threats at Phuc Yen. And Arkov was airborne too and might do some good.

"Tomb, Control. The target is 3 kilometers ahead now. Closure rate: 100 knots. Climb 10 degrees now." The controller directed the zoom maneuver. Tomb pulled his plane up through the cloud deck. Raggedly the other seven MiGs in his formation followed. In seconds, he and the others broke through into the brightness. The sun flooded his forward canopy. He lowered his tinted goggles and blinked several times to adjust his vision.

The American formation was 2 kilometers dead ahead now. Initially, they were merely dark shapes in the afternoon sunlight.

1509 hours
Bear Robinson's cockpit
Ford flight
Overhead Phuc Yen

Bear Robinson had a visual tally on Olds flight, 8 miles ahead at eleven o'clock level. He was about to call out his position to Clint

Adams on the UHF when his GIB squealed in a high-pitched voice, "Boss, two groups of pop-up bandits on the scope. Comin' in behind Olds flight. One right behind the other at ten o'clock—10 miles and 15 miles."

Robinson pushed the radio button to alert Clint Adams to the radar contacts, when he saw the first MiGs pop through the undercast at Olds flight's six o'clock.

"Olds, Ford. Bandits! Deep six! Four, six, no, sixteen!"

Adams and his wingman immediately broke left and reversed for a shot. Olds 03 and 04 split high. As Nelson went to afterburner on his two engines, Kuszinski quickly learned his one engine wasn't going to hack it. This wasn't his fight. He couldn't turn with the Phantoms or the MiGs. Nelson and Peterson were on their own from here.

"Olds 04's disengaging the fight. See you outbound, gents." Kuszinski rolled inverted and sucked his Thud straight down into the undercast. He decided to lurk below the clouds, possibly picking off a scared MiG pilot heading for China.

Adams wheeled his Phantom through a shuddering direction swap. In seconds, he was in the missile shot basket, and Martinez had a radar lock-on in this target-rich environment. Adams, in Olds 01, launched an AIM-7 Sparrow, then hit his heat switch and squeezed off a heat-seeking AIM-9 Sidewinder. Both failed to guide, but they scattered the MiGs in a near panic, much like breaking the opening rack in a deadly game of billiards.

Mike Nelson, in Olds 03, took a few more seconds to achieve a better shooting angle on an unsuspecting MiG-21. He turned back into the MiGs and stayed high.

"Moose. I'm boresight on the lead element. Lock on! Lock on!" Moose clicked the red paddle switch on his radar control stick with his right hand. Instantly, the firing logic came up on the radar scope. Mike Nelson launched two radar Sparrow missiles. "Fox One. Fox One."

Six seconds later, Mike Nelson's first Sparrow missile struck the MiG leader's wingman in the midsection. The MiG-21 disintegrated. The cockpit section, still intact and burning, corkscrewed through the undercast. No chute. Nelson and Peterson had their third MiG kill.

Flight discipline among the MiGs broke down almost immediately. For a moment, Tomb himself was confused. All he saw were F-4s! Wait, there was one F-105, heading straight down. What was this? A mixed flight? He had been victimized by tactical surprise, for the first time in his combat experience. There were mostly air superiority Phantoms. He had put his pilots into a hornet's nest. The surprise was complete. He cursed the Americans.

All Tomb saw were F-4s—three close in and another four just entering the fight in the distance. Immediately dead ahead, he saw three F-4s splitting and turning into his MiGs. They were swarming into aerial maneuvers, already reacting to his MiG attack. Despite all his planning and stealth, Tomb was furious that he'd had no missile shot.

Tomb watched in horror as two AIM-7 Sparrows tracked into his wingman's aircraft. Once he saw that he himself was not the intended target, he counterattacked against the strike force leader, Olds 01. Had he known that they had been fired by the pilot that had buzzed Phuc Yen, Tomb would have attacked Olds 03 like a fanatic. Then Mike Nelson fired a third Sparrow in the direction of the still-vulnerable North Vietnamese double ace.

Tomb racked his delta-winged aircraft into a series of evasive turns in an effort to get so far off angle from Olds 03 that the Phantom's spotlighting radar would break lock. All the while, he kept the pursuing missile in plain view. He was alone now. No wingman to protect him or draw fire for him. Yet he foiled the Sparrow missile attack with his maneuvers as the American radar missile slithered off behind him and detonated to no effect. His heart was pounding out of his chest, and his pulse was setting new personal records. He had never been caught in so deadly a duel.

Tomb decided that the Olds flight pincer play was squeezing him too tightly, almost like a vise on his stomach. For the first time, he felt the panic of not understanding the turn of events. Tomb thought that this was how his young pilots must often feel.

He felt an almost uncontrollable desire to flee the scene. "Discipline yourself!" Tomb growled into his mask, "Disengage, then return on your terms." Near the undercast, he executed a violent split-S, pulling his bucking MiG down through the clouds, and exiting the fight. Once under the cloud deck, he pulled his MiG hard to the right and leveled out. An unguided Sparrow missile exploded off to his left, probably aimed at him by the American flight leader.

1509
Blue Chip Operations Center
Seventh Air Force HQ
Tan Son Nhut Air Base

"General, Hillsboro reports that all hell's breaking loose on the Bolo tactical frequency."

"What the hell does that mean, Major?"

"MiGs, sir. MiGs popping up all over the place."

Tom Morgan looked at Max Crandall and slowly broke into a broad smile without taking the cigar out of his mouth. "Crandall, you're a frippin' genius. Now we're gonna find out if we're the stickers or the stickees."

1510 hours
Tomb's cockpit

Tomb looked around to get his bearings. Nothing going on below the clouds. Within seconds, he was back up through the overcast. For a few brief moments, twenty-four jet fighters—sixteen MiGs and seven F-4s and a F-105—had come together in the sky north of Hanoi. His MiGs had outnumbered the Phantoms two to one, but his pilots were not using that advantage. They were already mentally routed. Worse, more Phantoms would be joining the fight soon.

In the first 150 seconds, the complexion of the battle had already taken shape: confused MiGs beset by single or pairs of F-4s. And, man for man, Tomb saw that his pilots were totally outclassed. Some MiGs were fleeing immediately, just as he predicted. Right now, the disengaging MiGs looked like the smart ones. They would survive.

Tomb radioed to his remaining MiGs, "This is Tomb. Remember my instructions!" Still, his pilots were faring badly. Then, 5 kilometers west, Tomb saw a hapless MiG-21 in a near-level turn take a heat-seeking missile in the tail section, fired from two F-4s chasing from the rear. The pilot ejected. The burning hulk rolled over into a flat spin. The fatally wounded MiG fell into the cloud deck below, trailing heavy black smoke. Tomb fought the impulse to watch the MiG's mesmerizing final descent. It was dangerous to get fixed on destroyed aircraft.

Tomb hit his radio transmission button. "Control, Tomb. Return the exiting MiGs to the battle. Seal off the other arriving Americans. Attack the inbound enemy planes from two sides if you can."

"Acknowledged." The GCI channel became saturated with confused transmissions between the controller and the disoriented NVAF pilots, some of whom did not want to reengage the Phantoms. GCI Control sorted them out and vectored them toward inbound targets northwest of the main battle.

1510 hours
Clint Adams's cockpit
Olds 01

Adams and Martinez in Olds 01 closed in on another MiG after they saw the enemy formation leader escape into the clouds with an Adams-fired Sparrow on his tail. This second MiG was at their eleven o'clock, slightly low, in a left clearing turn. Adams pulled up and inside the MiG's turn, then he executed a classic vector roll over to the right.

Adams paused, inverted at the top, as the MiG continued his level left clearing turn. "The MiG hasn't seen us yet, Taco," Adams said calmly. "Most victims never see their attackers in these big dust-ups."

Adams reached down and again selected the heat toggle switch with his left hand. At precisely the correct moment, he completed his right vector roll, perfectly positioned for a Sidewinder shot, slightly low on the inside of the enemy pilot's turn. Remarkably, he hadn't pulled more than three Gs in this pursuit. The afternoon sun to Adams's rear outlined the tiny MiG against a brilliant blue sky.

Taco Martinez remarked, "What a beautiful silver plane."

"Fox Two." Adams broke his backseater's momentary euphoria by sending a single lethal Sidewinder off the wing pylon. With a thump, it scooted off in a plume of chalky rocket propellant exhaust. Seven seconds later, the missile hit the left-wing root of the unsuspecting MiG.

"Splash One." The MiG's wing broke off. The fuselage swapped ends, and the remaining cigar-shaped hulk hurtled into the clouds below. No chute.

"Sir, we have three Sparrows and two Sidewinders remaining. Still enough to be an ace today."

"Get a grip on yourself, Martinez. Find me another bandit."

1511 hours
Ivan Arkov's cockpit

Arkov was enraged at being caught by such a stunning surprise, but he knew how to fly the Russian-built MiG-21. He turned to take advantage of Olds 03 and 04, who had rolled back to provide cover for Olds 01. The Russian launched a heat-seeking Atoll as soon as the geometry permitted. This was the first missile fired by the MiGs today.

Moose Peterson saw the MiG-21's missile launch. The business end of the Soviet-made Atoll missile got the attention of the normally laconic Minnesotan. "Break left! Left!"

Arkov's Atoll couldn't maneuver with the F-4 as Mike Nelson took the pursuing Arkov through a high-speed scissors maneuver—a series of turn reversals—causing the Russian to overshoot out of firing position. Nelson pulled the pursuing Arkov into another vertical turning series that, by design, MiG-21s found difficult to perform at 10,000 to 15,000 feet.

After sixty seconds, Nelson gained the advantage on Arkov by reversing direction smartly several times. The unsettled Arkov slowly lost ground against the American. His wingman had also abandoned him several turns ago. Arkov decided to disengage. He turned for the undercast. This egress maneuver lengthened the distance between Nelson and Arkov, exactly what Nelson was working for.

"Moose, I'm boresight again. Give me a radar lock-on." The Swede was ready and locked up before Nelson stopped talking, giving his frontseater full firing logic for a Sparrow shot. Nelson had one AIM-7 left.

"Go for it," exhaled Moose. When Nelson heard Moose's words, he simply squeezed off his fourth and last AIM-7 radar missile of the day. "Fox One."

Arkov accelerated through the sound barrier as he disappeared into the undercast in a 45-degree dive. The supersonic MiG passed through the clouds in less than two seconds. Believing he had escaped, Arkov leveled off and throttled back. Arkov called the NVAF radar controller for a vector to reenter the fight. "Control. Red Leader 02. Request—" The radio transmission was strangled by a loud ripping sound and a blast of electronic noise.

"Damn, Mike! He's going into the clouds." Moose wanted this kill.

So did Nelson. "Radar missiles don't care about undercasts, Moose. They only care about radar lock-ons, closure rates, distances, and target proximity. Keep your lock-on. This one's gonna track. I know it. Let's go see." Mike Nelson's last AIM-7 Sparrow followed Arkov easily through the clouds.

Olds 03 broke out through the undercast just in time to observe the residual fireball and shredded MiG parts falling away. Arkov's wingman,

2 miles to the west, pulled up into the cloud deck using a looping maneuver, escaping further attack from Olds 03. "Splash One!" Nelson and Peterson would never know their fourth and most exciting air victory had been against a MiG pilot from the outskirts of Moscow.

1511 hours
Ford flight
On the west side of the air battle

Bear Robinson in Ford 01 and the rest of his four-ship blew into the air battle just as the bulk of the MiG force scattered.

Rod Wells called out on the UHF, "Ford 03, two MiG-21s, two o'clock high."

The Mikoyans were climbing to higher altitude, above 20,000 feet, where the delta-wing interceptors performed best. Robinson saw the ascending MiGs. "Tally." He took Ford 01 and 02 in pursuit.

Meanwhile, Wells saw four MiGs converging in what appeared to be a ground-directed attack on Ford 01. "Ford 01, Ford 03 has four bandits at your nine o'clock. We'll keep them off you." These MiGs saw Ford 03 and 04 turning into them, and they left Bear Robinson alone to pursue the climbing pair of MiG-21s.

1514 hours
Twenty miles north of the main air battle

Randy Starbuck led Rambler flight screaming down the north side of Thud Ridge, almost to Phuc Yen. Rambler was running late on its time over target. Rambler 02 had gotten hung up with a few disconnects while taking on fuel from the KC-135 tanker.

But now Starbuck was entering the fighting area. He'd come all the way to Pack Six on only one generator. Under Randy Starbuck's strict leadership, Rambler flight was religiously flying the ECM pod formation exactly as briefed, just as expected of the chief of 8th Wing Tactics. Rambler was stacked echelon left, 2,000 feet apart, 2,000 up between planes. Major Roscoe Stewart in Rambler 03 had a great view of the battle from his position in Rambler flight.

Randy Starbuck in Rambler 01 had been listening to the excited chatter of the massive dogfight for the past few minutes. He leaned forward in his harness, as if to pull his Phantom forward. He wanted to merge with the main battle. Starbuck griped on the intercom, "Shit, Snake. We're payin' for running late. Sounds like they need us." He was mentally kicking himself. He'd pushed up the speed to 0.95 Mach three minutes before.

Snake Cummings couldn't find the main battle on his radar. "Don't see them on the scope. How about a turn? Maybe to the southwest." Obviously the fight was not straight ahead, because Rambler's radar scopes were clear.

Starbuck took a calculated risk, "You're right, Snake. Let's use our technology to find the fight." He led Rambler flight in a right turn. After completing the turn, the trailing and stacking of the pod formation was now a serious liability. The Phantoms in Rambler flight found their naked butts staring right at Hanoi, very exposed to the MiG threat. Unknown to Starbuck, the NVAF ground radar controller was already vectoring MiGs to intercept Rambler flight.

In frustration, Randy Starbuck made a radio call, "Olds 01, where are you? Where are the MiGs?"

Adams, too busy to know, answered, "Find your own!"

Just then, Roscoe Stewart in Rambler 03 did just that. "Rambler, four MiG-21s crossing from two o'clock low, 8 miles." The MiGs had been setting up a stern intercept on Rambler, but Starbuck's unplanned turn upset the geometry of their attack. The NVAF radar controller on the ground couldn't detect this change fast enough on his scope and react in time to the maneuvering American targets. Now the four MiGs were on their own.

Starbuck radioed, "Rambler, close it up." The four Phantoms abandoned the inflexible ECM pod formation and moved into a two-pair fighting wing in seconds.

"Rambler 01 has the front end of the split." Starbuck took the lead two MiGs, while Stewart in Rambler 03 and his wingman pursued the second element.

Starbuck slid in behind his intended victim and squeezed off two Sparrows. The first radar missile didn't track. The second Sparrow pulled forward in a graceful left climbing turn toward the small, silver MiG. The missile impacted on the red star of the MiG-21's fuselage, breaking the plane's back. The pilot somehow ejected. "Splash One, Snake!" Starbuck exulted.

Roscoe Stewart had the next two shots, also AIM-7 Sparrows, aimed at the number three MiG. "Fox One. Fox One."

"Crap, where is it?" Stewart's first Sparrow did not ignite, breaking his perfect combat record for missile shots. The Sparrow dropped out of its semirecessed missile cove like a free-falling white fence post, but Stewart's second radar missile tracked right into the tailpipe of the MiG-21 for Stewart's third MiG kill.

1514 hours
Blue Chip Operations Center
Seventh Air Force HQ
Tan Son Nhut Air Base

Tom Morgan and Max Crandall stood together, their eyes locked on the expanded map of the Route Pack Six area.

"All those Fox Ones and Twos sound good so far, sir. Clint Adams seems to have the upper hand."

"I'm listening for the Mayday calls, Max. Just a few of those and the ratio goes down the tubes."

1516 hours
Rambler flight
Ten miles north of the dissipating main flight

The battle continued for Rambler. Snake Cummings in Starbuck's backseat saw a lone MiG wallowing 3 miles north. "Roll right, roll right," he urged Randy Starbuck.

"Got 'em!" Randy Starbuck got an opportunity for a second kill inside of two minutes. He barrel rolled into firing position against the disoriented, surviving MiG pilot.

Just then, Roscoe Stewart in Rambler 03 saw two trailing MiGs slide in behind Starbuck and his wingman. "Rambler Lead, two bandits at your six. Working a sandwich."

Roscoe Stewart converged on the MiGs, but lost sight of Randy Starbuck in Rambler 01. He was confused. "Is that Lead? He didn't break on my call. Shit, I don't know." Stewart saw the two MiG trailers continuing their slide in behind the unresponsive F-4. "Got to try something else." Stewart made a quick, desperate radio call, "F-4C, there's a MiG on your tail. Break hard right."

Starbuck was about to squeeze off a Sidewinder, oblivious to everything else right now.

Not so Snake. "Break, dammit! break!"

"Shit." Frustrated and pissed, Starbuck broke hard right. Every other F-4 pilot listening to this radio frequency did the same thing.

But Randy Starbuck wouldn't quit. He shook off his attackers, rolled back, and continued his attack on his original MiG. Snake helped, snapping up a radar lock-on inside two seconds. "Good lock-on, Snake. Fox One. Fox One again." He fired two Sparrows. The second missile followed the MiG-21 into the clouds. No confirmation.

Before their fight was over, Roscoe Stewart, in Rambler 03, got a clean shot at yet another lone MiG, but he was forced into a defensive break by two more bouncing MiGs. His last two Sidewinders had most likely done their work on the MiG-21 flying well above the cloud deck, but nobody saw the impacts.

Stewart turned back to his target. "Where's the MiG? Where are the missiles?"

His GIB answered, "Don't know, Boss, but I got a tally on a Gomer in a chute at two o'clock."

"That's ours. I know it! Shit." Roscoe circled the MiG pilot floating down in a good parachute.

"Anybody in Rambler see a Splash moments ago?"

"Not now, 03." Starbuck chided the flight, regaining a semblance of control in the process.

Nobody could confirm Stewart's second kill of the day. Lesson learned: don't take your eyes off the target if you want a confirmed kill—only if you want to live for another day.

1517 hours
Five miles east of Phuc Yen

Rod Wells in Ford 03 had a MiG-21 squarely in his optical sight. "Fox Two." He took a clean Sidewinder shot at his target.

The NVAF fighter exploded within five seconds. "Splash One!"

The pilot's chute was a "streamer." Wells watched the doomed pilot plummet into the undercast locked in his ejection seat, his green parachute hopelessly twisted in a Gordian knot of shroud lines.

1518 hours
Over Phuc Yen

By intuition and chance, Tomb had come upon Adams in Olds 01 again. The two aces were in a clockwise level turn opposite each other, feeling each other out. Tomb was near rage at being surprised in his own backyard. He wanted the American leader.

I have to control my emotions, thought Tomb. That was when he was at his best. This American was perhaps the best pilot he had ever faced.

A few cat-and-mouse turns later, Tomb was sure that he had come upon the American flight leader, the Eagle. This man was an aerial master, he thought.

In a minute, the engagement moved below the undercast. The two men were fighting in a different environment now, darting in, out, and around the small rain showers that were still building in the Southeast Asian heat. Adams used a vertical rolling scissors to take Tomb even lower but still held him at arm's length out of firing position.

Still, Tomb took several low-percentage, short-burst gun shots. He was an uncanny aerial marksman; and he liked the shots he'd taken. The pounding of the cannon shells and the sight of the red tracers encouraged him to drive home his attack. His spirits leaped when several of his 23mm cannon shells found their mark, clipping the green formation light off the end of Adams's left wing and damaging a Sidewinder missile fin on the nearby underwing pylon.

Adams, too, knew he was facing someone special. "That's Tomb," he muttered to Taco. "Got to be. Hold on! This son of a bitch can fly his 21."

Both Adams and Martinez tensed when Tomb's cannon shells chewed off #680's right wingtip light. Instinctively, Adams tightened his turn. But the MiG pilot's cannon shells found another, more vulnerable part of his F-4, pounding into the upper fuselage.

"Shit, Colonel. My cockpit's filling up with JP-4." Taco Martinez had stated the case clearly. One of the cannon shell fragments must have punctured the number one fuel tank, which was directly behind the rear cockpit. The cold, kerosene-like liquid was rising above the tops of Martinez's flying boots and seeping in between his toes.

"Go 100 percent, Taco." Both pilots flipped the white switch on their oxygen control panel. The 100 percent oxygen counteracted the fumes somewhat. Adams could hear Martinez increase his respiration rate, more apprehensive over his cockpit predicament than the deadly battle with this outstanding MiG pilot. Tough luck, but the fight continued.

The dogfight progressed northwestward into the foothills near Thud Ridge. "Stick with me, Taco. I'm taking it low, real low." Adams edged toward the ground, weaving among the cloud-shrouded hilltops, 50 feet below. This was a dangerous tactic, with little margin for error.

First things first. He needed to get out of the enemy pilot's gunsight. Then he'd worry about a missile shot.

Tomb wondered why the American brought the fight here where he had no missile shot. He must be on the defensive, trying to escape. The F-4 could turn tighter down here, but Tomb knew every meter of the terrain. Tomb had the fuel for the fight. And his guns did not care about the heavy ground clutter. There was no radar advantage here, and the heat-seeking missiles did not like the closeness to the earth, either. Here, too, the rain showers limited the American's ability to see Tomb's small MiG. Good, American, keep the fight down here, thought Tomb.

Tomb saw a chance for a front-quarter gun attack. He rolled into Adams from behind a shower. But the enemy Phantom darted into an adjacent rain cloud as the cannon tracers from Tomb's aircraft enveloped the F-4. Remarkably, Tomb's cannon fire missed the American.

Tomb lost sight of the American. Was he escaping? No! The F-4 had converted to the offensive while inside the rain shower, a most unlikely turn of events. The American was at his four o'clock, in the clear, firing a Sidewinder!

Tomb wrenched his 21 into an incredible corkscrew up, around, and down the far side of the rain shower's shaft, offsetting the rapidly closing AIM-9 missile. Still, the Sidewinder almost found its target, detonating close by. Tomb felt the warhead fragment slap into the rear of his MiG, punching holes in his plane's engine compartment. Tomb smelled engine and saw black smoke trailing behind him, signs that his vital oil line was breached. "How did this happen?" Tomb shouted into his mask. "The American was mine!"

Adams remained poised for the kill. "I'll smoke the little bastard when he comes out of that shower, Taco."

"We got one more Sidewinder, Boss."

Adams waited for Tomb to emerge. "Where's that son of a bitch?" But the wait got too long. Adams and Martinez anxiously scanned the entire area. Nothing. Tomb was gone.

1520 hours
Blue Chip Operations Center
Seventh Air Force HQ
Tan Son Nhut Air Base

The duty officer hit the paddle switch on his table mike. "General, Hillsboro reports that the fight seems to be breaking up."

"What's the straight poop, as you know it, Major?"

"We have at least a half-dozen MiG kills to sort out. And some probable kills to go with it."

"Lose any Phantoms?"

"None reported, but it was a big, confusing fight."

Morgan stubbed out his cigar butt. "Is Olds flight moving out of the area yet?"

"Half of Olds flight and all of Ford and Rambler flights."

The response irritated the raw-nerved Max Crandall. "What the hell does that mean?"

"No word from Olds 01 or 04, sir."

1521 hours

Adams made several clearing turns in one last effort to locate Tomb's MiG-21. No joy. He turned northwest and headed up Thud Ridge. In thirty seconds he was through the overcast and on his way out of the area. "Taco, how you doin'?"

"It's up to my calves now, and my teeth are chattering." Martinez had to be close to panic from the fuel's cold, stinging effect as it slowly penetrated his skin pores and body openings.

"Any pain, good buddy?"

"Smarts a bit, sir."

I bet it does, Clint thought. He could hear his GIB taking short irregular breaths.

"Don't move any switches. I'll do everything up here." Adams looked at his own boots. They, too, were sitting in an inch of fuel. Both men knew that with one errant spark it would be all over.

"Olds flight, Olds 01 outbound. We got a hit in our number one fuel tank, and gas is filling our cockpits."

"Copy, Lead, we're ten minutes ahead. We'll get the tanker moving and onload gas before you get here," responded Mike Nelson in Olds 03. Olds 02 was on his wing.

Adams's fuel gauge showed 625 pounds. The fuel leak had robbed him of the 1,000 pounds of fuel he and Taco needed to hit the tanker, 90 miles west.

"Hillsboro, Olds Lead, 0 over 600. Request the tanker stretch out to meet us."

"Copy, Olds. We're already working it," the console operator aboard the C-130 command-and-control aircraft acknowledged. In a minute, the KC-135 tanker turned northeast. It wouldn't be able to get too far into Laos in the next ten minutes. Bad luck for Olds 01.

Adams's mind flashed back to Laura and the kids. Dammit, he thought, I never got things straight with them. They'll never know how much I love them.

Adams calculated that he had just enough fuel for a zoom climb to 28,000 feet. He pulled the stick back and kept the engine power at an efficient 92 percent. He had 250 pounds remaining as he passed through 21,500 feet. "This is Olds Lead. We're zooming now for a final glide. Won't make the tanker."

"Olds 03 copies. We'll tank and come in for the rescue cap. Hillsboro, you copy?"

"Roger, SAR has been initiated."

"Olds Lead will flame out while still over North Vietnam in about one minute," Adams radioed. He and Martinez had two choices. They could ride into the mountainous jungle below to their certain deaths. Or, they could eject, and the aircraft would probably explode instantaneously, killing them both. Adams deployed his ram air turbine for electrical power after the engines flamed out. At least he could talk on the UHF radio.

"I think we're running out of options, Taco." The irony of it all, thought Adams, sitting in the very fuel that could get them to the tanker.

Time was up. Both engines flamed out. Olds 01 pitched over into a power-out glide at 300 knots. Adams kept his airspeed up to windmill the engine turbines that, in turn, provided minimum hydraulic pressure for the Phantom's flight controls. The F-4 glided 6 miles for every 10,000 feet of altitude lost. Olds 01 would impact close to the Laotian border about 15 nautical miles ahead. The tanker, Oboe 52, was still 50 miles away at 25,000 feet.

Adams got ready to pull the ejection handle sticking up between his legs. When he pulled the ring, the F-4's automatic ejection sequence would start. Even though Adams would pull the ejection handle, Martinez's ejection seat would fire first. There was a slim chance that Taco would separate fast enough to survive. At least I can save the kid, Adams thought. "Prepare yourself, Taco. You're going for a short trip into the jungle."

Adams braced himself against his seat and grasped the ejection handle with his left hand. He closed his eyes.

"Lead, Olds 04. I'm in your six o'clock. Been chasin' you for 50 goddamn miles. Lower your hook." Big Jim Kuszinski had hung back as a rear guard for awhile. Then he'd turned outbound when he'd heard Clint Adams's distress calls. The Polish Warrior had plenty of gas and a crazy idea.

Kuszinski's radio call jolted Adams back into the flight environment. "Copy. I'll try anything once." Instinctively he slapped down the tail hook lever with his right hand. If the Air Force had built the Phantom from scratch, the F-4 wouldn't have had the black metal tail hook. Fortunately, the Navy needed one for carrier landings, and the Air Force had decided it was too expensive to engineer it off their F-4C version.

Adams steadied out in a steep glide. Ten seconds later he felt a bump and forward momentum thrust life into his plane.

"Pull back slowly and level off, Lead," Kuszinski said. "Just call your control inputs as you make them." Adams leveled off at 20,000 feet.

Kuszinski had moved in behind #680 and placed his Thud's thick Plexiglas front windscreen on the flat underside of the protruding tail hook. Both surfaces matched at a near 45-degree angle. Kuszinski's 6-inch-thick front windscreen had the strength to withstand the high dynamic air pressure of low-altitude, supersonic speeds. Now it seemed strong enough to push a flamed-out Phantom already in motion. So far, Kuszinski's first law of physics was working.

But Clint Adams's hook, held straight down by trapped emergency hydraulic pressure, slipped off the Polish Warrior's flat forward windscreen and gouged into the right side of his canopy. Big Jim pushed his Thud over violently and pulled back his throttle to avoid a midair collision with Adams's gliding Phantom.

Kuszinski's right canopy shattered into a frosted glass pattern, but somehow it held. Again, he drove his front windscreen into the extended hook's flat spot. This time the contact was firm and steady. Big Jim would not allow himself to think about his fate should his tiny one-foot-long front windscreen give way. . . .

Kuszinski flew the most important and dangerous formation of his life. "Oboe 52, have radar contact at 50 miles. We'll call your turn. Descend to 21,000 now. Expect a toboggan refueling from 20,000 to 15,000."

"Oboe 52, Wilco."

As Oboe 52 reached 30 miles out with a 3-mile offset, the tanker rendezvous began. "Oboe 52, start your turn now. Roll out heading 210."

As the KC-135 tanker was halfway around his turn, Mike Nelson took radio control of the operation and transmitted, "Olds flight has a tally on Oboe 52."

Now Nelson broke the news to Oboe's crew. He spoke deliberately. "Ah, Oboe, this is gonna be an unusual refueling. Tell your boomer to look for one Thud pushing a flamed-out Fox Four. Tell him to be aggressive. The boomer may only have one chance. And this aircrew cannot punch out due to fuel in the cockpit."

"Oboe 52, Roger. Call the toboggan, Olds 03."

This was one cool tanker crew, thought Peterson.

Adams worked his way quickly to the precontact position by coordinating his control inputs with Kuszinski's. The hook had slapped into Big Jim's windscreen a dozen times, creating ever-widening cracks in the Plexiglas. If it ruptured, Kuszinski would need a new face.

Adams opened his refueling receptacle. He got the yellow "open" light. He could hear the door disturb the air flow over the top of the aircraft much better now that the engine noise wasn't in the way.

"Oboe, 500 foot per minute descent now. We're coming in." Kuszinski pushed up the throttles an inch. Both planes moved in at about a foot per second. Ten seconds later, Olds 01 moved into the back edge of the 3-foot cube, and the boomer plugged #680 on the first attempt. Kuszinski pulled off an inch of throttle as the tanker's boom pulled along Olds 01 to a slight degree. Adams saw the green light, meaning gas was pumping into his tanks at 3,000 pounds per minute.

"You have pressure, Olds 01." The boomer's call was a victory of sorts. If Adams could stay on the boom for just twenty seconds, he'd have 1,000 pounds of jet fuel, enough to drop off the boom, start his engines, and top off under normal conditions. The connected boom actually stabilized #680, now sandwiched between a pusher and a puller. Ten seconds. Just a little longer. Twelve. Fifteen. Eighteen. Twenty. Twenty-three. Adams grunted to Taco, "Get ready with the air start checklist."

Taco plunged his hand into the standing pool of fuel and pulled out his plastic-covered checklist, "Ready."

"Oboe 52, disconnect. Sorry."

"Olds 01 has 1,200 pounds. Be back after the relight." Adams dropped away, and Taco called out, "Number one throttle—Idle. Fuel control switch—Airstart."

Nothing happened. The powerless Phantom slid through 15,000 feet, 14,000, 13,000, 12,000. . . .

Adams vented his anger. "Shit, start, you fucker! Start!" Chris Cole's F-4 responded at this very moment, and the right engine cooked off, the engine rpm rumbling slowly toward 65 percent. Taco whooped and shouted, "The sucker must've been cold-soaked."

The damaged plane would fly quite well on one engine, but Adams started the other quickly. He raised the hook and pulled in the RAT. In the next two minutes, he climbed back to Oboe 52 for another 5,000 pounds.

"Okay Olds flight, 01 has the lead. Get your gas and let's go home. And Oboe, thanks for a great plug on the first pass."

"Rog. Standing by to top off one Thud, then Ford, and Rambler," transmitted the KC-135's copilot.

Adams turned to look at the Polish Warrior. "And Olds 04, much gratitude, my friend. That was one damn fine job."

"You're goddamn welcome," chirped Kuszinski.

1534 hours
Blue Chip Operations Center
Seventh Air Force HQ
Tan Son Nhut Air Base

"General," the major said, happily carrying the good news, "MiG activity has ceased according to Hillsboro. At least for now. Only the first three flights—Olds, Ford, and Rambler—encountered enemy air action. All the succeeding flights continued over the target area, prowling for more MiGs, but they only reported light flak and a few inaccurate SAMs. The biggest air battle of the war all happened in about fifteen minutes."

"That's a long time to suck Gs, Major," chided Morgan.

"Understand, sir. Things are still sketchy, but all engagements took place over or very near Chicago, er, Phuc Yen. We've got at least seven MiG kills and a handful of probables on MiGs with missiles following them into the clouds."

Tom Morgan turned to Crandall. "Max, your boys did a fine job up there today."

"Adams did it, sir. We just helped."

"Bullshit. It was a team effort. Let me tell you what we did today. The F-4 established air superiority over the MiG-21 in a quarter hour. Fifty percent of North Vietnam's operational MiG-21s are definite smoking holes in the ground. The actual toll may be 80 percent."

"Not a bad day's work," Crandall added.

"You got that right, Max. You stay here and watch the aftermath. I'm gonna go call CINCPACAF in Hawaii."

"Yessir."

Morgan paused, pondering one nagging point. "Did you say that one of our pilots pushed Olds 01 out of North Vietnam?"

"That's what Hillsboro relayed, but I'll check it out more thoroughly," responded Crandall.

"Do that, Max. You do that. Damn. I gotta meet that fella," Morgan commented, heading for the privacy of his inner office.

1535 hours
The flight line
Kep Airfield

Tomb slowly walked away from his damaged plane. Dried blood was caked in streams on the right side of his skull. The right shoulder of his flight suit was wet with a dark red stain. The American colonel's Sidewinder had done more than damage Tomb's engine turbine blades.

This time Major Duc Van Do did not ask the colonel how many planes would be returning. Instead he approached Tomb's damaged MiG after the colonel moved toward his tiny office. Duc had watched Tomb guide his damaged fighter down to the runway, flying final approach at 160 knots. The silver craft had been spewing a mixture of white and black smoke. Only someone of Tomb's superior airmanship could have nursed the wounded machine back to Kep. The NVAF maintenance officer took one look at the leaking MiG. The underside of the machine looked like a cheese grater. Duc declared it beyond repair by the NVAF. It was easier to crate it up and send it back to the Soviet Union.

Only four other MiG-21s returned that afternoon, out of sixteen that had taken to the air less than an hour ago. The surviving pilots were quite disturbed. Arkov was not among those who'd returned. Duc, like everyone else at Kep, would not miss the Russian.

1540 hours
Colonel Tomb's office
Kep Airfield

Tomb summoned Ngoc the moment he could get to the phone. The young officer knocked on the door and entered on a crutch, his left leg in a splint. Tomb motioned for the nurse tending his head wound to wait outside.

"What was it you wanted to tell me, Ngoc?"

"That the Ubon wing commander Adams was leading the American strike force today."

Tomb said nothing at first. He took on a detached expression. It was all clear to him now. His intuition had been correct all along—something was not right. Yet he had allowed others to prod him into action, especially that stupid Russian. Tomb had always prided himself in picking the time and place for his battle. Today, he had let other forces compel him into a trap. He stared straight ahead. Ngoc had held the knowledge to avert this disaster.

"Why didn't you advise me on the radio, Ngoc?" If Tomb had had this one fact everything might have been different.

"Colonel, the Americans would have known we had intelligence agents at Ubon Airfield. I would have exposed our operatives there."

Tomb grabbed hold of the front edge of the desk and squeezed it so tight that Ngoc could see his knuckles turn blue-white. "Do you believe that those agents would be in greater danger than my pilots were in today?"

Ngoc said nothing. He understood now that Tomb had wanted the information, despite the risks. He feared Tomb as never before. The battle must have gone badly.

Tomb pulled open the center drawer of the desk, exposing the old French revolver he had taken off a French officer's body twelve years earlier.

Major Duc and the maintenance team examining Tomb's damaged MiG-21 heard the single shot echo from Tomb's office, 50 meters away. They looked over toward the building. Nguyen Tomb was standing in the doorway holding a handgun. Two security guards shuffled past Tomb, carrying Ngoc's body, his swaying arms dragging in the dirt. A nurse nervously dabbed Tomb's head wound, which had started to bleed again.

1630 hours
The Aussie alert strip
Ubon RTAFB

Group Captain Harley Stockman and two other Aussies looked up to see the first eleven Ubon F-4s flying down initial approach, a flight of three followed by two flights of four. One Aussie aircraft crew chief queried his detachment commander. "'Scuse me, sir, can you tell if the Yanks had good hunting?"

"We'll know in a minute or two. Looks like they left some behind up north. They could have lost a few." Stockman figured if the Americans lost some planes, so did the Gomers. "But I bet you the lucky bastards gave out more bashings than they got." Stockman's envy was showing. He expected some victory rolls.

"Olds 03, Lead," radioed Adams. "I'm on a 5-mile final for a straight-in. Work a victory roll sequence after I touch down." Nelson double clicked his UHF radio.

Moose couldn't believe it. "How can he think about our victory rolls when he and Taco are swimmin' in gas?"

"I think that's why some command and some watch, Moose man." Nelson was catching on.

Alerted by Mike Nelson in Olds 03 twenty minutes earlier, the emergency crews, fire trucks, and ambulances were in place out at the runway, waiting to help their wing commander. The HH-43 Husky helicopter was airborne off to the side of Runway 23 at midfield with its fire suppression bottle containing 800 gallons of foam slung below its fuselage.

Adams touched down, rolled to the end, and turned off. #680 was immediately surrounded by fire suppression teams. Three men in head-to-toe silver fire suits moved to the Phantom. Adams shut down all power and unhooked every strap connecting him to the plane. Martinez did the same. They were not out of the woods yet. One spark could still ruin their day. The two pilots didn't open their canopies electrically. They let the fireman do it from the outside, pneumatically. In fifteen seconds, both men were out of the plane. Adams was okay. The JP-4 fuel had never gotten above his boots. Martinez was on his way to the hospital for a series of cleaning baths and some pain killer. Otherwise, he was fine.

Chris Cole exchanged salutes with Adams. "Thanks for bringing her back, Colonel. Did we get anything?"

"Paint another star on her, Sergeant. We damn near got a Dragon, too."

Mike Nelson took the Bolo formation straight through and off to the east, setting up a holding pattern. He aimed a radio call at the seven MiG killers. "If you have a confirmed kill, take a roll over the field. Stay 1,000 feet minimum. Peel off in sequence. Follow me."

The six remaining victors took their turns doing victory rolls at Nelson's direction, one at a time. As each succeeding F-4 pilot took his craft through the traditional aileron roll maneuver, the morale of the men and women on the ground went one notch higher. Sergeant Chris Cole and the other crew chiefs were shaking hands and slapping each others' backs.

1655 hours
Wing commander's office
Ubon RTAFB

Adams pressed the red phone to his ear, trying to make the lousy connection with Saigon more effective.

"Thank you, General Morgan. The 8th Wing did a fine job, and so did the supporting forces. Thank General Crandall and his staff. Bolo was well organized. And, General, there's a Thud pilot from Korat that deserves the Silver Star.

"Now, sir, about our plan to strike the MiG airfields. . . ."

AFTER BOLO

Operation Bolo was so decisive that MiG activity markedly declined through April 1967. Then, as it increased again, the White House allowed the American aircrews to strike and close the North Vietnamese fighter bases. In the initial raids, U.S. Air Force and Navy aircrews destroyed twenty-six enemy planes on the ground. This time, the F-4s, F-105s, and the Navy's carrier-based fighter-bombers did the job together. The combination of Bolo, the airfield attack, and aggressive American fighter tactics kept MiG activity under control into the winter months of early 1968.

Clint Adams and his 8th TFW had decisively hurt the North Vietnamese Air Force over Hanoi with Operation Bolo. But the pattern was already there; as in every major military engagement, America had won the battle, yet would lose the war.

The Eagle and the Dragon never met again over Hanoi. Nguyen Tomb flew very little for almost a year. He turned his energies toward rebuilding his shattered air force and protecting it from raids on his airfields. Clint Adams rotated back home in September 1968, leaving the 8th TFW at the apex of its combat capability.

MARCH 1968

12 March 1968 0645 hours
A Metro bus stop
Springfield, Virginia, in suburban Washington, D.C.

Clint Adams pounded his feet on the frozen ground as he waited on the corner for the Metro bus. The late winter wind easily cut through his blue Air Force overcoat. He looked at his watch; the goddamn bus was late again. He'd have to start driving his car to the Pentagon—if he ever found the time to get it running right. Twelve-hour workdays during the week and half-days on Saturday were wearing him down.

Clint worried about missing his 0800 appointment with his new boss, Major General Max Crandall, the Air Staff's new director of plans. Crandall hadn't forgotten the last phone conversation he'd had with Adams back in Southeast Asia. He and Crandall were not getting along, and Adams didn't want to give the bastard any ammunition by being late this morning.

Clint was existing in a state of professional limbo. He was a brigadier general-select, meaning he'd been chosen for one-star rank, but he hadn't pinned it on yet. Three more months, the personnel guys said, if ten more generals retired by June.

In the meantime, Adams continued in his present job as deputy director of force development. He had 100 staff officers working for him. Collectively, they put in long days trying to figure out how many fighters, bombers, and cargo planes the Air Force needed ten years from now. Who the hell knows? Adams thought. Who the hell cares?

He was miserable. Worst of all, Clint wasn't flying fighters, just pushing papers. Life after wing commander had been bad enough the first time. This second time it was just plain terrible.

For Laura's sake, Clint hadn't fought his Pentagon posting when he'd left Ubon. She had liked Washington when they'd been stationed there seven years ago. He owed her something, especially after leaving her at Shaw the way he had.

These days, Clint put Laura first, a just penance for all the times he had gone off into the night for the Air Force. He had realized he couldn't live without Laura even before he'd left Ubon in late September 1967.

When they'd met in Hawaii after he'd completed his combat tour, Clint was at the top of his profession: four confirmed MiG kills, running his lifetime total to seventeen aerial victories. The newspapers back home were running stories predicting he would become America's first Vietnam air ace. But they were wrong; time had run out for him. He had served a full year as the wing commander of the Wolfpack, flying 105 missions over the North. General Morgan and the chief were already uneasy about letting him continue to take risks for that fifth MiG by flying Downtown. When his one year was up, they pulled their best bona fide war hero out of the fight. But if they had let him, Clint would have stayed on for 200 missions North.

He had gone to Hawaii with all that behind him. It was Laura's turn now, and he knew it. With Amy already at Smith College, things seemed more manageable between them. Laura had surprised him, agreeing to one more assignment. Her sense of adventure, cultivated over two decades, got the best of her. At least at first.

Adams could see the bus as it crested the hill and lumbered toward him. He felt pathetic, standing there holding an attaché case, looking like the half-dozen other officers waiting for their thirty-minute ride to the Pentagon. Clint found a seat next to an overweight civilian he'd sat next to several times before.

He was thinking about his phone call to Laura last night. She wasn't happy either. Laura's two months in Greenwich before joining Clint in Washington had exposed her to the life she'd always wanted. She'd hated spending all those days alone in suburban Virginia, waiting for Clint to come home. She missed the kids. And the Bolling Air Force Base Officers' Wives Club just didn't do it for her anymore.

At first, Laura started taking long weekends to Greenwich, then month-long vacations. This time, she'd been gone over two months.

Clint had missed her when he'd been at Ubon; missing her from a closer distance was worse.

Their argument on the phone last night was especially painful. Laura had said she wouldn't be back. Her terms were simple, but nonnegotiable: if Clint would retire to Greenwich, she'd be willing to try their marriage again.

Adams had hung on for the results of the Brigadier General's Promotion Board last December. It was his second realistic shot; and he had made it. Now, as a selectee, he felt trapped. He hated what the Air Force was doing to him. But he also felt a deep-seated obligation to contribute in any way he could. Like he had said before, there was a war on.

Clint also thought about the letter he'd gotten from Randy Starbuck yesterday. Randy was flying B-52s at Loring AFB in Maine. Starbuck was fed up with bombers and the Air Force. He'd written to Clint to tell him he was getting out. He'd try for a fighter slot with any Air National Guard outfit that would have him. In the meantime, he'd work for National Airlines in Florida, where it was warm.

The man next to him wheezed and coughed as Clint unfolded his *Washington Post* and scanned the front page. He didn't expect to find anything interesting, but his stomach tightened as he read the headline in the third column:

Air Force Pilots Down Two MiGs in Dogfight over Hanoi

Saigon—In an interesting correlation of news stories, the French newspaper *Le Monde* wire service reported that U.S. Air Force pilots destroyed two North Vietnamese MiG-17s in a five-minute reeling battle fought out above the capital city of Hanoi as French Embassy officials attended a garden party below. Assistant Chief of Mission Henri Devou described the scene. "The larger American planes kept turning in behind the tiny MiGs about 5,000 meters (8,000 feet) above the embassy grounds.

"The Americans were shooting missiles everywhere," Devou said. "But the two little MiGs kept evading them. Finally, one missile hit its target, and the MiG disintegrated in midair. Seconds later, the other MiG was hit and fell into the nearby Red River. It looked like an air show, except that two men were killed."

Only hours later, the U.S. military headquarters in Saigon released a statement confirming that two pilots from the 8th Tactical Fighter

Wing at Ubon Air Base, Thailand, had destroyed two enemy jets earlier that day over Hanoi.

The U.S. pilots, flying two-place F-4 Phantom fighters, scored both aerial victories using infrared heat-seeking missiles. Major Todd Benning and Captain Paul Westman already had one MiG to their credit from earlier in the month. With three kills, the two F-4 pilots became the leading MiG killers still flying in combat, second only to Colonel Clint Adams, who earned four kills before completing his combat tour last fall.

"The second MiG—the leader—was hard to bring down," said Benning. "He knew his stuff. From the markings we saw on his MiG, that pilot had quite a few notches on his gun."

Based on Benning's debrief, experts are speculating that Benning and Westman probably brought down North Vietnam's top ace, Colonel Nguyen Tomb, who was believed to have 14 American kills.

Adams crumpled the newspaper into his lap and stared out the window past the fat bureaucrat snoozing next to him. The Metro bus bumped along in the rush-hour traffic that choked all four inbound lanes of Interstate 95.

The morning sun rose into the clear sky. It would be a nice morning to head out to the dogfight area for some air-to-air work, Adams thought. Tomb downed in such a fight? Not likely, Adams thought. But if it were true, at least Tomb had died well—not in this subhuman existence.

The bus jolted to a stop amid a sea of commuters. Clint Adams decided he would go straight to General Crandall's office when he got to the Pentagon this morning. Clint had had enough. He'd turn down his brigadier general's star. Laura was more important than this.

The Author

Major General Walter Kross, USAF, has commanded an operational flying wing and flew 158 combat missions in Southeast Asia, 100 over North Vietnam as an F-4 aircraft commander. In twenty-six years of active duty, he has accumulated over 5,200 flight hours—750 as an F-4 fighter pilot. His decorations include the Legion of Merit, as well as three Distinguished Flying Crosses and thirteen Air Medals earned in combat. General Kross is the author of *Military Reform: The High Tech Debate in Tactical Air Forces* (1985). Born in New York City, he lives in southern Illinois (with his wife, Kay, and his daughter, Karin), where he is Director of Operations and Logistics, U.S. Transportation Command, at Scott Air Force Base.